MASTER OF BENGAL

NORMAN PARTINGTON

Master of Bengal

A novel of Robert Clive of India

MACMILLAN

SBN 333 17179 9

First published 1974 by
MACMILLAN LONDON LIMITED
London and Basingstoke
Associated companies in New York Dublin
Melbourne Johannesburg and Delhi

Printed in Great Britain by
NORTHUMBERLAND PRESS LIMITED
Gateshead

Written with affection
for
Pamela Ann

Author's Note

THIS NOVEL is an imaginative reconstruction of Robert Clive's life and the beginning of Empire in India. In the middle of the eighteenth century, India was a conglomeration of states under the despotic rule of Muslim princes, who often kept in serfdom the meek Hindu, and who were determined that it should stay that way.

With the arrival of the French and the British, who were of course traditional enemies, European culture (a dubious benefit at times) was brought to Bengal and the Carnatic, not by political design but as a by-product from the expansion of trade.

The source of all British power in Calcutta and Madras was the Honourable East India Company which, during the dynamic period of Clive, was much like a humble grocer who, on eliminating his business competitors, finds that in the process he has become Mayor of the city, its Chief of Police, and its President of the Chamber of Commerce. It was an intoxicating discovery!

The grocer-cum-Mayor promulgated good laws and dispensed justice according to the best standards of that age. As Chief of Police he proved heroic beyond belief. But as President of the Chamber of Commerce he could not resist dipping his fingers into other people's cash boxes until, two generations later, the auditors in England called a halt.

Durban 1973   Norman Partington

Dramatis Personae

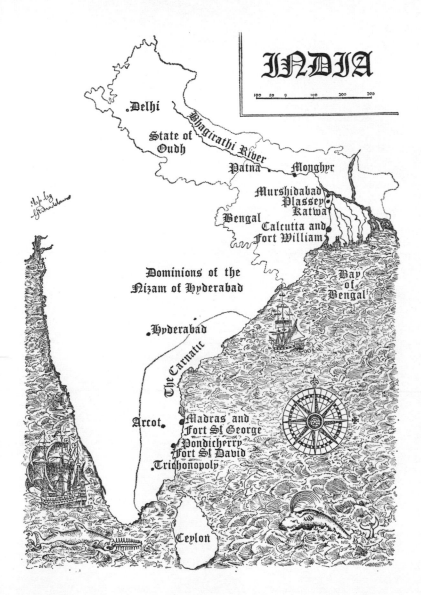

INDIA

100 50 0 100 200 300

Delhi

Bhagirathi River

State of Oudh

Patna Monghyr

Murshidabad
Plassey
Katwa
Bengal
Calcutta and
Fort William

Bay of Bengal

Dominions of the Nizam of Hyderabad

Hyderabad

The Carnatic

Arcot

Madras and Fort St George
Pondicherry
Fort St David
Trichonopoly

Ceylon

Map by
G.Etheridge

I

IT WAS an age of enlightened men – but not too many. A child of ten could be hanged for the theft of a silk handkerchief, but persons of substance did the Grand Tour and, over a period of a year or two, acquired a veneer of culture. The well-schooled wrote epigrams in Latin, struggled through the pastorals of Theocritus and could assess a fine horse at a glance. In the universities scholars patiently extended the boundaries of knowledge, keeping a wary eye on Holy Writ. It was a bawdy age, when even Ministers of the Crown boasted of performing acts of gross depravity.

Several thousand miles from England, where opportunity for profligacy was even easier to come by and social opprobrium even less exacting, in a bug-infested, fly-blown, hot room in the shabbiest part of Madras, a boy of nineteen celebrated his birthday by loading a flintlock pistol and attempting to blow out his brains.

Twice he placed the muzzle against his temple, twice pressed the trigger, twice the hammer struck the flint and twice the charge failed to detonate. His fine-boned but pinched face was haggard; after the second attempt he lowered the clumsy weapon, stared at it bitterly, then cast it from him. It fell into a corner of the room, spilling out the black powder and then the round ball, which rolled across the floor and lost itself down a rat-hole.

In frustration and relief he cried, 'I will live. God must have intended me for something!'

Some later opinions, more jaundiced than perceptive, have suggested that the real tragedy was that the flintlock failed; nevertheless the history of India moved into a more stimulating era as a result. Of all the figures in British-India few match the colourful, aggressive yet oddly sensitive personality of Robert Clive – that temperamental and moody genius who arrived in Madras in 1743 as a writer in the Honourable East India Company.

'By all the saints, Robert! What's that noise?' His friend Edmund's heavy face appeared at the door, the grease glistening on his short clubbed pigtail. He came in, and leaned his elbow languidly

13

against the wall. His white cotton blouse with its ruffled sleeves and frilly collar was stained with sweat.

Clive stifled an impulse to shout imprecations at him because the newcomer did not share his misery; he sank down on to his rope charpoy and rolled on to his back. His eyes focused on the filthy wooden ceiling where flies buzzed and mated.

'Leave me. I'm sick,' he groaned, turning his face to the wall. His friend came further into the room.

'Sick? What kind of sickness, Robert? You seemed all right this morning.'

'Sick of this accursed life!' Clive yelled at the peeling wall plaster. The visitor relaxed.

'Oh *that*. What you need is a woman. You'll have a brainstorm if you think too much in this heat,' he exclaimed cheerfully; but his eyes hardened as he caught sight of the pistol on the floor. Before he could pick it up Clive had swung his head round and was staring bitterly at him.

'A *mistress*, Edmund! On ten pounds per annum!'

'Who says you have to pay them anything. We're providing a service for these dear ladies – and if you can't find a lady there are plenty of nursemaids who'll gladly oblige a gentleman.' He winked suggestively. 'I've got two little charmers in my bed this very moment.'

Clive shot upright. 'Two! At the same time?' he exclaimed. 'Your tastes are as depraved as your attractions are remarkable.' Despite himself, he was curious.

'You shall have one of them,' Edmund declared handsomely. 'But I warn you, she must leave within the hour before her father returns home.'

Clive paused perceptibly before dismissing the offer with fine contempt. 'Go back to your loose women, Edmund. When I want a mistress I shall find one myself.' Edmund gave an expressive shrug and swatted a mosquito that had fastened on to his arm.

'As you please, my celibate friend – but it's a poor philosophy that compels a man to starve amid plenty.' Unseen by Clive he swiftly picked up the pistol and backed out of the room. A few faint giggles heralded his return to his own quarters. Clive closed his ears to them. 'Ten pounds a year. Twenty pounds in five years when I'm a *factor* and, when I'm thirty – if I survive that long –

14

maybe a merchant at two pounds ten per month! Surely I was intended for something better than this.'

He lurched off the bed, sat at the small table and dropped his head into his folded arms in an attitude of defeat. Day after day of numbing routine, copperplate entries in thick ledgers, money in, goods out, indigo, saltpetre, cotton materials, invoices, bills, advice notes, receipts. He would for years on end be standing at that tall desk, with twenty other clerks, half fainting in the perpetual heat, sharpening quills, refilling pots with cheap ink, the pepperpot of sand never used because the writing dried as soon as it went on to paper; listening to the inanities of the other writers as they boasted of their latest conquest (much of it wishful thinking), and wary of the sharp eye and caustic tongue of the chief factor as he spurred them constantly to greater effort.

In England he had been glibly assured that promotion was rapid in the East India Company. They had neglected to tell him why. The unnumbered silent congregation in the cemetery outside the city supplied the answer. Oh yes, promotion was rapid – if you survived!

He poured tepid water into a stone basin, splashed some on to his face and looked dolefully into the fragment of mirror which he had balanced on a protruding brick. Nineteen years of age! He looked ten years older, he told himself miserably. Deep shadows under the eyes, lean unhealthy cheeks a little swollen near the jaw; the mouth small and compressed and with a sore on the bottom lip; the chin aggressive, the eyes set wide apart but sunken and connected by deep furrows; the hair black, pulled from his face and ribboned in a small pigtail. Everything about him, even the pistol, was worthless!

Yet on the Monday morning Robert Clive was at his desk again. Edmund hissed at him across the huge ledger wherein he was supposed to be entering invoices: 'We shall spend Saturday and Sunday at my parents' home, Robert ... I think a little gracious living is needed to salt the tails of those daemons you've been harbouring.'

Clive's head jerked up in surprise. 'Your home?' he accused. 'You never told me you had parents in Madras.'

'It didn't seem relevant.' Edmund banged one ledger closed and opened another ostentatiously when he glimpsed the chief factor glowering in his direction.

Clive craned his head forward. 'I'd always assumed you were like me. I thought you'd been sent out from England to relieve your parents of your quarrelsome presence.' The parting scene with his own father was still painfully fresh in his mind.

Edmund laughed; a pleasant sound and rare enough in that office to cause the other writers to lift their heads. Edmund ignored them. This serious-eyed, intense youth – the antithesis of himself – roused a protective response in him. The other clerks were prissy-mouthed dullards. If Edmund subscribed to any philosophy it was that life was far too ludicrous and boring to be taken seriously.

Clive bent his head to stare at his friend through the gap in the ledgers. He was puzzled. 'But if your parents live here, then your father must be in trade,' he whispered. Edmund's blue-grey eyes twinkled with amusement.

'Of course, idiot. Why else would anyone choose to live in this stinking bazaar! Doesn't the name Maskelyne, the cloth merchant, mean anything to you?'

Clive was dumbfounded. 'Maskelyne!' he echoed faintly. So Edmund was the son of the Company's senior merchant, a distinguished member of the Madras Council. 'But he's ...' The intended word was 'wealthy', but it seemed ill-mannered to use it.

'Stinking rich,' Edmund supplied with curious derision.

'But why are you here as a *writer*; living like a pig in those lodgings? Surely your father could ...' He received a wicked grin in reply. Contemptuous of who might be listening, Edmund said in his normal voice: 'Think of it as a penance, and the means by which I shall learn an honourable vocation. That's my official explanation,' he added dryly.

He adopted a posture. 'My esteemed father, who commands my filial devotion (but alas, not my respect), owns to several mistresses, the existence of which my autocratic mother prudently denies – and with them I wish him well. But to this same dear lady the more modest escapades of her son would call forth denunciations and protestations. Frankly, Robert, it suits me to live as I do. The freedom it gives is sufficient compensation for the stifling luxury of home.'

Clive, who had never been indulged by his own parents, frowned; he found his friend's renunciation of comfort hard to understand. 'I concede that it may be more accommodating for you, particularly

16

in view of your tastes, but that is no reason for working here when you could obtain a much more fitting position in your father's business.'

Before answering Edmund took out a small knife and proceeded to shape a new chisel point at the end of his quill. He held up the result for inspection and, with a neat flourish, nicked a slit in it along which the ink would flow. Addressing the quill he said quietly: 'As I have no wish for my affairs to be brought under scrutiny I must respect that my father's are equally sacrosanct. He doesn't care a jot who knows about his mistresses but he's reluctant to make me privy to his business secrets *at this stage* – though content that I should control the business when he retires. You see, Robert, he feels that in his son's eyes he might fall from grace were I to learn to what degree he swindles the native.'

For a moment Edmund's eyes were filled with passionate intensity. Clive swished away a large fly; when he looked again the sardonic mockery had returned to them. 'Swindles!' Clive exclaimed. 'Your father has the most honoured name in Madras. I'm sure he makes large profits – but *swindles*!' His head shook vigorously. 'The Council would be the first to pronounce against him were this so.'

The chief factor appeared in the doorway and blew a small whistle. At the signal the ledgers were closed with sighs of relief, ink bottles capped, quills tossed down, and the writers began filing out of the huge office. Edmund came round the desk. He was a large, rawboned fellow, light on his feet, and stood several inches taller than Clive, who himself was above average height. He flung a sweat-stained arm around his friend's shoulder and gave a derisive laugh at his ingenuousness.

'What an artless fellow you are, my dear Clive! Do you really believe that the Council would call to order one of their own?'

They linked arms and walked out into the hot dusty street, screwing up their eyes against the fierce glare, their shoes scuffing up small puffs of dust. Clive had tightened his mouth.

'This I will not believe, Edmund. The Council, the whole of John Company in fact, is too scrupulously overseen by the directors in England. They would tolerate nothing that savoured of deceit or roguery.' He stopped abruptly and wagged an admonitory finger at his friend. 'A business could not survive were it to cheat its customers. For how long could we trade against the competition of the Portuguese, Dutch and the Frenchie, if we cozened and cheated! We are *shopkeepers*, plying our trade under the Emperor's mandate. We buy raw materials at an honest price and sell finished goods at a fair profit.'

They took their seats in the dim interior of the nearest punch shop and ordered the cheapest drink. Edmund sighed, as if his friend had confessed to a belief in fairies.

'Long may you live with such noble concepts, my dear Clive. India truly needs such men as you,' he exclaimed in mock reverence. Then he clapped his hands. 'But enough! A moratorium on the matter. We have better things to discuss. On Friday after our labours we shall hire two palanquins and ride in style to my home. Once there we shall spend two days in idle rapture and excessive eating.'

The glass almost slipped from Clive's grasp. 'Palanquins! Are you so demented by the sun? I would have to deny myself food for a month to afford even the shortest journey.' Edmund was unperturbed. His affection for Robert gave him licence to tease. He adopted a sententious tone.

'Robert Clive, mark you well. Treat not the dignity of my family with impunity. Were we to arrive at my father's mansion, conveyed by neither phaeton nor palanquin, without escort of bearers, peons, and hurcarrahs to sing out our titles, we should be spurned by the constables at the gate, my mother would refuse to receive us and would delicately expire from shame. No one in the Carnatic visits on *foot*! Would you destroy the fabric of our society by the impious act of *walking*!'

A glint had appeared in Clive's eye and Edmund saw that he had gone too far. 'Forgive my nonsense, Robert,' he quickly apologised. 'Be not fainthearted. My purse is just long enough for the little we'll need.' And an hour later, arms linked together and swaying slightly, the two young men wandered off to their lodgings; Edmund's booming laugh sending a wayward goat scuttering from their path.

2

LATE ON the Friday afternoon two palanquins were hired. Edmund paid the deposit, eased his bulk into the cupboard-like interior and set himself to be joggled through the baking streets of the city like a perambulating Punch and Judy show. Clive entered the other one. The half naked bearers set off, plodding and sweating with a lopsided gait that kept the passenger on a reasonably even keel. Their manner implied they were demeaned by the failure of the Europeans to commission an escort. These were not the style of client *they* were accustomed to!

It was Clive's first introduction to the sedan chair and the swaying motion combined with the sultry heat made him slightly sick. He opened the curtains and tried to concentrate on the scene outside.

Madras had a perverse air of imbalanced prosperity, princely wealth cheek by jowl with appalling poverty. On the one hand were the beggars who waved their twisted stumps in desolate appeal; the rags of the Hindu peasants; the wild-eyed yet cowering pariah dogs stalking the rubbish dumps at each street corner; the tarpaper bazaar shops heaving with clouds of flies; and the crumbling adobe huts so small that a man could not stand upright in them. And on the other, fronting the broad thoroughfares, were the residences of the wealthy, palatial and gleaming white, with uniformed guards at the gates and a dozen or more peasants tending the lawns. And with these were the squat yet eminently substantial buildings of the Honourable East India Company.

In marked contrast to the subjected Hindu were the superior Muslim traders, descendants of the fierce Turko-Islamic invaders who had swept through the great passes of north-west India to overwhelm the less warlike Hindu. These were richly garbed in long silken robes, brightly coloured turbans, curly-toed Turkish shoes, and had no more affinity with the Hindu than the European had with either.

Clive, accustomed now to the motion of the sedan chair, rather enjoyed his new viewpoint of a wearisomely familiar scene. Here crude carts trundled along behind some uncomplaining bullock, urged by some skeletal Hindu. There were peasant women in filthy saris carrying shapeless bundles on their heads; and the occasional Englishman in ruffles and breeches, riding in his phaeton, disdainful, sweating, aloof. And here also were the white and other pale-skinned ladies in their open carriages, holding down their hoops and stays while keeping parasols erect over their mobcaps. Now and again a gay young blade might overtake a carriage in his more dashing chariot. He would lift his tricorne hat, bow to the ladies, then spur on his horse. 'Hatmen' was the sobriquet, faintly derogatory, by which these men were known by the dark-skinned peoples.

And distinctive from all these was the Persian Muslim – so clearly the master of all. Brown-skinned or lighter, often Mongolian featured, sharp-eyed, warlike, taller and of more heroic proportions than the abject Hindu, and splendidly gowned, he stalked the streets with his companions, hand clasping the hilt of his dama-cened sword, watchful lest the shadow of a Hindu or Infidel defile his path, curtly salaaming whenever he caught the eye of an English-man (who invariably responded with a nod), suspicious, volatile, cruel, perverse, sentimental, proud; he knew his power and felt his position as overlord keenly.

'There's an undercurrent of violence, Robert,' Edmund had once said, indicating one of these Muslims. 'An unmentioned threat that many of us sense but won't admit to. Trade and profit, that's all that concerns us – and how to get back to England with a weighty purse before this damned climate arranges the swifter trip to the cemetery.'

In Europe the French and the British fought each other as they had been doing for centuries. With communications to India limited to the speed by which a four-masted barque could sail, their repre-sentatives in the Indian factories (or trading posts) were often at peace when their home countries were in conflict, and vice versa. There was never any lasting peace: each truce was but a lull to prepare for the next round.

In the Carnatic and in Bengal the trading posts functioned under the greedy tolerance and shrewd opportunism of highly volatile Muslim princes, and both England and France used every oppor-tunity to curry favour with their princely hosts. Neither had tested their muscles against the Rajahs, and had no desire to do so. As

Edmund had said: 'It would be a three-cornered contest in which any pair would defeat the third; and, as Britain and France will never ally, the outcome in India will depend upon which European any Nawab decides to favour.' And so with patronage and condescension the Englishman and Frenchman sought to woo the Muslim princes – and the princes waited to see who made the best proposition.

The name of Maskelyne in Madras conjured up images of splendour. Yet Clive was unprepared for the reality: uniformed chubdars at the wrought-iron gateway, palm tree lined carriageway, paved forecourt bordered with flowering shrubbery, tiled stone steps leading to the triple-storey flat-roofed building itself. It all breathed so eloquently of wealth.

As the palanquins were set down a contingent of consumahs, chubdars, peons swarmed around them, shouting, salaaming, struggling to be first to have the honour of opening the tiny doors. They genuflected until their brown heads all but touched the paving stones.

Prominent among them, his commanding voice the loudest, was the head steward, a Sikh of imposing stature. With dramatic flourishes of his hands he cleared a path to the visitors – and then he recognised Edmund. His performance disintegrated and he prostrated himself before the master's son. Edmund bent and lifted him to his feet and, to the ululations of awe from the watching servants, embraced him with touching affection. The Sikh was overcome with pride and happiness. To be thus singled out was to be touched by a god. He knelt, grasped Edmund's hand and pressed the back of it to his dark forehead. He was his slave forever. Edmund gently detached himself from the head consumah's embrace, beckoned to Clive, and together they walked up the flight of steps between a pathway of genuflecting servants. It was a performance Edmund submitted to each time he came home; not unwillingly, for the occasions were rare enough.

'We'll go into the main parlour and wait until mother makes her appearance,' he told Clive, watching with amusement his friend's efforts to rid himself of the fine coating of red dust on his shoes and breeches.

In the hallway, Clive stopped, overwhelmed by what he saw.

Deep carpets lay on polished wooden floors, valuable tapestries hung on the walls, a wide curving stairway spiralled a glittering path to the two upper floors, various ornaments filling the interstices of the balustrade, and where some space remained an expensive painting filled it on the walls.

Robert Clive, the eldest of thirteen children of a small landowner and lawyer in Shropshire, possessing a modest education and little else, felt at that moment as never before the bitterness and shame of being poor. The tiny rug on which he stood would have cost ten years of his salary; the piece of jade left so casually on a marble table, three years. And he, Robert Clive, what was he? A harum-scarum scribbler, tossed out of four schools for bad behaviour and packed off to India because his father could cope with him no longer. He touched the seat of his breeches and felt the glazed thinness of the cloth. The buckles of his shoes were of cheap metal, not the silver of a gentleman. His blouse was ill fitting and poorly sewn; his cravat was shabby; the dye of his jacket faded and the sleeves frayed. He wished most fervently that he had not come.

He felt Edmund's eyes upon him and made a show of diffidence. 'John Company pays its merchants to live in this style?' Edmund clapped him on the back. He understood.

'Private trade, you donkey. Indigo, saltpetre, spices, money loans. What the Company pays my father would hardly meet my sister's clothing account.'

'Loans?'

'An advance on the security of some peasant's harvest,' replied Edmund; he waited for Clive's reaction.

'One of the ten per cent per annum chaps, is he?' Clive remarked, not very interested.

Edmund gave him an odd look. 'I sometimes wonder at your innocence, Robert,' he said. 'Admittedly you've only been in this country a few months – still ... ten per cent per *annum* ... Really! Per *month*, it so happens to be. Hence all this.' He waved a derisive hand. 'By the time the rice or whatever is harvested, the miserable wretch owes twice as much as he borrowed. He can never hope to catch up with his debt. Eventually he's forced to sell his farm and become a serf-tenant on his own land. And that, my dear Clive, allows my father – and all the other loan sharks in

Madras – to acquire a few more sweat and tear stained acres in the Carnatic.'

Clive was shaken. 'And the Company permits it?'

'Parliament has condemned the practice many times, but John Company has too many Members in its pockets for anything to be done,' he rejoined scathingly. Clive looked sympathetically at his friend. Much about him was becoming clearer.

'So you and your father ...?'

'Precisely,' snapped Edmund. 'That is why I cannot wait to purchase a commission in the army.'

Whatever Clive was about to say was halted by the rustle of fine silken skirts as a girl of his own age whisked into the room. She stopped in alarm at the sight of them. 'Edmund!' she cried out, and would have rushed to embrace him had not the presence of a stranger inhibited her.

'Margaret,' Edmund responded easily, sauntering over to her and gravely kissing her on the cheek. He waved at Clive. 'May I present my good friend Robert Clive ... Robert, my sister Margaret.' The girl flushed slightly at the casual introduction. She held out her hand and Clive respectfully bent over it. And then she bobbed the stranger a brief curtsey before submitting him to a speculative study. The restrictive size of Madras society was such that no young lady dared risk ignoring the possibilities latent in any introduction to a presentable young man.

But was this a presentable young man? His clothes were ill cared for and of inferior cut. And his shirt! Really – both tailor and dhobi should have been soundly whipped! And yet – his face. And her own pale green eyes softened when she saw its pinched intensity and the determined look in his eyes.

'Won't you please be seated, Mr Clive?' she invited, settling herself graciously on the couch. She was about to say something else when....

'Margaret! Who is that with you?' It was a strident voice and came from upstairs. Thirty-seven brisk footsteps later, Margaret's mother flowed into the room on a tide of long skirts and a backwash of stewards.

The atmosphere underwent an immediate change. It now seemed charged as at the breaking of a monsoon storm. Mrs Maskelyne stopped abruptly as if deliberately affronted by the stranger's presence, and a pair of glacial eyes fixed themselves on him. Her thin nose, bony cheeks and sharp chin jerked upwards, and the fan of Chinese silk flicked open with a terrifying snap and fluttered with agitated movements as she made a lightning assessment of the visitor's worth.

Still holding Clive in her formidable gaze, she addressed her son. 'And who, pray, might this be?' she demanded.

Edmund was equal to the occasion. His tone expressed honest concern as he replied, 'My dearest friend, Mother. Allow me the honour of presenting him to you' – a sad look in Clive's direction. 'Mr Robert Clive, who has but recently arrived in Madras after a most terrible experience on his journey from Calcutta.'

Clive hastily bowed, his cheeks crimson from Edmund's outrageous lie. He managed to stammer something in return but received no more than a sniff of acknowledgment. Blithely, Edmund began embellishing. 'Mr Clive's father is involved in certain matters at Court, and his son is visiting this country in respect of those matters.' He gave his mother an oblique look that hinted at a multitude of delicate missions. 'I took the liberty of extending to him the hospitality of my home for a day or two until he recovers from his ordeal,' he added in a reverently hushed voice.

At the cabalistic word 'Court' a little of the edge was taken from her manner. The tempo of the fan decreased a little. 'You are indeed welcome, Mr Clive,' she found herself saying, her nostrils quivering with distaste as she took in the cheapness of the visitor's attire. Edmund caught her look and gave an anguished sigh.

'Dacoits, Mother. Terrible, too terrible. The whole of Mr Clive's apparel was stolen. The poor fellow was lucky to escape with his life. And that miserable tailor protests that the new linen cannot possibly be ready for another week.' Clive, flushed with embarrassment, was utterly incapable of meeting Mrs Maskelyne's eye. While she was aware of the strong possibility that she was being fooled, she dared not call her son to account lest the story be proven true. Glaring at Edmund, she addressed his companion. 'We shall look forward to your presence at dinner, Mr Clive. Come Margaret.' And she swept from the room.

Margaret eyed her brother but said nothing. She knew him for a lovable and plausible rogue to whom the truth was never permitted to become a burden; and when she saw the colour of the visitor's cheeks she was satisfied she had judged him correctly. She curtsied to them both, and dutifully followed her mother.

When they were safely out of hearing, Clive rounded on his friend. 'Court! *Court!* What kind of lies are these? Are you to fabricate a gilded mask for me? I warn you, Edmund, I will not wear it.' He was almost shouting and his hands trembled.

Edmund arched his eyebrows in injured innocence, flopped down on a chair and crossed his legs. 'But you yourself, my dear Robert, told me your father was a lawyer. Surely he would have connexions with some kind of court. It would only confuse Mother to supply needless detail.'

Clive returned even more vehemently to the attack. 'You are deliberately creating a false image. You are cheating – attributing to me a nobler quality than I possess.'

Edmund yawned. 'What is that to a fool, Robert,' he said laconically. 'Those who worship false idols deserve the litany of fake priests.' The acridity in his remark shocked Clive and had the effect of calming him. He flung himself down on to one of the couches and prepared to sulk. His pride demanded that he should leave at once – but he did not. The thought of seeing that lovely girl again detained him.

'Come Robert, I will not allow us to quarrel,' Edmund said, leaning forward to touch Clive's arm. 'If it will help restore your much abused dignity then I do offer you my most abject apologies. During the next two days I hope to persuade you to join with me in taking a commission; and as soldiers we shall have more pertinent matters to vex us than my Mother's delusions of grandeur.'

But Clive had something else on his mind. With studied disinterest he said, 'Your sister Margaret ... An attractive girl ... Does she happen to be ...'

'Spoken for? Betrothed?' Edmund cut in swiftly, one eyebrow knowingly raised, his mouth twisting into a lopsided grin. 'As yet – no. Offers have not been accepted – because none have been made. Why do you ask?' he added archly.

'Simple curiosity, that's all,' replied Clive lightly.

They both relapsed into a silence broken only by the soft padding and shuffling of seemingly endless platoons of consumahs and peons who drifted from room to room in their quest for what no one seemed rightly to know. When eventually the two men spoke again it was on a subject that haunted the minds of many perceptive people in the Carnatic – the news that war had once more broken out in Europe between France and England.

'It is the most heavily fortified place the French have,' ruminated Edmund, speaking of Pondicherry, a hundred miles to the south and the principal French factory in India. 'I once had the opportunity of meeting Dupleix and that general of his, Bussy. Astonishing fellow, Dupleix. Plays host to the princes with all the aplomb of an emperor – absolutely charms them. I tell you, Robert, it offends my English pride to give praise to a Frenchie, but candidly he's got the most astute mind in the Carnatic – and Bussy is his mighty right arm. They're a formidable combination.'

'We shall beat them,' Clive returned with all the assurance of the ignorant. Edmund looked at him dryly.

'Do not underestimate him, Robert. With the Carnatic the size of England, and most of the princes fawning around him, whether we like it or not he's the *de facto* ruler with that army of his in Pondicherry. It will take better leaders than we have now to upset him.'

But his friend's mind was wandering. 'She is rather lovely though, isn't she?' he said causing Edmund to stare.

'Who? Margaret?'

Clive nodded happily. Edmund's eyeballs rolled upwards and he heaved a mock sigh. 'Robert, my very dear friend, if you have been so bewitched then I beg of you, for the next two days exercise restraint. Whatever you do, keep Mother in ignorance of your feelings.'

But Clive's gaze was resolute. 'Know you now, Edmund Maskelyne, that one day I shall marry your sister, – and that no one, nothing, shall prevent me.'

3

'THE FIRST objective, General, must be Fort St David. This is vital before the next fleet of English ships arrive to reinforce the garrison,' said the Governor-General of Pondicherry. An elegant and slender man, fifty years of age with greying hair under a full-bottomed, well-powdered wig, Joseph François Dupleix was a diplomat of finesse who, by manoeuvre, chicanery and outright bribery had, over the years, made himself the European 'ruler' of the Carnatic.

It was as king he considered himself and as such he lived. His palace outstripped in size and magnificence any other in the south of India, and was designed to impress and overawe all the Rajahs and Nawabs who came to pay him court. Amidst a race of princes not noted for any lack of modesty, his personal appearance aroused envious admiration. And when he travelled beyond the fortified walls of Pondicherry his retinue was the size of a preposterously dressed army. Yet Dupleix was no mere fop.

'That's twenty miles south of Pondicherry,' mused General Bussy, a rugged soldier who towered over Dupleix. 'But taking the fort might not be the simple matter it seems.'

A delicate hand fluttered away his doubts. 'At this moment it is inadequately defended. The garrison is small. An attack, pushed with determination, and Fort St David will be ours.' He gave his General a conciliatory smile. 'Not that I *need* the fort, but I do insist that its threat be eliminated before we launch an offensive against Madras. It would be foolhardy to move the bulk of our strength a hundred miles to the north, leaving a weakened Pondicherry open to attack from Fort St David. First, General, cripple the fort.'

Twelve French senior officers were gathered in a semicircle about him in the marble and gilt splendour of his conference room. The Governor-General himself was seated languidly on a throne of teak and ivory, its arms shaped like the backs and heads of elephants and the back carved with the swirling forms of Shiva and Parvati; the whole placed on a marble pedestal so that the officers had to crane their heads to look into Dupleix's face.

Bussy was still hesitant. 'With respect, Your Excellency, I repeat, it may not be quite so simple as you imply. We shall breach the walls easy enough with the cannon we have; but the fort commander ...'

'General Stringer Lawrence,' Dupleix interrupted. Bussy nodded grimly.

'Yes. I have fought against him many times, and he has a positive gift for impossible situations. He'll use every trick he knows to hang on to the fort.'

This was most unlike Bussy. Dupleix cast him a mildly reproving look. 'Your own reputation is not without merit, my dear Bussy; and I have every confidence that your generalship will prove not a whit less than that of the Englishman. Fort St David will be taken ... And now for Madras.' He courteously signalled for Bussy to continue.

'No problem there, Your Excellency. The city is wide open. Fort St George in the centre of Madras could be a stumbling block, but at present there are hardly enough troops there to defend a single wall – and thankfully, the colonel in command is a fool, brave but incompetent. I intend to lay siege to the fort, seal it off and let the sun and time do the task for us.'

Dupleix stifled a yawn. He was content to leave military tactics to the professionals. 'You will take personal command, General Bussy? ... Good. Make whatever arrangements you wish and march when ready. Meanwhile I shall prepare a formal declaration for the British to notify them of our intent. Kindly see it is delivered into the hands of General Lawrence one day before you attack. I shall include in it our terms for his surrender.' He noted Bussy's arch look and added, 'I agree, Bussy, it is unlikely!'

'This Stringer Lawrence,' he murmured. 'A man of integrity, is he?' Bussy shot him a hard look, catching his meaning.

'He is a soldier, a man of honour – as such he would consider me if posed with the same question,' Bussy replied sharply.

Dupleix – not at all put out – merely sighed his regret. 'Then it appears you will have to rely entirely on force, my dear General. But the fort must be crushed before you turn towards Madras.'

In Madras two newly commissioned officers were admiring themselves before a huge mirror. Clive pretended to a joy he did not entirely feel, since his commission had been purchased with his friend's money. Edmund, however, felt free at last from what he considered the 'knavery of business'.

The attractive uniform was more suitable to a ballroom than to campaigning in a hot climate, and it concerned none that these two newly commissioned innocents were now licensed to lead soldiers into battle.

'Just think, Robert. If I had sufficient money I could have bought a colonelcy and raised my own regiment,' Edmund said wryly.

Clive sobered immediately. 'Money,' he echoed bleakly.

'After all, Robert, what does a man need to become a great captain,' Edmund persisted. 'Common sense, an awareness of the country, and a modicum of intelligence to outguess the enemy.' He gave a dismissive 'pouf' and drew his sword with a dramatic flourish. They fenced a while, laughing helplessly at their own lack of skill, then made pretence at being generals and controlling vast armies. And in the days that followed – while Fort St David was being battered to pieces – the two novice officers toured the fort in Madras and discussed how best it could be defended – or attacked. It was conceded that the young Clive conceived the more imaginative plans.

They examined the cannons, talked with the gunners and argued long over the merits of roundshot and grapeshot. They observed the few soldiers that comprised the garrison and criticised from the standpoint of their own inexperience. They decided how best cavalry could be used and studied the techniques of using a sabre. All in all it was not the ideal training for future commanders.

Two months later, when Fort St David was little more than rubble surrounding a battered keep, there still remained a small group of defenders tenaciously resisting in the more rugged inner fortress. General Bussy stared moodily at the devastation and at the field of corpses that lay between his artillery and the pulverized stone of the fort.

'A plague on the fellow!' he cried irritably, slapping away the dust and insects from his tunic, then putting the spy-glass to his eye. 'He's cost me five valuable weeks already.' He drew his hand across his forehead and it left sweat-stained gritty marks on the skin. He stared at the hand in disgust then beckoned to an aide.

'Cease firing. We leave for Madras tomorrow,' he snapped. The aide – a colonel of artillery – wavered before blurting out, 'His Excellency's orders, sir ...'

'Be damned to them!' Bussy rounded on him. 'Fort St David is no longer a military threat. God in heaven, am I to kill every last one of them,' he shouted.

The colonel scurried away. Soon the cannons were silent. The following morning, when the French columns, cavalry, bullock-carts, wagons, formed up for the long trek to Madras, General Bussy stood on the highest point of the hill overlooking the plain and the shattered fort.

'The Indians maintain that the English have no spirit for battle,' he said to himself with unutterable cynicism. 'Then for their sakes, I pray they never have occasion to find out for themselves.'

4

IN THE small town of Murshidabad, the capital of the Nawabs of Bengal, two Muslim youths in princely dress strode with all the assurance of rank into the palace courtyard. The taller of the two carried himself with great arrogance. The smaller youth conceded this claim to seniority but made no overt submission of himself. In the centre of the courtyard the consumahs were holding two horses superbly accoutred with silver harness and richly burnished saddles.

'That is my horse,' pointed out the smaller youth as the other prepared to mount. The bigger boy calmly stood on the bent back of a servant and then mounted, saying casually as he did so, 'Today it is mine – and tomorrow if I so choose.'

Kassim, the smaller youth, protested but could do nothing.

Across the courtyard, under the arches of the cloisters, from behind one of the marble columns, a young girl watched the scene with that silent concentration peculiar to the submissive Indian female. The quality of her robes, the necklaces and the number of gold bangles she wore placed her as a person of rank. Her eyes were only for Kassim.

As Kassim took the reins and prepared to bring round his horse, he glimpsed her face as it shyly peeped around the massive column. He cautiously glanced at his companion, saw that his attention was elsewhere, then gestured to her with his left hand, warning her not to be seen. She flashed him a conspiratorial smile and dodged her head back out of sight again. But it was too late. The older boy had spotted her.

He grinned maliciously, called out some jibe to Kassim (who scowled angrily) and gave vent to a peal of laughter. 'Sareen!' he called out, levelling his hand and finger in her direction. Slowly she reappeared, clearly embarrassed at being detected, and sank to the ground in obeisance to the older boy. He laughed even louder. 'Farewell Sareen. Mir Kassim has better things to do today than to gaze sickly into your lovely limpid eyes,' he shouted derisively, whirling his horse around and pulling on its reins so that it reared in a spectacular manner. 'Remember who you're promised to.' And with a great hoot of laughter, he whipped up the horse and sped out of the gates.

Kassim sheepishly waved a small hand to her and clattered after his companion. He soon caught up with him and they began racing, charging recklessly across the arid fields, creating clouds of dust in their passing, ignoring peasants – who hastily got out of their way – then speeding through a village and scattering some of its livestock.

Tiring of the race, the boys warily circled each other – still on horseback – and at the older boy's command, unsheathed small blunted swords and began attacking each other with great zest. They lunged, sliced, chopped, drew away, most skilfully, giving each other fairly hard whacks in the process. But the taller and stronger boy was not quite so agile, not quite so skilled, and lacked the fury of the smaller. Repeatedly he got the worst of the encounters; his countenance began to darken and his temper to rise. He tried all the tactics he knew, thrusting his beast against the other to knock the rider off balance, lashing out with his feet in close combat, thrusting for the face when they had agreed not to do anything so dangerous – but always Kassim got the better of him.

Eventually, after receiving a blow on the shoulder that really hurt, he became so enraged that he flung himself on to Kassim, knocking him to the ground and falling on top of him. Neither was injured, both lay winded for a moment. The older boy recovered first, leapt on to his companion, flattening him in the dust, and pulled from its sheath a long curved dagger.

The eyes of Kassim bulged at the sight of the blade as it reached for his throat. He screamed. But no one was at hand to hear his cries – and even if there had been none would not have dared to interfere, such was the authority of the older boy.

'This is one contest you lose, Kassim,' he snarled, forcing the blade nearer, pricking the throat so that a thin line of blood appeared.

'Siraj! don't ... please ... Your Highness, don't,' shrieked the

31

half demented youngster as he struggled frantically to move his face away from the blade. The dagger pressed again and made another tiny cut. Again the youngster screamed. The knife moved higher up his face so that the point was suspended over Kassim's right eyeball. It eased down so that the boy knew that even the slightest movement would destroy the eye.

'Should I remove this eye first, Kassim,' Siraj jeered, 'or this?' He grabbed at the youngster's groin. 'Perhaps I should make you a eunuch? Just one swift cut ... here.'

Kassim yelped. The knife returned to his face and the point was inserted in his nostrils. 'Just like the Marathas, hey, Kassim ... one quick cut.'

The young boy was in a state of collapse. Siraj-ud-daula was without control, without mercy, when crossed. He was capable of committing any cruelty. And the fact that Kassim and he were childhood friends counted not one iota in moments of stress.

The blood poured from Kassim's earlobe as Siraj nicked it with the edge of the blade. 'So what will you give me if I allow you to live, to retain your eyes, to keep your balls?' he smirked.

Kassim was sobbing. 'Anything, Siraj. Anything ... Take what you will,' he implored him. Siraj knew exactly what he wanted. His knife moved swiftly downwards, ripped open Kassim's tunic, scratching his chest slightly in the process. His hand slipped inside the torn garment, fumbled around and then pulled out a small golden block attached to a chain. It was simply a replica of the Koran – not particularly valuable nor especially decorative. But to Kassim it was precious and quite beyond price. And this Siraj knew.

'I shall take this,' he announced triumphantly, yanking it from Kassim's neck so violently that the thin chain snapped. He dangled it in front of Kassim's eyes, tantalising him, sheathed his knife, and, now calm and content, raised himself from the weeping boy. Tying the trinket around his own neck, he remounted his horse, from whose height he began admiring it with great ostentation.

'Sareen gave me that,' Kassim sobbed, brushing a hand across his eyes, a shade less fearful now the immediate danger had passed. 'Please, Siraj, anything else I have ... not that, please,' he begged, going to him and clutching at his stirrup.

'I know she gave it to you, Kassim my friend.' He bent towards him, his voice one of utter reasonableness. 'But now it is mine. You made a promise, remember? "Anything" you said ... so, I take Sareen's gift.'

He could have had a hundred similar baubles merely for the asking. But this one had a special value: it was Sareen's gift to Kassim – a bond between them that the Nawab would never allow to be consummated.

The bright sun sparkled on the golden trinket as Siraj whirled it around his fingers in exaggerated admiration. Then, well pleased with the outcome of the morning's expedition, Siraj took up the reins and prepared to ride back to the palace. The younger boy, now standing erect, glared up at his antagonist, his chest heaving, his eyes blazing with hatred. In a sudden overflow of anger he shouted up with passionate intensity, 'Mark you well, Siraj-ud-daula, *adopted* heir of the Nawab of Bengal ...' (that was the nearest to an insult that he dared). 'Mark you that you steal only what you are strong enough to keep.' He could think of nothing else to say.

Siraj gave a contemptuous laugh and his hand slapped at the sword in his scabbard. 'What I take I keep,' his voice rang out, 'and no one will match my strength when I am Nawab – ever.' With that he dug his heels into the horse's flanks and set off at a fast trot. His hand waved farewell. It was a derisive gesture. 'Give my humble respects to Sareen, Mir Kassim. Maybe we shall play again tomorrow, if I feel so inclined.'

The younger boy stared bitterly at his retreating companion. 'Good-bye, Siraj-ud-daula,' he said quietly. 'The day will come when I shall take back what you have stolen – and with it I shall also take your life.'

5

THE TWO officers paused momentarily in the doorway of the barracks, reluctant to leave its merciful shade. Edmund squinted speculatively at the sky. It had the hot coppery tints of a pan held over a fire. With one accord they moved out into the glare and made for the edge of the forecourt where the walls cast some shade. Clive was wearing his habitually preoccupied expression which tended to make him seem dour and forbidding to casual observers. Edmund turned his bright eyes on him.

'Presumptuous though I may be, my melancholy friend – yet claiming privilege as her brother, what may I ask progresses twixt Margaret and yourself?' he asked in a deliberately stilted manner as they reached the edge of the shrubbery-lined walls. Clive's lips tightened and he pulled up abruptly a few paces from where the tentacles of a giant creeper were slowly strangling its host tree. Still without replying, he whipped out his sword, tested the edge with his thumb and adopted an aggressive stance. Edmund prudently stepped back.

'We have spoken not a word to each other in six weeks,' Clive rasped out, bringing the sword across and cutting clean through the main stem of the creeper.

'By all that's in heaven! Cease this nonsense and tell me why not,' shouted an exasperated Edmund, as he was showered with parched leaves, fragments of bark and severed twigs. Clive took no notice. A number of soldiers, lounging and gossiping nearby, turned their heads, grinned and whispered to each other as they watched the young ensign's tempestuous display of swordsmanship. Clive had already gained a reputation for erratic, independent behaviour.

'Because ... she has made it ... abundantly clear ...' A slash of the blade punctuated each phrase. 'By hint and ... innuendo ... that any form of ... understanding ... between us ... will not be permitted until ... formal permission is given ... by her parents.'

In a perverse way it was quite a feat of swordsmanship. Every tendril and tentacle of the creeper had been sliced off so that only the stem itself remained clinging to the denuded tree.

Clive leant on his sword hilt, breathing heavily from his exertions, perspiration streaking his face. Edmund moved closer, thankful the performance was over.

'You have not, I assume, made an approach to Mother?' he asked in seeming innocence.

'Does such an inane question need an answer?' Clive snorted, levelling the green-stained blade of his sword at Edmund's chest. Edmund flung his arms up in mock appeal for mercy. 'I have offended you again,' he sighed.

'You're an idiot,' Clive snapped, but he was unable to be angry with Edmund for long.

'Sadly, I agree. But something was needed to lift you from the suicidal mood you've been in for the past few weeks.'

Clive shot him a look, wondering how much he knew of the suicide attempt. He cleaned his sword, sheathed it and, arm in arm, seemingly carefree, the two of them sauntered towards the massive gate of the fortress.

'I've been giving your problem much thought,' Edmund continued. 'Assuming that your affection for my sister, and hers for you, be genuine, how then can the joining of your hearts and bodies be achieved?' Clive glowered. 'You may abduct her and then gallop madly for the hills ...' He looked sideways at his friend; his lips were curled down even further than before. 'Or you must achieve both rank and money – *especially money* – sufficient to impress Mother.' His voice hardened subtly as he added, 'I can assure you that Mother will sell quickly enough if the price is right.'

The puritan Clive was still capable of being shocked at hearing a man speak thus of his own mother, and he said as much – to Edmund's cynical merriment.

'Probe for the substance, dear Robert, and disregard the façade,' Edmund returned, no longer teasing, 'and that advice includes the image we see in the looking-glass. We tend to imagine only that which supports the fine opinion we have of ourselves.'

He paused in his stride, forcing Clive to stop with him. He wagged his forefinger in a 'take note of what I'm saying' manner. 'Consider your present status: the youngest of ensigns in the army of the Honourable East India Company – a mere stripling. Your wealth exceeds no more than the coins you jingle in your pocket; your means only the paltry sum paid you as an officer; your prospects uncertain. Frankly, as a suitor for the hand of Margaret Maskelyne you wouldn't get beyond the chubdars at the gate,' he said with stinging honesty. In a lighter yet more saddened tone he went on, 'The truth is that Margaret will be sold to whomsoever makes the highest bid. Either obtain rank and funds, or take her by stealth.'

Clive had been shaken and deeply offended by Edmund's cynicism. It struck at the fundamentals of marriage, the sanctity of man's relationship with woman, and made a mockery of romance.

'How dare you speak in this manner!' he cried out angrily. '*You!* You with a private life of such shameless depravity. How could you give tongue to such malicious and iniquitous slander?'

Edmund looked down at his enraged friend. He put a conciliatory arm around his shoulder – which Clive was tempted to shake off. 'How indeed,' he returned sadly. 'Though I accept your rebuke, take no account of my own profligacy when considering my words. Simply get rich, Robert, if you desire Margaret. Neither my parents nor society will question the method once wealth and position have been attained. Money brings its own absolution, and society can be notoriously forgetful when it's expedient to be so.'

Clive stared at him. The advice was in such opposition to what he had judged Edmund's character to be.

'Are you saying that *any* means are justified?'

He was cut short by the sound of alarm bells. Whistles were shrilling and frantic shouts heralded the beginnings of panic. Clive held up a warning finger to silence Edmund then cocked his head to see if he could make out the sense of what was being shouted.

'Back to the fort,' Clive said, and together they rushed back through the stone archway just as the guards were putting their shoulders to the huge doors. An 18-pounder cannonball struck seconds later, knocking a block of stone from its place and leaving the gateway looking like a gigantic mouth with one tooth missing.

The two men ducked and hurried to their pre-assigned posts. Soon the shouts were nearer and clearer until there was no mistaking the cry. 'The Frenchie is here ... 'WARE THE FRENCHIE!'

A second cannonball smashed against the crenellated lip of the west wall, testifying to the accuracy of those firing. Then a third ball followed, and a fourth, and next a veritable barrage that sprayed the fort and the surrounding streets.

Collecting their muskets, ball ammunition and powder horns, the two new ensigns looked at each other in a bemused way.

'Perhaps we could persuade the French to train our own artillerymen,' Edmund said dryly, observing the haphazard way in which the fort's cannon were being brought to a state of readiness. At that moment an alarming thought struck Clive.

'Margaret! For God's sake, Edmund! The French'll be through that area within a couple of hours.'

'Get *down*!' Edmund yelled, grabbing his belt and forcibly pulling him below the lip of the wall. 'There's nothing we can do about it now. If they survive the cannon fire just pray to God that Frenchie's the gentleman he pretends to be.'

Clive knocked his hand away, but squatted by his side nonetheless. Common sense told him that Edmund was right and he felt angry at him for being so.

Edmund raised his head cautiously and took a quick survey of the scene. The walls of the fort had been manned by only a scattering of soldiers, their long red tunics and tall mitred hats creating bright splashes of colour along the top of the lichenous grey of the stone battlements. Tiny spurts of flame and puffs of smoke rippled along and between the embrasures in the parapets as the defenders recovered from the initial confusion and discipline reasserted itself. But so far as he knew there were no more than fifty or sixty men in the entire garrison. Not many to protect a city the size of Madras.

'Feeling any better?' Edmund asked, wiping the sweat from his face and loading his musket for the twentieth time. Clive shrugged and took a cautious look through the firing slit. The scene in the streets below was one of chaos. People were running in panic to escape the advancing French infantry; peasants and drovers abandoned their carts and fled for cover; screaming women swept up wailing infants and fled before the salvoes of musket fire and grapeshot. Peons dropped their sedan-chairs, spilling out the occupants in their frenzy to escape; horses pulling phaetons or chariots reared as a musket ball struck them, eyes wild with terror, and then plunged madly away, dragging wrecked carriages behind them.

Even as Clive watched, he saw one such horse stampeding down the central thoroughfare, blindly heading towards the oncoming soldiers, the woman passenger hysterical as the vehicle rocked crazily from side to side before eventually it crashed into an abandoned water-cart. The woman was flung over the horse and into the street. A French sergeant detached himself, rushed forward, picked her up and gently laid her in the doorway of a warehouse for safety.

Clive readily identified the various regiments as the French, in their familiar blue uniforms, regrouped at the end of the long street leading directly to the fort.

'They're Bussy's,' he muttered, eyeing the men as they fixed long bayonets to their muskets, 'and if he shapes to the pattern of his other battles, then it looks as if Madras is lost. I don't see why he need bother with the fort at all. He's probably got everything he came for right at this moment.'

Edmund jerked his finger over his shoulder. 'Hey ho for the Colonel,' he sang out derisively, looking down to the forecourt where the commander – awakened from his noonday siesta – was dashing from point to point with his braces trailing in the dust behind him. 'It's not to be wondered that the princes elect to side with Dupleix when they see buffoons like *that* calling themselves Englishmen.'

By the time darkness fell the French had destroyed the last remaining groups of British soldiers who had been outside the fort when the attack started. In the morning the contest for the fort itself would begin.

As the milky dawn lightened, a concentrated cannonade burst against the west wall. It created damage to the walls and havoc among the defenders as they were swept from the firing-ledges. Volley after volley of musket fire followed for several minutes and then a further cannonade began. Out of the thirty men along that wall, sixteen were killed or wounded in the first half hour.

It continued all the morning, then, without warning, ceased, and the defenders were left to consider their fate. Madras belonged to the victorious Bussy and, in one small day, power in the Carnatic became indisputably French.

On the fourth day, Bussy sent an emissary under a flag of truce. He was admitted to the oven that the sealed fortress had become. Commandant and emissary stiffly raised their hats to each other.

'It is the wish of General Bussy, sir, to avoid further bloodshed and hardship to the gallant defenders of Fort St George,' began the emissary, sweating mightily and pretending to ignore the rivulets that coursed down his cheeks. 'The entire city is now under French control. There are forty-two heavy siege guns at this moment trained on these walls; and an army of eleven thousand awaiting the command to open fire. Fort St David under the command of General Lawrence has been destroyed, and help from that quarter can no longer be expected.'

He paused a moment, and took a square of linen from his pocket to mop his face and neck before producing the inevitable scroll of parchment. He enumerated the surrender terms one by one, concluding with: '... and if the Commandant and his officers give their parole neither to escape nor take further offensive action against the French in Madras, General Bussy undertakes to treat them with respect and to allow them unrestricted freedom within the confines of the city.' He re-rolled the now soggy piece of parchment, which he handed with a bow to the colonel.

The colonel took the scroll and somewhat airily replied, 'Convey my respects to General Bussy, if you please. Inform him that though his terms be generous and honourable, I must first consult with my officers before reaching a decision.'

'It is my intention to accept these terms of surrender,' the colonel told a gathering of officers an hour later; 'but I will compel no officer to abide by this decision. Each of you will decide according to his conscience. But I warn you that should you give your parole it must be binding upon your honour to keep.' He looked with affectionate sadness on the seven surviving officers of his garrison, then added softly, 'Those of you who elect to follow my example will parade with me tomorrow when Bussy's emissary returns. Should any officer be absent, I intend to remain in ignorance of his reason and can therefore offer no explanation to the French. God be with you all.' Then he left the room as if conscious of the silent accusation in the officers' eyes.

'Cowardice and base treachery!' exploded Clive when he was alone with Edmund. 'I will have no part in it. Frenchie will get no parole of mine.' He pounded a fist on the table.

Edmund regarded him calmly. 'Impetuous hothead,' he drawled. 'Had you been the colonel you could have done no other than he. We have lost Madras, so why extend the agony?'

'Any surrender to the enemy is to be despised,' Clive rounded on him, 'and for an *Englishman* to do so is worse. A nation is judged by how its individuals react under stress. How can we gain the respect of the natives ...'

'I will not argue with a fool,' Edmund cut in mildly, clumping his long legs on to the table. 'Be content that you've been granted leave to make your own decision.'

'I have already made it,' Clive retorted.

'And so have I,' Edmund sighed, squinting sideways at his

scowling companion. 'We go over the wall after midnight.'

Clive's eyes widened and he rushed to embrace his friend.

'We must first see that Margaret is all right,' said Clive, his old anxiety flooding back. Edmund said nothing. He had closed his eyes and was quietly snoozing in the chair.

6

WITH BURNT cork rubbed on face, arms and legs, and dressed in dhoti and gown such as the peasants wore, the two ensigns were a passable imitation of any coolie. Just before midnight, with the help of two sergeants and a long coil of rope, they climbed through one of the embrasures in the south wall, and let themselves down the forty feet to the ground. The two sergeants waved them good luck and then hauled back the rope.

If there were any French patrols about in the city, the two men neither met nor saw any. Even so it was a tense business creeping through the silent streets, trying to keep their swords hidden under the rags they wore, always keeping one hand on the butt of their pistols.

It was nearly two hours later before they sighted the Maskelyne home. There was not a mark, not even a broken brick, to show that an invasion had recently swept through this part of the city. Hugging the side of the street they were about to rush through the open gates when the chubdars on guard raised their javelins and threatened murder on the two 'beggars'.

'Sahib!' one of them gasped when Edmund unwound his turban, revealing the white flesh that bordered the burnt cork, and then he prostrated himself on the ground. Having no time for the 'prodigal son' formalities, Edmund stepped over him and, dragging Clive with him, dashed up the steps, past the startled consumah at the door, and entered the house.

At all the noise, Margaret, clutching around her a thin cotton night-gown, came apprehensively down the stairs. She burst into tears at the sight of her brother, and rushed into his arms. When the dark shape of Clive materialised behind the bigger form of Edmund, she gasped, and, without thinking, flung her arms around his neck and began sobbing into his cheek – her tears making a striped disaster of his make-up. She held him close, and they whispered words of endearment that the dark and the occasion permitted, restraint and modesty swept away in the joy and relief in each other's safety.

'Margaret!'

The mother flowed down the stairs in bewildered outrage, tempered slightly by the sight of Edmund – though she would not embrace him while he wore 'that filthy stuff' on his face. Behind her came the tubby figure of Mr Maskelyne in long night-shirt and round woollen cap. He carried a lighted candle and was cross at being taken from his mistress's bed.

'But need you escape?' he remonstrated, after being told of their intentions. 'General Bussy has harmed no one save those who have opposed his troops. The people are not molested; nothing is taken from them ...'

'Save their dignity,' Clive muttered under his breath, determined not to quarrel.

'My father and other businessmen are allowed to go to their offices without let,' interposed Margaret, adding her plea.

'Were it not for the soldiers wearing blue uniforms instead of red, we should never know that a change of ruler had taken place,' said her father.

But all their arguments were to no avail. The two men were adamant. With money provided, to Edmund's shame, by his father, they slipped through the gates of the house and stopped the first bullock-cart they saw. The Hindu drover's eyes blinked open when he saw the handful of gold coins that Edmund was holding out to him but, after much gesticulating, he eventually abandoned both cart and beast and fled into the darkness, clutching the golden hoard to his breast.

The two men loaded the cart with a barrel of water and ample provisions, stuffed their swords under a pile of rags but retained their pistols in their belts. When they bid farewell to the family, Margaret hung back for a moment then tore herself from her mother's restraining hand and put her arms around both men's necks, kissing each on the lips.

Edmund, with some difficulty, climbed aboard the clumsy cart and – in the manner of the drovers – sat cross-legged, groaning.

41

The bullock swivelled its massive head around and stared vacantly at the ugly apparition that was its new keeper. Clive, his dress a sack that covered him from shoulders to sandals, took up the drover's stick, prodded the ponderous beast to get it moving, then walked alongside it with his head down in the subservient manner of the peasant.

For four hours they lurched, faltered, stopped, started again, sweated profusely through the dusty interminable streets of Madras. Occasionally they passed French patrols – and never earned even a second glance from them. Of all the sights in India the bullock-cart was the most familiar.

'So you think Fort St David is the best place to make for, Robert?' Edmund asked when, with relief, they passed the outskirts of the city and could resume their normal posture. Clive answered without hesitation, 'Yes,' and dabbed some more burnt cork on his face where the sweat had given him the appearance of a leprous albino.

'The saints only know what we'll find when we get there, if what Frenchie claims is true,' Clive moodily added.

For three weeks, travelling mostly through a dacoit-infested wasteland, making wide detours to avoid French outposts, skirting villages when they could, two unusually strapping 'natives' with a bullock-cart continued on their fantastic journey. Three bullocks died en route and had to be replaced by bullocks bargained for from suspicious Indian villagers, and, when Pondicherry came into sight, Edmund and Clive had the nerve to stumble and groan their way right through the centre of the city itself rather than take a wearisome diversion.

Twenty miles further on, their sandals having disintegrated days before, and in a condition bordering on exhaustion, the two friends halted as the desolated rubble of Fort St David was seen in the valley. The hope that had sustained them throughout their ordeal oozed away as they gazed at what had once been a proud landmark. No one, it seemed, could have survived the holocaust. Of the outer walls great gaps had been blasted wide enough for two elephants to walk through abreast. Three of the four bastions had crumbled to heaps of stone and in the ruin of the fourth they could see a number of Indian children who played and searched hopefully for anything of value.

Clive at once began a painful and loping run towards the ruin but Edmund grabbed him by the shoulders.

'Hold, Robert,' he cautioned, shielding his eyes against the sun. 'There's a flag flying above the keep ... It might be Frenchie.'

Clive pulled up. 'Can't make it out ... Let's get nearer,' he replied, grabbing the reins of the bullock-cart and urging the beast forward.

Several hundred yards further on, Edmund suddenly yelled excitedly, 'It's the Union Jack!' and turning, clasped his friend to his side in a great outburst of emotion. Faintly recognisable, at the top and rear of the still intact keep, on a mast that leaned at an angle, the familiar banner hung limply in the sultry air.

With their last reserves of strength the two friends hobbled towards the blasted walls of the keep. They started shouting as they neared the tiny entrance; dry, throaty croaks that were scarce human. A face cautiously appeared in one of the firing slits, its eyes widening in astonishment as they took in the sight of these two ragged apparitions dragging their way across the rubble-strewn ground.

The door of the keep opened – and a blunderbuss was thrust out at the two visitors.

'Idiot!' Clive shouted. 'We're British officers from Madras.'

The blunderbuss still pointed, then wavered slightly and eventually lowered.

An hour later, in two huge wooden barrels filled with water, Clive and Edmund relaxed in heavenly coolness and tried to give some coherent account of their journey to the elderly, small though wiry, man in the grubby uniform of a major-general who sat in a chair near them. Though marked by his own ordeal, Stringer Lawrence – an almost legendary figure at that time – was filled with concern for his unexpected guests. Occasionally he leaned forward to catch some muttered scrap of information from one or the other, and though anxious not to overtire them was pathetically eager for every bit of news.

'My boys,' he said at one point, in his somewhat reedy voice, his eyes smiling affectionately. 'If, in the future, you inspire those whom you command with the spirit you have shown these past few weeks, no limits can be set on what you might achieve.'

By the time they were bathed and dressed in remnants of borrowed uniforms, Robert Clive and Edmund Maskelyne had been promoted full lieutenants. And, with the three other officers in the keep, were invited to the General's dinner-table that evening.

The dining-room was sadly battered. The 'table' was a door that had been laid across blocks of stone, and the crockery had survived only by the grace of God. The food, notwithstanding, was ample and excellent, due to the credit of General Lawrence in the nearby villages, and to his gift for barter.

'Ten chickens and a sack of rice for one flintlock is the current rate of exchange,' he told them proudly. He was an entertaining raconteur with a fine sense of humour, and one who managed to be informative at the same time. The war with France occupied much of the conversation.

'The French army is the greatest power in India at the moment and there are few fortifications that could for long stand against a concentrated barrage of its artillery. Its cavalry is the finest in the world, and man for man, none could match the French foot-soldier for courage and skill in combat.'

His guests exchanged frowns. Edmund listened uncomfortably to this heresy, while Clive set himself to make vehement protest. Stringer Lawrence's eyes twinkled in merriment at their various attitudes. Finally he put the palms of his hands flat on the table and added in a conspiratorial manner, 'Well, that's the legend Dupleix has created – and I charge you well to note: it's easier to destroy an army than a story.'

The old man peeled a ripe fig and began to chew on it. As many of his teeth were missing the effort was rather messy. He mopped his mouth and chin carefully and continued with his discourse.

'And I'll tell you something else, all you young fellows. Legends have a nasty habit of being proved correct. However, do not give the enemy credit for having greater resilience than yourselves. When equally matched forces meet in the field, the side which keeps fighting just five minutes longer than the other is the one that wins the day. It seems obvious, yet it's strange how many commanders forget.'

The General squinted at Edmund. 'I've been fighting the French practically all my life, and I've a devil of a lot of respect for their prowess. But they can be beaten *if* you remember a few things: first, artillery wins battles, and the French artillery is excellent.

So, when your own time comes, use your cannon to the best advantage and try to stop the enemy from using his – especially if he's French. At all times, at *all* times, be ready for the rain. The commander who lets his guns and powder get wet has lost the battle. Drill this into your troops.'

The old man cast aside the debris of the fig and started on a new one. 'The French have one or two fine generals like Bussy. They've also got good common soldiers. But their regimental officers are neither inspired nor imaginative ...'

He seemed about to say more, but instead subsided into an introspective mood and the meal was continued in silence. When it was over the General took the two newly promoted lieutenants on to the battered ramparts. His hand roved sadly over the corrupted stone as he told them the story of the siege. He took little praise for what he had done, except to say, 'I managed to fox Bussy a few times, but the end was inevitable. I delayed the attack on Madras for four or five weeks, but otherwise ...' He made an empty gesture with his hand.

'It'll take some time to build again,' he went on, then gave his companions an ironical smile. 'It looks as if you two will be staying on here ... mainly because there's no other place in the Carnatic that you can go to just at present,' he added ruefully. 'But while you're here you might as well set to and learn the trade for which you've donned uniforms.'

Robert Clive and Edmund Maskelyne were at Fort St David for two years. They learned their trade from a master.

7

A L O W cloud of dust steadily built up on the horizon threatening the onset of a dry storm: a commonplace occurrence – but nonetheless feared – that sweeps the Indian plains with its scorching winds powerful enough to flatten huts. The peasants working on the arid land looked up from their labours in mild alarm. The women began rounding up their children, hoisting the youngest infants on to their backs and securing them with their saris, and urging the older ones to rush to the village and take shelter.

The men, no less apprehensive, forced themselves to work a little longer lest they appear as timid as the women. But in minutes all of them, carrying baskets filled with the meagre produce of the land, had broken into a jog-trot towards the collection of mud and thatch huts. As they shot uneasy glances over their shoulders towards the now huge and flat-topped cloud of dust, the wrinkles on their gaunt faces deepened. Had the phenomenon been a storm they would have felt the warning gusts of hot air, and the sky would have darkened. But no such portents had taken place. They exchanged worried glances with their neighbours.

At the edge of the village, near its only substantial building, a young boy and a lovely young girl talked to each other, oblivious to the world around them. Occasionally the boy timidly stretched out his hand and touched the girl's forearm, and she did not draw away as a properly modest Muslim girl should have done.

'Are you sure that no one other than your servant knew you were coming?' Mir Kassim asked – for at least the fifth time that afternoon. Sareen gave him a reassuring smile and shook her head, a gentle movement that caused the trinkets attached to the rings in her lobes to give a soft, bell-like sound.

'No one knows, Kassim, and the Nawab will not miss me until he holds court this evening. By that time we shall both be back in the palace.' She gave him a sidelong look from under her long black eyelashes. 'Siraj will probably guess when he finds that both of us are missing. But you must not worry, Kassim. We are here now so let us be happy for what little time we have.'

Kassim looked dubiously at her. It was not the first time they had arranged a clandestine meeting, but as Sareen grew older, more beautiful, and more ready for marriage, so would the protective screen around her be that much tighter.

'I heard my father talking to Alivardi Khan last night,' Kassim said unhappily. 'Already they have consulted the astrologer and he has suggested a date on ...'

He stopped talking, cocked his head to one side, and motioned Sareen to silence. His head slowly lifted as though he were sniffing the air – and it was then that the ground began to tremble. Telling her to stay, he ran to the crumbling temple and climbed the steps to the stubby little tower, and peered out of the window.

His frame quivered before becoming rigid with terror. His hands clutched the white-washed edge of the window as if they had become part of the stone, and a moment later he heard the frenzied screams of the peasants.

'MARATHAS! ... *MARATHAS!*' Soon the fearsome name echoed and re-echoed through the stifling air. The peasants' stick-like limbs took their emaciated bodies at a speed which only the most abject terror could produce. Some tripped and went tumbling head over heels, picked themselves up and continued with a limping rush towards the dubious shelter of the village.

The vibrations increased as a thousand horsemen charged towards that pathetic collection of huts, and when they were a few hundred yards from the last of the fleeing figures, the flattened cloud of dust seemed to widen into a crescent-shaped arc whose twin horns reached around to clutch and embrace the whole village.

Kassim was unable to move, unable to tear himself away from that window. He saw the leading horsemen overtaking and knocking flat some of the runners, striking out with flails or curved swords. Some of the peasants were simply scooped from the ground and flung across the withers of the horse with the beast hardly breaking step. Other wretches were brutally run down and stamped into the earth.

'Kassim!' called out Sareen frantically, shaking him out of his trance. He dragged himself from the window and rushed down the steps.

'Marathas!' he gasped, grabbing her arm and pulling her towards the horses they had left some distance away. She fled with him, looking from side to side as she made a swift appraisal of their chances of escape.

There seemed none.

'Stop, Kassim!' she cried. 'It's no use, we can't outrun them ... look! ... they're nearly all round the village now.'

Kassim glanced round fearfully. Sareen was right. The tiny collection of mud huts and the temple was practically surrounded and the nearest of the Marathas was less than a quarter of a mile away.

'Oh, merciful Allah!' he screamed inwardly.

'Quick ... between those two huts ... the well at the back,' Sareen gasped, grabbing at his arm and pulling him out of his shocked state. He ran with her, blindly accepting her lead – grasping at any suggestion she made, for his own mind was paralysed by memories of stories told of the Marathas.

'They always search the wells!' he cried, as they dashed over the rocky ground at the rear of the village. Sareen made no answer but simply held his hand tighter and kept on running.

And on came the Marathas. Of bigger stature than Hindus, sharp featured, wearing turbans, baggy pantaloons and coarse braided waistcoats, they were nomads who practically lived on horseback; the most ruthless and ferocious of Asiatic races. They cared nothing for national identities, owed no allegiances, paid no tribute, had no allies, spurned any kind of settled existence. Purely tribal in organisation, the Maratha roamed over central India and considered every other race as their legitimate prey. 'Money ...' They made only one demand. 'Where money?'

The village was surrounded. The Maratha closed in. The peasants dropped to their knees and begged mercy from a race ignorant of its meaning. The warriors leapt from their horses and began dragging men and women to the huts to make them show where they had hidden their gold.

Knives were drawn from their belts and, at the slightest hesitation on the villager's part, his head was pulled back, the blade inserted in his nostrils – and they were slit open. If that failed to bring money, his ears were cut off – and if that failed ... The barbarous treatment continued: men, women, children, maimed in unbelievably barbaric fashion.

The frantic peasants rushed into their shabby dwellings, scraping from the ground the few coins they had buried there. They were then allowed to live. Three of the horsemen, soured by the paucity of their gains, scooped out a hole in the sand, thrust a woman's head into it and refilled the hole – telling the husband she would be freed when he brought money. He brought them everything he had, and they released his wife – but she was dead. They flung young children into the village trough and held them under water until some relative pushed money into their hands. Most of the children were drowned, but to the Maratha it was of no consequence.

Later, a few of the bandits scoured the village to see what else they could find. Five of them headed for the village well – a favourite hiding-place as they knew from experience. It was simply a deep hole in the ground some five feet in diameter, surrounded by a wall of stone. They peered into its dank darkness but could see nothing. They tossed heavy stones over and listened for any cries. There were none.

They had begun debating which of them would make the descent, when the leader of the Marathas fired a musket into the air to signify withdrawal. The well was abandoned and within minutes the whole tribe of horsemen formed an indistinct shape amidst a rolling cloud of dust as they headed for some unknown destination.

'It is safe now, Sareen,' Kassim said, sheathing his knife and climbing back over the edge of the well before reaching back to assist her. The young girl, still shaking from her ordeal, both of them barely protected from the stones dropped down by a narrow outcrop of rock that had formed a ledge, hauled her saturated body over the rim and fell sobbing into Kassim's arms.

They could think of nothing save collecting their horses and getting away from the scene of the massacre as fast as possible. When Kassim returned a few minutes later leading one of the horses (the other had seemingly gone with the Marathas) Sareen was crouched on the stones of the well, her hands over her face, her body racked with convulsive sobs. Steam rose from her garments as the burning sun dried them. Kassim helped her to mount then climbed up behind her, taking the reins with one hand and putting the other around her waist – a liberty he had never dared take before.

He spurred the horse to a fast walk as they passed through the centre of the grieving village. Bodies slumped everywhere; weeping relatives filled the air with their cries, the wounded screamed their agony.

Sareen could not bear to look. She draped the sari over her face, closed her eyes, and sobbed quietly, her head resting backwards against Kassim's shoulder.

'Why cannot they be found and destroyed?' she wept, when they had covered some miles and she was able to speak.

'Because the Maratha never allow themselves to fight battles with disciplined soldiers. They sweep down, kill and torture, take all the money they can and then rush away. The Nawab always has a force of troops out to search for the Maratha ... but they find only the villages they've left ... just bones that the vultures have fed on.'

Kassim gave a heavy sigh. 'The Nawab will be especially angry when he learns of this. That village had yet to pay its tax, and now there will be no money.'

Sareen barely heard what he said; she was preoccupied with other things. Eventually she said, very quietly, 'I was so afraid when we were hiding. I saw you with your knife, and you looked so fierce. Yet I felt proud that you were prepared to fight to the end for me ... I felt proud ... and I loved you, Kassim.'

He made no immediate answer. His hand felt the softness of her flesh through the sari, and she put her own hand over his and held it there. Then he leaned forward slightly, let his chin rest lightly on her shoulder and whispered sadly as though confessing to an error of judgment, 'I could not have saved you, Sareen, if we had been discovered. When they started to throw down the rocks and it seemed that we must be found, I took out my knife ... for I was going to kill you lest you fall into their hands. I had the knife ready to plunge into your breast when I heard the musket shot – and I stayed my hand.'

He closed his eyes momentarily and gripped her tightly. The hooves of the horse made rasping and hissing sounds in the yellow-ochre dust which sounded obscenely loud.

'And then I would have ended my own life,' he added quietly.

8

DURING THE two years of Clive's sojourn in the wrecked fort of St David he saw nothing of Margaret, though he received carefully worded letters from her – letters, so Edmund told him, that would pass the censorship of Mother. He replied to them – also in the same cautious vein.

Whilst Clive read solidly through the remnants of Stringer Lawrence's library and avidly soaked up every drop of the General's knowledge on warfare and statesmanship, Edmund blithely went his way as a generous-hearted libertine whose success with the local women caused his name to be bandied about with something like awe.

The two men remained the closest of friends. Clive, often morose, serious-minded, well-informed, occasionally revealing flashes of brilliance in military exercises, found his character hardening around an ambition that he would not reveal even to his friend. Edmund was quite content – and mildly surprised – that he, too, had been promoted captain along with Clive.

As for Dupleix, he reigned supreme in the Carnatic; behaving towards the defeated English in a gracious manner with scrupulous fairness, yet not allowing them to forget who was master. To the watchful princes he presented on the one hand the discredited English, and on the other the strength and prestige of the French, making clear where alliances would be most advantageous. And alliances were formed.

In England, in the late 1740s, in a small country town in Oxfordshire, a young man in the habit of a Franciscan monk was being thoroughly horsewhipped by his father. So beside himself with rage that the small veins on his forehead stood out like pulsating strings, he raved at the young man.

'I'll teach you to trifle with that kind of blasphemy,' he cried out, tearing at the coarse brown cloth of the habit and punctuating each word with a blow from his cross-woven leather whip.

The victim made frantic efforts to deflect the blows and to fight off his antagonist, but was too securely held by the stronger man. He shrieked each time the leather cut across him, and pleaded hysterically for mercy.

'I promise you ... *promise* you, father! I will not go again.'

'You promised me on three other occasions,' the father stormed. ' "I will not go again ... I will not go again ..." ' You gave me your solemn oath you would neither don those accursed robes nor visit that infamous Dashwood's place again. Each time you defied me and broke your word.'

The habit was now completely stripped off and the thrashing continued with even greater intensity. The boy – for he could not have exceeded eighteen years of age – was howling demonically. Livid weals appeared on his flesh. Eventually the father, his temper partly assuaged by the sight of the cruel hurt he had done his son, flung the riding crop from him and stood threatening, his face flaring red, his body trembling with nervous exhaustion.

His powdered wig had been flung aside and was impaled on a thorn bush; the sweat on his face had mingled with the white talcum and formed ugly rivulets down his cheeks. The boy had collapsed into a writhing heap, and rolled over to allow the coolness of the damp turf to soothe his hurt.

The father, tense with emotion, eyes suffused with gritty tears at what he had felt obliged to do, raised a quivering hand and pointed a finger of indictment at the sobbing form on the grass.

'No more ... no more will I believe you though you swear your oath on the Holy Book,' he rasped out. 'Go! I have listened to the last of your falsehoods. Leave my house. Take what money I'll provide and redeem your honour and Godliness in some other land, for I and England have seen the last of you. And this vow take with you: that should my path ever cross that of the satanic Dashwood I shall shoot him for the dog he is and rid this country of a pernicious evil.'

He stopped, overwhelmed by the sentence he had pronounced on his own son, then turned away and stalked back into the house, the tears flowing unashamedly down his face. At one of the windows his wife and daughter peered out, their faces bloodless, and the moment the father had passed indoors and out of sight, they rushed to help the boy outside. They fell on him, weeping and hugging him, though quite unable to commute the sentence ordained by the father.

A month later – as part of a fleet of five ships carrying reinforcements for the coming offensive in the Carnatic – a four-masted barque was directed to the more northern port of Calcutta. Sitting in the stern of the ship, leaning his back gingerly against a bulkhead and glowering at the fading coastline of England, was a passenger: the young, calculating, hard-eyed boy intended for the trade as writer in the service of the Honourable East India Company. His name was Warren Hastings.

Eight months after this event, in the rebuilt Fort St David, a newly arrived English general called a meeting of his officers – including the new Captains Robert Clive and Edmund Maskelyne – and to them revealed his plan for the defeat of the French and the restoration of British prestige in the Carnatic.

He was an assertive, self-assured officer but not an impressive one – judging by the tactics he was proposing to adopt. 'Pondicherry is the key, gentlemen,' he declared, stressing the name of the French citadel in case the listeners had never heard it before. 'Once we have taken that fortress we shall have destroyed the very foundations of

French power in India. The remaining trading posts will fall into our hands like ripe tomatoes once we have severed the main vine ...'

'He seems more fitted to gardening than soldiering,' murmured Edmund, looking sideways at his frowning companion. Clive brusquely shook his head, motioning his friend to silence as the general continued.

'After making a thorough survey of all possibilities I have come to the conclusion that a direct frontal assault on the main walls, after a preliminary bombardment by warships anchored off the coast, will be all that is needed to force the surrender of this Monsieur Dupleix. Gentlemen, we shall leave Fort St David for Pondicherry in ten days' time.'

Stringer Lawrence – whose age had deprived him of commanding the expedition himself – rose to his feet and shuffled out of the room in a black mood. Dupleix would make mincemeat of the popinjay, his attitude said.

'I fear the worst,' said Edmund later. 'Our esteemed new commander is mistaking confidence for performance.'

'The man is a fool,' snapped Clive in reply.

9

AGAINST PONDICHERRY, with much noise and raising of dust, the gallant general repeatedly stormed forward with his troops. Each time they were driven back by the accuracy and rapidity of the French musketry and cannon fire. After three weeks of banging ineffectually against the rugged defences, all that he had achieved were casualties for his men and a touch of sun-stroke for himself.

Clive – already an outstanding tactician – groaned his frustration. 'If England has no better generals then we are indeed lost ... and rightly so!' he exclaimed to Edmund, during one of the periods of recuperation after yet another retreat from the walls of Pondicherry. 'I am inclined to think that the board of directors shows no more wit in appointing its generals than the public does in electing its politicians.'

Edmund gave a sour laugh and crawled nearer to the tree to

obtain what benefit he could from its shade.

'The first weapon of the army is its artillery,' he declared sonorously in a passable imitation of Stringer Lawrence.

'And so it is,' Clive replied, swishing away a cloud of determined insects, 'but the calibre must be big enough to knock down the walls.'

'Provided that one *hits* the walls,' retorted Edmund dryly. 'Bang, bang, bang, and the dear old admiral pops off his guns: one ball for Bussy's private lavatory, another to plough up the Governor's garden, and the third to kill two of our own men. Really! We'd be better off if the admiral defected to the French.'

'They're the only guns we have so we'd better hang on to them,' said Clive; then flinging out an arm in exasperation, he cried, 'This nincompoop of a general, so eager to get into battle that he cannot wait a few days for his own artillery to arrive. "Charge the walls!" he yells out, then draws his sword and rushes headlong for the best defended fort in India. We'd be more successful hoisting him up and using the thickness of his skull to batter down the gates.'

Edmund roared with laughter, causing the general – who was quaffing soda-water some yards away in the shade of a pink, heavily tasselled umbrella – to glance, irritably, in their direction.

'Dupleix and Bussy must be helpless with laughter,' Clive went on bitterly. 'Were I an Indian prince I should immediately seek an alliance ... with *anyone*, other than the English.'

'To think,' began Edmund in a ruminative mood that was rare for him, 'that in seventeen forty-eight the two greatest Powers on earth feel obliged to blow themselves to pieces simply to acquire jurisdiction over a few square miles of eastern squalor. All that the merchants require – ours and the French – is a lengthy period of peace. Heaven knows! I disapprove of much they do ... but it's more to be desired than this.' He waved his hand at the battered walls and the exhausted troops.

Clive narrowed his eyes and rasped, 'There is more at stake here than simple profit. In Bengal and the Carnatic we have the only secure base from which we might trade with the entire East, and Dupleix will not rest content until the last English trader is sent from these shores – or buried under its parched earth.'

'That sounds like simple profit to me,' Edmund murmured. 'But are you suggesting that "John Company" has not a mind to do the same to the French? Are we not two jackals snarling over the fat carcase of the Indian cow?'

'Indeed we are not!' Clive almost shouted. 'And I find your analogy false and downright offensive. India is a savage land ruled by barbarians. Use your eyes and *see* the condition of its peoples. The European in Bengal and the Carnatic represents its only hope for a truly civilised future.'

Edmund hooted and flopped over on to his back, causing the general to send over an aide to warn them that this was 'no concert hall' and 'to behave themselves'. When the aide had left – with a flea in his ear from Edmund – Edmund rolled over and pointed a finger at Clive.

'A century ago, India was among the great civilised nations on earth, under its Emperor Akbar. There was peace and justice here, and now ...' He gave a sardonic laugh. 'How we English delude ourselves. We are never at a loss for a noble reason by which to cloak our desires.'

Clive scrambled to his feet, his face set with anger. Had it been any other man but Edmund he would have struck him and called him out on the field of honour. He controlled himself with difficulty and shook his fist at his friend.

'Whatever India might have been a century ago, it is not now. It is a patchwork quilt of ruthlessly governed fiefs, with the princes constantly at war in their greed for another's land. Had you studied as many books in Madras as I did, instead of seducing every woman that took your fancy, your knowledge of India might be more profound. This country, I tell you, is corrupted by its traditions, its religion, its princes, its racial fears. *God give me strength,*' he added with surprising passion, 'and one day I shall impose on it the rule of law, and of *justice.*'

Edmund rose slowly to his feet, taken aback and oddly impressed by this outburst. He felt that for a brief moment a shutter had been raised and he had been privileged to take a swift glance at a man's naked soul. He gave Clive a twisted smile and hastened to make amends.

'Perhaps you're right, Robert,' he said, putting his hand on the other's shoulder. 'Take care of yourself,' he added affectionately, when the brisk tattoo of a drum put an end to further conversation.

All around them men were springing to arms and forming into

line of battle. The two captains touched hands and returned to their respective troops. The general's exotic umbrella was folded and put away, and from the sea commenced the dull booming of cannon as the warships once more opened fire.

Hot pieces of metal as large as a man's head were sent crashing into Pondicherry. Columns of red-black smoke and dust spurted up and then hung wearily in the sultry air. The accuracy of the gunners seemed to have improved for much of the shot actually struck the red sandstone walls, but apart from creating more gravel and dust the barrage was seen to have no measurable effect.

To the stirring sound of drumbeats and the shrilling of fifes, the four long lines of red-coated fusiliers and grenadiers in their tall mitres, muskets levelled with bayonets fixed, advanced at a disciplined march towards the menacingly silent and still unbreached ramparts. It was picturesque, impressive, even noble, and all so terribly futile.

As they came within a hundred paces of the thick walls the entire ridge of crenellations suddenly rippled with puffs of smoke, and tiny spurts of flame leapt from many muskets. As if a long stick had been pushed against a line of tin soldiers, nearly the full length of the first wave of fusiliers crumpled to the ground, and terrible cries were heard. Yet the movement continued. The pace remained steady as the second, third and fourth lines trudged resolutely forward.

Another ripple of fire. Another line decimated. But by the time the defenders had reloaded their muskets, the grenadiers had reached the base of the wall. Pulling out their large matches, they lit them and applied them to the fuses of the globe-shaped grenades they carried. Like a male corps-de-ballet, at a word of command the whole line pirouetted round and tossed the bombs over the wall. At the same time the fusiliers kept down the heads of the defenders with brisk musket fire.

The grenades exploded with noisy violence, causing many casualties among the French but influencing the battle hardly at all. This was repeated over and over again until all the bombs had been expended, then the drums beat a retreat and all the soldiers retired to replenish their supplies and to prepare for the next round.

Four times that day did this clod-pated general launch these self-destructive attacks, and four times was he repulsed. That the men did not mutiny under such insane leadership was a credit to their discipline.

It was late afternoon when Clive and Edmund saw each other again, both miraculously uninjured – though Edmund was missing an epaulette due to a badly aimed shot. They embraced, and as they came apart, Clive, glancing over Edmund's shoulder, suddenly stiffened. The great doors of the fortress were slowly being pulled open.

He pointed, unable to speak, as five men emerged, all wearing the uniform of the Volontaire de Bussy, whilst the warrant-officer in the rear carried above his head a white flag of truce. As soon as the five were clear of the wall the gates closed behind them, and Clive even heard the thud as the great bar was slammed across. They paused a moment as if taking note of their surroundings and then, with admirable courage and elegant diffidence, began marching purposefully towards the English lines where a pop-eyed English general stared at them in growing exultation.

Their long, pale blue coats, red lapels and bibs, floppy bear-skin hats, were as stifling as the British uniforms. But if the heat was a torment to them they disdained to admit it. The French officers marched across the recent battlefield, respectfully avoiding the still unburied corpses, as if on a Parisian boulevard in the cool of a spring afternoon. They carried no firearms and their swords were sheathed.

The general rose slowly to his feet, cautioning the men to hold their fire, and, with ill-concealed elation at Dupleix' intention to surrender, adjusted his posture to that of 'victor magnanimous to the defeated' and calmly awaited them. With massive dignity he posed there, hand on sword hilt, other hand on hip, and set himself for the supreme moment of his career. When the deputation was no more than twenty paces away, one of his aides gave an audible gasp as he recognised the officer leading it. He whispered urgently to the general, and the general's eyebrows shot up with even greater jubilation. 'My God!' he told himself. 'Pondicherry must be in a terrible condition if Dupleix is sending his top general on a mission like this.'

The officers snapped to a halt in a little flurry of dust. General Bussy drew himself up and doffed his hat in a respectful salute. The English general did likewise and then courteously invited the Frenchman into the shade of two stunted trees. Bussy stared at his erstwhile opponent for a second or two as if summing him up, then he snapped his fingers and an aide placed a scroll of parchment into his hand. Bussy never once took his eyes off the English general.

With a small Gallic flourish he unrolled the scroll, glanced at it as if to refresh his memory, and then began to speak. It was a loud voice, a commanding one, and it rolled out with the timbre and assurance of a town-cryer.

'Pour le Général des armées anglaises,' he began, switching immediately to English the moment he had made his point. 'I am commanded by His Excellency, Joseph François Dupleix, Governor of Pondicherry and of all factories, trading posts, owing allegiance to France in the Provinces of the Carnatic and Bengal . . . to declare and to command that this present engagement and contest of arms between les armées Françaises and the forces of England do now cease forthwith . . .'

The English general gravely nodded but found it difficult to conceal his excitement and satisfaction at the marvellous drama with which the surrender was being negotiated. General Bussy gave him an oblique glance, guessing at what was in his mind, then went on, with even more theatre than before.

'Be it known to you that, this day, news has reached our hand that, on the Eighteenth day of October, Seventeen Hundred and Forty-Eight, the nations of England and France did sign an agreement for peace, and a treaty was concluded to this effect at the town of Aix-La-Chapelle.' He looked up and gave a benign smile, then added, rather more warmly than before, 'As subjects, and in oath bound to our respective nations, we are therefore required to lay down our arms and declare peace between ourselves as from this moment.'

The English general's face was a study of astonishment. His mouth gaped vapidly as the document was placed in his hands. He unrolled it but the words swam before his eyes. Edmund, seeing his difficulty, sprang forward and offered to translate. He did so, modulating his voice – with some difficulty – to the gravity of the moment.

'I do not believe it,' spluttered the general when Edmund had finished. He pointed a threatening finger at General Bussy. 'It is a trick ... a trick, I say. Dupleix is trying ...'

'Monsieur,' Bussy cut in with heavy patience, 'a French ship put into Madras some three days ago with documents from my government and a copy of the Aix-la-Chapelle Treaty. It took a fast horseman no more than two days to reach Pondicherry. His Excellency invites you to inspect them at your convenience.'

The general refused to listen. It was all a conspiracy to cheat him of his victory. He began ranting, 'The papers are fraudulent! It is a stratagem to avoid defeat ... to ease the pressure of my forces on Pondicherry!'

Bussy's mouth tightened and his eyes began to flash. 'Monsieur, His Excellency has no need of *stratagems* to defeat the British. Were we not restrained by this Treaty we should continue this battle until the vultures picked the bones of the remnants of your army; until the whole maidan in front of Pondicherry was strewn with corpses.'

At this challenge the general swelled with outrage. He swore, grasped at his sword hilt, and began to draw the blade. Bussy backed warily and reached for his own sword. Edmund swiftly moved between the two angry men and firmly clamped his hand over that of the general's, gently forcing the blade back into its sheath.

'Sir, you may not violate the truce under which you have received the deputation. General Bussy's person is sacrosanct,' he said quickly; adding in a swift appeal to reason, 'Might I suggest, with respect, sir, that it would be wiser to confront Monsieur Dupleix and there examine the full text of the Treaty?'

The French general, eyeing this performance with quiet amusement, cast a glance of curiosity at the English captain and muttered an aside to him in French.

'When you weary of this pompous fool, Captain, come to see me. I can use a good liaison officer or an aide,' he said, his eyes twinkling. Edmund squinted at him, batting back without a moment's hesitation, ' 'Tis a greater fool, Monsieur le Marquis, who presumes his enemy to be one.'

The Governor-General of Pondicherry greeted his English visitors with elaborate courtesy some two hours later. In the sumptuous conference room, across an acreage of marble table, the two former adversaries took the measure of each other. Disdaining the invitation to be seated, the English general, with his senior officers, stood erect and aloof. But both Edmund and Clive noticed the absence of triumph in the Frenchman. In fact, to Dupleix, the Treaty of Aix-La-Chapelle was a deliberately engineered ruse by the English, and a disaster for France – especially with regard to the current situation in India.

He came to the point quickly. 'The substance of this ... remarkable document,' he said, stretching the many sheets of parchment between his fingers as if they were the throats of the signatories, 'is that all factories, towns and territories, formerly under British influence, are to be restored to her control.' He paused for a dramatic moment then added caustically, 'It would seem, gentlemen, that our chess-board has been tilted, and that we are to set out our pieces as they were two years ago.'

His head jerked round in annoyance as the sound of a cannon boomed across the water, and he glared at the visitors. 'Perhaps one of your staff, General, could inform Admiral Watson that the battle is over,' he said acidly. 'We might then conclude our own peace treaty in less hazardous conditions.'

A man was hastily despatched to the English Admiral.

Documents were frowned through, niggled at, but eventually signed with the minimum of grace by both parties. A relaxing of tension followed and glasses of excellent French wine were offered and grudgingly accepted by the English.

Another game in the interminable contest was over. It belonged to France. With good cards and devious play, Dupleix had gained every trick – but the Treaty of Aix-La-Chapelle had ordered him to refund the winnings. Yet his undoubted achievement had been prestige, for in the shadows beyond the card table the Muslim princes placed side bets on the French. Among themselves the Rajahs and Nawabs chuckled derisively at English pretensions to military prowess.

'Well, well, well. We live in an age of miracles,' exclaimed Edmund cheerfully when later he and Clive were discussing the Treaty.

'No miracle,' Clive replied sombrely. 'An interregnum only, during which Dupleix will pay court to the Nawab whilst strengthening his position in the Carnatic. Once his base here is secure, French influence will reach out to cover the whole of India.'

Edmund shrugged. 'And is it all that important? India is big enough for two traders.'

Clive shook Edmund's arm, and sighed, 'Dupleix, my naïve Edmund, is the first of the Compagnie des Indes Orientales: a state enterprise concerned with the expansion of French colonialism. It is not simply trade that Dupleix is after, but political control.'

'And is not the East India Company the same?'

Clive shook his head vigorously. 'Trade and profit only ... although,' he mused, 'were the opportunity ever given, I think that I, too, might consider political control. Commerce can only function under a peaceful and progressive government – and a government can only progress when a strong and just body is in control.'

Their discussion was interrupted by a major of cavalry. 'Ah, so here's where you're skulking,' he cried good-humouredly, handing each of them a sealed envelope. 'Orders, I think, for your reassignment.'

They slit open and read their letters. Clive, a little glumly, said, 'Back to Madras for me.'

Whilst Edmund, miserably, added, 'They're sending me to Fort William ... in *Calcutta*.'

10

THE PHAETON went bowling down the central thoroughfare at a speed too great for the safety of others on the street. Its passengers – a lieutenant of foot soldiers and a young lady – were clearly exhilarated by the experience, until a sedan-chair and its carriers emerged from round the corner of the intersection. The driver of the phaeton screamed imprecations and tried to stop. It was too late. The peons fled at the sight of the carriage bearing down on them, leaving their own passenger to his fate. A wheel of the phaeton just grazed the bars of the palanquin, snapping them off but leaving chair and occupant mainly unscathed.

The lieutenant leapt from the carriage and began berating the peons. He was a large man with heavy jowls and small eyes, yet fairly good-looking. His attitude changed immediately, however, when he recognised the rank of the sedan-chair's occupant, and he became deferential.

'I did not realise, sir ...' He watched Edmund uneasily as he climbed shakily out of the chair. 'Lieutenant Mathieson, sir,' he introduced himself, doffing his tricorne hat and pulling himself erect.

'You're a bloody, inconsiderate and reckless fool,' Edmund began before noticing the lady in the carriage – at which he calmed remarkably. The lieutenant came forward with studied courtesy.

'Allow me to introduce you, sir,' he offered, assisting Edmund to the door of the coach. 'Captain ...?'

'Edmund Maskelyne ...'

'May I present Captain Edmund Maskelyne, Miss Wilkinson,' he said with a flourish.

'I trust you are not injured, Captain,' she enquired solicitously. No, he was not injured, he replied, allowing a shadow of pain to cross his face.

She seemed to be his own age, but that might have been deceptive. Her eyes were warm brown and had exceptionally long eyelashes. The hair was almost black, whilst her olive complexion suggested mixture of ancestry. Even by upper-class Calcutta standards, she was richly gowned and wore a fetching sun-hat in a fashionable style. He was impressed.

With some concern she looked past him to the sedan-chair and then pointedly at the lieutenant. He hastily pulled from his outsize purse a few coins and handed them to the eager peons.

'Your palanquin has been damaged, Captain,' she said – which seemed a remarkable observation to Edmund, seeing that bits of it were scattered on the street. 'I should be honoured if you would allow my phaeton to take you to your destination.'

'Fort William, Miss Wilkinson,' he returned quickly, 'if it is not out of your way?'

It was by no means out of her way, but first she would have to drop Lieutenant Mathieson. He is late, Captain, hence the speed at which we were travelling, she explained.

So the phaeton belonged to Miss Wilkinson. That was something to think about, and so was the faintly ironical smile that Mathieson gave him when he left the carriage at the gates of a mansion in the northern part of Calcutta.

Edmund glanced at her much-ringed hand when the phaeton started off again. There was nothing there to signify prior claims. She was sitting next to him on the narrow seat and the fine scent of her presence titillated his nostrils. 'A handsome woman' he now considered her rather than a beautiful one, for she was a shade older than he had first imagined. Nonetheless, there was an attractive and lively quality about her that made a strong appeal to him.

'Lieutenant Mathieson,' he said cautiously, 'a close friend of yours, Miss Wilkinson?'

She looked sideways at him and flicked her eyelashes.

'An acquaintance,' was all she said, leaning over to adjust her long gown and in doing so affording him a glimpse of her fine breasts. The vehicle turned a corner a little too fast and Miss Wilkinson rocked against him.

'Sorry,' he apologised as he put his hand up to catch her.

'Such a terrible driver,' she laughed.

'You are English, Miss Wilkinson?' he asked, thoroughly enjoying the journey.

She hesitated a second, but the pause was sufficient for Edmund. 'My father was,' came her reply.

The reddish-grey walls of Fort William came into view. Miss Wilkinson stirred a little, realising the end of the journey was near. She sized up her handsome companion.

'Have you been long in Calcutta, Captain Maskelyne?' she asked.

'A little less than three months. I'm still finding my way about the city.'

'Then you must allow me to show you around some time.' She took him up immediately. Almost too quickly, he thought, for an unmarried lady. 'Calcutta's quite a large city, you know, though there are only three hundred English citizens here and one soon gets to meet most of them.'

'If you feel you would not be ... compromised, Miss Wilkinson, by being seen in my company, perhaps you would allow me to show you around the fort ... unless, of course, it is already familiar to you,' he ventured, full of gallantry.

'Not at all, to both questions, Captain. I have never been inside and I should be most pleased to accept your invitation.'

On reaching the fort, Edmund assisted her up a large step that led to the main building, and did not miss the shapely ankle she revealed in the process. She gave a little sigh at the slight exertion and proceeded to straighten her clothes with little pats and tugs. Despite the metal pannier over which her gown flowed, Edmund guessed at the quality of figure underneath.

'It isn't very impressive, is it, Captain?' she said, and, looking at the fort through her eyes, Edmund knew what she meant. Candidly, only the redoubts at the corners – shaped wedges some ten feet higher than the outer walls – offered any security from serious attack.

'No, it isn't,' he agreed, putting his arm round her to lift her up another step. 'There is a ditch that runs part way around the city – ostensibly to keep out the Marathas. But it would be useless in a determined attack.' He indicated the wide stretch of water a few hundred yards away. 'Calcutta's main defence, its harbour,' he said grimly. 'Whilst warships are there the merchants sleep soundly in their beds.'

'All this land used to belong to the Marathas,' she said suddenly, 'and the English bought it from them.'

'Not strictly correct, Miss Wilkinson,' he replied, giving her that infuriating superior male smile. 'We own it by a firman of the Emperor, granted to us after we'd held it against Moghul troops. We collect the taxes on his behalf, keep our share, and send the balance to the Emperor in Delhi. That agreement has never been rescinded,' he concluded, feeling pleased with himself.

'My goodness, Captain Maskelyne, you are well informed,' she returned in mock astonishment.

'The land we obtained from the Marathas was in the Carnatic,' he continued. 'They offered to sell the English as much land as could be covered by the firing of a cannon ball. So ...'

'So the English brought the biggest cannon they could find,' she interrupted triumphantly.

He grinned. 'Absolutely correct ... and in that area we built Fort St David ...'

She suddenly clutched his arm in fright. 'What was that?'

Quite enjoying the sensation of being 'protector', he asked innocently, 'What was what, Miss Wilkinson?'

'That noise,' she glared at him. 'That shouting and wailing.' Then she cocked her head and listened more carefully. 'Somebody seems to be singing.'

64

Disengaging himself, he smoothly slid an arm round her waist – as a precaution against attack, his attitude seemed to indicate.

'Come. I'll show you.'

There was an element of mischief in his manner as he led her across the courtyard and on to the wide covered verandah of a large stone building. They went down a flight of rough granite steps and then along a wide corridor on one side of which a series of low arches opened out to face the harbour. On the other side were a number of thick doors for what appeared to be storerooms, and at the far end of the passage-way was yet another door in front of which a sentry was leaning indolently.

The noise of wailing was much louder now.

With some trepidation, Miss Wilkinson allowed herself to be taken along. The sentry sprang to attention when he saw the Captain approaching. It seemed to her that the door was of exceptional thickness; it was secured by two bars and two heavy padlocks. At the height of a man's shoulder was a grille about twelve inches by ten inches, and – to her astonishment – through the bars across it a fist had been thrust with a metal cup dangling from the little finger.

The sentry whispered urgently to the owner of the fist and the cup was speedily withdrawn. At Edmund's suggestion she peeped hesitantly through the grille, and saw that the room was a small stone cell. A man was slumped in the corner of the cell and another man was standing and looking shamefacedly at her to her acute embarrassment.

Edmund questioned the sentry and looked surprised at his answer. 'Sergeant Grimsby, again!' he exclaimed, naming the soldier who had assisted his escape with Clive from the fort in Madras – two, or was it three years previously?

He hurried Miss Wilkinson back along the corridor, his mind on Sergeant Grimsby, who appeared to be a regular occupant of the cell. He answered her questions in an off-hand manner.

'It's the black hole, as the soldiers call it. Every fort has one.'

She grimaced. 'What a horrid name.'

They climbed the stone steps, and she breathed deeply in the open air. 'And you put soldiers in a place like that,' she accused. He spread his hands as if to say, 'What other choice have we got?'

'Only until they sober up. They get their pay on a Saturday morning and then they go on the spree. Some go to cockfights in the afternoon. Some go to ...' he hesitated, 'places of ill-repute; others spend their time in the punch shops. By midnight many of them are roaring drunk. If they get back to barracks without too much noise we take no notice, but if they get into a fight and the patrol has to bring them in, we toss them into the black hole until they're sober.'

'And what happens then?'

'Two days later they're taken before a senior officer and tried. If found guilty they're sentenced to loss of pay or a flogging.'

'A flogging!' she exclaimed, knowing that Zamindars had power to order a man to be flogged to death for some crimes. He guessed immediately what she was thinking and hastened to correct the impression.

'Not to that extent, Miss Wilkinson. Twenty lashes laid on hard is the usual punishment ... for instance, that fellow in there now, Sergeant Grimsby, has been a soldier for fifteen years and boasts of having received three *thousand* lashes in his time, and he's still hale and hearty ... though I can hardly recommend the treatment for good health,' he added dryly.

She felt slightly nauseated at what she had seen and heard, and it was a relief to be out of that dreadful corridor and into the sunshine once more.

'I think that I must leave now, Captain Maskelyne.' She forced a smile.

As he assisted her into the phaeton a few minutes later, he removed his hat and said, 'Might I have permission to call on you at some convenient time, Miss Wilkinson?'

She made a play at considering this, then turned her head to look him full in the face.

'Tomorrow, Captain Maskelyne,' she returned, with most unfeminine assurance. 'I shall send my carriage for you at three in the afternoon.' Then flashing him a most immodest glance, she was gone.

Edmund waited until the phaeton had turned the far corner then, in an excess of glee, stuck his hand into his pocket, extracted a coin and spun it into the air, catching it with a great flourish. He noticed a small Hindu child observing him with the quiet melancholy of the racial outcast and, impulsively – for it was a golden coin – flicked it in his direction where it was caught with skill and disbelief. Still in this mood of gaiety, Edmund turned, rushed through the gates of the fort – and promptly sent sprawling a young writer who had been coming from the opposite direction.

Profuse with apologies, Edmund bent down and helped the rather slender fellow to his feet. He whipped out a handkerchief and made some effort to dust the powdery filth from his clothes.

'I do beg your pardon and hope you are not injured in any way,' he said with concern.

The young man was grimly offended, and from his thin lips he grunted something inaudible and manifestly uncomplimentary about 'irresponsible *officers*', and jerked his body free from Edmund's ministering hands. Giving a chilling bow, no less insulting than a blow, he made to stalk off – and promptly went down on his knee as his ankle gave way.

Edmund, crimson with self-reproach, rushed forward again to assist the injured youth to his feet.

'You have indeed suffered harm, my dear sir,' he exclaimed. 'Pray allow me to assist you inside where I may summon a physician.'

With bad grace, though the tightness of his face was evidence of his distress, the unprepossessing youth allowed the captain to place an arm around him. Edmund could easily have carried the injured man, but he 'walked' him to the officers' quarters instead, suspecting that the lesser indignity of the smaller man would produce less scornful abuse from him.

Even conceding that he had been needlessly injured, there was a smouldering resentment in the youth that Edmund felt was excessive. Yet the image of Clive flashed through his mind, and recalling what he had been like when living miserably as a writer, he was filled with compassion for the youngster.

Within thirty minutes the victim was sitting in Edmund's most comfortable chair, watching balefully as the physician completed the binding on his ankle.

'Twisted,' said the doctor dismissively, for at least the fourth time. 'No more than twisted. Keep your weight off it for a few days an' you'll be able to dance a quadrille with the best of 'em,' was his final laconic advice, before bowing to each of them curtly. Edmund rushed after him simply to be reassured of the patient's condition – and to hand him a few coins.

'Edmund Maskelyne, captain of foot soldiers, sir.' Edmund introduced himself formally when he returned to the young man. The youth – who seemed about nineteen or twenty – cocked his angular, smooth-cheeked face, squinted cynically at his 'host', and answered insolently, 'Warren Hastings ... writer and exile, and captain of sweepers.'

Edmund was taken aback and his cheeks pinked at such unnecessary churlishness. On any other occasion he would have flung the boorish fellow from his room. But Edmund had never forgotten the sight of that discarded flintlock on the floor of just such another embittered writer's lodgings.

He was no longer moved to compassion, for Hastings was not the kind of person who called forth feelings of such quality in others, but he felt sympathy for the life the youngster must be enduring.

'I was a writer myself some years ago,' he offered, in an attempt to establish some rapport with his prickly guest, 'and I must confess I left the profession with the greatest relief.'

'And you're a captain now,' Hastings was quick to reply. 'Dressing in a fine uniform, ladies hanging breathlessly on your arm, a fat purse, a real career in front of you ... *everything*,' he almost spat out, his eyes warily studying Edmund's face as if calculating the extent he dared go before the big fellow retaliated. Edmund said nothing. The youth continued his lamentation, his voice slipping easily into a whine. 'Think that any lady would look at me? Would she spend five minutes with a man who couldn't afford even one glass of punch?'

The strain was beginning to tell, but Edmund still made an effort to be polite. 'You wouldn't have much difficulty in taking a commission whenever you've saved a little money,' he said, with just a slight hardening of tone. 'Nearly all the officers were originally writers. You could do the same.'

Warren Hastings gave an ugly laugh, then swiftly cut it short, aware he had gone too far. 'Become a soldier!' Then he recalled the muscles in the arm that had half carried him into that room, and wisely became less aggressive. 'No, Captain Maskelyne. I have no desire to become a soldier.'

Edmund walked over to the door, removed his sword and belt and hung them behind it, a slight hint that now he required the room to himself. Hastings made no move to go.

'Life will not be easy for you, Mr Hastings, if clerical work is your sole ambition,' he said, as he straightened the sword straps.

Hastings snorted. 'I have no intention of remaining a writer. I have other plans.'

'And they are?' Edmund asked, from politeness rather than curiosity.

'To leave India as soon as I can. To get away from this *stinking* land,' he said vehemently, 'and return to England with as much gold as my trunks will hold.' It was the popular sentiment voiced by all the junior writers – and the senior ones as well.

'Admirable ambition,' Edmund said tonelessly. 'I wish you well.' He began unbuttoning his tunic, underlining the hint. 'Have you been in India very long?'

The patient cast him a sour look, rose to his feet and tentatively tested his ankle. He moved forward two paces.

'A whole lifetime ... a *lifetime* ... for that's what seven weeks in this damnable country seems like.'

Edmund, only fractionally sympathetic now despite the persistent image of Clive, replied with the local cliché. 'The first weeks are the worst. Soon you'll find there's merit in the country, and promotion is very rapid out here.' He produced his large watch and consulted it with a frown.

'I will leave you, Captain.' Hastings took the hint at last, hobbling towards the door.

Now that the patient was finally leaving, Edmund became solicitous again. 'Allow me to call on you tomorrow, sir, so that I may reassure myself as to your welfare ... and again, my deepest and most profound apologies, Mr Hastings.'

Something of his tender, unaffected honesty struck a responsive chord in the youth. He looked back at his host with curiosity, and with a kind of tolerance that conflicted with habitual contempt.

'You're a strange man and a kind one, Captain Maskelyne,' he said quietly. 'Misguided, I think. But I warn you kindly, it won't be gentlemen like yourself who'll make the running in this country – and neither will it be complaisance nor compassion that'll create a nation out of India,' he added softly, moving outside into the brilliant sun of Bengal.

II

CLIVE DISMOUNTED, handed the reins to a waiting chubdar, climbed the steps to the verandah of the punch shop – where he was greeted effusively by the proprietor – and sat at a table overlooking the street. He ordered a glass of wine and soda water and found he had a full thirty minutes to wait before Margaret drove past in her father's carriage.

Despite his rank of captain he was still *persona non grata* to the Maskelynes. He took a sip of wine and grimaced. It was costing him a fortune to sit at that table every other day, in the hope that he would see Margaret. His income was three pounds sterling per month. Adequate to keep a gentleman in style, but not a married one – and most definitely not one proposing to marry Margaret Maskelyne.

There was a jingling of harness and into view came the splendid carriage of Mr Maskelyne and the parasol of Margaret, held vertically above her head. His heart leapt, and he rushed towards the carriage which had halted in front of the shop. He was about to help her down, but she beckoned him into the carriage instead. He climbed up beside her with alacrity, and allowed his hand to drop gently on to hers.

'They're both away for the next two hours,' she whispered in gleeful conspiracy. 'I decided we'd drive into the country.'

Clive sat upright in the carriage and looked grave – until they had driven sufficiently far out of the city, when he turned towards her and slid an arm around her shoulders. Her head moved towards his and their lips touched briefly.

'I received a letter from Edmund,' he said, pulling two folded sheets of paper from his pocket and spreading them out on his lap. She averted her eyes, and asked diffidently, 'How is Miss Petal Wilkinson?'

Clive shot her a startled look. 'You know of her?'

'Of course,' she answered, adding primly, '*I* receive letters from him as well ... perhaps with some of the ... details missing, but I've a shrewd idea of what's going on.'

Clive pulled at the lobe of his ear and gave her a secretive glance. It seemed wrong for such an innocent creature to be privy to Edmund's escapades.

'Did he mention ... what she was?' he asked cautiously, and was shocked by the amused glance she gave him. She patted his hand.

'Yes. She's the owner of Calcutta's most exclusive bawdyhouse.'

'Bordello,' he corrected swiftly, thinking the name less vulgar, and wondering if Edmund had told her also of the two 'charmers' there, Jasmine and Lotus, about whom he had written with much enthusiasm. 'Of course, there is no question of him marrying,' he added, hastening to reassure her.

'No, he won't marry,' she replied quietly, implying that, apart from her profession, the one-eighth of Moghul blood in Miss Petal Wilkinson would be prohibitive. No Englishman induced social ostracism for keeping one or two of these light-skinned Eurasians as mistresses, but society would not countenance marriage with one. 'Even if his affection for this lady were such as to make it desirable for him, the Governor's permission would be needed to make their liaison legal.'

Clive was silent for a while, as he gazed at the arid land worked by hundreds of toiling peasants bent double as they poked at the soil.

'Does he say anything new in his letter?' asked Margaret, moving away from a distasteful subject yet envious of her brother's freedom.

'He first wrote me of Miss Wilkinson over a year ago, and though he's still attached to her and visits her regularly, I sincerely believe it is solely because the woman is intelligent and provides him with excellent and stimulating conversation.'

Margaret flicked him a sceptical glance but made no comment.

'However,' Clive went on, wondering how much he had a right to say, 'another lady has come into his life.'

'Another!' Margaret exclaimed, feeling cheated at not being the first to know.

Clive considered her for a moment or two, then realised he had committed himself and would have to tell the rest. 'It's either Anna or Anne, I'm not sure which. The writing was smudged. But it seems an unrequited love so far. The lady apparently is affianced – or else there is some understanding with a fellow-officer of Edmund's, some lieutenant by the name of Mathieson.'

'He's such a blind fool,' cried Margaret angrily, not really believing that Edmund could be in love. 'Of all the women in Bengal – all those spinsters who sail from England simply in the hope of snaring a husband – he has to choose a woman already betrothed. Really, Robert, he's a most irresponsible fellow.'

Clive lowered his head, wanting to be loyal to Edmund but unwilling to quarrel with his sister.

'I think we should be returning, Robert,' she said, waywardly transferring to the bearer of bad news the displeasure rightly earned by another. He agreed immediately, finding that for him, too, the excursion had gone sour.

12

INSIDE THE great hall in the palace at Murshidabad the aged Nawab of Bengal, Alivardi Khan, seated on a throne that glittered with gilt and semi-precious stones, benignly surveyed the assembled nobles. But always his gaze returned to the two principal figures.

The audience of dignitaries in robes of colourful splendour muttered and hissed in approval as they craned their necks to see over the heads of those in front. Then came a loud 'Ah!' and they clapped their hands together as Mir Jafar – the Nawab's senior general – gravely pronounced the words of marriage to the sixteen-year-old Sareen.

The now seventeen-year-old Mir Kassim, and the nineteen-year-old Siraj-ud-daula – ostensibly friends again, though the stolen trinket still hung from the older boy's neck – watched the ceremony with different feelings. On a balcony that ran down one side of the huge room, the two youngsters had made themselves comfortable, leaning forward with their heads practically level with the Nawab's throne, but some twenty feet distant from it.

Siraj was bored, and loudly proclaimed the fact. The Nawab frowned at him and he subsided into fidgeting silence. His companion was staring at the young bride with such intensity that one or two of the noblemen who observed him whispered to each other and shook their heads.

Sareen, in a gown of blue and gold, her head and face covered with red satin so that only her eyes could be seen, raised them sadly to the balcony. She bit her lip, praying that she would not weep and thus be shamed, then lowered her head, deliberately cutting him from her view. She knew that nothing could alter what had been ordained since she was six years old.

Siraj-ud-daula sought to liven things up. He leaned to one side and gave Kassim a push, hissing spitefully, 'How terrible to see the girl you love married to your *father*.' He smothered a laugh when his companion turned on him with eyes blazing. Siraj prodded him again, his voice mockingly sympathetic.

'Have no fear, Kassim. Your father is old, and Sareen will be eager for you when you creep into her bed.' But he recoiled nervously as Kassim knocked over the chair and stood facing his tormentor, his fingers clasping the hilt of his curved dagger. He stretched out his left hand and thrust a finger under the older boy's nose, his voice quivering with an emotion barely held in check.

'One word ... one word more, Siraj-ud-daula, and you die *now*,' he gritted out.

Siraj's left hand shot out and gripped the wrist. He exerted pressure sufficient to cause the smaller boy to wince, then in pretended abjectness began to plead, 'A thousand pardons, Kassim. Little did I realise how deep was your affection for the lovely Sareen.'

Kassim grabbed at his knife and drew it from its sheath, the little drama unnoticed by the throng of people below. Siraj flung up both hands in mock contrition, taking a gamble that Kassim would not strike. Kassim lunged at his chest, but Siraj was too quick. His left forearm came round, blocking Kassim's wrist; his other hand, with almost contemptuous ease, wrenched the knife away. He tossed the blade on to the floor.

'Do not kill me, Mir Kassim,' he begged, in mock helplessness, then cocking his head to one side, added, in a low and ominous tone, 'for if you so much as cut my flesh, Alivardi Khan will have you buried in the sand up to your neck, and kite-hawks will descend to pluck out your eyes and the jackals will crunch at your bones. Truly, Sareen would not care to witness such a thing happening to her *son*.'

'I am not her son,' Kassim screamed, though his voice barely rose above a whisper. 'She married my father, but I am the son

73

of his principal wife.' He was in tears.

'Ah yes,' Siraj sighed, 'the seraglio has a new ruler. But what perfection she is, Kassim. Think of the delight in those breasts, those deep mysterious thighs ... and that silly old man having it all.' Then he became consoling and stretched out a hand to touch Kassim's shoulder. The hand was roughly shaken off.

'But have no fear, my dear friend Kassim, Alivardi Khan cannot live for ever. I will see that he does not,' he muttered imprudently with a hard glint in his eyes. 'And when Siraj-ud-daula is Nawab of Bengal, I shall take her for my own bed and shall grant you the privilege of sharing her charms ... Hah!' he cried as Kassim rushed at him. But the furious boy only suffered the ignominy of being picked up and gently bumped on the floor, and then left to lie there whilst his antagonist strode away, laughing to himself.

Mir Kassim picked himself up, tears flowing down his cheeks, took one last look at the scene below where Sareen, the ceremony concluded, was being led from the great hall in procession for the celebrations that would last until dawn.

Hatred for his father at that moment ranked second only to his loathing for Siraj-ud-daula. Minutes later, in the privacy of his own apartments, he took down from a shelf an exquisitely bound copy of the Koran. He opened it and placed both hands on its pages, and stood there for a moment or two before kneeling and pressing his forehead to the floor in the direction of Mecca. He stretched forth both his arms in supplication and howled his grief to Allah.

'May the miseries and torments of a thousand years, the agonies of hooks and burning irons, the treacheries and malice of enemies, burn his flesh, tear out his heart, cut from him his fingers, hands, arms, legs. May the name of Siraj-ud-daula be a stench in the nostrils of pigs, and may the fragments of his body be carried to hell in the hide of a swine.'

13

IN 1751 two major events took place: France and England went to war again, and the Nizam of Hyderabad died, leaving unresolved who would be the next Nawab of the Carnatic.

Both European nations ranged behind their own candidate. England chose Mohammad Ali; France supported Chanda Sahib. All the other princes crowded the ringside ready to place their own weight on the side of whichever champion seemed like winning. The odds were all in favour of France, for no one had forgotten the poor showing of England at Pondicherry, the destruction of Fort St David, or the easy capture of Madras.

The result of the 'election' was of paramount importance to the foreigners. The contest began in earnest when the English nominee, Mohammad Ali, found himself besieged in his capital of Trichinopoly (200 miles south of Madras) by the forces of Chanda Sahib assisted by the French. Day after day, in the sun-baked high walls of the Trichinopoly fort, Mohammad Ali, with a few hundred loyal subjects plus two dozen English soldiers, held out against several thousand native troops of Chanda Sahib and a few hundred unenthusiastic French soldiers. Only slight damage was suffered by both sides, yet it was evident that at some stage the defence would collapse; Mohammad Ali would be taken and executed by Chanda Sahib, and a French-inclined Nawab would rule in the Carnatic.

Clive, itching for battle, weary of Madras, and frustrated in his efforts to win Margaret, went to see Stringer Lawrence who was also in Madras.

'If Trichinopoly is not relieved within the next few weeks, England will be finished in the Carnatic. Dupleix will be the real ruler of this state and we shall have to submit meekly to whatever he orders the Nawab to tell us to do,' General Lawrence said, his thin cheeks sucking mightily at the hookah between pauses.

'I often wonder why the princes tolerate us at all,' observed Clive glumly, at which Lawrence gave him a shrewd smile.

'Do you cease dealing with your grocer or negotiating with your banker simply because you dislike the hats they wear?' he returned, shaking his crusty head. 'We cause them trouble, but the benefits we bring them more than balance the irritation of our presence.'

His companion seemed not to have heard. He was staring curiously at one particular volume among the many books behind the old general. It was a short history of the Maratha nation. Lawrence turned to see what he was looking at.

'Something worrying you, Captain?' he asked. 'Captain Clive ...'

This time he obtained a response.

'Sir? ... Yes, forgive me ... I was thinking of the Marathas,' Clive replied, going to the bookcase, pulling out the volume and checking the index for the name he was seeking. He found it and returned to his seat. His eyes sparkled with unconcealed excitement.

'Very well, Captain. You've set the stage, now produce the play,' the General drawled, making due allowances for youth and enthusiasm but finding his patience wearing thin.

'A prince called Nizam-um-Mulk; you remember the name, Sir?'

A finger scratched a grey head thoughtfully from under a lopsided wig. 'Vaguely ... had a few battles with the Marathas, didn't he?'

'He did – and lost.' Clive leant forward in his eagerness to explain. 'The Marathas have never liked pitched battles against superior forces. Their tactics have always consisted in swift movement, so that they can engage small segments of the opponent's army, defeat them and then ride away. By this process they eventually defeated their enemy, or at least caused him to retire.'

'But this is what I've always advocated, Clive,' the old soldier replied, wondering what his companion was leading up to. 'Do you see yourself in some kind of Maratha role?'

Clive got to his feet and began pacing the room nervously. 'Not in that way, General Lawrence, but if you glance through that volume you'll see what I'm getting at. The Marathas were too slippery for the Nizam-um-Mulk, so he attacked Poona which was then the heart of the Maratha nation. He reckoned they would return to its rescue and, with his superior forces, he could defeat them in a set battle in conditions best suited to his own forces.'

'You hardly need finish the story, Captain. Let me guess,' Lawrence interposed. 'The Maratha leader – Baji Rao, I think his name was – about-turned and headed straight for the Nizam's own capital at Aurangabad. Denuded of practically all the Nizam's soldiers, it fell easily to the Marathas, and so the Nizam pulled out of Poona and returned to Aurangabad.'

'Exactly, sir. He never did defeat the Marathas – and he never again dared leave his capital unprotected.' The young man's face glowed with enthusiasm.

'A glass of soda-water, Captain?' Lawrence offered, stirring himself from his chair and pouring a glass for himself – a ruse to give himself time to catch up with his subordinate's galloping imagination. He took a sip. The soda water was as flat and tepid as he felt himself to be.

'You presume that by attacking Chanda Sahib's capital you'll force him to withdraw from Trichinopoly?' he mused.

'I do,' Clive replied, without a second's hesitation.

'And his capital is ...?'

'Arcot.'

Lawrence took out a pair of tiny spectacles and fitted them on his nose; thus equipped he scrutinised a small notebook on his desk. 'Have you any idea of the forces Chanda Sahib has left at Arcot?' he asked, squinting up at Clive.

'Yes, I have, sir ... between eleven and twelve hundred men to garrison both fort and town.'

'And do you know how many troops you'll have available?'

'Two hundred British and three hundred Sepoys.'

Lawrence took off his spectacles and began cleaning them energetically. The idea was madness.

'Captain Clive,' he said after a while, holding his spectacles up to the light, 'soon the rains will be here ...'

'The monsoon will not stop me, sir,' Clive interrupted.

'Pray allow me to finish. As I was saying, the rains will soon be upon us, and you are proposing to tow all your artillery through a quagmire and then attack a major fort. If you were not so enthusiastic, Clive, I should be tempted to laugh,' he said, with a kind of pitying admiration, before adding briskly, 'How many guns will you have?'

'Three cannon, sir ... all that's available,' Clive told the astounded General.

'*Three!* You propose to attack a fort with *three* cannon?' he expostulated and, for several minutes, the subsequent history of the East was in the balance. Eventually he got to his feet, tottered around the desk and put an affectionate arm around Clive's shoulders.

'Against all my military experience I give you permission to try this crazy scheme of yours, Captain,' he said with much misgiving. 'Let us pray that God is your companion – for I assure you you'll get damned little help from any other source.'

On the 26th of August 1751 the expedition for the attack on

77

Arcot got under way in conditions of blistering heat and threatening storm. Riding his grey horse at the head of the column, with few illusions as to the task that faced him, Clive was a proud figure and, for the first time since arriving in India, a contented one. If he had fears at all they were that he be caught in the monsoon before they reached Arcot.

But the sun exacted its toll. The great column slowed and became slower as men collapsed in the heat, prostrate under the weight of the equipment they carried and the constrictions of their uniforms. The two days Clive had calculated for the journey became three. On the fourth day the column was but two-thirds of the way towards its destination. And on the same day the monsoon broke.

With a resounding crack of thunder and a dazzling flash of lightning, the heavens opened in a hissing, cloud-splitting thunderstorm. Animals reared in fright and a number of sepoys fell to the ground and wailed to Shiva to spare them. A deluge of water fell to the earth, pounded into the dust and saturated it. Clive the visionary became Clive the demon. Disregarding his lieutenant's pleas to halt the column and make camp, he dragged his horse about and with its hooves plunging deeply into the mud, rode slowly up and down the long line of struggling men and beasts exhorting them to keep moving. Occasionally he leapt from his mount and put his own hands and shoulders to the cannon wheels as the bullocks ploughed their way forward through the descending gloom.

No commander with his wits about him would have attempted to march under those conditions. But Clive shouted, pleaded, he urged, he encouraged and – as much by his example as anything – he kept the column moving forward foot by foot and yard by yard. By the sheer power of his will he forced five hundred soldiers and all their followers through that awesome monsoon fury against every military principle.

The troops, red tunics and white gaiters now black with mud and saturated with rain, trudged along, placing one foot after the other in the holes made by the feet of the man in front, yet kept their powder-horns covered and their muskets inverted. In the cloud-shrouded dimness of the fading afternoon, the whites of the sepoys' eyes, like those of demented cats in a salt mine, revealed their fear.

For mile after mile, blinded at times by gusts of rain, bending low with arms across their faces, the column pushed a way through the storm. Clive dared not let up a single moment, for he knew that once the men stopped he would not get them in motion again. His own mount had sunk to its knees and refused to get up – so he abandoned it and commandeered another horse for his constant patrolling along the flanks of the column.

As the day drew to a close the rain at last eased off and stopped, and the very air seemed to lighten. Clive called a halt at a village, where the column ate what food it still possessed and rested for the night, making what shelter it could in the saturated conditions.

The villagers in their wattle and daub huts, cowering first from the storm and now from the 'invasion', peered fearfully at the soldiers and whispered to each other. Truly they must be giants among men to have survived in the open and marched unscathed through the worst monsoon in memory. And that strange Englishman on the horse, he who never seemed to tire or be still, of what inhuman nature must he be? A rumour was born.

The rumour became magnified as the villagers mingled with the sepoys, and the sepoys told of their ordeal and of how this preternatural Englishman had – with his own hands – seized the column and pulled it through to safety. The sepoys also mentioned that they were on their way to attack Arcot and that Arcot was finished – for nothing could prevail against the power of their leader or themselves.

But the preternatural Englishman was himself exhausted. He allowed the soldiers to rest a full day in the village – and in that time the news of their coming sped onwards.

Near the end of the sixth day the column reached the outskirts of the small town that was Chanda Sahib's capital. Dispersing the men in battle order, Clive, with a patrol of ten men, entered Arcot to test its defences. There was an air of quiet that seemed more threatening than meeting the expected fusillades of musket fire and grapeshot. They had gone nearly a quarter of a mile when Clive called a halt. From one of the substantial houses on his right – imposing enough to be owned by some senior official – there came sounds of argument, of shouting, then a scuffle. Eventually the door was flung open and there appeared, in the robes of a senior constable, a huge Muslim. He carried a bunch of flowers.

He salaamed deeply to Clive, then obsequiously presented him with the bouquet. Clive took the flowers and responded with a respectful bow and traditional greetings. Within two hours the column was marching through the streets of Arcot, heading for the fort.

Not a musket was fired at them, not a sword nor dagger drawn. Instead, the soldiers and camp attendants, even down to the drovers of the bullock-carts, were bombarded with garlands of flowers from nearly every house which they passed, the townspeople dropping to their knees as the stern figure of Clive on his horse went by. The doors of the fort were open wide, the twelve hundred of the garrison had already fled the town, and the column passed under the great stone archway more like a carnival than an invasion force.

The moment the gates of the fort had closed safely behind them, Clive flung his arms above his head and cried out from sheer exuberance. The cry was taken up by the men and the whole fort resounded to their cheers and laughter. Clive dismounted and allowed himself to be led, past hands outstretched to pat and touch him, into the inner keep and to the apartments of the former commander.

'Leave me now in peace,' he told his senior officers kindly as he looked around the spartanly furnished, stone-floored office; 'and attend to the men. Secure the fort and arrange a meeting of officers for one hour after sunset.' The officers doffed their hats, sprang to attention and filed out of the room. As the latch of the teak door dropped into place, Clive flopped into a chair and lifted his feet on to the desk.

He was bewildered by the suddenness of it all. From the obscurity of an ordinary captain of foot soldiers, he was now commander of a victorious army, master of a fort that had surrendered to him, controller of a major town, the victor of the enemy's capital, and a man whose word was law over an area bigger than London.

He had thought often of this moment, but only as a drummer-boy imagines himself a general; and yet, subconsciously, he had prepared for it by intensive reading and by his military studies under Stringer Lawrence. And now it had happened. Power had been given to him. No! Nothing had been *given*. He had been inspired by an idea. He had planned – and had pushed through that plan against major opposition. With brute energy and determination he had driven a pathetically small force through a tempest, and he had captured the capital of Chanda Sahib. It would be the heaviest blow so far delivered against Dupleix.

Robert Clive that day found the taste of power pleasant indeed. He had revealed the ability to command and to coerce a large concourse of men to exert themselves to the limits of endurance, simply by demonstrating to them the extent of his own determination. He also discovered that the prospect of governing and administering a sizeable territory filled him with enthusiasm rather than dismay. These were revelations indeed for a young man of twenty-six.

A few hours later he sternly addressed his officers. 'Do not be deluded by what you have witnessed this day,' he warned. 'We have neither friends nor allies beyond these walls, for these are Chanda Sahib's people. Even before the flowers you sport around your necks have wilted, there will be gathering against us such an army as will shake the earth in its fury to regain its homeland.' The listeners began to look disconsolate as Clive went on in this harsh vein, laying down rules for the provisioning of the fort against the coming siege, and for their conduct towards the people of Arcot: 'Courteous and fair at all times, unless knives are drawn against you, then evade no fight, but carry it with all your strength against your adversary.'

'Tell the worst to Britons and they fight best of all,' said one ensign, sotto voce, to another.

'Tell the worst to foreigners and they fight not at all,' grinned his companion, colouring when Clive called them to order.

'Preserve your humour for when your bellies are empty and Chanda Sahib is hammering at the gates,' he snapped caustically, then continued, 'We have a period of grace that will last, I hope, for five or six days. During this time I want this fort readied for an onslaught of – not ten times our number, but one hundred times. So now see to your guns, sharpen your blades, make your peace with God.'

14

FOR THE first few days the patrols through Arcot received generous contributions of foodstuffs from the townspeople. Later it required armed expeditions to obtain what they needed. And, when news of Chanda Sahib's approach was known, out came the knives. Trichinopoly, however, had been relieved; the English nominee, Mohammad Ali, saved. Clive's first exercise as a commander and strategist had been splendidly successful. But having saved Trichinopoly he must needs save himself.

From the highest tower of the fort, Clive watched the newly arrived army of Chanda Sahib setting up camp, arranging its cannons, preparing battering rams. And, bearing in mind Lawrence's dictum about keeping the enemy off balance, he forthwith led a party of troops outside the gates on a rampage through the town. It so startled Chanda Sahib and his French cannoneers, that they shifted back their artillery to a more secure redoubt – thus reducing the effectiveness of their guns.

The siege of Arcot commenced. With the reverberating sound of massive drumbeats, the French artillery discharged great cannonballs. From the more distant redoubt the penetrating power of the balls was not as good as it could have been. Still, great chunks of stone were knocked from the lips of the walls, and in one of the salvoes two of the castellated 'teeth' were sent flying across the forecourt to demolish the stables.

Plumes of smoke and dust arose with each hit, and at the sound of each detonating explosive the defenders ducked their heads involuntarily and crouched behind the nearest cover – often too late, for by then the roundshot had struck. With three small cannon at his disposal, Clive returned the fire. He succeeded in collapsing a few buildings and creating dust clouds sufficient to confuse the enemy's marksmanship. Casualties were suffered by both sides, the attackers getting the worst of it due to their less protected position.

'The walls are standing up well, sir,' one of his officers reported, somewhat alarmed to see the commanding officer binding up his arm with a bandage. 'You're injured, sir,' he exclaimed. Clive shook his head irritably and told the fellow to put his finger on the knot.

'A spent musket ball ... broke the skin and bruised the bone – nothing at all,' he said.

On the third day of the siege, he was breakfasting with his Welsh second-in-command.

'Luckily at the range we've compelled Frenchie to shoot at he'll not be able to bring a concentration of fire sufficient to knock down one of the walls,' said the Welshman. 'But Mr Clive, sir, it's the main gates I'm afeared of ...'

'Wrong angle for cannon fire,' Clive replied curtly.

'But not for battering rams or ...'

'Or what?'

The answer was provided by an ensign who flung open the door in great excitement.

'Elephant,' he cried out, military courtesy forgotten in the heat of the moment, then rushed to the window which overlooked the walls and street. 'There, sir!' He pointed.

The two senior officers took one glance and at once hastened from the room, the Welshman to his cannons and Clive to the battlements above the main gate. He took his stand at one of the archery slits that gave him a commanding view. The scene outside was spectacular indeed though there was little in it to give him comfort.

Nine of the great beasts, armoured with long strips of leather draped over their sides to which were fastened scores of thick metal plates, were lumbering in an ungainly manner down the broad street. On each of their massive foreheads a round shield had been fitted from which projected a long iron spike, and on each back, crowded into an armoured howdah, were five warriors with guns and bows. Sitting on the neck of each beast an excited mahout urged on his charge and from his exposed position looked nervously towards the fort.

Crowding the sides of the elephants, overflowing into the streets beyond, were the foot soldiers of Chanda Sahib. They carried spears, swords, bows and arrows and were heralded by the unnerving sound of beating drums and the blowing of conches. Some of the warriors carried muskets, but not many, for the primary weapon of India was still the elephant surrounded by spear and sword-carrying foot soldiers, with archers in the rear to give support.

Elephants could batter down the gates of enemy forts. To counter this the defenders learned to affix long iron spikes on the gates. But there were no such spikes on the Arcot fort.

'Aim for the legs! AIM FOR THE LEGS!' Clive yelled, levelling his own cumbersome 'Brown Bess' musket and waiting until the first elephant came within range.

Gently he squeezed the trigger. The musket recoiled sharply, and with a puff of smoke and a spurt of flame a two-ounce ball of lead hurtled on its way and struck the leading elephant on its knee-cap.

The great beast trumpeted angrily, lifting its leg in pain and all but flinging the soldiers in the howdah to the ground. Several more musket balls struck it on the legs and feet. The elephant performed an enraged lumbering dance on the dusty street. The mahout, clinging for dear life to its ears, struggled to calm the maddened beast but to no effect.

All along the wall of grey basalt muskets rippled and crackled in small gusty explosions; the faces of the defenders streaked burnt carbon. Clive, racing from one end of the narrow ledge to the other, exhorted his men to greater effort. His hat and wig had been knocked off in the excitement, and the sun beat down on his boyish face, drenched in sweat.

When no more than twenty paces from the unprotected gates of the fort, the three leading elephants decided they had taken enough. Swinging their huge bodies around, they loped off down a side street and soon broke into a maddened charge. The enormous animals brushed against small houses and demolished them; the howdahs were ripped from their backs and their screaming occupants were flung under the feet of the elephants following. The remaining elephants, though uninjured, were caught up in the atmosphere of panic. They blundered along in a vast cloud of dust, cutting a swath of havoc and destruction right through Chanda Sahib's capital.

Bewildered and dismayed to see their primary weapon so swiftly blunted, and so easily turned against themselves, the army of foot soldiers and cavalry milled around in a state of uncertainty until, prompted by fusillades of musket fire from the fort, they turned on their heels and fled in disorder.

Clive sat down on the ledge and wearily leaned his head against the hot rough stone. But the soldiers were exuberant. They shouted with joy, slapped each other on the back and embraced, laughingly. They peered over the walls and shouted insults at anyone they saw.

'Is it permitted to tap a cask of wine in celebration, my lord Captain Clive?' one of the junior officers asked him respectfully. Clive opened one eye and looked blearily at him. He was tempted to retort, 'We have beaten off the enemy – not defeated him,' but had not the heart to dampen his enthusiasm.

'One cask, when the sun goes down,' he said ungraciously, then waved the fellow away before preparing to write his first instalment of an epic letter to Margaret.

'I have won my first real battle,' he tried to tell himself several times, looking down at the blank sheet of parchment and at the dry quill in his hand. Eventually he tossed down the pen, let his head sink into his arms on the table, and closed his eyes. What should have been a moment of exhilaration had become a mood of depression.

Two hours later he was still seated at the table, dinner uneaten and pushed to one side, an empty bottle of wine on the floor, his face thrust into his hands. His head pounded with the sounds of revelry. Suddenly, unable to bear it a minute longer, as if each distant raucous laugh served only to emphasise his lonely misery, he flung himself out of the room and screamed at the first officer he saw to quieten the men. Taken aback, the officer at first hesitated – but soon fled as Clive made to seize his throat and shake him into obedience.

The clamour and the singing dwindled and faded. Clive returned to his bunk and attempted to sleep. It was impossible. His mind churned with disconnected images and worries. He sat up and lit an oil lamp. Perhaps his condition was only that suffered by every commanding officer. But he was not persuaded. Was it then the gravity of their situation? Stringer Lawrence had once said, 'The besieged can never win – they can only hold out until relief comes. With sufficient ammunition and provisions, they only survive (in steadily diminishing numbers) until the enemy tires or is driven away by outside help.' And what was his other dictum? 'Carry the battle to the enemy.'

Clive lay down again, eyes wide open, his mind a confusion of undefined anxieties.

15

TO THE hard vengeful eyes of Mir Kassim, Siraj-ud-daula seemed in a state resembling paralysis. He himself felt drained of all emotion as he saw Siraj being assisted to his knees, sweat coursing down his face, his eyes two black tunnels driven into his head. Behind Kassim were the bars of large cages which comprised the dungeons of the palace of Murshidabad, and in front was the small courtyard surrounded by high walls.

Armed guards stood at intervals all round the courtyard. In one corner – on a throne brought down for the occasion – sat the aged and inscrutable Nawab of Bengal. On a patch of grass far to the left of Kassim lay the discarded blood-soaked bodies of seven high-ranking Muslims, and in the opposite corner, like a pile of fleshy cannonballs, were their heads.

A stocky mulatto, naked to the waist, and with a reputation for animal savagery, came up behind the kneeling Siraj, put his hand on the victim's head and pressed it forward until it rested on the chunky segment of tree used traditionally as the block. The executioner's assistant presented him with the freshly cleaned scimitar and bowed himself out of the way.

Sombrer took his stance at right-angles to the half-fainting Siraj, tested the edge of the blade with his thumb, then looked enquiringly at the Nawab. Kassim's fists clenched and he almost ceased to breathe when he saw the finger of the old man flick upwards.

The mulatto raised the scimitar far above his head and then down until it paralleled his back. His powerful muscles tensed, then the blade came over in a wide arc, moving so swiftly that the eye could not follow. The whine of the blade was followed by an appalling thud as it buried its edge in the wooden block.

It skimmed the hairs of the victim's head so closely that two of his curly black locks were trimmed off and floated to the ground. The watching Alivardi Khan lowered his eyes and then, without a change of expression, fixed his gaze on the executioner's face. Sombrer struggled to free the blade from the grip of the block, recovered it and stood back, resting the point of the scimitar on the ground. He folded his hands over the hilt – and waited.

Not a word was spoken. Not a sound came from the guards. But Kassim gave a muffled exclamation and sprang to his feet, staring with accusing disbelief at the Nawab.

For several seconds the head of Siraj-ud-daula remained where Sombrer had placed it on the block. Then slowly it began to turn. The eyes flickered open. They caught a glimpse of the sword resting on the ground between the executioner's feet, and the executioner himself, standing quietly and making no move to repeat the blow. A trembling movement began at the neck and continued all the way down his body. Siraj lifted his head and turned slowly to face the old man. The texture of the victim's flesh was that of curdled cream.

Alivardi Khan studied the kneeling form for a moment or two before saying quietly, in a voice strained with bitterness and compassion, 'I have spared your life, Siraj, my son.' And as Siraj-ud-daula closed his eyes and rolled over in a dead faint, the Nawab wrapped his cloak around his shoulders and stalked away and out of that bloody chamber. Kassim respectfully bowed as he passed by, glared balefully at the back of the departing ruler and then spat venom on to the ground before rushing away to his own apartments.

Sareen looked anxiously at him as he went by. 'Is he dead?' she asked. Kassim shook his head, too angry to speak. Sareen looked down at her hands. Her expression did not reveal what she was thinking.

An hour later, the prostrate body of Siraj-ud-daula was brought into the throne room by the guards and unceremoniously dumped at Alivardi Khan's feet. He immediately upbraided them for their lack of respect to the prince, then dismissed them. He waited, with cold composure, until the crumpled figure had revived sufficiently to kneel and to comprehend what was being said to him.

From the height of his throne he looked down, severely yet with strange affection, on the youngster he had nearly sentenced to death. 'You are a fool, my son. Evil spirits have seized your heart and twisted your mind. You have repaid my love for you with treachery, with the gratitude of a pariah dog, and you have brought about the deaths of seven once-trusted warriors.' He tucked his cloak a little tighter around him despite the heat. Men of eighty feel the cold, and Siraj's treachery had made the years remaining to him that much colder.

'I am an old man, Siraj, a very old man, and soon you would have been Nawab of Bengal. Yet not content with all that I have given you; despising the honour that I selected you to be my adopted son and heir; contemptuous that you live in the style and rank of a prince ... you sought to hasten my death.' His aged voice began to quaver with emotion. 'Indeed, Siraj-ud-daula, a pig would have shown more affection – and you are no better than that most unclean of animals.'

Siraj flinched at this most foul of Muslim insults, but did not neglect to keep his head low in an attitude of contrition and unworthiness. His forehead touched the floor three times as he debased himself before the Nawab. But Alivardi Khan was no less wary than he would have been in the presence of a sleeping tiger.

The Nawab went on speaking. 'Amongst all my family, Siraj, I chose you because I believed you would have the courage and wisdom to govern my people. It has grieved me to find that you are greedy, cruel, ungrateful; a despoiler of women, even those who belong to other men; a vile creature who lives only for himself. And knowing this I have often feared for Bengal and for its people.' He paused for a while, then added, 'It is my weakness that I now fear to change the succession, for it has long been accepted that you will be Nawab after me ... and to place another in your place would lead to much slaughter. This I would not wish.'

Siraj, still prostrate, pricked up his ears. Still to be appointed Nawab! Alivardi Khan must be senile. Had any person done to him what he had done to the Nawab they would have begged for death once his torturers had got to work on them. He listened with renewed attention.

'There is no one in Murshidabad with your skill of government; no one who more commands the obedience of the people – and there is no one whom I loved more dearly than you, Siraj-ud-daula. I have spared your life though all those whom you sought to lead in bloody rebellion against me now lie in the execution chamber. I have not lived all these years without knowing how to keep long ears and develop sharp eyes. I was aware of your evil purpose though I knew not the method – until I was so informed.'

Until I was so informed. The phrase burned into Siraj. Who had informed? Who had known that had not already suffered death? Who hated him to such an extent? – There were all too many. A name came to him – Kassim. Could it have been ... Mir Kassim – his friend?

'I decreed that you suffer the torment and fears of execution without death. This you have done, and it is sufficient. Now hear me, Siraj. You will again take your place as my heir and you will be accorded the rank and dignity of this office – but as my once

88

beloved son you will cease to be. I will not again look upon your face until the hour of my death.'

The Nawab of Bengal, a prince among princes and loved by his subjects as the wisest of the wise, rose shakily to his feet and stared down at the prostrate figure. There were tears in his eyes though his face was resolute.

'This is my command, Siraj-ud-daula, heir to the kingdom of Bengal, that you do, when summoned to my presence, keep your face and head covered with cloth with nought but holes in it for eyes. Take care never again to address me save to answer whatever question I may place, and never again look upon my person.'

The old man, his voice now trembling with emotion, then leaned forward, stretched forth his hand and gently touched the black hair of the youth; a touch so fine that the fingers did not even brush the scalp.

'Now raise your face ... my son ... so that I may gaze upon it for the last time and carry the image of it in my heart to calm the bitterness you have caused there.'

Siraj-ud-daula rocked back on his heels and tentatively lifted his head. His eyes met those of Alivardi Khan. They looked. The father looked down on the son and the adopted son gazed calmly into the face of his benefactor. There was hatred in the heart of Siraj-ud-daula that boded ill for the future of Bengal, and for the man who had betrayed him.

16

AFTER FIVE weeks of sporadic attacks, the situation at Arcot was stalemate and seemed likely to go on forever, or until the English starved to death, for there was no sign of relief from either Madras or Fort St David. Clive himself alternated between ebullience – following the repulse of some sustained offensive – to moody introspection and depression during the periods of waiting. His energy was unflagging for he was reluctant to delegate responsibility. When water and provisions were doled out he felt obliged to supervise. It impressed the men and they viewed him as some kind of father protector but his officers felt such conscientiousness was excessive.

Chanda Sahib's elephants were not used again; his cavalry proved ineffectual against high walls; the French artillerymen appeared to be short of ammunition, while the foot soldiers could do little.

'The whole enterprise will come to naught if I do not inspire the men with some aggressive action,' Clive wrote to Margaret. 'Already there are signs of starvation and lethargy. My men are sloppy in their dress, peevish in their behaviour, sullen when obeying orders. Many are so weak that they cannot for long stand on guard and they slump down at their posts and mutter under their breaths when spoken to.'

He also told her that the sepoys best survived the terrible siege due to their atavistic gift for masterly inactivity. 'Yet these same sepoys,' he went on, 'when supplies have dwindled, insist that the white soldier eat the rice as they themselves can subsist equally well on the water the rice is boiled in ... So now, my dearest Margaret, I have decided upon a venture, both audacious and foolish, to give heart to my men and to instil fear into the enemy, and thus prove to this Chanda Sahib that not only are we still a contained force to be reckoned with but we possess the will and power to strike back at him.'

Clive outlined his plan to his dubious officers, concluding with, '... and within twenty minutes of our leaving the fort, one hundred sepoys under the second-in-command will search and bring back whatever provisions they can find in the town.'

Long after sun-down, by the light of a dozen flickering torches, a small group of men prepared their equipment for a mission that they felt was doomed to failure. Clive selected forty of his best horsemen and forty of the most able sepoys. Each sepoy was appointed to a horseman and, with his hand gripping the pommel, the native soldier would, at a half-run, be carried into battle. It was a well-proven technique.

The horsemen took only lance and sabre, whilst the sepoys armed themselves with their favourite curved sword. Soon after midnight the war-party crowded behind the main gate, keyed up and nervously waiting for Captain Clive to lead them through. He appeared on his massive grey, wearing nothing but shoes, breeches and blouse, with a pistol in his belt, a cavalry sabre by his side, and a grimly confident expression on his face. It would be unlikely, he had told them earlier, that the sentries would be alert or expecting attack.

No decent soldier fought after the sun had set.

The huge gate was quietly pulled open and the expedition filed out. Clive was invigorated at the prospect of being attacker instead of the besieged. All his old vitality and enthusiasm had returned.

For two miles the party threaded a silent way through the ill-lit streets until they approached the open maidan – now dotted with the small mushroom tents of the enemy. The embers of many fires still glowed in the ghostly light of the plain. There was no one on guard. The camp was so open to attack that Clive cursed himself for not risking his entire force on the venture. Silently walking his horse around the perimeter, he arranged ten horsemen with their accompanying sepoys in line abreast facing ten lines of tents, and grouped the remainder of his force in equal numbers behind.

He had just wished his men good luck, when one of the nearby camp fires was blotted out by the figure of a Muslim soldier. The man had removed his pantaloons and was on the point of relieving himself when his eyes lit on the silent horsemen. He gaped, then screamed.

'GO!' Clive sang out, unsheathing his sword and heading for the first avenue of tents. The ten pairs of horsemen and runners set off after him down their own avenues, swinging swords and slicing through the guy ropes of the tents. The folds of canvas collapsed on the sleeping occupants.

Thrusting swords and lances into the bulky, writhing shrouds from which arose screams of terror, the night riders committed fearful massacre. A form rose from the ground, the tent draped around him, and was at once impaled on the point of a lance. The sepoys occasionally let go the pommels and, rushing over to a tent, made great rips in the canvas and plunged their blades into the flesh beneath. In and out went the bloody swords, and then the sepoys rushed to the next tent to repeat the deed.

Clive slashed his great sabre from side to side, caught up in the madness and exuberance of killing, and when the squadron had reached the end of the line of tents, he wheeled around and led it back along new avenues to repeat the awful process. Again and again the lances were thrust in, the guy ropes slashed, the tents collapsed, until hundreds of men had been sent to their death or submitted to crippling injury.

By this time the whole camp had awakened and the sound of

crying was terrible to hear. When Clive saw that all his squadron had returned to the point from where the attack had started, he rallied them and led them off at high speed back to the fort, the sepoys running and skipping along as they clung to the parent mount.

A horse stumbled and fell, throwing its rider and killing him. As the gates of the fort closed behind the triumphant squadron, it was discovered that this had been their only casualty. A double celebration was called for when it was seen what the other sepoys had collected in their foraging expedition into Arcot: vegetables, sacks of rice and a small herd of goats and oxen.

On this occasion Clive allowed the festivities to go on unchecked and, in the morning, hardly a man in the fort was sober enough to stand on his feet. Even Clive, a puritan regarding drunkenness, was reduced to a bleary-eyed confusion long before his jubilation had dissipated.

The next day he told his senior officers of the next expedition he had planned. 'The French guns. With those out of the way we can hold out here until the last grain of rice is consumed.'

Three nights later, down ropes thrown from the rear walls, shinned another raiding party. Again led by Clive, it headed for the Arcot barracks where the French artillerymen were known to be. The sentries were awake, and the fire from the barracks became intense, but Clive held his ground and then advanced to where the great siege guns were located. While some of his men kept the French occupied, the rest shot their way through the guards round the battery and spiked seven of the guns.

A few days later, with a hand that shook from weakness and nervous exhaustion, he wrote to Margaret, 'Only the Lord God knows how much longer we will survive. We have water but little food; our ammunition will last for several weeks but only if we use it sparingly. I grieve at the sight of the men; their wrists are those of skeletons, their faces spectrelike, and their eyes look out at me like those of faithful animals unjustly whipped. Surely, Margaret, after nine weeks in this burning and terrible fort, it is not too much to expect relief.'

As he recapped the ink-horn and put the letter in his drawer, his senior lieutenant tapped on his door and entered the room. His face was ashen.

'A relief column from Madras ... it's been ambushed and destroyed ... totally,' he cried out. Clive motioned him silently to a chair and heard him out.

'How did we take Arcot so easily?' he asked suddenly, to the lieutenant's amazement.

'Well ... because they thought we ...' His voice tailed off.

'Because,' Clive supplied, 'they thought we were *giants* – supernatural creatures. And so they fled and left open the doors of the capital. Rumour, you fool, rumour. They were deceived.'

The lieutenant was speechless.

'And what is it that these people fear most of all?' he demanded. 'The Marathas. Name me a town that would not be abandoned were it known that a Maratha horde was on its way.' The lieutenant still looked blankly at him. Fired now with enthusiasm, Clive leapt to his feet.

'Let it be rumoured around Arcot that the English have made treaty with the Maratha chiefs, have promised them rich spoil, and that even at this moment many thousands of tribesmen are riding to our aid and will be here in less than five days.'

'They will not believe it, sir,' stammered the lieutenant. 'With respect, Captain Clive, no one makes treaty with the Marathas, and they will not believe it.'

Clive laughed. 'They will believe. When you touch on a man's innermost fear you render him incapable of thinking rationally. The Maratha is the spectre who lurks in every mind. Merely whisper his name and you will induce panic in the listener. The people of Arcot will believe, because they are conditioned to believe what they have always feared.'

Clive began pacing the room, ticking off points on his fingers and rapping out instructions to the bewildered lieutenant. '... and let six sepoys be dressed in the rags of the townspeople and lowered over the walls after darkness. Instruct them carefully in what they are to say and how they must say it to be convincing ...'

After dismissing the lieutenant, Clive walked out into the scorching heat. He raised his head to where the banner of St George and St Andrew fluttered limply at the top of the mast.

'If help is denied me from those whom I serve,' he prayed softly, 'I shall look to You, my Lord God, to see that I do not fail my country nor those in this fort who look to me for deliverance.'

17

THE HEADLINES blackened the full width of the *Calcutta Gazette* and caught Edmund's eyes immediately. 'THE SAVIOUR OF ARCOT' they blazoned out. 'Noble Hero makes triumphal entry into Madras.'

He bought a paper, and read, 'Captain Robert Clive, the inspired and tenacious hero of Arcot who, with dauntless courage, spurning the pitiless torment of his condition, and with the Englishman's proper devotion to duty ... gallantly held the Arcot fort for ELEVEN weeks against repeated attacks by the merciless hordes of warriors led by the evil Chanda Sahib.'

The eulogy spread across seven columns. Three columns described the final battle, recounting how the rumour of an alliance with the Marathas had induced Chanda Sahib to launch a total effort against the fort the very next day. Elephants, their legs protected against musketry, were about to force down the gates, when bags of curry powder were emptied over their heads, causing them to stampede as before.

The French delivered mighty cannonades at the battlements, muskets were fired, shoals of spears and arrows were hurled at the defenders, and a hundred scaling ladders were placed against the walls. But Clive had proved himself a Titan, rushing from one threatened point to another giving encouragement and direction. And when the sun vanished over the horizon, Chanda Sahib and his troops had faded with it. In the morning, Arcot was deserted.

With the retreating troops of Chanda Sahib went also Dupleix' hopes for the Carnatic, for on its return to Trichinopoly the disorganized army met a new force under Mohammad Ali. Chanda Sahib was executed, and the watching princes again shifted alliances and made overtures to the English 'hatmen'.

Edmund stretched out his long legs, unashamedly proud of his friend. He grinned as he read of Clive's victorious entry to Madras, and his grin widened as he perused the social page in which it was stated that '... one of our distinguished citizens, Mr Maskelyne, ... will give a sumptuous banquet at his home in honour of the great Captain Clive ... Mrs Maskelyne, with the delicacy and restraint for which she is noted, told our reporter that, and we quote: "There has always been a measure of affection and a certain understanding between my daughter, Margaret, and Mr Clive" unquote.'

'So you've made it at last,' Edmund exclaimed with some amusement. 'Now that you've met my mother's price! Anyway, dear Robert, after what you've done at Arcot there's no one in the Carnatic that'll outbid you for sister's hand.'

A shadow passed across the newspaper. Edmund frowned, saw to whom the shadow belonged, and offered him the paper. 'Here. Read deeply, Hastings,' he commanded jovially. 'Let the example give you hope. At least here's one friend of mine launched into fame.'

Hastings made no reply but took the newspaper, scanned the eulogies swiftly, and yawned. He dismissed the entire Arcot episode with the remark 'Anyone with connections such as Stringer Lawrence who was in the right place at the right time with the same good fortune, could have done as well.'

Edmund was riled, but before he could make a tart reply, Hastings had spotted the name in the society column.

'Maskelyne?' He darted a look at Edmund. 'Any relation?' The tone was almost accusing.

'Parents,' Edmund replied, then thinking this too curt, 'plus a sister; soon to be the wife of Robert Clive, if I'm not mistaken.'

Hastings studied his companion with new interest. 'They are betrothed?'

'Not yet, though I don't suppose it will be long before marriage settlements are arranged,' Edmund replied.

Hastings curled a finger around his jaw. 'There is a curious bitterness under that mask of impartiality, Edmund,' he said blandly, cautiously fishing.

'I, bitter?' laughed Edmund. 'Nonsense. I'm simply a cynic in matters of marriage.'

'Have you ever considered matrimony yourself?' Hastings persisted, as Mathieson joined them. Mathieson nodded his respects to the Captain but disdained to recognise Hastings.

Edmund regarded the newcomer with wary ambivalence. Neither Mathieson nor Hastings were company he would normally seek yet, because of Anna (the girl to whom he had lost his heart and to whom Mathieson was betrothed) he had a compulsive interest in him.

'Matrimony, you say?' He laughed with gay derision. 'Not likely.

95

Women are champagne, Hastings; sparkling, effervescent. Marriage makes it all go flat.'

Warren Hastings – with one eye on Mathieson – rejoined with smooth malice, 'Ah! Then what a remarkable vintage Miss Petal Wilkinson must be.'

'Do not overstep the bounds of good taste,' said Edmund stiffly, softening the rebuke by clapping him gently on the shoulders. Mathieson looked on with thinly disguised repugnance.

'And what are friend Mathieson's views on matrimony?' Hastings asked.

Mathieson looked down his nose from his superior height and said rudely, 'My views are not for dissemination, Hastings,' then he doffed his hat to his superior officer and bid him good day. As he was about to walk away, a thought occurred to him. 'Is our meeting for tomorrow still convenient, Captain Maskelyne?' Edmund confirmed that it was, and Mathieson took his leave, flinging over his shoulder as he went, 'If ever you are dismissed your employment, Hastings, do make an appointment with me. I'm always in need of writers of some kind or other.'

Hastings smiled sourly. 'Mathieson seems unduly sensitive. Perhaps he feels some guilt regarding the lovely Anna,' he murmured.

Edmund stiffened, but dared not call Hastings to account lest his own love for Anna be revealed. 'Come,' he said, with forced gaiety. 'We shall take a phaeton and call on Miss Wilkinson. The visit might sweeten some of the vinegar in your belly.'

Hastings stared up at him, his eyes glinting with amusement, confident that now he was in possession of both of the officer's secrets. 'Why not,' he said cheerfully, adding cryptically, 'though what Dashwood and his Franciscans would think of this lark, I shudder to think.'

As they waited for a phaeton, Hastings said more seriously, 'It is rumoured that Miss Wilkinson has some connection with the Nawab, Alivardi Khan. Would you say this is true, Captain?'

Edmund's patience was wearing thin. 'Yes,' he said bluntly, fixing him with a cold stare. 'She is the Nawab's spy in Calcutta.'

Hasting's eyes shot open. 'Spy,' he echoed blankly, thrown out of his usual composure.

'Spy,' reiterated Edmund. 'An agent for Alivardi Khan among the English, whose task it is to report whether or not we are keeping our agreements with him.'

'But ... but ...' stammered Hastings, completely at a loss.

Edmund smiled derisively and added, 'But she also warns the Council against steps which she feels the Nawab would object to. In this manner she is not so much a spy as a well-intentioned liaison officer who functions for the benefit of Muslim ruler and English trader. Other than that, my dear Hastings,' he went on acidly, 'she is the loveliest and most generous-hearted brothel owner in Bengal – and she also happens to be my friend.'

18

THE AREA around the Maskelyne home was so crowded with private transport and the streets so thickly thronged with servants and onlookers that late arrivals were compelled to abandon their dignity and thread a way on foot through the dust, the heat and the press of human bodies in order to reach the gates.

But when the guest of honour arrived, a passage slowly opened through the crowd to allow his coach to proceed in a manner befitting his dignity. Both the host and his wife were awaiting him in front of their own great doorway; their daughter was at the bottom of the steps.

When the coach pulled to a halt Mr Maskelyne hurried down the flight of stone steps and actually opened the carriage door himself, then stretched out both arms as though he would embrace the occupant.

'My dear Captain Clive, what a signal honour you do me,' he cried, clasping his guest's hand in both his own. 'Words fail to express my joy at seeing you safe and well after your truly heroic ordeal at Arcot. To think that one of India's most intrepid heroes ...' He was gently nudged aside by Margaret.

As their eyes met, their hands touched and held, the tumult, the people, the house and servants, melted away. 'Robert,' was all she said. He looked at her tenderly before assuming the posture of honoured guest once more and allowing himself to be led up the steps to the apprehensive, foot-tapping Mrs Maskelyne.

'You of course know my wife, Captain Clive?' said Clive's host.

'Indeed I do,' Clive replied with imperious suavity, bending distantly over her hand. Mrs Maskelyne smiled glacially and gave a deliberately theatrical curtsy.

'And Margaret, of course,' said her father unnecessarily, bringing his daughter forward like an auctioneer displaying the *pièce de résistance.*

Clive kissed her hand – and took an unconscionably long time doing so.

'Would you come inside, Captain Clive?' Mrs Maskelyne invited.

Clive hesitated only momentarily, then said, 'It is of no great consequence, Mrs Maskelyne, but it is now *Colonel* Clive ... a gesture from the Council.'

Her eyes sparked angrily. She was put out of countenance – by what she knew to be revenge at her own slights – but too much was at stake to allow her even the mildest display of temper. She quickly recovered her composure and smiled engagingly.

'I am justly corrected,' she gushed. 'Perhaps, Colonel Clive, you would care to escort Margaret around the gardens. It will give you an opportunity to relax for a few moments before the ordeal of being presented to all the other guests. As for myself, I have positively a million things to attend to.'

She managed to retain a fixed smile as she hurried away. Clive nodded curtly to the departing skirts, and rather more graciously to the father, then offered Margaret his arm.

'She will be sold to the highest bidder.' He recalled Edmund's cynical comment as he caught the arch look that passed between Mr and Mrs Maskelyne. But it mattered not at all. He had met the mother's price....

'Robert, I asked you a question.' Margaret's voice cut into his thoughts.

'I am so sorry.' He fished in an inner pocket and brought out a thick wad of papers, giving them a curiously sad look before handing them to her. 'The letter I wrote you in Arcot,' he said simply. 'Read it when you are alone.' She took the letter with bowed head, and when she raised her eyes again he saw they were moist.

He hastily began to speak. 'Assuming that my presence in the Maskelyne household is no longer to be viewed with repugnance,' he began lightly, pinching her arm and casting her a sideways look, 'may I beg permission of your father to pay you court?'

Though his voice was deliberately teasing she knew he was serious. She could feel herself flushing, yet trying to match his tone she replied, 'If that is what you wish, Mr Clive, then indeed you have my permission.'

The newly-promoted colonel sighed. It was settled.

Later, standing with Margaret, flanked by Mr and Mrs Maskelyne, he stood in the great hall meeting the guests. His hand ached and a smile was frozen on his face. Ninety-two guests! It was a blessing when dinner was finally announced.

Passing into the dining-room, where three vast tables sparkled with table-ware, and punkahs overhead flowed backwards and forwards causing flames in a galaxy of candles and bright oil-lamps to dance merrily, the walls lined with stewards in white gowns and blue sashes, Clive, with a sudden flash of the devil at the solemnity of it all, nipped Margaret on the bottom.

Her eyes shot open and she gave a little squeak – swiftly turning it into a cough – and struggled to regain her composure. They took their seats and the guests did likewise.

Mr Maskelyne signalled for the wine – all three hundred bottles of it – and soon a hubbub of talk and raucous laughter filled the huge hall as a gargantuan meal was set before the guests.

An hour later the ladies, perspiring in their long dresses that swathed out over metal panniers, giggled and swayed, pulling even lower the Caroline-topped blouses that revealed their shoulders and much of their over-powdered breasts, while the gentlemen told bawdy jokes and glanced speculatively at the giggling females.

The temperature of the room increased with the heat from densely packed bodies. Glasses were knocked over and plates began to shatter as drunken arms waved. Sweat poured from many faces. Men peeled off their jackets and loosened waistbands, dragged the ruffles from their necks, then leaned over and assisted the ladies to tug down their blouses, to unbutton or unhook their dresses. By the time brandy was brought to the table at least half the ladies were nude to the stomach with their breasts swinging freely, and often little drops of perspiration suspended from the nipples.

Disregarding glasses, the men drank straight from the bottles. One gentleman cooled a protestingly overheated lady next to him by pouring a glass of claret over her shoulders; she retaliated by upending a brandy bottle down the front of his trousers, at which he screamed with laughter and stood with the bottle protruding in a most vulgar manner.

The din was deafening. Two ladies were engaged in a competition that seemed to involve dipping their breasts into wide-mouthed goblets and trying to lift the glasses as high as possible off the table. Their partners encouraged them by making wagers, and later licked their nipples clear of the drops of wine.

Mrs Maskelyne sat next to her daughter like a stone Krishna, mute and unforgiving. Her livelier husband had thrice staggered to his feet to deliver a toast, and thrice had failed to remain upright and simply collapsed into inane giggles. Even Margaret had her eyes screwed tightly closed, whilst under the table she clasped Robert's hand and rubbed it against her thighs, uttering little moaning noises. As for the Hero of Arcot, his head was resting on one arm whilst his mouth blew tiny bubbles as he peacefully slept amidst the debris of flowers, glassware, plates and cutlery.

A lady gave a joyful yelp somewhere near the bottom of the table, bringing Mrs Maskelyne to life. Lurching to her feet, she gazed blearily around, waved an airy hand in farewell, then allowed herself to be hustled to her room by two of her maidservants.

An even louder uproar awakened Clive. He saw several of the guests peering under the table and shouting encouraging remarks. He and Margaret bent down to see what was happening, and fell into each other's arms hysterical with laughter at what they saw. A senior merchant of sizeable girth was having grave difficulty with his tight trousers as he sprawled on top of an equally well-known Madras lady. Her ballooning skirts were draped over her head like a small bell-tent, almost smothering her. Booze alone triumphed, for whilst it stimulated passion it inhibited performance, and it left the drunken merchant wailing at his impotence and cursing at fastenings that he was incapable of undoing. The lady had fallen asleep.

By four a.m. the party had divided into three groups: those still sober enough to play cards, those who had collapsed into a soporific stupor, and a number who fornicated in any place where they might lie down without fear of being trodden upon.

As Margaret had gone to bed, Clive seated himself in the vestibule and prepared to play whist. Two merchants and a fellow officer played at the same table, each with his bottle of brandy. The cards were dealt, the game proceeded. Clive, neither drunk nor entirely sober, was puzzled. The tricks did not add up.

At the next hand the major of grenadiers trumped a winning card when, according to Clive's fuzzy accounting, the fellow should still have possessed a card from the suit being played. Rage welled up in him. With a sweep of his arm he sent cards, bottles and glasses crashing to the floor.

'You cheat, sir!' he shouted thickly at the major, lumbering to his feet. The major blinked stupidly.

'What was that?' he demanded.

'You cheated. I saw you cheat,' Clive repeated aggressively.

It dawned on the major that he was being insulted. He, too, stood up, tipping over the table as he did so. 'You accuse me of cheating?'

The accusation was repeated. Harsh words followed and a blow was struck.

As the sun streaked the horizon, Clive and the major faced each other at the extreme end of the garden near the high wall. In the hands of each was a duelling pistol. On one side stood the referee, a senior officer. He looked from one protagonist to the other, and made the customary attempt at mediation.

'Gentlemen, will you not agree to resolve your differences other than by a duel?'

'Only by an apology from Colonel Clive,' declared one.

'Only by his admission of cheating,' declared the other.

The referee sighed, 'Then, gentlemen, take aim.' The heavy pistols were raised, none too steadily.

'FIRE!' called out the referee.

Clive squinted along the arm that terminated in a flintlock pistol. Somewhere in the distance a dark figure seemed to leap about, split into three and then merge into a shapeless blob. He squeezed the trigger. The gunpowder ignited, exploded, and the ball hurtled forth – shattering a kitchen window pane. The major lowered his pistol, turned round and frowned. Then he turned back to face his opponent. Unable to see him very distinctly he ambled over and stopped within three paces of Clive. His pistol rose in the air until the round pipe of the muzzle threatened to ram Clive's nose.

'You will ask ... ask for your ... life, sir,' he hiccoughed. Clive gaped at the slowly moving pistol; it occurred to him that he was in some danger. He spluttered, 'I then ... ask for my life, sir.'

This seemed to satisfy the major, but as he prepared to lower his pistol something else passed through his hazy mind.

'You will apol ... apologise ... and retract ...' he commanded again. But this was too much for Clive. His stubborn rage welled up in him again, and he flung open his arms and cried, 'Be damned to you, sir. You cheated ... I still say ... you cheated. Fire your pistol and ... and ... and may the devil take you!'

The major shut his eyes and then tried to open them, but could not remember how it was done. He became aware of the pistol in his hand and of Colonel Clive staring malevolently at him. With an oath he flung the weapon high over his shoulder, shook a fist under Clive's nose, and mumbled, 'You are mad, sir ... quite ... quite ... raving mad, sir.' Then he walked away with as much dignity as he could muster, leaving his erstwhile opponent to vomit up what remained of his courage.

The story quickly went the rounds of Madras of how the great Clive – with a loaded pistol pointing in his face – had challenged his opponent to fire and 'be damned'.

19

EDMUND FOLDED the letter that had just arrived by boat from Madras, put it in his pocket and went out to hire a chair. Soon after he was entering a palatial building whose garden was congested with pergolas and festooned with creeper. The hurcurrahs and chubdars greeted him with grave respect as a familiar visitor, and led him up the flight of marble steps into the vestibule.

'Edmund! How delightful.' He grinned at Petal Wilkinson's superbly contrived entrance. She floated delicately towards him and kissed him affectionately.

On most European women Petal's outfit might have been ludicrous, but on her it was stunning. She wore Turkish slippers and pantaloons of fine silk that insidiously caressed her hips and legs. Her midriff was bare, whilst over her shoulders was a Chinese jacket on which dragons writhed. Her hair was coiled into a single pigtail that reached to her waist, and small golden chains dangled from her ears. Two ropes of pearls were wound around her slender neck, and golden chains on wrists and ankles jingled provocatively as she walked.

She gazed at him speculatively, trying to gauge his mood. 'First a little Madeira, and then you can unburden yourself of all your problems,' she said, slipping her arm through his and leading him into an inner room. 'I see that you have neither come for Jasmine nor Lotus, nor even me – except to talk to,' she said gaily.

'You are the most fascinating woman I've ever known,' he said sincerely.

She looked sideways at him. 'You are a brutal charmer, Edmund Maskelyne – and I love you for it. Now come and sit next to me and we shall talk of whatever you will – even of Anna if you so wish,' she sighed ruefully. He put his arm around her waist and nuzzled her neck, with little more sexual intent than if she had been his sister – and Petal Wilkinson was wryly aware of it.

'I received a letter from Robert,' he said a few minutes later.

'Colonel Clive? And what has he been doing now? Conquering more French territories? Taming some obstreperous prince?'

He looked up sharply at the rare acidity in her voice. He had long ceased to be amazed at the extent of her knowledge for she freely admitted to having many sources of information, just as she made no secret of her relations with Alivardi Khan.

'Don't you approve of him, Petal?' he asked

'I've never met him, so how can I say? And as you haven't seen him for ... three years? ... how can you tell if he is the same man you once knew?' she said, tossing her pigtail over her shoulder in a vexed movement. 'When you were at Fort St David, he was just a boy – a stripling. Now he's famous. He has a dozen great victories to his credit, and he's honoured, feted – and feared wherever he goes.'

Edmund was puzzled by her waspishness. 'Well, I agree to some extent,' he conceded reluctantly, 'but you make him sound ...'

'Not a very admirable kind of person?' she finished for him, cocking her head to one side and giving him an apologetic smile.

'Well, yes.'

'Did you know that the Madras Council listens to his so-called advice almost as if he were ruler? And that since he took Arcot two years ago he has become a very rich man indeed?'

'Whatever fortune has come his way has been justly earned,' Edmund snapped. 'Robert is an honourable man. He'd never stoop to extortion.'

She looked steadily at him, loving him for his loyalty and pitying him for his naivety. 'I did not say extortion,' she corrected him softly, adding in a slightly harder tone, 'But let us not be blind or deaf, Edmund. Colonel Clive accepts very lavish gifts from those who seek his favours.'

Edmund would have sprung to his feet in protest, but was prevented by Petal, who sat on his lap, placing her head on his shoulder.

'My adorable Edmund, please listen to me and do not get vexed. If your friend accepts gifts – which I know he does – it is no more than any other important man would do in his position. But you must admit to this, and I in turn will admit that I have heard nothing to suggest that he has ever abused his power nor used it for unworthy and selfish ends.'

She nibbled his ear. 'Now give me your own news.'

'He's asked me to be his groom when he weds my sister,' Edmund said grumpily.

'And must you be sour about it?' she chided.

'No. Actually, it pleases me. Though why he should have waited so long ...' his voice tailed away. But before he could say more, two young girls entered the room.

Whilst Petal Wilkinson was predominantly European, the two girls, Lotus and Jasmine, were just as clearly Asiatic, with their subtle yellow-brown skins and the high cheek bones of the Mongol. Their long yellow gowns were slit at the sides to reveal their thighs at each step.

Edmund stretched out his arms and they came forward and knelt at his feet.

'I am going away for a few weeks,' he told them, touching their cheeks with his hands. 'So what would you like me to bring you from Madras?'

'Just yourself,' murmured Petal, touching her forehead to his. Lotus and Jasmine's requests were more exotic.

Four weeks later Edmund strode down the gangway of the barque in Madras harbour and into the welcoming arms of his sister and Robert Clive. It had been nearly four years since they had seen him and the change in all three was marked. Clive studied his friend whilst Margaret chatted excitedly about the forthcoming marriage. Edmund's gay bravado and handsome roguery had been toned down, and Clive noticed a new introspective quality.

Edmund in turn had been making his own observations. Margaret seemed to have lost much of her stiff reticence. There was a twinkle in her eye and a contentment about her that pointed to a sexually awakened woman. But the change in Robert was more pronounced. He was heavier; his face had filled out and his waist was thicker.

The uniform and accoutrements he wore were of the finest quality and his lace was immaculate. His bearing was that of a man who wielded power and who neither feared, nor would render obeisance to, anyone. This was the new Clive: the conquering soldier now moving arrogantly, into the world of statesmanship. And yet towards Edmund he displayed no superiority. He clasped him by the arms and embraced him warmly. 'My first, my best – and sometimes, I think – my only friend,' he said with a wry grin.

'And when is the wedding to be, Robert?' Edmund asked, his eyebrows arching in admiration at the sight of the postilioned team of matched horses that drew Clive's coach.

'In two weeks. It will take them that time to clear the church of packing cases.'

'Wholesale reliquaries?' Edmund grinned.

'Idiot!' Clive replied cheerfully, both men slipping easily into their former relationship. 'Overflow from the last convoy.'

'May the saints preserve us!' Edmund exclaimed a few minutes later when the coach halted outside Clive's new house. 'Are you seeking to outdo Dupleix with this ... this *palace*?'

Clive accepted the remark as a compliment – which in a way it was. 'Four storeys, eighteen bedrooms in the centre wing ... I've forgotten how many others,' he said.

'What are your intentions, Edmund, after the wedding?' Clive asked him later, as they sat on the rear porch.

'Go back to Calcutta, I suppose. There is much to do there, especially with the fortifications.'

Clive idly drew a little circle on the ground with his gold-hilted cane, and commented softly, 'The sooner the better. Dupleix will not remain idle whilst we channel all French trade into British hands. Eventually he will ally himself with some prince, most likely the Nawab of Bengal, and sally forth again.'

'Alivardi Khan is a man whose honour I would vouch for,' objected Edmund.

'Whilst he lives,' said Clive heavily. 'It's his protégé you'll have to watch – Siraj-ud-daula. Even here in Madras we know of him. He's a firebrand, Edmund; a prince so unstable that peace or war could depend solely on whether his concubine pleased him the night before.'

Edmund was silent. He knew about Siraj-ud-daula from Petal Wilkinson, who had expressed the same opinion.

'What numbers have you in the garrison, Edmund?' Clive asked.

'Seventy.'

Eyebrows were raised at this. 'You can't defend Calcutta ... you can't even hold Fort William with that number,' Clive said sharply. 'What quality are your sepoys?'

Edmund shrugged a little uncomfortably and wondered whether it was Robert or Colonel Clive who was interrogating him.

'Good soldiers. I think we can rely on them. They live a better existence under "John Company" than they would do elsewhere.'

'Bengalis fighting Bengalis,' said Clive, with an arch look.

Edmund protested. 'They're Hindus, and they've no affection for the Nawab ... though admittedly they've never been put to the test.'

'Then pray they won't be,' retorted Clive, thrusting his cane at the back of a nearby chair.

'And your own future, Robert, what of that?' asked Edmund, unwilling to pursue the subject any further.

Clive spread his hands and sighed happily. 'England. Margaret and I will be sailing almost the moment the wedding festivities are over.'

Edmund shot upright in his chair. 'England! But how can you?'

Clive regarded him with amusement. 'It's little more than a brief vacation – a couple of years, I would say. I need it ... God knows, I need it, Edmund,' he added with curious fervency. 'For nearly four years I've held a sword in my hand, and I'm tired. Dupleix and Bussy have been trounced and should lie quiet for a little while, so let India grant me a period of grace before the cauldron starts to bubble again. There is so much to be done in this country, Edmund, and if I'm to do it, I must first rest.'

20

BY 1753 – the year of Clive's marriage and his departure for England – the Mogul Empire was a decayed thing. Its titular head, the Emperor, resided in Delhi and theoretically possessed dominion over the vast bulk of India. But in truth his power extended little beyond the territory of his own state and there were subject princes even stronger than himself.

In the centre, the south, and the east, were the dominions of the Nizam of Hyderabad, whose own subordinates were the Nawabs of Bengal and of the Carnatic – as independent of him as he of the Emperor. Ranging over these states were the nomadic tribes of Marathas, subservient to no prince and a scourge to all.

The other group in this complex was the European traders with their private armies, bitterly squabbling among themselves, not for political power but for predominance in trade.

The revenue of the country belonged to the Emperor. Its collection he left to the princes and to the Zamindars (a kind of magistrate) and to the position of Zamindar he appointed both French and English governors in their respective factories. The amount of revenue received by the Emperor was the drops that remained after his agents had siphoned off their commissions. But he rarely complained, deciding wisely that it was better to receive little than nothing at all. The princely 'robber barons' bent the knee, made a pretence of listening to his commands, handed him a pittance of the tax collected, and otherwise ignored him. He was content to leave well alone.

The Nawab of Bengal, Alivardi Khan, was a prince of rare quality. He reigned wisely, for he was tyrant to neither Hindu nor hatman, and he encouraged the Europeans and benefited from their skills and trade. They reciprocated with respect and obedience.

Regarding the British he made a classic analogy: 'They are a hive of bees from whose honey you might reap much benefit. But disturb that hive and they will sting you to death.' He repeated this many times to Siraj-ud-daula, but Siraj rarely listened.

What dignity the old Nawab possessed, Siraj matched in massive displays of temperament; where the Nawab was honourable, Siraj was sly; whatever devotion the old man showed to his only wife, Siraj mocked by taking anyone's wife. Yet he did not lack courage. He lacked conviction, certainly; he was impulsive; vacillated when he should have been firm; was stubborn when compromise was called for. And he demanded loyalty from those he abused and treated with contempt.

In the small palace belonging to Mir Jafar, the Nawab's senior general and Kassim's father, a troupe of entertainers attempted to divert Siraj. His elderly host stood by his side, obviously ill at ease. Siraj watched the trite routine of the jugglers, musicians and dancers, fondled the bodies of the girls and then, tiring, pushed them aside. He was bored with every pleasure and diversion that Murshidabad could provide. What of Sareen? He had not seen her for several months – as if she were deliberately being kept from his sight.

'Mir Jafar,' he smiled blandly at the elderly man, 'your lovely child wife, Sareen, is she sick?'

The general's hand moved deprecatingly. 'Indeed not, your highness, she is most well,' he replied, his mind searching desperately for anything to distract Siraj. 'My armourer has produced a new blade for me; pray allow me to show you ...' he began.

Siraj looked up at him in amusement. 'Summon her to our presence,' he said quietly. The bearded Muslim stiffened and made no move to obey. Siraj, pretending mystification, stared up at him. 'Did my command fail to reach your aged ears, Mir Jafar?' he said with ominous mildness.

The husband pressed the palms of his hands together apologetically, then bowed and backed out of the room. The moment the door had closed behind him, he angrily kicked a servant out of his way, and then yelled at him to bring Sareen immediately. But when his wife appeared, so did his son. The father glanced first at Sareen and then at Kassim, and though Sareen lowered her eyes demurely as she faced her lord, Kassim met his father's eyes and held them challengingly.

'Siraj demands her,' Mir Jafar muttered, avoiding his son's gaze and stepping between the two young people.

'Siraj!' exclaimed Kassim, thrusting his father aside and moving determinedly towards the closed door. Mir Jafar grabbed Kassim's arm.

'Madman!' he screamed at him in a whisper. 'Have you considered what Siraj would do to you?'

The boy flung him off, but when Sareen laid her hand restrainingly on his, he simply stared into her face with outraged surprise. She looked steadily at him for several seconds before turning away and walking with dignity towards the closed door, leaving Kassim to stare after her.

She sank to her knees and paid obeisance to the prince as he reclined on a pile of soft cushions, and stood tall again as he gestured for her to rise. As was customary for a woman in purdah, her blue and gold sari covered her body and most of her head, leaving a small aperture for her eyes, which were lowered as was modest and fitting. Siraj leaned back, cocked his head to one side and gave her a long appraising look. Sticking the point of a knife into a portion of mango, he lifted it to his mouth. Still chewing, he said calmly, 'Remove her clothes, Mir Jafar.'

To Mir Jafar such a command presented no dilemma; the alternative to obedience was an unimaginable death. With eyes averted from Sareen's face, he proceeded to unwind the sari. The girl stood still, face lowered in mute submission. When he had finished, the sari lay about her feet and she was naked save for the twist of silk around her hips. Siraj pointed at this and flicked his finger. Sareen flashed a glance at Mir Jafar, and disdainfully removed the garment herself.

The guards looked on with growing excitement. Siraj-ud-daula caught his breath. This slip of a girl whom he had known for many years was now ... 'The first blush of sunshine after the rains,' he sighed.

He rose to his feet and went to her, his greedy eyes moving slowly from her calm, lovely face, down her golden-brown body to her feet. He cautiously put out a hand to touch her as if fearful she might crumble beneath his fingers. She gazed steadily over his head and did not flinch. Taking courage, he stroked her shoulder and then let his hand move down to caress her right breast. Involuntarily she shuddered as his finger touched the nipple, and he shot a glance of curiosity at her face – but her mask was impenetrable.

By some supreme effort of will Sareen had stepped outside her body. This made him angry.

'Leave us! All of you,' he barked out, causing a flurry of exits by guards and servants. Mir Jafar left unwillingly, biting his lips in mortification.

'Sareen,' Siraj-ud-daula whispered the name as he might have whispered 'Allah.' But only an eyelid flickered to show that she had heard him. She sensed the heat of his body behind her. His hands touched her shoulders gently, so gently that it became a caress: then, almost without seeming to exert pressure, he compelled her to bend forward.

Through the thin panels of the door, Mir Jafar listened with his ear tight against the woodwork, his hand clenching the hilt of his knife. He clasped his hands over his ears to shut out the erotic sounds of love-making, berated himself for cowardice and spat contemptuously on his own honour. He became alarmed that Sareen might not find the experience as distressing as she had feared.

The sun was low on the horizon and the large rooms were darkening before Sareen reappeared. She started when she saw her husband waiting but swiftly recovered, setting the muscles of her face into the same enigmatic expression as when he had last seen her. Rage again welled up in him and he felt the urge to strike her and demand whether she had taken pleasure in this cruel betrayal. But she looked calmly into his face and awaited whatever punishment he might inflict on her. His hand drew back; he could not strike her. He swung on his heels and rushed away in frustrated anger.

In the weeks that followed, it became evident to him that though he still owned Sareen, and occasionally possessed her, she was nonetheless lost to him. Her slender body became a voluptuous commodity: taken lawfully by one, usurped by another, and given willingly to a third.

'Mir Jafar,' shouted Siraj raucously and, swallowing his pride, the husband forced himself to open the door and go in. Sareen, the sari loosely draped around her body, made a deep salaam and then moved gracefully out of the room. Siraj was lolling back on a disorder of cushions, practically naked, and eating fruit with noisy enjoyment. He was in splendid humour.

'Most fortunate among men, to have the eye to find the one jewel in a bowl of coloured glass,' he said extravagantly, shaking off a thick circlet of gold from his wrist. 'Give Sareen that – with my affection,' he said, tossing him the bangle, 'but mind how you do so, lest she suspect it to be payment. Say that it is a gift, a token from Siraj-ud-daula, for a princess he respects.'

Mir Jafar felt the weight of the bracelet in his hand; its warmth from Siraj's wrist burned his palm. Sareen had no need of such trinkets, but she must wear this one, for Siraj would look for it on his next visit. He groaned.

Siraj rose to his feet and flung an arm of good fellowship around the older man. 'Clear the heaviness from your heart, Mir Jafar, and take joy in the prospect I offer you,' he sang out cheerfully, squeezing his companion tightly.

'Prospect, your highness?'

'A fine prospect ... we leave for Calcutta in three days.'

'Calcutta! But to what end, your highness?'

'As ambassador from the Nawab – to see a Feringhee woman,' Siraj replied, giving Mir Jafar a meaning look. 'And whilst I am listening to her news, you, my good friend, shall be entertained by the loveliest slaves in Bengal. They will excite your old bones and bring forgetfulness of Sareen – at least for a little while.'

'A Feringhee woman!' Mir Jafar was astounded. 'You, a Muslim! You would abuse your Faith, ignore the Koran?'

Siraj let out a peal of laughter. 'Calm your fears, Mir Jafar. The slaves will not offend your sensibilities. As for the Feringhee, Miss Wilkinson, the Nawab tells me there is sufficient of the Believer in her blood to cause no offence to our Faith.'

Mir Jafar was not convinced. The debauchery of his own wife humiliated him and outraged his honour, but to embrace a non-believer was an act of unimaginable blasphemy.

'Take care, your highness,' he warned. 'Blood which has mingled with other races oft takes only the evil of that race and not the good. Mixed blood is always bad,' he declared, with utter conviction.

'Cease your complaints, old general,' Siraj retorted harshly. 'Mixed blood always flows to the stronger side – when the fear of its being shed tilts the balance.'

21

FAINTLY POSTURING on the upswept stern of the Indiaman that was to sail him to England, finely attired in his lime-green claw-hammer coat with its gold embroidery, lace ruffles, buff waistcoat, bottle-green trousers, Colonel Clive overshadowed his bride as a peacock does the hen. His left hand rested lightly on the golden-hilted, diamond-encrusted sword at his belt: a gift of friendship from Alivardi Khan.

He waved to the assembled crowd of well-wishers on the quay, and thought wryly of the gossip they would later indulge in. The wedding day had been a disaster despite the immaculate guard of red-coated soldiers, the flattering spectacle of the entire Madras Council at the banquet, or even the beauty of Margaret on that supreme day in her life. It had been a disaster, and he flushed to think of it.

During an unseasonable downpour the church roof had leaked gallons of water on the guests. A drunken oaf of a minister had forgotten his words and – and during the exchange of rings – had let slip a bottle of brandy from under his cassock. It had smashed on the floor and soaked himself and Edmund with stinking liquor. An outraged Mrs Maskelyne had slipped on a patch of camel dung as she made to enter her carriage, necessitating a hurried change of dress when she got home, and the breeches of one of the Council had split when making too extravagant a bow to bride and groom. Truly it had been a memorable wedding! If only he could now forget it.

However, it was over. He put his arm round Margaret and waved his hand a little more enthusiastically. He took mild pleasure in knowing that he represented the zenith of achievement for every downtrodden writer and humble ensign. He was returning home as a soldier of high rank with an unmatched reputation for victorious campaigns, and with a trunk filled with gold – £40,000 – an incredible sum. And every penny of it, he convinced himself, obtained by means lawful to the Honourable East India Company.

The last figure he saw standing silent on the quayside was that of Edmund Maskelyne. Clive raised his hand, and as Edmund raised his in response, an unspoken affection passed between them.

The voyage to England was long. Margaret was sea-sick for much of the time and Clive was bored and sexually frustrated. Even after arrival in England, Margaret felt compelled to retire to her bed for several weeks to convalesce whilst her husband faced alone, and not unwillingly, the adulation of the populace.

The press was hysterical. Parliament made long and extravagant speeches in his praise, and George II invited him to dinner. But the novelty of his return gradually ceased to excite the public interest, and, though this piqued him somewhat, he was pleased to be left alone to indulge himself in the style of life he had dreamed of when first he entered the Maskelyne home as an impoverished writer. His life became as grandiose as that of an Indian potentate. He purchased a house so large that one hundred and thirty servants were required to keep it functioning, and kept a small fleet of carriages, and a large stable of horses.

In an age when a skilled artisan received twenty pounds for a whole year's work, the sum of forty thousand was considered unspendable in a lifetime. Robert Clive spent thirty thousand during the first year. And rather enjoyed the sensation. Companions, eager to help spend his money, were many; and compliant ladies made known their willingness to become his mistress. In England, as in India, a mistress or two invoked no social opprobrium - provided one was discreet.

Though Margaret desired nothing but her husband's affection and unlimited funds to continue this grandiose existence, Robert himself soon fretted at the absence of challenge in this sybarite life. He began adventuring at the gaming clubs in London; the plumpness and pallor of his cheeks increased, and a paunch became noticeable.

He was in St James's one evening, when an acquaintance introduced him to a tall, thin man, with a large skull-like head from which the eyes seemed to bulge, and deeply carved lines flanking the nose and mouth. The acquaintance hinted to Clive that the newcomer was 'high up in the government', and intoned his name in a somewhat reverent manner as 'Sir Francis Dashwood'. It meant nothing to Clive.

They played cards until three in the morning, during which

time Clive lost one hundred and seventy guineas to the stranger.

'You're quite a magician at cards, sir,' said Clive ruefully over a bottle of port when they had ceased their play.

'A social skill, hardly worth the learning, Colonel,' he returned deprecatingly. 'Money has an especial fascination for me, but to acquire it at gaming seems needlessly playful and tedious a method.' He had a cool, disinterested way of talking, and he held his head at a slight angle; and though one bulging eye never seemed to remove itself from Clive's face, the other seemed capable of taking in everything that was happening around the room.

'Oh? Money is your ... profession? vocation?, Sir Francis?' prodded Clive, pouring out two more glasses. The thin man gave him a faintly cynical smile.

'Indeed it is. As Chancellor of the Exchequer it is my unenviable task to convert a public debt of one hundred million into a credit balance – and it is with this in mind that the government and myself have the keenest interest in Bengal and the Carnatic ... and of course in you, Colonel.'

Chancellor of the Exchequer! How close can one get to the fountainhead, Clive thought to himself, though he was careful not to show that he was impressed. He gave a deprecatory laugh.

'You have a problem, sir, indeed you have. But don't look to India for its entire solution. There is more to do there than simply robbing its treasures,' he said.

'Robbing its treasures! My dear Clive, we contemplate no robbery. It is towards increased trade that we direct our endeavours,' protested Dashwood. 'At present we have a foothold in Madras and in Calcutta, and a fingerhold in Bombay – but the whole mass of India still awaits our traders.'

'Much trade you would do with a tribe of Marathas surrounding the factory,' Clive was tempted to retort, but voiced instead that which had occupied his mind from the moment he had sailed from Madras.

'Trade will develop only when the country is secure, Sir Francis. India now is a spawning of warrior states, each under the dominion of some barbarian prince who imposes his will upon a population writhing for freedom and justice.' He glanced at his cadaverous companion to ascertain the reaction. There was none. The codfish eye was still fixed unblinking on him.

114

'If we are to exercise our right to trade we must also be assured of the right to trade in peace. And political control is the only means by which this can be guaranteed.' He warmed to his theme when he saw that he had captured Dashwood's interest. 'There is in India the promise of a vast new empire that some day may well prove to be worth the effort of taking. We shall impose law, justice, a sense of direction, of nationhood, on what is at this moment a continent given over to internecine feuding.'

'Noble words, Colonel,' murmured Dashwood dryly. 'I confess I admire your confidence.'

'I have reason to be confident,' retorted Clive. 'I have proven that our soldiers have the measure of the Asiatic army – irrespective of size,' he added, rather boastfully.

'And you consider that such an empire would be to England's financial gain?'

Clive eyed him for a moment or two before replying.

'I appreciate that as Chancellor of the Exchequer you must measure everything in terms of profit or loss,' he said at length, 'but you'll get no rich harvest from India unless first you plant good seed and husband it well. And you will get no lasting co-operation from its peoples until you first prove to them that ...'

'Sir Francis? ... a letter from your office,' the porter murmured, interrupting the colonel with great circumspection. 'The messenger declared it was urgent, otherwise ...' he glanced pointedly at the clock which showed a few minutes to five a.m.

Sir Francis read the missive then motioned Clive to remain as he saw him moving to leave.

'It would seem that affairs are speeding up in India, and to our advantage, Colonel,' he said, waving the letter somewhat triumphantly. 'The Admiralty has just relayed news that General Bussy and Dupleix, having launched a major offensive on Trichinopoly, suffered a complete rout by this General Stringer Lawrence.'

'Trichinopoly! Lawrence has beaten them?'

Dashwood nodded, then held up a finger to show that he had more to say. 'Following on this debacle the French government – apparently disenchanted with their representative out there – has recalled him to Paris ... in disgrace.' He sat back happily.

Clive's reaction was unexpected. He leapt to his feet in outrage.

'Disgraced!' he cried out. 'Dupleix disgraced! by all the saints in heaven, what contumely is this? A plague on those popinjays who sit, cowardly snivelling, in their Parisian boulevards, for daring to call such a man to account.'

Dashwood cocked his head and a faint smile played about his thin lips. 'Forgive my amusement, sir, but your nature seems contrary. To show distress at the fate of a man who has done naught save attempt to bring your own fate to a speedy close appears overly Christian, or overly foolish.'

The soldier stared down at the civilian with all the contempt of one who takes risks for one who only talks of them.

'Dupleix was a great Frenchman, the one man I feared in India,' he said quietly. 'And if France can so ignobly use a faithful servant, might not this government be equally treacherous towards those who have served it well?'

The fire crackled in the grate and a clock chimed the quarter hour.

'Governments are rarely as grateful as their hero-redeemers think they ought to be,' observed Dashwood, looking at the fire. 'It is not sufficient for such a man to rely on the record of his fine deeds. He must also be watchful, for the more his image brightens the public's eye the more numerous, envious, and dangerous his enemies become.'

Clive flung himself into his chair and allowed deep waves of depression to wash over him. His companion, sensing his mood, leaned forward and touched Clive on the knee.

'I think a little distraction might be called for, my dear Colonel. Perhaps I might suggest a cure for your melancholia, if you will allow me.'

Clive opened one eye but made no reply. Dashwood, encouraged, went on. 'I have a retreat in the country – an old disused abbey at Medmenham – and a number of years ago I founded a ... a kind of monastic order: the Franciscans, I call it, an amusing play on my own name. I feel that a man with your breadth of view would not find the experience of a visit entirely unrewarding.'

He stood up and his long thin form leaned over the seated Clive; a skeletal hand touched his shoulder.

'A few hours in the tranquillity of my abbey will soon restore your humour, my friend. Permit me to call on you on the morrow and together we shall ride through some of England's fairest countryside, along the banks of the Thames, to Medmenham. There, if you so wish, I shall elect you to the Brotherhood of the Franciscans and appoint you friar.' He smiled. 'You will find yourself in a medieval world with which the modern cannot compare ... and I do assure you, Clive, that life itself will be given a new dimension after you have been to Medmenham.'

22

FROM THE back of his stallion, Kassim watched with smouldering impatience as the eleven dhows taking Siraj and his retinue to Calcutta cast off and floated to midstream of the wide, greasy Bhagirathi river.

'May such a storm arise that you, my cowardly father, be cast into the waters to drown ... and for you, Siraj-ud-daula, may your throat be choked with weeds before the Bhagirathi sucks you into its mud,' he called out – but only when the dhows were rounding the bend of the river. Then he spurred his horse and galloped back to the palace, his mind set on an audience with the Nawab.

It was granted him. He walked solemnly and tight-lipped down the long corridor to the throne room, and as he neared the door a thickset mulatto appeared from out of a side corridor. He salaamed obsequiously to Kassim and went on his way. Kassim swallowed hard. That was Sombrer, the executioner, and to meet him was a fearful omen. For a moment his resolution faltered. What if the Nawab took exception to his complaint? What if he considered himself affronted and immediately ordered Sombrer to dispose of him?

He squared his shoulders, tossed his head defiantly, strode into the chamber and prostrated himself before the Nawab. Alivardi Khan listened without interruption as the slender youth poured out his grievances.

'Arise, Mir Kassim, so that I may look on you ... Come closer.' The Nawab beckoned not unkindly, his voice betraying nothing of his thoughts. The youth stood as directed. The aged eyes studied his face, noting the fine down of whiskers sprouting from the chin as if desperate to claim manhood; the rich mahogany skin under the silk turban – glistening now, he suspected, more from apprehension than from heat. Yet he saw that the boy stood his ground under the scrutiny, and it pleased him.

'Is it not strange, Kassim,' he began slowly, using the diminutive to put the youngster at his ease, 'that your father has not sought my aid in this matter of which you complain?' It was a question that had not so far occurred to Kassim, and it was not easy to answer without giving offence. Yet he replied boldly.

'Mir Jafar fears too much the wrath of Siraj-ud-daula, your highness.'

'And you do not?'

Again Kassim wavered then, straightening his back, he replied, 'Indeed I fear him, your highness ... but I place my faith in the justice of the great Alivardi Khan.'

The old man sipped at the drink of fresh juice a servant had brought him. It served to refresh him and give him a moment or two to think. He knew of rumours concerning this Kassim and Sareen but had dismissed them as palace gossip, engineered to have malicious fun at the expense of a senior general.

'Speak with your heart, Mir Kassim,' he said a little sharply, 'and tell me. Do you covet this girl Sareen – the wife of your father?'

Kassim flinched, and the image of Sombrer's scimitar rising high above his neck flashed through his mind. He clenched his fists. 'I have shown honour to my father, your highness,' he replied evasively. The Nawab stroked his yellow-grey beard and his gaze hardened.

'You answer, Kassim, where there is no question. Now you shall tell me what I must know: have you lain with this woman?'

Kassim flopped to his knees. 'My lord, I have not lain with Sareen ... but she is mine, *mine*, since we were young. She has affection for me as I for her.' His eyes filled with tears.

The old man dismissed his outcry with a curt gesture. 'A woman is a chattel, stupid boy,' he said with some irritation. 'But that chattel belongs to another – and *that* is what matters. You are aware of the Koranic law concerning another's goods ...'

'But, my lord, Siraj-ud-daula takes what ...'

'Silence!' the old man barked at him. 'Siraj is the heir to the throne of Bengal, and to him many things are permitted.' Then, as if vexed with himself at giving way to anger, he said less harshly, 'So in truth, Mir Kassim, it is from greed for the wife of

118

another that you beg an interdict from me – and not from filial devotion. You accuse Siraj-ud-daula of rape, yet would seek to do no less yourself. How then can you honour your father, Mir Kassim?'

Kassim decided to fling himself on the mercy of Alivardi Khan by leaving nothing unsaid of what was in his heart.

'I honoured my father in all things, your highness, until, knowing what Sareen was to me, he took her for himself ... to warm his old bones in bed,' he added in a savage mutter. 'I won with love what my father sought to buy with treasure. Sareen and I pledged ourselves to each other,' he went on fervently, and with such effect that the Nawab was silenced – though what he was hearing greatly offended his own code.

The old man stayed the youngster's protestations by raising his hand. In the silence that followed, he said gravely, 'I could grant your petition but by so doing I should add to your peril, Mir Kassim. Neither you, your father, nor Sareen, would escape Siraj's vengeance once he is Nawab. But of greater consequence is your proposal to abuse the Faith.' He fixed the petitioner with a hard stare, then said, 'Speak now, Mir Kassim, of what is written in the Koran on this.'

Kassim looked at him tragically and recited miserably, 'Henceforth, you shall not marry the women who were married to your fathers. It is an evil practice, indecent and abominable.'

'From your own lips you have proclaimed the law; and you will now tell me of the punishment ordained for one who commits adultery, Mir Kassim.'

The youngster closed his eyes and in fear again recited, 'If any of your women commit fornication, call in four witnesses to testify to their guilt, and if proven, confine them to their houses till death overtakes them.'

The frail old man sat back in his throne. 'Go now, my son, and pray ... In the Name of Allah, the Compassionate, the Merciful, and offend not against the law.'

Kassim touched the marble floor with his forehead three times, then rose and backed out of the audience chamber. Minutes later he was relating the whole story to Sareen in the privacy of her apartments in the seraglio. She kept her eyes upon him all the time but made no comment until he had finished. Then, with bitter cynicism, she began to quote, 'Men have authority over women because Allah has made the one superior to the other. Good women are obedient. They guard their unseen parts because Allah has guarded them.'

In sudden anger she cried, 'And does the Koran not also declare that God withholds his blessing from arrogant and boastful men? And does it not make mention of helpless women?'

Kassim flung his arms around her in sudden panic lest she commit further blasphemy, and she was still for a moment. Then with cold anger she started to remove her clothes, and when she was completely naked she stood before him, her lips quivering but her eyes bright with determination.

'If I am considered to be no better than a chattel, to be numbered and valued among his gold and his silver, his silks, his horses and his cattle, to be handed to whomsoever my master chooses for their pleasure – then I declare myself absolved from the oath I swore when I was taken to wife,' she declared to the dumbly stricken Kassim. And in the same tone, 'Lie with me, Kassim. Take me and do with me what you will. My flesh has been dishonoured by those who indulged themselves against my desires. But to you only, Kassim, I do offer myself willingly.'

She lay on the bed and a few moments later slid her body under his, closed her eyes, and lost herself to the bitterness of her passion. She had no illusions as to the risk she was taking.

23

MATHIESON, NOW a captain of foot soldiers, was a tough looking fellow, with bright blond hair and a small scar on his right cheek. He knew all the latest songs of ribaldry and sang them well. He was sardonic, crude rather than witty, hearty rather than friendly. Edmund dubiously accepted him as a good fellow, but at times he found Mathieson too much.

They were drinking in one of the punch shops that dotted Calcutta.

'Utterly divine, quite the most beautiful creature on earth,' Mathieson was boasting. 'But, of course, you've met her,' he added, casting a sly look at his companion. Edmund nodded moodily. 'I saw her parents a few weeks ago; catchpenny type,' he went on blithely, 'not without money. But by little hints and sidelong glances they made it pretty clear that if Anna caught me it wouldn't be unwelcome in that household.'

Edmund, writhing at such boastfulness, asked pointedly, 'And how do you propose to keep Anna on a captain's pay?'

Mathieson stared at Edmund as if he were half-witted. 'Captain's pay! Well, Maskelyne, if that's all that *you're* living on, more fool you. With all the opportunity here to make money ...' He shook his head in wonderment. 'Do you know that I have a staff of six writers working for me? I tell you, the moment I get my majority I'll resign, parcel up my fortune and be off to England – another wealthy nabob,' he exclaimed proudly, as if expecting applause.

Edmund shot him a hard look. 'And what exactly is your business?' he forced himself to ask, knowing well what the answer was likely to be.

'Rice – food of the peasants, and luxury to me,' Mathieson replied cheerfully. 'I advance money on security of the next harvest, the farmer pays me in rice – at my own valuation, of course. It's stored in my warehouse and later sold during a shortage ... and believe me, there's always a shortage in Bengal,' he added, tapping his fingernails on the table.

Edmund knew the rice game; nearly everybody in Calcutta played it. And though reluctant to quarrel with Mathieson, he could not stop himself from saying acidly, 'And what kind of modest profit do you expect this year?'

Mathieson told him, without the slightest embarrassment, that he normally bought rice at three pounds for one-tenth of a penny and would resell it during the famine at three pounds for three pence.

'Rather a large profit,' Edmund exclaimed. 'No wonder that after three or four years at the game even the meanest trader can sail home a wealthy man.'

Mathieson looked pained. He wasn't the first to make a fortune that way, and he wouldn't be the last.

Edmund toyed gloomily with his glass. He had severed relations with a number of companions on this same issue. Warren Hastings had been such a one, though he admitted that he was no real loss, but at this rate he would soon have no one to speak to. Was he being unreasonable? Was he entitled to dismiss anyone from his company whose business morals he objected to? And did Anna know of Mathieson's trade?

Anna. The name stabbed at him. She was not as tall as Petal Wilkinson, and her figure was less slender than those of Lotus and Jasmine. Her light auburn hair was pulled too severely away from her pale oval face, and when she had smiled at that first meeting he had noticed that a fragment of tooth had been chipped from the left incisor. But there was a freshness and a sparkle about Anna that recalled for him the blossom that grew wild in the foothills of Nepal. He had been entirely captivated.

Circumspectly he had enquired of Mathieson if he was betrothed to her. His reply had been typical, and spoken in an airy and dismissive way that was infuriating.

'I have as yet made no formal request for her hand ... but if looks, kisses, meaningful sighs can be construed as significant, then the sweeping of my hat and the bending of the knee would be a mere conformity to ritual.' The arrogance of the fellow was detestable. Yet wasn't his own deceit equally so? he asked himself. Was it not true that he tolerated this boorish fellow simply to retain contact with Anna?

He saw through the window a familiar carriage drawing up, and, with a nod at his companion, he went out to it.

'Sahiba Wilkinson wishes you to come, my lord Maskelyne,' the coachman told him with some urgency, opening the door of the carriage. He climbed in the phaeton with alacrity and bid the driver whip up the horses.

A worried Petal Wilkinson met him at the door of her sumptuous bordello, forgetting even the habitual kiss in her hurry to take him inside.

'Siraj-ud-daula was here,' she blurted out, her hands clasping and unclasping as she sought to calm herself.

'Here in Calcutta!' Edmund was appalled. A visit from the heir to Bengal required the turnout of the entire Council and a host of guards to provide a formal welcome. This was a blunder on someone's part. He began to say as much, but Petal cut him short.

'Please, Edmund. It isn't important,' she all but snapped at him. 'He was here for no more than a few minutes ... half an hour ... an hour ... I don't know,' she went on, getting more and more excited. 'Then a message came from someone from Murshidabad – and he rushed off ... rushed off back to the boats.'

He looked at her in amazement. 'He came all the way here – and then sailed off again?'

She looked up at him, and she had tears in her eyes.

'Alivardi Khan is dead ... dead,' she moaned, terror creeping into her voice. 'Siraj-ud-daula is now Nawab of Bengal. God have mercy on us all!'

But Siraj had not returned to the capital by boat. It was much too slow – and anything might happen whilst he was away. On teams of horses he made the journey to Murshidabad in two days, and found the capital thronged with people wailing and beating their breasts and foreheads as they mourned the noble Alivardi Khan. Siraj smiled happily to himself and at once arranged for the most ostentatious of funerals.

Four score of elephants, richly caparisoned, with gold tips to their tusks and howdahs like small mosques on their backs, lumbered their ungainly yet majestic way through the main streets of the hot, dusty town. Twenty thousand of the great Khan's warriors in full armour accompanied the beasts. And in the midst of it all, on a monstrous flat-topped juggernaut – almost unseen for the flowers that covered him – lay the body of Alivardi Khan. Twice the traditional number of animals were sacrificed, and double the amount of contributions from the public was demanded.

The customary period of mourning was abandoned after twelve hours. Within twenty-four every vestige of the former Nawab's existence had been obliterated from the palace. Entertainment was the order of the day. Alivardi's family was banished to a distant palace and the seraglio restocked with specially chosen females. But even that was not enough.

Siraj summoned Mir Jafar to his presence. The elderly general came – filled with apprehension. He was greeted affably.

'It pleases me, Mir Jafar, to confirm you in your appointment as general in my army,' he told the prostrate figure. 'Not as supreme general, for that rank I shall bear myself.' He then bid the much-relieved warrior rise and face him. 'Still, I shall need to consult with you often and therefore require that you be near at hand. The Nawab's palace is of sufficient size,' he went on, smiling and trying to look agreeable, 'and I have set aside apartments for you and your family.' He paused for a moment as if considering within himself, then as an apparent afterthought said, 'I shall arrange for Sareen to live in my own quarters amidst a richness and splendour that even you could not equal ... though in deference to Islamic law you will be permitted to visit and to take her as wife whenever you ... whenever it suits my convenience,' he hastily amended.

If the new Nawab elected to have Sareen as his plaything, then the husband could only touch the floor with his forehead and proclaim his joy at being so signally honoured. And this he did.

Kassim raged when told of the arrangement. 'When the sky is rent asunder; when the stars scatter and the oceans roll together; when the graves are hurled about; each soul shall know what it has done and what it has failed to do,' he ranted the awesome Cataclysm of the Koran.

Then he bent his head in passionate misery, knowing there was nothing he could do about it. Whether his father knew of his own affair with Sareen, he cared not at all, but in deference to him he kept silence.

'Siraj ordered me to discover the man who betrayed him to Alivardi Khan,' Mir Jafar said quietly.

'And you will tell him, father?' Kassim challenged contemptuously. The father looked searchingly at his son, and saw in his eyes nothing but hatred. He turned away, murmuring, 'What father can shed the blood of his own son?'

Sareen, in obedience to the Koranic dictum, performed her duty. She appeared not to care which of the three made their claims on her. To Siraj-ud-daula she went in obedience but with some apprehension; to her husband with cold impassivity; and to Kassim with tenderness and anticipation which fell short of love. For Kassim, too, had failed her as protector.

24

EVEN SIR Francis Dashwood, a man of substance himself, could not resist a flutter of envy when he called on Robert Clive to convey him to Medmenham Abbey. The length of the driveway seemed interminable, whilst the size and noble proportions of the mansion itself reduced visitors to insignificance. Two footmen assisted him from his carriage, two others swept open the huge double-doors at the top of the flight of steps, and a splendidly liveried butler with imperious disdain led him into the cavernous hallway.

'You do yourself well, Clive,' he remarked to his host.

'It will suffice for the brief period I shall be in England,' said Clive airily.

'For a house this size, what staff do you employ?'

Clive took his cane and hat from the butler and led the visitor out of the house.

'I really couldn't say, Dashwood. The butler attends to domestic matters, and the steward the rest of the estate ... this your coach?' He nodded his head in approval at the postchaise with its four matched greys, its two postilions, its coachman and footman. Dashwood smirked.

'Yes,' was all he needed to say. Such a rig effectively classified the owner. Clive wandered over to the horses, ran his hand over the team-leader's haunches and rubbed its muzzle with undisguised affection. He climbed into the coach, adjusted his tricorne hat and settled into a corner.

They reached the 13th century abbey without mishap. There it stood, its corroded stones and picturesque Romanesque architecture fitting its surroundings as if painted by a French baroque artist.

'It used to be a Cistercian abbey ... but that was before Henry wanted to legalise his mistresses and changed the country's religion to do so,' Dashwood said, casting a sly look at Clive.

Clive paid no attention to this remark. 'And it belongs to you?' he asked, thinking it an odd possession for one whom he would have least suspected of devout proclivities.

'Yes.' He hesitated, then fixed his companion with a look. 'I assume you are not ... of the Roman faith, Mr Clive?' he queried.

'Did you think that I was?' replied Clive, with just the right touch of indignation.

Dashwood gave him a pacifying smile. 'Assuredly not, my dear Clive. Simply a precaution,' said he cryptically, preparing to open the door and step out as the coach halted. 'You see, the Order I've formed – the New Franciscans – is not exactly ... in accordance, shall we say, with the Roman faith.'

Clive stepped out after him and wandered over to the deeply-carved, weathered grey stonework of the porch. He shaded his eyes with his hand in order to read the inscription over the archway – and gave a puzzled frown. The carving was comparatively new, and the inscription, curious to say the least, read:

' "Fay ce que voudras," ' he mouthed slowly, 'Do as you wish.' He glanced sharply at Dashwood who was standing to one side, a faintly mocking smile on his face. 'Odd kind of motto for a religious Order, Dashwood,' he remarked. 'Seems more like the creed of a libertine.'

The skull-like face cracked into a mirthless grin. He offered no explanation but took Clive by the arm and pushed open the door. The gloom inside contrasted so greatly with the brilliance of the day that at first he could see nothing. A candle was lit. He saw that he was in the vestibule of the abbey, and in front of him was another door presumably leading to the nave.

Dashwood was fumbling inside a huge cupboard set against the wall. In a moment he was handed the complete habit of a Franciscan monk, and noticed that Dashwood had taken another for himself. Making some wry comment, Clive began pulling on the habit. His companion put a hand on his arm.

'It will be intolerably warm, Mr Clive,' he said from out of the gloom, his bulging eyes catching glints from the candle. 'I suggest you first remove your outer garments.' And, to Clive's astonishment, Dashwood stripped naked before putting on his habit.

'Not to that extent,' he muttered, peeling off his jacket and waistcoat before slipping the coarse brown cloth over his head.

When they were ready, Dashwood whispered, 'In here,' and opened the inner door. There was a strangled excitement in his voice that Clive could not fail to notice. The two 'friars', with cowls over their heads, passed out of the darkness and pulled up short on the other side of the doorway.

Clive's eyes widened. The whole of the nave, the double transepts, choir stalls, altar, were ablaze with light from scores of giant candles. A sour acrid smell of burning wax and incense filled the air. The windows had been boarded over, and beneath them, standing against the walls of the two aisles, were two silent lines of monks, their faces hidden by their cowls even though each one held a flickering candle in front of him.

It was medieval. Clive's lips felt dry.

One of the monks, seeing the newcomers, detached himself from a line and hurried over.

'We've been waiting an intolerably long time for you,' he hissed to Dashwood from the deep recess of his hood.

Sir Francis gave him a disdainful bow. 'My apologies, my lord. We were delayed,' he told him off-handedly, gesturing towards Clive and adding in a stage whisper, 'Allow me to introduce Colonel Robert Clive of India ... my friend, Lord Sandwich.'

The monk made the curtest of acknowledgments, rudely turning away from Clive and hissing again, 'Pray let us begin. We have wasted enough time.'

Dashwood took up a lighted candle and handed it to Clive, then took one for himself. Quietly advising his companion to remain near the end of one line of monks, he then slowly paced down the centre of the nave, bearing his candle aloft and, in a high-pitched voice, began intoning a strange Gregorian chant.

When Dashwood reached the centre of the nave the monks in the left aisle paired off and followed him in procession, taking up the chant as they did so. At the same time the monks in the right aisle extinguished their candles one after the other until all that remained was a glowing circle of light around the altar – which Clive was shocked to see covered with black cloth.

The 'high priest' Dashwood turned at the steps leading to the altar and commenced a ceremony that was a travesty of the Roman Mass. Clive was no longer in any doubt as to the nature of these 'New Franciscans', but though he could feel the nausea rising within him he was compelled to watch, riveted.

The monks who had been in the right aisle had by now formed a line facing the high priest at the altar steps. Four acolytes took up position behind him and, as Dashwood slowly raised his candle to the fullest extent of his arms, the acolytes hurried behind the ten monks and commenced tearing off their robes. Clive gasped as the ten stood revealed as girls and boys aged from seventeen to twenty years – all of them totally naked.

With raucous shouts and song, the youths formed a circle and began swirling around the altar, swaying, leaping and throwing back their heads, their breasts or male organs bouncing and flopping as their owners danced around in an ever-increasing frenzy. The other monks began shouting and encouraging the dancers to an even wilder activity. Boys and girls, sweating in passionate excitement, chests heaving and bodies glistening danced as if possessed.

Then Dashwood snuffed out his candle.

Immediately the roisterous, Bacchanalian revelling stopped. There was a frightening hush. The high priest pointed a long thin finger at one of the girls. She was seized by the four acolytes – one to each limb – and hoisted horizontally and laid flat on the altar. Then Dashwood selected a boy, and he, too, was seized and raised high above the compliant girl.

Clive was transfixed by the scene. His eyes widened as he watched this terrible perversion. And then a drop of hot wax fell on to his trembling hand, breaking the spell. In sudden fury he flung the candle to the ground and stormed out of the abbey, knocking over a standing candelabra in his hurry to escape. Outside he breathed deeply to clear his lungs of the incense and the evil waxy smell of the abbey.

Uncertain as to what next to do, he could only wait for Sir Francis's appearance. He waited an hour. Dashwood said nothing when he rejoined Clive, though he gave him many a questioning glance.

The journey back was strained. When eventually the coach halted outside the Palladian façade of Clive's home, he thrust open the door and climbed out. Once outside, he turned and fixed his host with eyes that glowed with fury, though when he spoke his voice was unnaturally even.

'You have gone to much trouble for my entertainment, Sir Francis.' His throat was tight. 'Your private corruptions are your own affair and have nothing to do with others ... yet ... if England be obliged to seek its masters from men of your ilk, then indeed I must cry "God help and God forgive this land." '

He stepped back a pace without waiting for the affronted Dashwood to make reply, rapping on the carriage wheels to call the coachman's attention to him.

'Drive off, coachman ... and by all the saints! if ever you return with this fellow I'll set my hounds on you.'

The lackey's mouth dropped open but he wasted no time in carrying out the order. The horses were whipped up and the coach began trundling down the driveway. As it moved off, an infuriated face appeared from out the coach window, the mouth opened and

Clive just heard the words shouted to him.

'One day I'll destroy you, Clive ... mark my name! ... I'LL DESTROY ... YOU ... THIS I VOW!'

25

To HIS shame, Edmund found himself inventing reasons to accompany Mathieson, and was ever conscious of the shallow basis for the friendship. His obsession with Anna was absolute. He thought of her incessantly, and saw her as often as he could induce Mathieson to invite his company when he visited her home.

On one particular day the two men were in the gymnasium of Fort William. They were duelling with blunted sabres, weapons capable of inflicting nasty wounds if carelessly handled. Stripped to the waist, wearing only tight blue breeches and shoes, Edmund and Mathieson laid into each other with good-humoured zeal.

Edmund's clumsy strokes were easily parried by the more skilled Mathieson. Finally, irritated, he launched a mighty chopping blow that – with a sharpened blade – could have split a man's skull. Mathieson laughingly turned it aside and, derisively, thrust forward and poked his opponent, none too gently, in the chest.

The sergeant-instructor, who had been watching with a jaundiced eye, intercepted the swords with his own weapon and brought the bout to a halt. He shook his head with infinite sadness.

'Cap'n Maskelyne, sir,' he pleaded. 'For gawd's sake, that's no axe yer wielding. Not that way ... *this*!' He took a stance in front of Mathieson, executed what seemed to Edmund to be a *grande jette*, rolled his wrist and, his sword flicked upwards like a chameleon's tongue, lightly prodded the topmost rib of Mathieson's chest.

The sergeant lowered his weapon and looked grievously at Edmund. 'Really, sir, if ever you're faced with any o' them black johnnies an' yer use yer sword like you've just been usin' it ... well ... we can allus make salt pork from what'll be left of yer. Frankly, sir, I tell you honest like, you'd be better off wi' a club.'

Edmund's pride was wounded. 'To the devil with you, sergeant. I'm out of practice, that's all. This sabre's a different weight from the one I'm used to,' he expostulated. 'Besides, I've never pretended to be other than an average swordsman. Have you ever seen me with a musket?' he challenged, wanting to redeem himself.

The instructor gave him a pitying look. 'Aye, I've seen you, sir, and right glad I was I were standing behind yer.'

'I was off form that day, sergeant,' Edmund replied huffily, 'and the barrel wasn't true.'

The instructor, taking pity on him, adopted a conciliatory tone. He rather liked Captain Maskelyne, as did most of the soldiers.

'Why not take a tip from an old campaigner, Cap'n Maskelyne,' he said. 'Just tell the men what to do. They'll foller yer awright, 'cos they respect yer. They all say yer the best officer in't fort ... but for gawd's sake don't git inter any 'and-to-'and fighting. Just point out what t'others have to shoot at then let 'em get on wi' it.'

Mathieson laughed uproariously at Edmund's discomfiture and clapped him on the back.

'Come, Maskelyne, let's away from this fiendish oracle. Get your tunic on, we've the fortifications to inspect.'

'What fortifications?' Edmund grunted sourly, handing the sergeant his sabre and slipping on his blouse. Then he tossed a ribald salute to the instructor, who just grinned back at him, and walked out with Mathieson to the outer walls.

'Has it ever occurred to you that if we were faced with a resolute attack, Calcutta would crumble like sticks on a funeral pyre?' Edmund said quietly from the top of the fort, staring out over the harbour. 'Any support from warships would be of little help – their field of fire covers only half the city ... Isn't that Anna?' The excitement in his manner was so marked that Mathieson shot him an odd look before turning to see where his companion was pointing.

The phaeton was drawn up outside the main gate. The girl sitting in it, despite the heat, looked exquisitely fresh in her long white gown. But Anna was not as composed as she seemed. She nodded and smiled a greeting as the two men approached, but when Edmund discreetly moved out of earshot it was obvious that Mathieson was getting the sharp edge of her tongue.

'Women!' he exclaimed, throwing up his hands in mock despair when the carriage had driven Anna away again. 'Furious because

I didn't call last night. Wouldn't believe me when I said I was on duty.'

'But you were not on duty.'

'Of course I wasn't, idiot. I went to the cockfight. We've got a bird there that we've fitted with some new metal spurs. It practically tore the ...'

'You went to a ... and you could have been with Anna!' Such was the anger in Edmund's voice that Mathieson could no longer doubt what he had vaguely suspected. He moved to face his companion squarely, but some small voice warned him to take care. His dilemma was thankfully postponed by the appearance of Sergeant Grimsby.

'Beggin' your pardon sir, but the fort commander wants you immediately,' he addressed Edmund, glancing from one to the other as if sensing the charged atmosphere.

'Thank you, sergeant. I'll come immediately.'

Mathieson shrugged. 'I'll come with you, if you don't mind, Maskelyne.' His tone was placatory.

The fort commander was a contented, tubby man with a strong dislike for any upset of routine. He was clearly agitated.

'I sent for you, Captain Maskelyne, because of your acquaintance with a Miss Wilkinson,' he spluttered.

Edmund's eyes hardened. 'Sir,' he said coldly.

'Yes, your friendship with Miss Wilkinson,' the fellow gabbled. 'We have a problem ... a grave one, I can tell you ... and I want you to go and see her ... or him, I should say ... find out what's it's all about.'

'All what about, sir?' Edmund relaxed a little when it seemed no offence was intended by the commandant's bluntness.

'The new Nawab – Siraj-ud-daula. He's *here in Calcutta,*' cried the commandant, surprised that Edmund needed to be told. 'He's got three hundred men with him and we've no idea if we're expected to treat his visit as a state occasion or what. He's given no intimation of what he's come for, and damn it, that's what you've to find out, Maskelyne – unofficially, of course.'

'Palanquins, Edmund?' drawled Mathieson, when they were outside again. Edmund considered.

'No. We shall go in style: cavalry escort, banners flying, the lot. That's how Dupleix would have done it, and that's how we're going to do it.'

Later in the afternoon the two captains, with all the panoply of royalty, set off in a four-horse open carriage with a splendid troop of cavalry in front and another one behind. Lances stood erect with pennants flying.

'The rumour is she's bound to him,' said Mathieson, breaking the cool silence between them.

'Bound? A slave, you mean? ... hardly likely. Miss Wilkinson's a white woman,' Edmund rejoined in mild irritation.

'Perhaps it would be more correct to say that her ancestry is dubious. However, slave or not, it's common knowledge she gave allegiance to Alivardi Khan. Whether or not she's prepared to do the same for Siraj-ud-daula remains to be seen.'

Edmund was silent.

When the colourful procession drew up at the white gateway of Petal's mansion, it was immediately surrounded by a threatening regiment of Siraj's guards. They pushed against the coach with less than welcoming expressions. The sergeant-major of cavalry looked around uneasily and barked out an order.

Lances were raised and placed into the leather rests behind each mounted soldier, then sabres were drawn and put ostentatiously to the 'slope' on shoulders. At a second order sixteen men dismounted and forced open a short passageway from the carriage to the gate. Angry murmurs arose from the armed crowd, which began pushing a little harder, causing the horses to become restive and the soldiers to grip their sabres tighter. It had all the makings of an unpleasant incident, when the eunuch steward of Miss Wilkinson rushed down the steps screaming imprecations at Siraj's guards and shouting that the visitors were friends of his mistress.

This had the desired effect. Edmund and Mathieson were granted admission to the house, where they soon found Miss Wilkinson.

'Be careful,' she whispered before taking them into the main room to meet the Nawab. 'He's in a dangerous mood.'

They removed their hats and made obeisance to him. He was reclining on Petal's couch, and eyed them with unmistakable hostility. Four armed men stood against one wall. Sombrer the executioner, with his great scimitar, was immediately behind him, and standing in the farthest corner were Mir Jafar and Mir Kassim.

'His Excellency the Governor of Calcutta sends his greetings and offers his respects to his Exalted Highness, Siraj-ud-daula, the Nawab of Bengal, and begs to know his wishes and how he may be of service to him,' Edmund said with grave formality, meeting the hostile glare with one of cool dignity.

Siraj, thrown out of joint by the unexpected visit, struggled to make up his mind as to the attitude he should adopt. He had already discovered that being Nawab brought as many problems as pleasures. The Hindu multitudes were seething under their Muslim masters; the Marathas were continually making raids on Bengal. But his most urgent concern was the rivalry between French and English, each of whom was growing strong enough to threaten his own position.

He decided to be difficult.

'Why are the English extending their fortifications?' he shouted, saying the first thing that came into his mind. 'Why does all the money come to Calcutta and none to Murshidabad?'

'Your highness, the fortifications which Alivardi ...'

'I know all about your fortifications! Walls and ditches supposed to keep out the Marathas. No Marathas come here; they're afraid of my armies.' His voice rose in pitch.

'The money you claim comes to Calcutta, your highness, is investment by other princes. It is not taxes ...'

Siraj shot upright, his eyes blazing. 'Hold your tongue, hatman! Keep silent when your prince is speaking. I order you now, not one more stone will you add to the fort. And all the money ... ALL ... you have enticed to this English factory will be sent to Murshidabad. Murshidabad is the capital of Bengal, not Calcutta. And I, Siraj-ud-daula, am Nawab, not your president of Council.'

Edmund kept his temper with difficulty.

Miss Wilkinson moved forward swiftly and dropped to her knees in front of the Nawab in an attempt to pacify him. He brushed her aside with a contemptuous swing of his left hand. Edmund took a pace forward – so did the guards.

'Siraj-ud-daula,' he gritted out, 'you will grant me the courtesy of allowing me to speak.'

The Nawab's eyes shot wide open. This hatman was trying to beard the lion in his own den. He sprang to his feet and drew himself to his full height. The guards unsheathed their weapons.

'My lord, I beg you,' Petal screamed, flinging her arms around his legs. He kicked her away, but the distraction served to calm him.

'You will leave, hatmen! Leave, LEAVE!' he yelled. 'Tell your governor of my commands ... and tell him I shall *crush* Calcutta if he disobeys.'

Edmund stole a look at the sobbing Miss Wilkinson, then jerked his head in a travesty of a bow and stalked out of the room, followed by Mathieson.

In the carriage once more, the courage drained from his stomach. 'God in heaven,' he breathed. 'I never wish to be *that* close to death again ... the man is a fanatic! He's going to attack Calcutta, Mathieson, and damned soon ... Mathieson?'

Mathieson was vomiting into his lace handkerchief.

26

AS CLIVE stormed into his hallway, after his return from Medmenham Abbey, a man of his own age, uniformed as a lieutenant of cavalry, sprang to attention and took off his hat.

Clive, a little taken aback, stopped abruptly. 'Who the devil are you?' he snarled.

'Eyre Coote, sir, lieutenant.'

'I'm not blind to your rank! What business have you with me?' he snapped, aware of how badly he was behaving but unable to stop himself. The large, rotund officer with the bright red hair flushed, yet continued to stand his ground.

'It is an impertinence, Colonel Clive, but I would beg a few moments of your time. I have a desire to go to India, sir.'

'Then go and have done with you. Make war on Frenchie and the Coolie; get sunstroke and cholera; play the rice game and pray you live long enough to spend the money – but don't impose your absurd presence on me.' Clive stabbed the marble floor with the point of his cane and made to walk past him.

'I have been court-martialled, Colonel.'

This was an admission sufficient to capture any soldier's attention. He paused and scrutinised the lieutenant.

'What did you say your name was?'

'Eyre Coote, sir.'

The name meant nothing to him. 'And for what reason were you court-martialled?'

'It was at the battle of Falkirk ...'

'The Jacobite rebellion!'

'Yes, Colonel. My regiment was under heavy assault ... some of them ran for it. The rest of us held out, but I was made responsible. The verdict ... you can guess what it was,' he said quietly, with no appeal for sympathy.

'You were judged guilty – and rightly so,' Clive said severely. 'Every officer is accountable for his men. What was the sentence?' he asked after a small pause, during which he continued his assessment of the visitor.

'Reduced to the rank of lieutenant, sir.' He then added disarmingly, 'It was also hinted that I take my services elsewhere.'

Clive's manner became less caustic. 'So you have elected to go to India.'

'Yes sir. With respect, Colonel, my intention was to beg leave to join your command once you return.' The statement was made with such sincerity that Clive had to repress a smile. Return to India! He had less desire for India than a fox for a pack of hounds. 'You *have* decided to return, have you not, sir?' the visitor pressed him anxiously.

Clive pondered a moment before answering slowly. 'Go to India as a conqueror, Mr Coote, and you become its captive. Two years ago I thought I had snapped the chains.' Clive held up his left arm as if for inspection. 'I was mistaken. I stretched them only.' He laughed cynically and lowered his arm. 'Yes. You may take it that I shall be returning to that fevered, blistering land. Get off to India with you, Mr Coote, and make your peace with the conditions that prevail there. When I take up my command again, you shall be welcome. You can be assured that for many years to come a man with a sword will be needed.'

Clive had at last made up his mind.

In 1755 a somewhat overweight colonel, thirty years of age, his fashionably gowned wife, plus three score of trunks, took ship back to India. They left with the cheers of the populace ringing in their ears, the blessings of Royalty, the unctuous wishes of the Company directors who had promised Clive the governorship of Fort St George – and the silence of the Chancellor of the Exchequer, who now occupied the office of Postmaster-General as well.

The journey to India by four-masted barque was so lengthy that it was possible for a lady to conceive in Plymouth and for the child to be born as the ship dropped anchor in Bombay. The infant was baptised Edward, and Clive congratulated himself on having arranged his affairs with splendid foresight for, devoted though he was to Margaret, he felt she would need something to occupy her mind whilst he went about creating an empire.

27

THERE WERE six weeks of uneasy calm following the meeting between Edmund and the Nawab of Bengal. Then the storm broke. Siraj attacked Calcutta with thirty thousand troops.

Mathieson, with his patrol, caught between the harbour and the fort during the opening barrage from the Nawab's artillery, wavered uncertainly. Then catching sight of Mir Jafar's division of two thousand warriors, he led his men to the harbour where they climbed into longboats and rowed swiftly to the ships anchored in the Hooghly river – all thoughts for Anna and the rest of the garrison pushed from his mind.

Within an hour the commandant had been killed by artillery fire, and Edmund Maskelyne took command as the next senior officer. Many civilians had fled to the fort, and though he searched anxiously, Anna was not among them. Organising the defence as best he could, soldier alternating with civilian along the walls, he waited for the first attack. And when it came it seemed to the defenders like a tidal wave of brown-skinned warriors. Hordes of them rushed the pitifully low walls – walls so low that a man could jump up and touch the parapet with his fingers.

The first wave was broken, and the second and the third, but Siraj's troops continued to press forward. The fort's two cannon blasted grapeshot, scything great gaps in the congested ranks of the attackers. But by the time a cannon had been reloaded, the gaps had been filled. The soldiers, demonstrating masterly skill with their slow-loading muskets, were firing six balls a minute – an incredible rate of fire. Yet ten times their number would not have been enough. As one man fell, a score of others were there to fill his place. It was not possible to push them back. Bayonets thrust and ripped upwards, swords hacked down on turbaned heads as the invaders swarmed up ladders. Butts of muskets flailed around, cracking skulls and flinging bodies in screaming arcs to the ground.

There was a momentary respite as the heavy guns of the warships began laying down a barrage. Buildings crashed into rubble in one entire section of Calcutta as the forty-two pound roundshot pounded them. Mir Jafar's regiment, assigned to that area, panicked and within minutes were fleeing to safety. Mir Kassim rode after them, slashing about him with his whip as he tried to turn them back, but they kept on running. But even the guns of the warships were unable to bring relief to the garrison of the fort.

Edmund signalled a retreat into the strongly fortified central building: he had not forgotten the example of Fort St David. Swiftly the remnants of the garrison and the civilians rushed across the courtyard into the keep and barred the thick door. Edmund took up his position behind one of the archery slits. Beyond the outer walls he witnessed the gathering of ten thousand warriors as they prepared for the final attack.

A few miles from Calcutta, beyond reach of the warships' guns, an impatient Siraj-ud-daula, resplendent in the full chain-mail armour of a princely warrior, paced up and down, seizing eagerly on each fragment of news brought to him. Tactics were changed, regiments ordered from one place to another then, at a whim, the whole strategy was adjusted – to the utter confusion of his commanders. Had it not been for the sheer number of his warriors, he might well have lost the battle.

'Your Highness! My Lord! The fort has been overcome!'

The news sent him into a paroxysm of joy. He pounded his thighs in exuberant delight.

'Only a few remain alive in the inner building,' came the less pleasing rider.

'Destroy them! Let them be killed,' he cried. 'Tell Mir Jafar that none must live.'

The messenger fled to deliver the message, shouting the substance of it to all who came near him as he searched for his horse. One who heard him was Mir Kassim who was just then slowly dismounting. He walked straight to the huge tent of the Nawab, pulled aside the flap and went in. His face was twisted with pain.

'Why have you left your regiment?' Siraj accused, and then he noticed the stain on Kassim's tunic. 'Kassim! You are hurt, my friend.' His voice dropped to a whisper as he came forward, his eyes showing genuine concern, his arms outstretched.

'Oh! what comedy!' thought Kassim. 'He abuses me; steals from me; debauches the one I love; ridicules me and holds me in contempt. Yet if another does me slight injury he fulminates and would slaughter them if need be ... though he must *know* that it could only have been me who betrayed his assassination attempt to Alivardi Khan. Now look at him! Like a peon on his knees, tearful over a mere scratch.'

'Siraj,' he said quietly, laying a hand on his shoulder. 'Do not let the soldiers in the keep be slaughtered. It would be an evil thing and would do you no credit. And to the English, my lord, it would be unforgivable. Death in battle they understand and accept – but murder whilst captive they would avenge. Those who came after them would not rest until ...' A significant gesture finished the sentence.

Siraj rose to his feet. The faintest of shadows crossed his face and he stared, puzzled, at Kassim as if trying to capture the sense of what had been asked of him. The bloodstain appeared to have attracted all the Nawab's critical faculties to the exclusion of everything else.

'Siraj? ... Did you understand what I asked of you?' Kassim urged softly.

'The English ... in the fort. Yes, take them prisoner,' he said distantly.

Kassim dropped to his knees, pressed the hand of Siraj against his cheek in a gesture of loyalty, then hastily backed out of the tent before he changed his mind.

He stumbled and grimaced with pain as he tried to mount his horse, and the stain on his tunic widened.

'Lift me on,' he commanded two of the guards, and clenched his teeth as they struggled to get him across the saddle. He slashed his whip across the stallion's flanks.

138

Edmund glanced swiftly through the archery slit then ducked back again as a fusillade of musket shots spattered against the stone, two of them finding an entrance and chipping plaster from the inner wall. In the ground floor of the keep, where the outer door was, beams of wood had been hammered into place so that nothing short of a battering ram would have gained the enemy entrance.

At the fourth hour, when Edmund was checking the ammunition, there was a sudden quietening in the crowd outside. Risking a peep through the slit he saw that a passageway had been made through the throng of warriors, and coming down it, limping slightly, was Mir Kassim, whom Edmund knew.

'Sahib Maskelyne,' he called up, keeping clear of the direct line of fire from the keep.

'Mir Kassim,' replied Edmund, keeping out of sight.

'Sahib Maskelyne ... if you surrender, your lives will be spared. His highness, the Nawab, has so promised.'

'And what is to happen to us if we surrender, Mir Kassim?' Edmund called down to him, beckoning those with him to keep watch at the other slits in case of trickery.

'You will be imprisoned for a few days and then released – to this I swear.' And to show that he trusted Edmund, Kassim deliberately exposed himself to the archery slits.

Not to have shown himself equal to Kassim in trust or courage would have been unthinkable. Edmund duly presented himself at the slit.

'Your highness, Mir Kassim,' he shouted through the aperture. 'Will you give your oath on the Koran that if we surrender to you no one here, or any other civilians you find in Calcutta, will be harmed?'

Kassim's pledge was such that no Muslim could doubt its sincerity.

The door of the keep was opened. Edmund emerged, followed by fifteen civilians and twenty-seven soldiers – all that was left from the garrison of two hundred and fifty. They stood nervously, hemmed in on all sides, blinking in the fierce sunlight. Mir Kassim salaamed, gasping with pain as he did so. Edmund swept off his hat and bowed.

'I would beg of you one favour, your highness,' he said respectfully. 'I need to visit a certain house in this city to assure myself of a lady's safety.'

Kassim's mouth creased into a knowing smile. 'Miss Wilkinson?' He waved both hands reassuringly. 'No harm will come to Miss Wilkinson. She is under the protection of Siraj-ud-daula.'

'This I assumed,' Edmund dryly replied. 'But it is another lady with whom I'm concerned.'

The young nobleman scratched his embryo beard and tried to look wise. He clapped his hands and summoned a captain of his guard. 'Escort this officer Sahib to where he desires to go, and bring him and the Feringhee woman to the prison. See that no injury is done them ... but see also they do not escape,' he added threateningly, then gave a curt bow to Edmund and made to stalk away. He had taken no more than two paces when he staggered, and would have fallen had not Edmund caught him.

'Take him inside the keep and allow him to rest,' Edmund ordered.

As the carriage, with its mounted escort, trundled through the city, the Englishman was sickened at the carnage. A baby sat crying outside one home, its mother dead beside it. Bodies lay spreadeagled under shrouds of dust and filth.

During the few hours that were left of that 20th June, 1756, pulling and pushing, urging, the warriors of Siraj-ud-daula carried out his injunction to seize every European they could find in Calcutta – save Miss Wilkinson – and to lock them up. They took them into Fort William, propelled them along the long corridors of the still undamaged main building, down the stone steps, pushed them the length of the arched corridor – and forced them into the tiny room known as the Black Hole. It was the middle of a Bengal summer and the land shimmered with waves of heat.

Among the first arrivals were two Calcutta cloth merchants. They were dragged protesting down the steps, the door of the prison was opened and they were unceremoniously pushed into the gloom of the stone dungeon. Eighteen feet long and fifteen feet wide, it was smaller than their own dining-rooms at home. They were shocked by what they saw and commenced banging on the door to summon the guard. He peered dully at them through the tiny grille. It fitted his head like a picture-frame.

'There are *ladies* in here – three of them!' one of the merchants expostulated. 'It's indecent to put us in the same room.'

The guard screwed up his eyes and could dimly make out the three women. They were cowering fearfully in a corner, barely visible in the deep shadow. There were neither seats nor benches, only the rough stone floor on which many an English soldier had sprawled until he sobered. The merchant again hammered on the door and began abusing the guard, to no avail. His only reaction was to draw the bar, open the door – and push in six more prisoners.

'This house,' Edmund said, pointing to the Vernier residence where Anna lived with her parents, relieved to see that it was undamaged. The carriage halted and Edmund sprang from it and rushed inside the gates, followed by apprehensive guards, fearful lest he might effect an escape. He dashed into one room after another, shouting her name, his terror rising at the continued silence.

He found her eventually. She was cowering in her bedroom wardrobe, wild-eyed with terror, a kitchen knife in her hand as sole protection. She shrieked as he opened the door. Grasping her by the shoulders he shook her, saying over and over again, 'It's all right, Anna, it's all right – you're safe. It's me, Edmund.'

She flung her arms around his neck, sobbing and incoherent. He tried to calm her, but when she saw Kassim's guards at the door she gave vent to another outburst of screaming, and it was only with difficulty that he got her out of the house and into the carriage. She had been in a state of suppressed hysteria since that morning, when her parents had been killed in the first attack by Mir Jafar's regiment.

The carriage passed through the gateway of the fort where it halted. The door was flung open and they were beckoned to get out.

'Take me to see Mir Kassim,' Edmund demanded, refusing to move.

'Mir Kassim, sick,' was all he was told, and without further ado both he and Anna were seized and bundled up the steps, along the corridor, down the stone steps – to the Black Hole.

'NO!' shouted Edmund, thrusting back with all his strength as the door was unlocked and opened. A wave of steaming, nauseous heat blasted out to meet him. The stench was unbearable, but no less terrible were the cries that accompanied it from the darkness.

The newcomers were pushed inside and the door slammed.

Edmund caught hold of Anna so that they should not be separated. When his eyes became accustomed to the dimness he estimated that over thirty people were crowded together in that tiny room. They were all standing: some shouted indignantly; many of the ladies were weeping; many begged for water; and there were others who remained silent, and prayed.

With grim presentiment of what was to come, Edmund grasped Anna, put his arm around her waist, and slowly forced his way backwards through the crush, pulling her with him, until he reached the wall nearest the grille. He had to stop his ears against the storm of protest. Thrusting her back against the wall, his body already saturated with sweat, he began inching out of as many garments as he decently could, and told Anna to do the same. She looked at him in horror and shook her head, determinedly clinging to her modesty though she might be deprived of all else. 'They can't keep us here. We shall all die,' she whispered in rising desperation, recoiling as the woman next to her slumped to the floor.

The door opened again. Edmund counted the new arrivals as they were forced into the crowded cell.

'Thirty-eight! Oh my God!' he croaked, his voice barely audible, for the heat was now a fearful thing and his throat was parched.

'For mercy's sake, release us. Give us water. WATER.' And Edmund too, proud as he was, joined in the general clamour.

But the dull-witted guards outside had no orders save to keep locked up those given into their custody. They were doing their job as instructed by their officers. The huge covered butt of water that stood in the corridor served only as a seat on which they took turns to rest. In their peasant ignorance it did not occur to them that the dungeon had been designed for three or four prisoners at most, and that there were incarcerated in it seventy-three human beings.

Edmund, who understood Persian, tried to reason with the guards, but discovered that their language was a Bengali dialect understood by no one other than themselves. Eventually it penetrated their thick skulls that their prisoners wanted water. Through the tiny grille they passed a tin mug filled with the precious liquid. So many hands reached out to grab it that it spilt. They grappled for the tin mug until it buckled and crumpled and the only water obtained were the few drops that one or two fortunate prisoners licked from their arms and hands. The cries were piteous. Three men scrambled on the floor to lick the wet stone, but having got down they could not get back again so great was the press of bodies. They were suffocated.

'For God's sake have mercy,' someone screamed, and the cry was taken up by others.

'Miss Vernier ... Anna ... ANNA ... hold on,' Edmund shouted, trying to make himself heard above the pandemonium.

She made a brave attempt to nod, her eyes brimming with tears. 'Captain Mathieson ... is he ... where ...' she tried to ask, with some pathetic hope that at any moment he would batter down the thick door and rescue them all.

'I do not know ... he was not ... in the fort ... I think he's safe,' he managed to gasp.

She opened her lips to attempt some new question when he was crushed against her as the mob seemed to expand in a surge of frenzy. She was nearing collapse.

'Anna, for God's sake, please,' he urged her with frantic desperation. 'If you are to survive you must disrobe ... please, Anna ... as much as you can ... you will suffocate else.'

By some extreme effort she raised her head to look up at her protector. He was barely visible inches away in the squalid and frightening murkiness of the dungeon. She nodded weakly. Aided by Edmund, she managed to tug at her collar, which was threatening to strangle her.

28

ROBERT CLIVE tapped on the door, opened it and tiptoed into the room where Margaret was breast-feeding the baby. He quietly lowered himself into a chair and sat watching them. They had been in Bombay for two weeks and Margaret had recovered from the rough sea voyage. Her eyes crinkled in a warm smile as they met his, and she moved her body so that he could see the child better. He smiled back, but there was some quality in the smile that disquieted her.

'Do you like it here, Margaret?' He opened the conversation innocuously enough, and she cautiously admitted to an improvement on the past months.

'Why, Robert? Are you eager to leave?'

'No, dearest, I'm not anxious to leave ... but I am compelled to – much earlier than I had anticipated,' replied her husband, with a regret that Margaret could only partly believe.

She studied his face intently. 'When ... and why?' she asked.

'On the next ship. I thought you and the child could follow in a few weeks' time when you feel more rested,' he put in quickly. 'The governor informs me that trouble is expected in Calcutta: the new Nawab of Bengal. It's possible he's already attacked the city. If he has, then he'll have taken it. The garrison there is too small to hold out.'

'Edmund!' she exclaimed, blanching. Robert touched her cheek consolingly. 'Edmund's a fine soldier. Don't worry about him. I'm sure he'll have escaped to the ships in the harbour,' he said, knowing that Edmund would do no such thing whilst he had a fort to defend. 'I'm taking ship for Madras, dearest. I'll pick up the latest news from there, and make my plans accordingly.' He gave her an encouraging smile and an affectionate squeeze, but his thoughts were less cheerful.

If Siraj-ud-daula was already in Calcutta, then Bussy would take advantage of the situation. Clive had no urge to meet the Nawab head on, but knew that he might have to.

In the commandant's office in Fort William, Mir Kassim and his father glumly watched as the Nawab raged. Behind them, cross-legged on the floor, sari covering face and body, was the silently observant figure of Sareen. Her presence was a testament to her status in Siraj-ud-daula's household.

'There is treasure here! I *know* there is treasure. Your men are fools, lazy; they have not searched,' the Nawab shouted.

'We have torn Calcutta apart, your highness,' Kassim repeated wearily, his forehead knitting together with pain. 'There is no treasure here other than the baubles taken from Feringhee homes.'

Sareen stole a concerned glance at Kassim. She longed to clean and dress his wound, but dared not whilst Siraj was in such a rage. Her eyes moved over to the other figure. Mir Jafar sat with head bowed, a cowering hound that takes a beating from its master without protest.

Siraj began banging the knuckles of his fists together, seeking some physical outlet for his rising frenzy. Sareen rose decisively to her feet, slid quietly over to him and – with thoughts of the consequences for Kassim and Mir Jafar should Siraj not be calmed – took his agitated hands ... and deliberately pressed them against her breasts.

Siraj pulled back from her as if he had been stung. He raised a hand to smite her to one side, but she held tightly to the wrist, keeping the palm firmly against her flesh. Kassim began struggling to his feet, but Mir Jafar laid hands on his son's shoulders and forced him back on the couch, shaking his head vigorously as he did so. 'Now is not the time for a confrontation,' his eyes warned.

Siraj stood as if transfixed, his hands firmly held against Sareen's breasts, making no effort to tear them from her grasp. She looked him squarely in the face and he glared back into hers. His anger had cooled, yet to prove that he was not to be dominated by any woman, he wrenched his left hand from her grip and struck her across the cheek. Sareen rocked to one side, fell to her knees and diplomatically bowed her head in submission.

Siraj drew himself erect. He was master once more. He glowered fiercely at the two commanders of his army.

'Search Calcutta again on the morrow. If nothing be found bring two important hostages to Murshidabad. They will soon tell me where the gold is hidden ... or else ...' He broke off, leaving the rest to their imagination. He seized the kneeling form of Sareen and lifted her roughly to her feet. 'Sareen and I will return to the capital. Leave a strong force to hold Calcutta and when you are satisfied it is secure, return yourselves to Murshidabad with the two hostages.' But a moment later he changed his mind, and commanded, 'No. You will send the prisoners tomorrow to Murshidabad under escort.'

Later, in the giant howdah, Siraj unwound Sareen's sari, pulled her across his lap and leaned over her. The tiny golden Koran she had once given Kassim touched her forehead as it hung from his neck. 'Take care, my Sareen, that you do not presume too much on my affection for you,' he said softly. She lowered her eyes in contrition and obedience, then raised herself and put her head against his shoulder, closing her eyelids in pretended bliss as he stripped her completely.

29

'ANNA ... SWEET Anna, my love,' Edmund cried urgently, when he saw her hand fall weakly away from the buttons at her throat. '*Take ... off ... your ... clothes.*' Trancelike, her head moved in the vaguest of nods to show that she had understood. '*Anna!*' he barked as her head lolled forward. It jerked up, eyes full of alarm, staring in shocked bewilderment at him. Her cheeks had reddened to the colour of raw meat. They were jammed so closely together that the sweat from their faces could find no channel down their bodies.

'Edmund ... Edmund?' she pleaded faintly. 'Oh God, help me ... Edmund ... help me.'

The door of the cell opened again, and seven more people were thrust into its stinking interior. It took seven of the guards, their shoulders against the thick wood, to jam the door back into its recess and to keep it there whilst the double bars were slid into place. The screams and cries that accompanied the closing of that door were perhaps the last coherent sounds of entreaty heard that night.

'Edmund?' The faint cry roused Edmund from his stupor. He was a big man and a powerful one. He braced his body against the wall, pushed with all his might to give himself space to free his other hand. Then leaning so that his left elbow rested against the rough stone, he brought his right hand over and, cursing at the buttons and hooks, tore Anna's blouse from her body. Bits of metal gashed his fingers as he reached for her corsets; he ripped at them furiously until they broke free and he was able to force them over her hips to the ground. Nothing mattered except the fight against suffocation. He thrust a hand behind her back, skinning his knuckles on the stone, and savagely broke the fastenings of her skirts. Soon she was naked but for her pantaloons. In their exhaustion the two

146

bodies pressed and fused together in the fearsome heat of that Bengal night.

Many perished before the midnight hour. There were no more screams, no oaths, no mutterings – only a sigh or a moan that preceded the absolute silence of death. The faint glow from the tiny grille revealed a scene so horrifying that it suspended belief. A number of corpses lay on the floor, trampled upon by those still upright. Even the dead stood upon the dead, their lifeless bodies kept vertical by the relentless pressure all about them. To the foulness of the air was added the stench of urine and excrement which the body discharged at the moment of death.

Anna, whose back was so crushed against the stone wall that it was pitted and torn, gave fitful moans between snatches of breath like a man drowning. Edmund, vowing that she should survive though his own death resulted, put all his tremendous will and strength into the fight to save her. He so manoeuvred his arms that he got the elbows against the wall and thereby formed a little cradle in which Anna might breathe. He croaked encouraging words to her; and periodically his head lowered and pushed against hers to waken her when she threatened total collapse.

By four in the morning nothing stirred in that awful vault. The mass of humanity had congealed like ripe dates when compressed in a little box. Edmund, his elbows wracked with pain, and grateful for the stimulus it provided in keeping him conscious, gently touched Anna's cheek with his lips. Her eyes were closed; her head lolled sideways, resting on Edmund's right arm. Only the subconscious urge to survive stoked the mechanism that kept her lungs functioning. The five creatures in immediate contact with Edmund and Anna had given up the ghost long before. Their heads drooped or lolled sideways or backwards; their mouths gaped open, their tongues protruded. One had his teeth clenched together, his jaw resting on the uncomplaining shoulder of his wife's corpse.

One of the guards, disturbed that he could hear nothing, took courage and hurried off to Mir Kassim. The young nobleman, though sick with pain, immediately rushed to the prison cell. He flung the guards aside and unbarred the thick door. It sprang open and a homogeneous lump of flesh swelled out of the doorway like over-yeasted dough rising from a baker's tin.

Kassim's eyes started from his face with horror and he screamed imprecations at the witless soldiers who had allowed this to happen. Trembling in fear, the guards started prising the bodies apart, examining each to see which was dead and which still lived – and exclaiming excitedly, as if to lessen their offence, when they found one that breathed. But the pile in the corridor grew higher, wider and deeper as corpse after corpse was laid upon it.

'Captain Maskelyne!' Kassim rushed forward and knelt at his side when the body was brought out and it was seen that his fingers were moving.

'Anna ...' His lips formed the word, causing Kassim to glance swiftly about him to find one to whom the name might apply.

'Your highness ... the Feringhee woman there,' one of the guards drew Kassim's attention. It was Anna, propped against the wall, her eyes closed. A guard was brushing water over her lips.

'Anna?' Edmund croaked, making an effort to crawl to her. 'Anna.'

'She is alive, Sahib Maskelyne,' Kassim assured him, putting his arms under Edmund's armpits and gently pulling him to the woman. Her eyes flickered, opened; her head turned slowly, the gaze focused indistinctly on Edmund's anxious face, her lips twitched, and then she collapsed.

When Kassim made the final count he learned that in that small cell one hundred and forty-six of his captives had been compressed for sixteen hours during that sweltering night.

Twenty-three only were alive the following morning.

Three days later the guards were executed on Mir Jafar's orders. The prisoners had been set free; the dead had been buried. Edmund and Anna rested at her home.

'You cannot take those two. They've suffered enough,' Kassim shouted angrily at his father when he learned of the Nawab's order. Mir Jafar spread his hands.

'He is the senior officer, Kassim. If there is gold here he will know of it.'

'There is no gold, no treasure,' Kassim said scathingly. 'It exists only in Siraj's mind. Will you take hostages to Murshidabad just for his amusement? And to what secrets do you think the Feringhee woman is privy?'

Mir Jafar retorted with some asperity, 'I take her in charity – she pleads to stay with him.' He gave a knowing smile as he added,

'The woman may be useful in persuading this captain to reveal what he knows.'

Kassim rose unsteadily to his feet and limped towards the door. He paused and levelled his finger at his father.

'He will not be harmed. I gave my oath on the Koran when he surrendered that they would not be harmed. And now ...' his voice shrilled to a wild pitch, 'Now I have been shamed ... one hundred and twenty-three murders in that hole – my sacred vow broken, broken, *broken!*' He paused to draw breath and added with cold vehemence, 'If the Feringhee officer or his woman be injured, both Siraj and Mir Jafar will answer for it.'

30

CLIVE SAT morosely in his seat in the Council Chamber of Madras. He had listened with growing unease as the various members had suggested how to fling Siraj-ud-daula out of Calcutta and to exact revenge for the Black Hole affair. He was sickened by the intrigues and machinations of those who seemed concerned only with financial loss or gain, and was even less impressed by a few who had recommended negotiating with Siraj-ud-daula through an intermediary named Omichand – a toad-faced, grease-ball of a half-caste merchant whom Clive had long known and despised.

Though governor of the Madras fort, Clive was subject to the Council's decisions – even though his influence was considerable. Eventually he could take no more of their endless vacillating. He crashed a fist on the table and stood up.

'You would make peace with a tiger by handing it a rabbit,' his voice rang out. 'The coward's way to treat with Siraj-ud-daula. When you speak let your voice come from the mouth of a cannon! This only will he respect.'

'Ha!' the president of the Council sneered. 'And does the gallant Colonel volunteer to lead a mere thousand soldiers against twenty times that number?'

Clive gave him a level stare then slowly surveyed the entire Chamber.

'Give me permission,' he spaced out his words, 'and I will retake

Calcutta though there be twice twenty thousand to oppose me.'

Seven days later, Clive, with six hundred British soldiers, nine hundred sepoys, and three companies of marines under a certain Captain Eyre Coote – the court-martialled officer who had imposed himself upon Clive in England – set off in five warships commanded by a doughty admiral named Watson.

The sea journey of nine hundred miles was calculated to take four weeks. Unfortunately, monsoon winds in the Bay of Bengal persisted in blowing in the wrong direction, and it was two months before the fleet hove to and anchored in the Hooghly river just within cannon-shot of Calcutta.

During this time Edmund and Anna were languishing in the prison cages of the palace at Murshidabad. Though threatened daily with torture, nothing had been done to them. Even so, the chains with which Edmund had been manacled were a constant source of torment. The dungeon was a long low room divided down the centre by a wall of bars. The guards were on one side and the two prisoners on the other. They had sacks of straw to sleep on, a bucket, and a well-filled tub of water.

Anna seemed indifferent to her own fate. She still fretted about Mathieson, and treated Edmund with a concern that was almost maternal. She abused the guards until they brought fat to rub on Edmund's chafed limbs, changed the old straw for new, or put fresh water in the butt. She washed, fed, tended him. Often they slept with hands touching or legs interwined. There were times of personal embarrassment, in which Anna, curiously enough, suffered the least.

To have become Edmund's mistress seemed not to have occurred to her. She considered herself affianced to Saul Mathieson, and to hear her speak of him pained Edmund as much as his chains. He tried to delude himself that Anna only thought herself in love with Mathieson and would some day recognise where her true affection lay.

Kassim came to see them occasionally. He brought them gifts of food and did what he could to make their confinement less arduous – but beyond this kindness he feared to go. The Nawab's word was law. And though it appeared that Siraj had forgotten his prisoners, Kassim dared not count on it.

Sareen, too, visited them and brought gifts. On one occasion she came upon Anna bathing Edmund with such tenderness that a responsive chord struck in her own sensitive heart. She stayed and watched – no longer to Edmund's humiliation, for modesty had ceased to have any meaning.

Kassim and Sareen walked slowly around the high wall of the fortifications. They often walked there, secure that they could not be overheard and, if seen, it was of little consequence. The Nawab was undoubtedly aware of their liaison yet did nothing save flaunt his own conquest of Mir Jafar's wife whenever the mood took him.

'You must free them,' she told Kassim calmly. 'You have the power and the means to do so.'

'I dare not. The guards would tell Siraj that I was responsible and he would have me executed,' he retorted sulkily. It was not the first time that Sareen had spoken of the prisoners.

She pulled herself away from him. 'You gave your oath on the Koran they would not be harmed,' she exclaimed, striking where she knew it would hurt most. 'You gave the word of a prince. Are you to prove a reed? An empty vessel?' she taunted, going as far as she dared. 'Does the Koran not say; "Deliver us, Lord, from this city of wrongdoers; send forth to us a guardian from your presence; send to us one that will help us." Are not those the very words of the Angel Gabriel?'

He looked sideways at her under lowered lids, knowing well that she had searched Holy Script for some passage to give weight to her plea. But it was not easy to bandy words with Sareen despite her submissive demeanour.

'Does my life count less to thee than the Englishman's?' he tossed back, pouting his lips.

She raised her head with fine dignity, replying softly, 'My own life is of less consequence to me than yours, Kassim, and gladly would I lay it down should the need be there. My virtue also, so precious to a woman, has been squandered for the lust of Siraj-ud-daula, used by my husband as a counter to gain favour. Only you, Kassim, have entered this flesh of mine for no gain save love. This love I accept and have returned with passion. Do not now stain the purity of our love by dishonouring yourself in my sight.'

Kassim lowered his head with shame.

Shortly after darkness had fallen, the young prince, with six men of his own regiment, arrived at the prison. They were admitted without question, for Mir Kassim was the son of Mir Jafar, and a general himself.

'Unchain the Englishman,' he ordered peremptorily, peering expressionlessly through the bars of the cage where Edmund was lying with an apprehensive Anna in his arms. Edmund squinted up at Kassim, trying to read his face, but lifted his arms willingly for the manacles to be struck off.

Kassim looked strained, so, taking a chance, Edmund spoke to him in English. 'I have waited long for you to recall the oath you made, Mir Kassim,' he said quietly. 'As a prince of the Faithful, are you now to redeem that vow, or do you obey the Nawab's more evil intent?'

Kassim was stung to snarl a reply but bit it back in time; instead, he ignored Edmund and addressed himself to Anna. Whilst he was speaking the senior prison guard, convinced now of his suspicions, crept silently behind Kassim. The other guards quietly took up positions with their backs to the wall and awaited a lead from the chief guard.

'You are to be released, Sahiba, both of you. My men will take you outside the palace where you will find horses. They will guide you to the river. Go aboard the dhow that is awaiting you and it will take you back to Calcutta ...'

The chief guard went for his sword, but it was barely half-way out of its sheath when one of Kassim's men plunged a dagger into his back. Confused, the others immediately dropped to their knees and, with loud wails, protested their allegiance to Mir Kassim. He disdained even to look at them.

As Edmund, assisted by Anna, got shakily to his feet and limped out of the cage, Kassim continued his instructions. 'Once you are in Calcutta you will be safe even though the Nawab's army is in control there. No one will seek you. This I swear. Do not bring yourselves to their notice, that is all.'

Edmund hesitated, turned and then bowed deeply to his rescuer. 'I trust that one day we shall meet in happier circumstances, Mir Kassim. I shall not forget what you have done this night,' he said softly.

Kassim responded with a curt nod, then waved them off dismissively.

When the prisoners had gone the young prince sardonically

scrutinised the jailers. They looked terrified. One of the guards, bolder than the others, blurted out, 'Your highness, what is to happen to us? The Nawab will have Sombrer remove our heads when he learns that the hatman and Feringhee woman have escaped.'

Mir Kassim imperiously motioned him to silence. Glowering contemptuously, he seized him by the ear until he yelped with pain, then flung the frightened man away from him. The guards wailed still louder, convinced their end was near. But, instead of blows, each received a small bag of gold coins.

Kassim, a ferocious expression on his face, cautioned them. 'There is money sufficient to make you rich men – scum though you be. Be out of Murshidabad before dawn. Ride north to Oudh. Once you are out of Bengal you will be safe.' He gave a mirthless chuckle. 'Three hours after sunrise I myself will inform Siraj-ud-daula that his prisoners are gone.'

Kassim had no qualms about being the one to deliver the unwelcome news to the Nawab; in fact the prospect was not without appeal. For though Siraj would rage and scream he would not vent his spite on Kassim beyond harmless insult. Siraj's ambivalent friendship still baffled Kassim. With one hand Siraj would humiliate him, and with the other sign him title to land on which a million people lived. But Kassim himself had no such ambivalence towards the Nawab. From the day when Siraj had stolen his Koran trinket his purpose had been inflexible: revenge.

31

THE RUMOUR sneaked into Calcutta from the south-west and from there spread among the Nawab's troops with the speed and effect of a cholera epidemic. Warriors on the outskirts of Calcutta began stealing away, those in the city under more rigorous control prepared to fight, nervously glancing over their shoulders towards the harbour, fearing the day when it would be filled with great sail-of-the-line. Even the commanders of regiments prepared escape routes for themselves.

'Sahib Clive! ... Clive is coming! ... the Great Conqueror is on his way.'

By the time Clive actually arrived in Calcutta, his reputation had spread a sense of defeat among the Muslim warriors. Disembarking with his troops before the ships reached the Hooghly river, he converged on the city at the same time that Admiral Watson prepared the ground with a bombardment. The first shot struck the keep of Fort William. After the fifth shot had hit the fort, its defenders were ready to quit. They cowered, ducked and ran as hot balls of metal reduced to rubble entire sections of the walls.

The cannon then ranged over the city itself. Many of Siraj's troops fled – and ran straight into Clive's forces, as he had planned. Most of them ended their lives on the Bengal plain where, for weeks thereafter, the jackals and the vultures gorged themselves.

Midway through the second day of the attack, the young Eyre Coote and his marines took to the longboats and rowed ashore as the second claw to Clive's pincer movement. Waving cutlasses and pistols the tough marines fought their way over the beach and into the streets, progressing in a crescent-shaped movement in the general direction of the fort. But by this time resistance had become so ineffectual that many of them found nothing to do.

And, having nothing to do, a group of marines launched a private invasion on one of the punch shops. Two hours later most of them had wandered off to rejoin their comrades, leaving behind them, amidst a litter of empty bottles, three very inebriated marines.

The leader of this gallant trio was confusedly convinced that they had some duty to perform. The three of them argued as to what it might be.

'It's the fort,' one of them insisted, trying to focus his eyes on the multiple images of his companions.

'Then ... we shall ... cabdgure it ... cabdgure ... hit!' declaimed the leader, staggering to the door.

His companions followed him as he weaved an erratic way through the streets, pistol in one hand, cutlass in the other. He was heading for the heavily defended Fort William intent on carrying out 'his dewddy'. By some small miracle the hardy trio reached the walls of the fort unscathed. Quite undaunted at the prospect of tackling an entire fort all by himself, the leader climbed on to the shoulders of his companions to reach for a hand-hold halfway up the wall.

Belching violently, this intrepid marine crab-crawled to a place

154

where an entire chunk of masonry had been blasted away, leaving a gaping hole. Through this he wriggled and then dropped unconcernedly on the ledge overlooking the crowded courtyard. The Muslim soldiers stared up at him aghast. The marine, swaying on his feet, calmly raised his pistol, aimed, and shot the gunner of one of the cannons. Very pleased with himself, he then drew his cutlass, brandished it in a most blood-curdling manner, gave a loud hiccough and brayed at the top of his voice, 'The ... fort is ... mine.'

At that moment his two companions thrust their purple, bleary-eyed heads through the aperture behind him and began yelling encouragement to the cutlass-waving conqueror. He acknowledged their cheers with a bow that nearly toppled him from his perch.

The defenders could take no more. They dropped their weapons on the ground and surrendered, all seven hundred of them. When Colonel Clive arrived on the scene, he was astonished to find the gates of the fort open and standing at each post, as if on guard, were two marines who manifestly had difficulty in remaining vertical. Barring his way was the third marine, who solemnly presented a huge bunch of keys to the bewildered Clive. Behind him, in attentive ranks, stood the former Muslim garrison, the palms of their hands clasped together in an attitude of reverence.

Eyre Coote was livid. The three marines had made nonsense of his own part in the invasion.

'A hundred lashes at least, Colonel,' he insisted to Clive, who had the gravest difficulty in keeping a straight face.

'I agree they must be punished, Captain Coote,' he rejoined soothingly. 'Discipline must be preserved. Nonetheless, they *did* execute the task to which they were assigned in quite a handsome manner, and this must be taken into consideration. Furthermore,' he cocked his head to one side and glanced sideways at the angry Coote, 'they are lawfully entitled to prize money.'

Four days later the three marines were stripped to the waist and given five lashes – laid on hard. In addition, they were awarded five hundred pounds each as prize money.

Calcutta was in English hands once more and with its recapture there trickled back into the city all those who had taken refuge on the ships. The administration of the area was returned to the Council. Clive made dispositions of his troops to secure the city, then considered what his next move should be against the Nawab.

As he was preparing to leave his office five days after Fort William had fallen, the door opened and the gaunt figure of a tall man stood silhouetted in the aperture. Clive looked up from the document he was studying, taken aback at the rudeness of the fellow, and opened his mouth to admonish him.

'Edmund!' He was round the desk and flinging his arms around his friend. 'Praise God you're alive. No one knew where you were. I sent patrols around the city to search for you.' He was all but gabbling with relief.

Edmund told his tale wearily: the ordeal of the Black Hole, the ghastly imprisonment in Murshidabad, the journey in the dhow down the Bhagirathi with a frail Anna, the constant threat from warriors fleeing Calcutta. He looked haggard; his flesh hung loosely over his bones; his eyes, once bright with fun, showed now a haunted quality, and at the corners of his lips were two deep lines of bitterness and cynicism.

'And Anna?' Clive asked.

'Mathieson came back,' Edmund said, not wishing to enlarge on how the hero had burst in on them at Anna's home, looking as if he had fought his way single-handed through the Nawab's army.

'And who might this Mathieson be? I don't recollect the name.'

'A brother officer – affianced to Anna,' replied Edmund, dismissively.

Clive studied his friend, but asked no more questions. Edmund would tell him whatever he wished him to know. He changed the subject.

'A house has been put at my disposal, Edmund. Would you be my guest for a while? ... I would count it a favour,' he added quickly.

Edmund considered. 'For three days only, Robert. After that I would prefer my former quarters at the fort.' He forced a twisted grin as he added, 'It would be too grave a risk for such pig-headed creatures as us to be in too close a proximity for any length of time.'

Becoming serious again, Edmund asked, 'Have you given much thought to Siraj-ud-daula?'

Clive dismally shook his head. 'Depends upon the Council. They favour negotiations through a fellow named Omichand ... claims to have the ear of the Nawab.'

'I know him,' Edmund rejoined in a way that caused his friend to glance sharply at him.

'You seem doubtful.'

'Like sending a vulture to make treaty with a jackal.'

'That makes Omichand eminently qualified, wouldn't you say, Edmund?'

At the Nawab's palace a distracted Mir Jafar pushed into Siraj's bedroom exclaiming, 'The English have defeated ...' Then stopped abruptly and averted his eyes in confusion. A naked Siraj leapt off the bed in a fury and launched a stream of invective at this invasion of his privacy. With fist upraised he berated the General until the sense of what he had said brought him to an abrupt halt.

'Defeated! ... Defeated what?'

'Calcutta, your highness ... The Englishman Clive has returned ...'

He got no further for Siraj sprang for his throat. 'Clive is in England,' he yelled, shaking him furiously, then, realising what he was doing, he released him. Mir Jafar smoothed himself down, modestly keeping his eyes from the bed where Sareen lay under a thin silken sheet.

'He is now in Bengal and has retaken Calcutta. And there is more, Siraj-ud-daula,' he said spitefully. 'The Marathas have raided seven villages. They took little money but many lives. Your own tax collectors ...'

'Tell me not of the Marathas!' the Nawab shouted. 'Order Kassim to take his regiment of Pathan horse and go after them ... it is of Calcutta I wish to hear.'

The Nawab angrily dismissed Mir Jafar when he had ended his account of the defeat. He then paced up and down the room, moaning with self-pity at all the problems that beset him.

'My Hindu officers are conspiring to mutiny; my cousin Shaukat Jang seeks to usurp my kingdom; the French demand my support against the British; the Marathas lay waste to my land and people; the British seek vengeance for Calcutta; Mir Jafar is against me; and Kassim I cannot wholly trust. Oh Allah, Allah, what must I do?' and he flung himself on to the bed across Sareen's thighs.

He was so childlike, so piteous, so genuinely wretched, that Sareen was touched. She dismissed his heroic posturing as she had disdained his arrogance, but this cry for help moved her to respond.

She fondled the back of his neck, gently massaged the area between his shoulder blades. He moaned pathetically and lay still. And he listened to advice that previously she had given only by casual remark or innuendo, but that was now given directly and authoritatively.

'Before the Clive Sahib marches against you, Siraj, you must contact the Sahiba Wilkinson. Let her say to the English that you will make treaty with them.'

He rolled on to his side and stared up into her face. 'You would have me lay my belly in the dust and crave forgiveness of these hatmen?' he cried indignantly.

She silenced his protest by clasping his head against her breasts and rocking him gently. 'They will not seek vengeance, only peace, my lord; for one day, both you and they may need each other against the Afghans in the north who have captured Delhi.'

He pulled his head away, observing her face with some curiosity. How could a *woman* know of such things? Then, still wondering, he put his head back where it had been and tenderly nuzzled her breasts.

'No,' he decided sadly, snuggling closer to her. 'I can raise an army of a hundred thousand warriors. I can sweep the hatmen into the sea. Nothing can prevail against the might of Siraj-ud-daula.'

'My lord, was it not Alivardi Khan who compared the English with the bees?' she told him softly, running her fingers through his hair. 'Beware of the greater swarms who might come after them.'

'Phastsh!' he spat vulgarly, sitting up in sudden vexation. 'I have been told by wiser people than you that in all Europe there are only ten thousand Feringhees.'

'Then you have been told falsely, my lord Siraj,' she contradicted calmly.

'Omichand himself confirmed that number,' he declared petulantly, adding as if to verify the accuracy of its source, 'And he is admitted to the secret meetings of the Council. He would not play me false.'

'Omichand, my lord, speaks as his listener wishes to hear.'

32

IN THE anteroom to the great Council Chamber in the centre of Calcutta, heavy with dark furniture and gilt decoration, reeking with polish and perspiration, a newly-promoted General Robert Clive sat in grave dignity at the expensive desk and studied the document in his hand. The phrases were subtle, the sentences finely constructed, the details evasive, but the intent of the writer was clear. He laid the parchment flat on the desk, and leaned his head on his hands – taking care not to disturb the splendour of his full-bottomed periwig.

In the same room were Admiral Watson, plump, sprawling in a deep chair, sucking at a hookah, in mental isolation from all the 'land-wallahs'; Warren Hastings, now a hustling opportunist in the Council, who was leaning forward with an elbow on the desk, staring intently at Clive as if ready to pounce; Captain Mathieson, standing behind Hastings like an attentive aide and wearing a frown of concern on his face. Eyre Coote, promoted major, was gazing at his toe caps and clearly wishing he was elsewhere; and Captain Edmund Maskelyne, perched on the ledge of the high gothic window, was gazing, with a seeming lack of interest in the proceedings, at the view.

'To reduce this ... *flimflam* to its essentials the Nawab offers a treaty with what he claims to be generous concessions on his part,' Clive stated at last without looking up. 'He will restore all former privileges and all former territories; he grants us permission to fortify Calcutta as we wish; and he reaffirms our appointment as Zamindar.'

'Damned crust of the fellow!' expostulated the Admiral, spluttering in his hookah.

'What does he require in return, sir?' Eyre Coote asked.

'An alliance against any who threaten his realm,' Clive said evenly, watching for the general reaction.

'Are you in favour of it, General Clive?' Mathieson asked, his eyes seeking approval from his new mentor, Warren Hastings.

'Briefly, yes,' said Clive lightly, without looking at him.

'Rather we made treaty with a cobra than with Siraj-ud-daula,' Warren Hastings interposed smoothly, his eyes intent on examining a badly trimmed fingernail. 'He rules by whim and impulse.' He glanced around the room as if counting his supporters. 'I move that this offer be rejected and that we march on him forthwith before he has time to recover from the Calcutta debacle.'

'Heroic gestures come easy to those far from the sound of cannon,' murmured Eyre Coote, meeting Hastings' angry glare with a cool one. But as the politician opened his mouth to castigate the major, Admiral Watson intervened with a blunt, 'Be quiet, Hastings. This affair needs reasoning – not rash posturing.'

'Captain Maskelyne,' Clive called over to the indolent figure by the window. 'Have you no contribution to make to this gathering?' Edmund obliged him by turning his head in Clive's direction. 'You, more than any here, have intimate knowledge of this confounded Nawab.'

Edmund lazily uncoiled himself from the ledge and stood up. His manner was deceptively mild as he faced his friend but there was iron in his voice. 'My only question, *General*, is to what authority do we pretend for decisions of such import? Is the purpose of this gathering to usurp the functions of the Council? Have you, by military conquest, taken upon yourself legislative as well as administrative powers?'

Clive rose from his seat, his face crimson with anger and the shock of betrayal. 'During this period of disorder following our expulsion of the Nawab's troops,' he replied, controlling his voice only with difficulty, 'I have rightly declared this city to be under martial law, and as the senior officer in Bengal it was my duty to suspend the Council's rights to administer and to make treaties.' He pointed an admonishing finger at an unresponsive Edmund and added, 'This will only apply during this period of transition. It is a temporary state of affairs as well you know.'

He resumed his seat, and dropped his head sulkily on his chest. No one dared to speak, and in the silence that ensued Edmund perched again on the ledge and stared sourly at the incandescent streets, where even the dust seemed unwilling to stir.

The silence was at last broken by Clive, who said in a more conciliatory tone, yet with an edge to it, 'Though our efforts to find a peaceful and a just solution to the problems that beset

Calcutta apparently have little favour in your eyes, I would, none-theless, still value your opinion, Edmund.'

A strange bubbling noise from the Admiral's hookah attracted the attention of all save Clive and Edmund, who stared glumly at each other – Clive in mute appeal for the breach to be repaired; Edmund in sadness that the breach was unavoidable.

'Make a treaty with the Nawab, Robert,' said Edmund gravely. 'Admittedly he's unreliable but it may work out. Reading his offer – and knowing how volatile he is – I would say that Mir Kassim and that woman, Sareen, have been using their influence. Besides, the note came through Miss Wilkinson – and I doubt that she'd be party to any fraud.'

An unpleasantly derisive laugh followed this protestation of faith. 'Trust Miss Wilkinson,' Hastings sneered. 'Why, she opened the gates of Calcutta to her master.'

Edmund coloured. He was still sensitive to the fact that he had often escorted her around the fortifications, but refused to believe she had given the information to Siraj-ud-daula.

'There is no proof of that, Hastings,' he snapped. 'But we do have proof that she saved the lives of fourteen people by shielding them in her home during the invasion and during the ... the Black Hole episode.' He still found difficulty in saying the name.

'Enough of this brawling,' Clive said, coming from behind his desk and walking over to Edmund. 'I shall have a draft treaty drawn up, and if you all approve I'll submit it to the Nawab. Thank you, gentlemen. The meeting is closed.'

As they started to file out of the room, Clive called back Edmund and Eyre Coote.

'Be good enough to accompany me around the fort. I have other matters to discuss,' he said, motioning them to silence until the others were well out of ear-shot.

A few minutes later the three men were outside in the hot sun and casting a jaundiced eye at the efforts of several hundred coolies as they laboured to rebuild the damaged walls of Fort William. The half-naked Indians collected the mortar in buckets and the stones in baskets, and bore these on their heads to the wall, where masons took the offerings, plastered it crudely and then laid a block of stone on top of the prepared area.

Major Eyre Coote poked his finger into dried mortar between

two huge stones. It crumbled at his touch.

'God help us if the Frenchie ever lays his cannon against this,' he muttered sourly.

'Exactly,' said Clive. 'That is why we must treat with the Nawab before attending to the French – and before the French make an alliance with him.'

A fat, long-robed, Muslim-Portuguese drew abreast of them, and Clive curtly acknowledged him.

'My lord Clive,' the fat half-caste bowed obsequiously. 'Sahibs.' Another deep bow, and he hurried off. Edmund turned his head to avoid acknowledging him.

'How much value do you place on his promises, Edmund?' Clive asked when the fat fellow had gone.

'Omichand? Depends whether our offer is higher than that of the French or the Nawab.'

Eyre Coote, mildly piqued that a captain should so often be consulted by the General, drew Clive back to the matter in hand. 'You were about to discuss the French, sir,' he reminded him, shooting Edmund a look warning him not to interrupt.

'The French, yes, I have decided the time is ripe for Chandanagar.'

'Chandanagar!' echoed Captain Maskelyne, trying to keep the surprise from his voice.

'Yes. I know what you're thinking, and I agree with you. But General Bussy is occupied in the north of India, and it's imperative to reduce the French stronghold before he returns and takes the initiative against us. We're still at war with France, don't forget Edmund,' he added in mild reproof, resting a hand on his friend's shoulder – to Eyre Coote's annoyance.

'What can you muster, Major Coote?' Clive asked, knowing the figures as well as he, but sensing the man's chagrin.

'A thousand English and one thousand five hundred sepoy, General, a meagre force for Chandanagar.'

'I have managed with less on other occasions,' Clive retorted, with a touch of acerbity.

'I shall be ready to move within six days, sir, if that meets with your approval,' said Eyre Coote squaring his shoulders. 'And I understand that Admiral Watson can sail at twenty-four hours' notice.'

Although Clive was no more than three years older than Eyre

Coote, he felt at times like a grandparent talking to a young fire-brand. '*We* shall be ready, Major. I trust that you had not gained the impression that I would stay in Calcutta?' he reproved, his eyes twinkling, then he clapped him on the back in a hearty manner and laughed. 'No, Coote, the only senior officer I shall leave here is Captain Maskelyne.' Clive turned to Edmund and smiled. 'After what you have been through, you deserve a rest at the fort.'

On this note, Clive dismissed them and returned to the mansion the Council had set aside for his use. He wandered into the library, but with no purpose in mind. It was a vast room, and, like the rest of the house, elaborately furnished, over-decorated, filled with the treasures of the former owner – and unbearably impersonal and lonely.

He lowered himself into a deep chair and brooded. Margaret and the child might be away several weeks, and he missed them more than he would admit. He was aware that to all who knew him, save Edmund, he appeared an unfeeling, rather callous soldier-administrator, a man capable only of dispassionate reasoning and rigidity of decision. It was his own fault. He had deliberately created the image in order to achieve what he had achieved. He wished that Edmund would visit him more often. Surely the dis-parity in their respective ranks was no barrier to a continued friend-ship.

He picked up a recently published novel, *Tom Jones*, idly flicked through a few pages and then tossed it back on to the table. What indolent and secure lives some people led, he thought, to spend so much of it in writing. Pulling himself out of his chair, he browsed among the rows and rows of books. He fingered the spines but could summon no enthusiasm to extract a volume and read it. Possibly Edmund was sulking because he had not been given his majority? But he was such a ... not a poor soldier, something of a disinterested one. Had he possessed the inclination and ambition he would have been a colonel by now.

He flopped into another chair, bored and restless, stretched out his hand and idly pulled open a drawer. He picked up the long object inside it, gave it a cursory examination, and then tugged at a bell-pull. The butler arrived, bowed and stood attentive.

'What is this?' asked Clive, holding out the object.

'An opium pipe, my lord. It belonged to the former owner. I

understand that it is excellent for the relief of ague, disturbances of the liver, swamp fever, and agitations of the spirit.'

'Agitations of the spirit,' Clive mused. He looked at the pipe curiously. 'Are you skilled in its preparation?'

The butler assured him that he was. He had always prepared his former master's pipes.

Two hours later Edmund called. His manner declared that he, too, was suffering from an agitation of the spirit. The butler ushered him immediately to the library.

The air in the library had a sickly sweet smell which Edmund recognised. Clive was lolling back on the chaise longue. He raised a limp hand in greeting and then let it flop back again as if the effort were too much. He smiled benignly. More anxious than angry, Edmund called for a bowl of water and a cloth. He knelt by Robert's side and started to sponge his face. The patient gave him a beatific simpering look, made to put an arm around his neck, and started to retch.

By the time Edmund left, Clive was in bed, washed and fast asleep, and the visitor had obtained what he had come for: permission to take part in the expedition to Chandanagar.

In high spirits, Edmund rode off to tell Anna the good news. She was pleased to see him and kissed him affectionately. Edmund occupied a unique place in her heart. Had she considered it possible to love two people at the same time, she would have loved Edmund as she loved Mathieson. But she believed in the monogamistic love of woman as stressed in the kind of novel she was addicted to.

She paled when Edmund told her that he was going to Chandanagar.

'Promise me you'll take care, Edmund dearest ... promise me,' she urged, biting her knuckles in agitation.

'Come, come, Anna; the affair will be a trifle. I shall survive,' he sought to reassure her. 'By the time Watson has finished his bombardment there'll be nothing left for us to do – other than accept the surrender.'

She would not be consoled for there was something else troubling her. At last she blurted out, 'Saul ... Captain Mathieson; is he going as well, Edmund?'

He clenched his hand, and for an uncharitable moment he felt her concern all along had been for Mathieson.

'He is going,' he told her a shade stiffly. 'But he will be safe. This I promise you. I give you my word he'll come back safe and sound.' He attempted a cheerful smile.

Later he went to see Mathieson, and found him in his private office adding a long column of figures in the fat ledger in front of him. Mathieson gave a sigh of satisfaction, tossed down the quill and gazed benevolently at his visitor.

'Seventy thousand pounds sterling, Maskelyne. What do you think of that for just four years' trading?' he crowed with huge pride. Edmund, determined to be amicable, made a non-committal reply which Mathieson barely heard. 'And not only rice. Take a look at those.' His finger tapped at the list of names like a woodpecker's beak driving into human skulls. 'Seventeen yet to meet their commitments – and they're not likely to with the harvest they've had.'

The avarice of the man, and Anna's blindness to it, was so galling that Edmund could have struck him. All pretence at amicability dropped away.

'Why in all hell's name, Mathieson, do you hold on to your commission? It couldn't be for the pay.'

The businessman eyed his visitor, knowing well what was eating at him, and rejoined smoothly, 'Rank carries status, Maskelyne. I shall wait until I have my majority – until my fortune reaches a hundred thousand – then be off to England with my bride. I rather fancy myself as squire with a comfortable seat in Parliament. I shall probably make vociferous protests against the rice trade and point accusing fingers. Of course, if I decide not to go to England ...' he broke off, as Edmund rose abruptly and stormed out. 'If I decide not to go to England,' he said, as he stretched his arms pleasurably and yawned, 'I shall probably become an administrator of some territory. I must confess, the idea does have a certain appeal.'

Siraj-ud-daula had also received a visitor, whom he treated with cool suspicion. A man like Omichand was not given to making tedious journeys simply for the love of travel, but Siraj trusted him no more than he did the British.

'And when is the attack on Chandanagar to be?' Siraj demanded, wondering how he might best take advantage of the situation. Omichand told him.

Siraj rose to his feet, walked over to the high window, and gazed out unseeingly. Omichand, still on his knees, looked apprehensively at his back.

'Will the English hatmen win this battle, dog?' asked the Nawab carefully.

'Allah alone can see into the future, your highness,' said Omichand, adding hastily when he saw the Nawab turning angrily towards him, 'Chandanagar is strong and the French are renowned fighters, holy lord, and if they were to receive help from the mighty Nawab of Bengal, then the issue would be in no doubt. The English would be defeated, and the position of the great Siraj-ud-daula would never again be threatened.'

'Fool!' cried the Nawab. 'How can I assist the French without incurring the wrath of the English?'

'It is not impossible, holy lord. Promise to send help to the English, but so delay it that the battle is over when it arrives. Meanwhile you secretly despatch another force to aid the French. When the army of Siraj-ud-daula is behind the walls of Chandanagar, who then can know its identity?'

The merchant sneaked a glance at the Nawab to ascertain how his suggestion had been received. Then, reassured, he added the clincher. 'By this means, your highness, no matter which way the battle goes you may justly demand patronage and favours from the victor.'

Siraj brightened, smiled patronisingly, and with the toe of his shoe he nudged the plump merchant to indicate he had permission to rise. Omichand sighed with relief and lumbered shakily to his feet.

'For what reward will you ask, dog, should this plan of yours succeed?' Siraj asked with an amiable sneer.

'I ask for nothing further than to be allowed to serve your highness,' whined Omichand in his most obsequious manner, 'though I would not take it amiss were I to be granted trading rights throughout Bengal, with freedom from all taxes and revenues, your highness. Then I would consider myself well satisfied.'

33

THE BILLOWING sails of five frigates made an imposing sight as Watson's squadron weighed anchor and moved slowly up the Hooghly river. To an observer on the low-lying ground there was the curious illusion of warships ploughing a course through the arid land, the dramatic figureheads on the bows thrusting aside the rocks and sand in their haste to reach Chandanagar.

On the flagship Admiral Watson presided sombrely at a meeting in his sea-cabin, a poorly drawn map in front of him. General Clive, Eyre Coote and Edmund were studying the map attentively.

'I shall disembark here with the main force,' Clive was saying, indicating a point ten miles south of Chandanagar. 'Major Coote will take command of the marines – with Captain Maskelyne his deputy – and make a shore landing near the city itself after the Admiral has breached the walls with the squadron's guns. The moment the bombardment ceases I shall attack with cannon and the main body of men. As you see by the sketch I've made, the fort is conventional in style with most of its battlements on the riverside where, quite logically, the French anticipate the heaviest assault. Perhaps Admiral Watson has some observations to make?' His enquiring look at the obese sailor was received with a discouraging yawn.

'If success is dependent on the bombardment from my ships – then be prepared for failure,' said he, to the listeners' consternation. And as Clive moved to protest, the Admiral held up a warning finger. 'Do you seriously believe that any fortress would allow ships to get close enough to pepper its fortifications? Unless I'm very much mistaken, the Hooghly at Chandanagar will be like a bottle with a cork rammed in it.'

'By that time, sir,' Eyre Coote interposed diplomatically, noting Clive's disconcertion, 'the General will be distracting the French with a land attack.'

The Admiral pulled himself to his feet. The expression on his weather-beaten face suggested he was dealing with amateurs. 'Young man, one shot won't halt an army, but a well-placed ball can put

167

a ship clean out of action – and no amount of courage on the part of the crew can do a damned thing about it. When ship fights ship the odds are even, but when a ship engages shore defences it's God help the sailor. We'll do our best, but don't make the navy an essential part of the plan.'

Clive drew himself erect – not an easy thing to do with the beams of the low ceiling almost brushing his head. 'Admiral Watson, we need your ships and we need the guns on the ships. Without them we shall fail. And if we fail, Bussy will ally himself with the Nawab and we shall be driven out of Bengal – and after Bengal, the Carnatic. Everything ... everything, Admiral, depends upon you getting within cannon range of Chandanagar – and staying there until you've reduced the walls to rubble.'

Two days later the main force disembarked. For ten miles in the blistering heat they dragged their 24-pounder guns, brushing aside one French outpost after another until they came within sight of Chandanagar. Here Clive began a preliminary barrage to distract the defences from the river. Great chunks of metal struck the ramparts with tremendous thuds but apart from flaking off crusts of masonry had no appreciable effect. He raised the elevation of the cannon and fired over the walls. Smoke and dust rose from the thin-walled buildings inside the fort, but again with no visible effect.

The ranks of men behind him poured out volley after volley of musket fire, aiming at the crenellations from which peeped hundreds of faces. The French artillery responded with the accuracy that Stringer Lawrence had always warned against and, within four hours, had destroyed three gun teams with roundshot and an entire company of men with grapeshot.

Clive looked balefully towards the Hooghly, but its vacant passivity only mocked him. Not a sail could be seen. He had nothing but contempt for Siraj-ud-daula's promise of help. Since he had left Calcutta there had been repeated messages from the Nawab saying that his force was on its way to join with him against the French, but each message had concluded with an excuse for the latest delay.

He shot a glance at Mathieson who was directing his cannon with admirable skill – though from the bottom of a deep trench. Had Clive not been so preoccupied he would have castigated the fellow for not showing a better example to his men.

And as if this were not enough, there was the problem of Chandanagar itself. Its firepower was enormous, much more than he had expected from the number of soldiers that comprised the garrison. Had the notion not been so patently unlikely, he would have said the French had been reinforced by at least a couple of thousand warriors. But from where could the commandant have got such troops? And where the devil could Watson have got to? Two more days of this and the attack would have to be called off.

'Ahoy! ... boom ahead,' the lookout called from the masthead of Watson's flagship, bringing about a flurry of activity as the sails were reefed to reduce speed. The Admiral and several other officers put telescopes to their eyes and focused on a formidable obstacle. Stretched across the narrowest part of the Hooghly river were four demasted hulks connected to each other by a tangle of ropes and chains. To make the whole rigid the two outer ships had been sunk so that they rested on the river bed with only the upper decks showing above water, and from river bank to river bank across the boom were a series of gangplanks to facilitate the rapid movement of French soldiers.

'Boom defended – boom defended,' the lookout warned, and the telescopes refocused on several mouths of cannon pointing at the squadron as the defenders confidently prepared to engage.

Signals fluttered from the flagship's mast and, in unison, the warships dropped anchor just out of range of the boom's cannon.

'That's a right pickle of salted herring,' grunted Watson, though Edmund thought he sounded less disturbed than he ought to have been. 'Well, gentlemen,' he said, after spending some time studying the construction of the boom, 'into my cabin – we have a little problem on our hands. Let's assume you have stomach enough for the solution,' he added, casting a dubious eye over the commissioned landlubbers.

Three hours after darkness the squadron's longboats beached gently against the river bank. A hundred and fifty sailors and marines, flintlock pistols and cutlasses in their belts, quietly splashed their way ashore.

'Keep in single file, and absolute silence,' warned Major Eyre Coote in a whisper. He himself would have passed for a pirate in his dark clothes, with black cloth knotted around his head, twin pistols in his belt and cutlass in hand. 'One and a half miles to go.'

He gave the men an encouraging grin.

For the next forty minutes the band of adventurers scrambled, lurched and thrust their way forward through the scrub and bush that lined the river bank. Occasionally a grunt or a whispered curse was heard as a marine slipped or a branch clawed at a sailor's face. They plunged knee deep into the shallow tributaries, slid down banks, grappled their way up the opposite sides.

They concertinaed in the darkness as Major Coote suddenly halted and crouched down. For thirty minutes he remained still, waiting until the thin crescent of the moon appeared and showed up in silhouette the low wall that guarded the shore moorings of the boom. He could hear the low voices of the defenders no more than forty yards away and from the number of round shapes dimly seen projected above the wall he guessed the number to be fifty or so.

The French were alert and ready for attack, though hopefully not from that particular quarter. The Major silently split his men into three groups and assigned each one to an area of the defences. When he felt they were in position he took out his pistol, aimed it at a French sentry, and blew off his head.

At the signal his men, with unearthly cries, dashed forward, converging on the low wall, some of them firing as they ran and others waiting until they were at grips with the enemy before discharging their weapons. The guards were momentarily stunned by the suddenness of the attack, and though they swiftly recovered and turned to meet the invasion, they were overwhelmed the moment the sailors and marines leapt over the wall and set about them with swinging cutlasses. The sharp, slightly curved blades flashed in the ghostly light of the moon and bit deeply into flesh. Shrieks of panic and agony rent the air. Now and again some pistol would blast out and, at such short range, a body would be flung backwards as the hot metal smashed into it.

From the boom-ships came scattered firing and a scampering of feet as reinforcements hurried over the decks and across the connecting planks to aid their companions on shore. But as they arrived on the scene the second group of Major Coote's marines came forward to intercept them, and the fighting moved on to the first of the boom-ships, where the slaughter continued as evenly matched combatants struggled for mastery.

During this diversion on the shore, four longboats from the squadron were rowing silently towards the centre of the great boom where, due to the current, the strain would be greatest. Three of the boats were filled with armed sailors under Edmund's command, while the fourth boat, on tow, had been loaded to the gunwales with scrap timber sprayed with pitch. In the bow of the latter boat stood two sailors holding grapnel and chain.

Rowing as well as they could against the current, the tiny armada reached the boom undetected. The fire-boat was released. The grapnel was thrown on to the deck of the boom-ship and, moments later, the longboat flared up like a great bonfire, putting an impassable wall of flame between the shore and the centre of the river.

Sailors from two of the longboats swarmed aboard the boom-ship, now isolated from the shore by flames, and engaged the few guards remaining. At the same time the sailors from the third longboat commenced hacking and sawing at the mass of ropes and chains holding fast one ship to the other.

Seeing what was happening, many of the defenders fighting ashore disengaged and ran back to save the boom, but they were met by a seething mass of flames. At this point Eyre Coote's third group went into action and swiftly demolished what little resistance was left.

Howls of rage intermingled with the sound of shots, screams of pain and the fearful crackling of the flames as the fire took firm hold on the boom-ships themselves. Within forty-five minutes of Major Coote's initial attack, there came a tremendous rasping, fracturing sound as the final chain gave way. Very slowly, swinging easily with the strong current, the two centre ships – one of which was ablaze all along its decks – gradually drifted apart like the majestic opening of lock gates on a canal.

A resounding cheer went up, followed by the shrill call of a trumpet. The fighting was broken off with difficulty and then followed the retreat.

As the night faded into dawn Admiral Watson, standing on his poopdeck, was gladdened at the sight of the boom now split into two useless halves. The way was open for the last few miles to Chandanagar.

'Up anchors,' he called to his flag-captain, then he turned to welcome the landlubbers who had captained the expedition. His opinion of the army had moved up a notch.

Further upriver a depressed General Clive stood with hands thrust deeply into his pockets. The lookout wearily put the telescope to his eye once more.

'Five ships ... five ships approaching!' he called from the tree branches, his voice almost drowned by the sound of the cannon. 'English ships!' he all but screeched, as he identified the banner fluttering at the masthead of the lead ship.

Clive fell to his knees, clasped his hands together in an act of reverence unusual for him, and gave thanks to God. As he rose to his feet, the lookout cried, 'Fireships, fireships!' He pointed dramatically to the north of the river.

Clive sprinted over to the tree, shinned up it, and grabbed the telescope. 'Oh God in all His mercy!' he prayed, shaken at the sight. The boom had been merely the first line of the defence system; now the second was moving fast with the current downriver, three large vessels ablaze from bow to stern, their rudders lashed to keep them on course. Flames, smoke and sparks were shooting high in the air leaving a reddish-black cloud behind them as they converged on the British squadron. In the narrows of the river there would be no room to manoeuvre. The opposing ships must plough into each other to create an inferno that would spread across the river like a torch plunged into kindling. 'May heaven help you,' whispered Clive fervently.

On board the flagship, Watson rapped out orders while keeping his eye on the approaching threat. He sent aloft a splendid fluttering of signal pennants to warn the captains of the other four ships of impending disaster.

The first of the fireships was little more than two hundred yards away when the Admiral caused his own vessel to swing to starboard. As it came about, a full salvo from the port cannon blasted accurately into the fireship's hull near the waterline. The stricken vessel staggered under the broadside, continued its movement forward for what seemed an eternity, then began settling in the water, spouting up great jets of steam as it did so. The second fireship, following close behind, crunched hard into the stern of the sinking ship, was slewed around by the force of the current, sent off on a course tangential to its former one, and beached itself on a sandbank near the shoreline.

The third fireship, unimpeded, sailed calmly on. As it passed the flagship the heat and sparks compelled the watchers to fling arms across their faces or duck behind cover, and started small fires that had to be quickly doused. Watson, jacket held protectively before him, gazed hypnotised as the fireship rammed hard into the hull of the third ship in his squadron.

The two craft staggered under the impact and then, locked together in an obscene embrace, shuddered downriver as the current took them. Flames swept over the warship, shooting up the rigging and masts; the sails burst free from their ropes, sending great gouts of fire into the air and across the deck.

Panic developed among the younger sailors. They rushed for the longboats or leapt into the river as flaming rigging and spars crashed around them. The captain leapt down from his quarterdeck, drew his sword and rushed among the terrified sailors, crying, 'Are you Englishmen or women?' His cry rallied the sailors, who began to launch the small boats in a less frantic manner.

The vessel was soon abandoned. The two doomed ships, firmly welded together, floated away downstream in a devil's inferno. The sight was compelling. Edmund found himself riveted by the spectacle and, to his shame, praised God it was them and not he that were now being consumed by the flames.

Involuntarily, he ducked as the fire reached the powder barrels. The two ships blasted outwards and upwards in a rapidly expanding globe of flames, timbers, rigging, spars and bits of hull, to land hissing and sizzling on the river or to start more fires on the land. He followed the flight of a 42-pound cannon as it arched through the air to strike the topgallant of another ship and snap it off. The sound of the explosion was deafening. Edmund clapped his hands over his ears, and when he took them away it was all over.

'We shall make do with four ships,' Admiral Watson later told his senior officers. His sole reference to the tragedy had been to remove his hat and to murmur, 'May Almighty God rest their souls,' after which, with seeming brutality, he dismissed the incident, and concentrated on the forthcoming engagement with the Chandanagar batteries.

As the officers filed out of his cabin, a messenger brought the news that they were within one mile of the fort. Watson gazed soberly through his window, and without turning round said quietly, 'Signal the squadron to open fire when within range.'

34

INSIDE THE fort the French commandant was lifted off his feet by the first salvo from the warships. The northern bastion was totally demolished and its gun crews reduced to lumps of mangled flesh. The southern bastion returned the fire and, amidst French cheers, a ship was struck. Wisps of smoke appeared, the deck seemed to heave and a flame enveloped the masts and rigging.

A French officer crowed something about the shot hitting the magazine but before the commandant could make reply he was distracted by shouts of anger and what sounded like fighting within the fort itself. With two of his officers sprinting behind him, he hurried to the firing-ledge near the northern drawbridge. Here ten French soldiers were making valiant attempts to keep back a horde of native warriors. Even as the commandant watched, three of the Frenchmen fell to the ground under a flurry of sword-thrusts while the other seven backed against the door.

Another salvo caused havoc along the top of the battlements; a Frenchman was flung clear across the courtyard as a roundshot took him and a portion of the wall with it.

'Let them through!' cried the commandant. 'Let them pass.' The French guards jerked up their heads, saw who was speaking and thankfully lowered the drawbridge. They were swept to one side in a frenzied rush of brown-skinned warriors as they fled to the safety of the plains.

'What price the Nawab's help!' exclaimed the commandant derisively as the last of the two thousand men Siraj-ud-daula had sent scurried through the archway and clattered over the draw-bridge.

The cannonade continued for three hours. When it ceased the commandant walked, grim-faced, around the crippled stronghold, and no matter where he looked his gaze fell upon the blue-uniformed fragments of what had been Frenchmen. An entire wall facing the river had been pulverised so that the moat was seeping into the underground rooms. Of his artillery only three small-calibre guns still functioned. His decision was reached on humanitarian grounds. Chandanagar surrendered.

Some days later the defeated commandant, standing erect, coolly faced his enemy across the lopsided desk in his quarters. The Englishman was angrily drumming his fingers on the desk.

'General Renault. Three days ago when you surrendered your command, you and your officers gave their parole neither to attempt escape nor to take aggressive action against us,' Clive began with ill-controlled agitation. 'Yet this parole has been broken. Monsieur, during the night three of your officers – by what means I am unable to discover – blasted a hole in the outer wall of the barracks, and, with some thirty or forty common soldiers, escaped. Perhaps,' he said acidly, 'you would give me the benefit of your observations?'

The ex-commandant swayed back on his heels and a shadow of a smile played round his lips.

'General Clive, sir. My face strikes no chord of memory?' came the surprising rejoinder. Clive, taken aback, gaped at the fellow and shrugged his shoulders in bewilderment. 'Then Monsieur, take your mind back to Madras, to the French officer who called upon you to surrender, and to whom you gave your parole not to escape – though you did indeed escape and made your way to, I believe, Fort St David.'

Now he remembered him. The French officer with the high-pitched voice who had read out the terms of surrender.

'You are misinformed, General Renault,' Clive corrected him. 'I and my companion gave no parole at that time and were therefore entitled to make our escape.'

'Precisely – as did my three officers, General Clive,' snapped Renault. 'When the others made their promise, these three were in hiding. They have escaped, as their honour required them to do.'

Clive laughed ruefully. 'Touché, Monsieur.' He stood up and gallantly offered his hand. 'Perhaps this evening you will do me the honour of dining with me?'

Some days later, in the howdah of the largest elephant in Murshidabad, its decoration so rich and flamboyant that its warlike purpose was reduced to the level of pantomime, Siraj-ud-daula struck an heroic posture. His right arm embraced the bare waist of Sareen – a silent and introspective Sareen, for she had exhausted herself in trying to dissuade him from his latest impulsive venture.

A splendidly robed figure on horseback cantered up to the elephant. 'The army is ready, your highness,' called Mir Jafar sullenly, glowering at the thought of what might be going on in that closed howdah. The Nawab disengaged himself from Sareen, leaned through the curtains, proudly surveyed the line of thirty war-elephants and the mass of warriors that pressed near, then dramatically flung out his arm and shouted, 'On to Calcutta!'

The stirring call was received with tumultuous huzzahs. Accompanied by the snorting of beasts, the cries of drovers and mahouts, the great army began trudging forward, light-heartedly intent on glory and plunder. For two days the colourful assemblage lumbered across the plains and through the forests, the howdahs rocking and swaying like top-heavy ships in a stormy Bay of Bengal, the great pads of the elephants and the thousands of horses' hooves stirring up great clouds of dust to choke the foot soldiers, whose enthusiasm soon waned as their discomfort increased.

On the fourth day, as Siraj rested in his tent with Sareen, in a foul mood at the miserable progress his army was making, a messenger entered and dropped trembling to his knees. Siraj unrolled the parchment and read:

To His Exalted Highness the Nawab of Bengal,

I have been apprised that you and a goodly number of warriors are but three days' journey from Calcutta. I know not if you come as friend or as foe, but if the latter then so inform me and I shall at once take the field to destroy you. If you come as a friend to assist me against the French, then know also that I need not your aid, for Chandanagar is mine. Against other enemies I have no fear for I can defeat them were they ten times stronger in number.

With respect,
Your loyal subject,
Robert Clive, Major-General.

Siraj sprang furiously from the bed. He ripped the parchment into fragments, flung them into the messenger's face and dealt the poor fellow such a blow that he sprawled to the ground, and was only able to flee the tent when Sareen hastily intervened. Even she received a few slaps for her presumptuousness.

She returned to the bed and calmly waited for the storm to blow over. When at last Siraj flung himself sobbing across her lap, she patiently extracted from him the substance of the message. Though secretly relieved, she adopted a sympathetic manner and gently stroked his head.

'You must return to Murshidabad, my lord.'

'I will not be a coward!' he shouted, maliciously pinching her thigh so that she winced.

'Bengal knows that its Nawab is no coward,' she soothed, 'and now Bengal will also know that he is wise. Your name will be praised. You will be honoured, and blessings will be cast upon your memory for having saved the lives of so many.'

At last she convinced him. He even began to savour the notion of being the people's saviour.

He pulled himself from her arms, flung open the tent flap and bawled for Mir Jafar. 'Turn the army round; back to Murshidabad,' he majestically commanded Sareen's husband. 'In my wisdom I have decided to spare Calcutta and bring peace to Bengal.'

Only by the flicker of an eyebrow did Mir Jafar show his derision at this abrupt turnabout. But the Nawab caught his look, and in cheap revenge he flung wide the canvas flap, offering Mir Jafar a full view of his wife inside, naked as she awaited His Exalted Highness's pleasure.

As the vast army retraced its steps, two miles further on Mir Kassim was interrogating a group of exhausted French soldiers and their three officers.

'And your purpose in seeking asylum with the Nawab?' he asked, viewing them with the suspicion he reserved for all hatmen. The senior officer answered proudly, 'We are artillerymen, your highness, and it is our desire to aid the Nawab of Bengal against the English. To this purpose we shall teach the Nawab's warriors the correct usage of artillery, and we shall also fight at his side whenever he calls upon us to do so. Only by the best use of cannon will it be possible to vanquish the Nawab's enemies, and in that, your highness, we have great skill.'

35

CLIVE'S EYES shone with happiness as he located Margaret on the topmost deck. She was holding up her baby, Edward, in a manner that proudly said, 'Look how big he's grown since last you saw him.'

'So that makes me an uncle,' said Edmund with wry amusement. He was impressed by Margaret's maturity, forgetting that it was three years since last he had seen her. Though composed and self-assured, as befitted the wife of a hero, she looked quite gay and fashionable in her large feathered hat and her flounced skirt.

'She is lovely,' murmured Clive to himself, inordinately proud of the effect she was having on the numerous spectators who had come to welcome the ship.

He and Edmund had been a week in Calcutta attending meetings in the Council chambers wherein the 'Inner Council' (as some called it derisively) had been setting to rights the future of the city – and possibly of Bengal.

'Robert, dearest, sweet,' Margaret gushed happily, flinging herself into his arms and hugging him tight, before extending an arm so that Edmund might somehow creep into the embrace. 'It's been so long ...'

Twenty minutes later her eyes glowed at the sight of the mansion given to her husband by an appreciative city. 'It's so big,' she enthused, thrilling to the way the guard of soldiers snapped to attention when General Clive's coach drew up in front of the main doors.

Margaret was very proud of her husband. She loved being the wife of such a famous man and luxuriated in his reflected glory. Even the captain of the ship which had brought her from Bombay to Calcutta had treated her with the deference accorded to royalty, and in Madras the whole Council had lavished a welcome on her when the ship had called to reprovision.

'Are we to stay in Calcutta very long, Robert?' she asked him over lunch. Edmund pricked up his ears curious to see how Clive would answer.

Imperiously, Clive dismissed the flunkeys and said nothing until the door had closed behind them. 'Be prepared for a long stay, Margaret,' he said quietly. 'I cannot leave India until the constitution I intend to write is not only on the statute book but has become firmly rooted.'

Edmund listened with growing astonishment and no little foreboding as his friend continued to speak. The *grand seigneur* that Clive had become, Edmund humorously accepted. But to think of writing constitutions was to usurp the office of emperor.

'The first task will be to depose Siraj-ud-daula,' said Clive calmly, causing Edmund to gape with incredulity. Clive might well have stated that he intended to replace the King of England. 'I shall treat no more with this prince. The bond I made with him he dishonoured. Perfidiously, deceitfully, he sided with the French against us – and, whilst we were thus engaged, sought to march on Calcutta. With such a false creature as Nawab there can be no enduring peace in Bengal.'

Edmund blandly asked, 'Assuming the Nawab will obligingly abdicate, who then have you in mind to replace him, Robert?'

Clive, in no humour to quarrel, ignored Edmund's sarcasm and answered, 'Mir Jafar. He has a popular following.'

'But wouldn't he remain loyal to Siraj-ud-daula, Robert?' Margaret ventured nervously.

Clive wavered a moment in deference to his wife's sensibilities, then said delicately, 'The Nawab has taken advantage of Mir Jafar's wife. Such abuse of privilege allows no claim on loyalties. I own to no knowledge of the General's nature, but were I he then I should be filled with loathing and inspired only towards revenge. Perhaps you know something of him, Edmund,' he said, turning to his sober-faced brother-in-law.

Edmund, who was not happy with Clive's proposal or his choice, said carefully, 'Miss Wilkinson implies that Mir Jafar might be receptive to an approach, but ...' He broke off and took up his wineglass, unwilling to say more.

'But? ... You were saying?' Clive spurred him on.

'Well, frankly, I'm in favour of his son, Mir Kassim.'

'Kassim!' Clive smiled, and shook his head. 'In his way, Kassim is as much a firebrand as Siraj-ud-daula. We need a man like Mir Jafar – devious, but shrewd enough to know his friends and amenable to suggestion. However, at the next Council meeting I want to suggest that Miss Wilkinson drops a hint in the ears of Mir Jafar to learn his reaction to the proposal.' He banged the table in dismissive good humour. 'Now I think we should put aside all this intense discussion and indulge ourselves with family gossip. I'm sure Margaret is simply aching to tell us of Madras ... aren't you, dearest?'

The outcome of the meeting was an endorsement of Clive's suggestion. Only Warren Hastings declared in favour of Mir Kassim.

Some time later, Captain Mathieson and Omichand were conferring over a sheaf of papers. The Captain was annoyed. Omichand was unctuously and unsuccessfully providing explanations.

'It is to my deep shame, Sahib Mathieson, that the profits on our last transactions did not fulfil our expectations. But what can a poor merchant like myself. ...?' He whined on at length, clasping his fat hands together. 'I cannot compete when English traders sell their names to my rivals. The Emperor's firman permits English traders to be excused customs duties. They buy cheaper and thus make huge profits, and for a fee they will lend their name to some native merchant, and he,too, will be excused customs duties. Now if the Sahib Mathieson would only put his name against my notes ...' He glanced sideways at the Captain. Their eyes met and a look of understanding passed between them.

Mathieson seized a quill and paper, wrote swiftly, and then handed the document to Omichand.

'Here. Now future dealings in Bengal will be carried out under my name, and we shall share the profits equally. Do not try to cheat me, Omichand, for if you do ...'

Omichand wailed that such an arrangement would reduce him to starvation, yet swiftly tucked the document into the folds of his robes. There were ways of cheating that even this astute Englishman had never heard of. 'It is agreed. It is agreed,' he said sorrowfully.

Mathieson raised a hand to clap him jovially on the shoulders, then thought better of it. 'Good. And once a new Nawab is appointed I see no reason why we shouldn't expand our future business throughout the whole of Bengal,' he said, unthinkingly.

Omichand's nostrils quivered. He busied himself collecting the sheaf of papers together.

Most casually he ventured, 'But Siraj-ud-daula is a young man, Sahib. He will live for many years. There can be no new Nawab.'

'No tyrant is so secure that he cannot be deposed, Omichand,' Mathieson replied offhand, standing up and peering into a mirror as he adjusted his hat.

'Only Mir Jafar is powerful enough to depose him.' said Omichand softly, and from Mathieson's expression he knew he had hit on the right name.

'Take care, Omichand, lest your tongue lick the wood of the block,' said Mathieson with contrived jocularity in an attempt to rectify his indiscretion. Omichand laughed, and secretly treasured the valuable information. No more mention was made of the subject, and when the two men parted it was with mutual protestations of goodwill and friendship – which neither of them considered worth a couple of straws.

When, a week later, Clive read the sealed letter brought to him, he swore loudly, and barked at a junior officer, 'Get me Major Maskelyne.'

'Who the deuce is responsible for this?' he shouted when Edmund arrived, tossing the letter accusingly at him. Edmund took the folded paper and began to read it. Half-way through, he flopped down in the nearest chair and let out a subdued whistle.

'Thirty lakhs of rupees plus five per cent of the Murshidabad treasure! Ouch!' he exclaimed, tossing the letter on to the desk. 'And to think I had always considered Omichand a rather petty kind of knave.'

'Blackmail!' Clive ranted, pacing the large room in such an agitated manner that his wig slipped a little and remained perched at an odd angle on his head. 'That unctuous, fawning, servile, stinking pig of a Turk dares to blackmail me.'

'And he's smart enough to know that if we're silly enough to turn him down, he can sell the information to the Nawab – which would mean the immediate execution of Mir Jafar and a few other people as well,' Edmund observed quietly. 'Thirty lakhs and five per cent ... and the rumour is that Siraj has forty million pounds in his treasury. It seems that our Omichand is an ambitious man indeed – astute enough to demand that the agreement be incorporated into whatever treaty we make with Mir Jafar.'

Clive swung round and pointed a quivering finger at Edmund. 'I will submit to no blackmail, to none whatsoever. And were he here at this moment I should strangle him with my bare hands.'

'Rest assured that Omichand will keep out of our way until this matter is settled to his satisfaction. But, of course, there is a way you can defeat him – though it is not an honourable one.'

'Honour!' Clive spat. 'Speak not of honour when dealing with such a blackguard. Tell me your plan, Edmund, and though it stinks of the cesspit, I shall use it.'

36

A FULL moon picked out the white buildings of Calcutta with romantic and serene clarity, throwing into shadow the less pleasant aspects of the city. On the balcony that clung to the second floor of Miss Wilkinson's house, six lesser shadows moved stealthily towards her open bedroom window. A few moments later a hand, black as ebony, softly moved aside the silk hanging that served as curtain and a dark body climbed into the room. Four shadows followed. As they slid quietly over the sill the moonlight glinted on broad-bladed knives.

Petal Wilkinson lay deeply asleep. She was naked, and the sheets were tangled about her knees and thighs. The shadowy figures arranged themselves around the foot of the bed and nudged each other, grins on their heathen faces, at the rare sight of the naked form of a white woman.

One of the figures leaned over and squeezed the big toe of Petal's left foot. It was a method designed to wake a sleeper without abruptness. Two or three seconds passed before her eyelids flickered. They opened, closed again and then shot wide open. She gasped and opened her mouth to scream. Another shadow drew his knife and held it close to her face and a third clapped a dark hand over her mouth. The leader whispered with urgent sincerity, 'We mean you no harm, Sahiba ... no harm. We will not hurt you but you must not call out.'

Her frightened eyes looked into his. Slowly she nodded comprehension. The hand was removed.

'You are to come with us. His Highness the Nawab has ordered that you be brought to Murshidabad and that you are not to be injured. Please dress and make no sound.'

Petal, normally an imperturbable woman, was terrified, but she controlled herself, and, when the knife was returned to the owner's sash, slid off the bed.

They watched with interest as she dressed and then, with much salaaming and gesturing, escorted her through the window and on to the balcony.

The ride to the Bhagirathi was short, and there the kidnappers took her aboard a waiting dhow for the hundred and thirty miles voyage to Murshidabad. A woman of much spirit, Miss Wilkinson soon recovered and set about enjoying the journey. What could be more enchanting than to recline languidly in the bows of that most picturesque of craft, under a tropical moon, summoned by a prince of Bengal? But such fantasy served only to heighten her apprehension. Had it been Alivardi Khan she would not have worried. But Siraj-ud-daula. It might be that he had need of her professional services, but she doubted it. When Siraj felt sexual urges he was not likely to wait several days for their gratification.

Eventually the dhow nudged against the wooden quay at Murshidabad. From there she was led straight into the Nawab's presence. Her sense of unease was heightened by the effusiveness of his welcome and the frequency with which he apologised for having so rudely summoned her. He bade her sit by his side, had his servants bring her the choicest food and wine, and talked at length about nothing in particular. He even deigned to break bread with her, which was an honour indeed. Then he began to tap his forehead as if to chide himself for being remiss. 'You have had an exhausting journey, Sahiba Wilkinson,' he said with magnificent concern. 'You must rest. I shall have a bath prepared for you and my own masseur will ease from your limbs the strain of your travels.'

She gave him a sideways look, but had no choice but to comply. If Siraj was leading up to a sexual orgy – well, it would be infinitely preferable to other things she could think of. Her suspicions refused to be allayed even when he led her to his own enormous sunken bath, and stood by contentedly whilst servants removed her garments and poured scented oils into the bath.

Siraj took a seat near the pool, his back resting against a column of finely mosaicked stone, and watched with obvious pleasure as she stepped into the deep bath accompanied by two female slaves.

'Alivardi Khan had great regard for your virtue, Sahiba,' he said. This tickled her, though she took 'virtue' to mean 'honesty' or 'loyalty'.

'Alivardi Khan was a great prince of India, your highness.'

'And I, Sahiba? Must I have equal regard for your virtue?' he went on smoothly.

Thinking up a diplomatic answer to this was more difficult. 'I am a loyal subject of Bengal,' she replied ambiguously, climbing out of the bath to be immediately engulfed in large, soft towels.

When dry, she lay down on a few cushions, where she was massaged by the eunuch. Privacy seemed the least prized thing in the palace, she thought wryly, looking round at the guards, the servants, the slaves, and, of course, Siraj himself. The masseur was a professional; he first sprinkled her body with an oil extracted from crushed flowers, and then with his hands and huge flattened thumbs kneaded the muscles of her back in small circles. Methodically and with expertise, the eunuch worked his way down her body, using the tips of his fingers, his thumbs and the palms of his hands according to the muscle groupings, until each fibre and ligament seemed to sigh with relief.

'I have been hearing rumours from Calcutta, Sahiba,' said Siraj. 'Do you know of such a rumour?'

Petal turned her head slightly and murmured some vaguely negative reply. The question was repeated. This time her sleepiness vanished and she became alert.

She was about to make some clearer reply when she heard the swish of an elephant-hide whip as it curled through the air. It cracked across her bare back. She screamed and tried to roll away from the next stroke – but found that her limbs were held firm by four of the guards. Again she shrieked as the whip cut across her back.

'I know nothing – nothing!' she screamed, giving way to panic.

'Turn her to face me,' he ordered calmly.

He raised the whip and struck her again, and again. Petal half-fainted with pain. Her body was lathered in sweat and criss-crossed with weals.

'They say, they say ... the English are to ... to put a new ... Nawab ...' she sobbed at last, and Siraj wearily lowered his arm. Flogging was a tiring business.

'Who, Sahiba Wilkinson, says this?'

'Those people ... the Council ... some who came to me,' she moaned between sobs, her voice barely audible.

'Sahiba Wilkinson. Did they say *who* is to replace me?' His teeth showed under the small moustache he was growing, and though he smiled his eyes glittered venomously.

She groaned and bit her lips to try and stop the tears, and as her head rolled to one side the whip came down again in a gentle reminder that the Nawab was awaiting her reply. It was a light blow and merely flicked at her thighs, but it was sufficient to break down the last barrier of resistance. She babbled, 'The General, your highness ... the General. Oh please, your highness, it is all I know. They told me nothing more ... just a general ... They did not say which one ... just a general, your highness.'

'One of my generals, indeed.' The revelation seemed to entertain him. He made a mental list of his generals, musing as to which of the seven would be the most likely. He stood for a moment deep in thought, his whip cracking and flicking at nothing in particular. He made no further attempt to hurt his victim, for his intuition told him that he had extracted all the useful information Miss Wilkinson possessed. Then, in his characteristic fashion, his manner changed abruptly. He became excessively solicitous to Petal, and abused his menials for their slowness in attending to her.

He knelt by her side and began to stroke her hair, crying out to his servants, 'Take the Sahiba to her room, fools! See that she is healed with your best ointments. Call my surgeon and let him attend her. Send for the Princess Sareen and tell her to see that the Sahiba has all she needs.' He rose to his feet, hesitated, and then impulsively slipped one of the golden chains from around his neck and fastened it about the sweat-stained neck of his victim. It was an act of penitence no less genuine than his earlier act of violence. He solemnly made obeisance to her, saying, 'Think not too harshly of me, Sahiba,' and then bowed himself out of the room.

Petal lay for several minutes in a state of numbed shock, listening to the faint sound of her inquisitor's voice giving commands that she be returned to Calcutta when recovered. When the masseur returned and began applying his lotions to her injured flesh, she fainted.

Three weeks later an uneasy Mir Jafar gingerly sat down on the edge of a chair in Petal Wilkinson's vestibule. He would have preferred cushions on the floor. Near him, on a soft couch, Petal herself reclined. Her body was still marked and the pain had not entirely disappeared. As hostess, her sole task was to ensure that her guests were plentifully supplied with refreshment and that the meeting was kept secret.

Robert Clive, with grave dignity, placed before the nobleman a long scroll of parchment – prepared only four days previously from the stomach skin of a sheep that had been ritually slaughtered. It was white and unstained, and the writing was in English and in Persian.

'The treaty for your approval and signature, your excellency,' he said, as one ambassador to another. Mir Kassim, behind his father, leaned over, and read the clauses one by one. His face remained impassive.

Clive enunciated each item carefully, occasionally glancing swiftly at the seated nobleman. 'All privileges and rights allowed by the Emperor and by the present Nawab, Siraj-ud-daula, are hereby confirmed ... an alliance with the English for mutual defence ... All French possessions in Bengal are to be placed under British control ...' He stopped as Kassim interrupted him.

'To use the skin of a lion you must first slay it,' he said sardonically. 'The French still hold Pondicherry – and I am told that Bussy has returned.'

Clive shrugged impatiently. 'Your excellency, when he is the new Nawab, will continue to receive all revenues from these factories of course ...' His voice tailed off as he saw that Mir Jafar had reached the most contentious clause of all. His brown eyes blinked in disbelief and he stared at the Englishman in shocked surprise.

'Three million pounds in compensation!' he exclaimed, dropping the quill pen.

'It is a just figure, your excellency, for Siraj's destruction of Calcutta and for the incident of the Black Hole. The sum is to be divided between the inhabitants who suffered as well as the Council – and myself.'

'But this is preposterous, Sahib Clive,' he spluttered, spreading out his hands. 'There is not that sum in the whole treasury of Murshidabad. I cannot guarantee to pay what I do not possess.'

Clive fixed him with a cool and cynical stare. 'With respect, your excellency, we have evidence that the treasure of Siraj-ud-daula consists of gold and valuables to the value of forty millions, and in view of this, three millions is not too excessive a price for gaining you the throne of Bengal,' he said, turning his gaze on the son as if daring him to contradict.

Kassim refused to meet his eyes, but jabbered excitedly in his native tongue, far too fast for any of the Europeans to catch the sense – although Miss Wilkinson flashed him an angry look before resuming her impassive role. Mir Jafar rounded on him and for several moments there was an angry exchange of words before the old man abruptly waved Kassim to silence.

'My son protests,' the elderly nobleman explained needlessly, 'yet I am compelled to agree to the terms. When the day comes that I am made Nawab you shall be granted permission to explore the treasury. If the money be there, you shall be paid; if not, then you must be patient until revenues are collected from the land.'

Though the offer was not to his liking, Clive had no option but to accept. He seized a quill and applied his signature to the bottom of the parchment. Mir Jafar appended his own name, and then followed the signatures of the members of the so-called 'Inner Council'. When all was signed and sealed, Clive visibly relaxed and became more affable.

To Edmund it seemed ludicrous that Robert Clive, a great soldier, and an Indian prince of dubious merit, should solemnly negotiate the transfer of a state over which they possessed neither lawful ownership nor control. 'First bell the cat,' he murmured.

'You are confident of the outcome of this coming contest with Siraj-ud-daula, Sahib Clive?' Mir Jafar asked anxiously – for what must have been the third time that evening.

'On that matter I, too, would like to be reassured,' Kassim cut in truculently, narrowly watching Edmund.

'My confidence, Mir Kassim,' Clive rejoined arrogantly, 'is based on your father's commitment that he will abandon the Nawab once the battle has commenced and will bring his forces to join with mine. Without the benefit of Mir Jafar's regiments I could not hope to win the day against the Nawab.' He paused, then leaned forward and asked aggressively, 'Is my confidence based on shifting sand, Mir Kassim?'

Kassim, grossly affronted, was stung to reply, 'Did you not witness my father as he placed his hands upon the Holy Koran? Did he not swear an oath to give you aid on that day? For me, Sahib Clive, it is enough – and for you it is an abundance of guarantees.' He glared savagely at his father, curtly salaamed to the gathering, and stalked from the room.

37

SIRAJ LAY sprawled across his outsize bed. By his side knelt Sareen, who was neatly trimming his fingernails. She seemed to be calmly concentrated on her task but her emotions were turbulent.

Siraj had told her of Miss Wilkinson, of the beating, and of the information he had extracted from her. She had no doubts as to which of the seven generals was aiming to usurp Siraj and now she was faced with the cruellest of dilemmas.

Her own husband might well be executed, and though she felt nothing but contempt for Mir Jafar, she had no desire to see hurt done to him. More important, would not Siraj also execute the son, Kassim, assuming that Kassim would naturally be involved in his father's treachery?

She caught a glimpse of Siraj's face. He was staring at her, a look of enquiry in his eyes. He smiled when their eyes met and offered the other hand. At times he seemed so young, though he was two years older than herself. Handsome? Yes, she conceded as much, though he was not quite so good-looking as Kassim, whose solemnly intense gaze burned into her each time they met. And they met often, and quite openly. Siraj must know of their clandestine affair, yet he never questioned her.

Siraj often baffled her. He was so unpredictable. Of his love for her he made no secret, and he made clear to the several women who inhabited the seraglio that Sareen was first, though without official status.

How could she allow Mir Jafar to proceed with a scheme which must mean the death of Siraj? Sareen was not vindictive. Her thoughts never toyed with revenge. During the early days, Siraj had been rough with her. He had debauched her in the presence of others with shameful crudity, and once, in a rage, had ordered a huge guard to rape her.

But all that had now passed. Her physical attraction for him had actually increased with time, and though he still took her whenever the urge possessed him, it was never with brutality. He often showed her tenderness – yes, even love. He had also developed an immense respect for her intelligence, her powers of reasoning and dispassionate observation. So manifest was this respect that he often asked her advice.

'The English conspire to make for themselves a new Nawab,' he said suddenly, speaking his thoughts aloud and disturbing the flow of her own. He squeezed her nipple tightly in his agitation. She pricked his thumb with the scissors in mild retaliation and he gave a mock squeal of pain and hugged her close to him.

'And do they say who is to take the throne, my lord?' she asked with pretended diffidence, keeping her eyes hidden from him. He removed his hand from hers and gently raised her chin so that she was forced to look at him.

'I think you know, Sareen,' he said quietly, at which she replied, 'Then I do pray, my lord Siraj, that both you and I are wrong.' He sighed, though whether at her answer or in admiration of her loveliness, she could not tell.

He was thinking that he should make her his wife ... possibly after he had defeated the English. Mir Jafar would repeat the formula for a divorce. And then there would be such a marriage ceremony! Yes, he would discuss the possibility with Mir Jafar when next he saw him.

'Mir Jafar,' he said aloud, and did not miss the look that Sareen gave him. He was about to declare his intent when, to his consternation, her calm face crumpled and she burst into tears. In complete abandonment she flung herself upon him, buried her face underneath his whiskery chin, and gave herself up to her grief.

Some weeks later in Calcutta, the sun burned down on the bright tunics of men on parade. They jumped smartly to attention the moment General Robert Clive appeared on his large dappled grey, followed by his senior officers.

There were seven hundred British soldiers gathered on the

maidan: grenadiers with tall mitred hats; light-infantry in jackets of blood red, led by Major Edmund Maskelyne; Highlanders in their colourful kilts of Royal Stuart tartan; and behind these a company of Lowland Scots, carrying the great double-edged, two-handed claymores. Standing alert in front of this splendid throng were the drums, the fifes and the pipers. On the opposite side of the maidan were two thousand sepoy infantry under the command of Major Eyre Coote. Finally, there were the hundred and seventy artillerymen, fifty sailors, and twelve cannon under the command of Captain Mathieson. Truly it was a magnificent sight.

Clive raised his eyes to where a single 20-gun frigate of Admiral Watson's squadron lay at anchor. He found some comfort in the sight, though it was the only ship Watson had been able to provide that was capable of negotiating the shallow Bhagirathi all the way to Murshidabad. To control the river was to keep Clive's left flank protected on his march north.

At last Clive signalled for the march to commence. The first platoon strode forward, followed by the next and the next. Soon the colourful army was moving dustily and steadily northwards. In the wake of the fighting force came the mobile village needed to keep an army in the field: a horde of bullock carts, coolies, carriers, elephants, women.

On the 14th June 1757 Clive reached Khulna, eighty miles from Murshidabad. He called a halt to rest the force and to weigh again the doubts that plagued him.

'If he goes back on his word then we're lost,' he declared moodily when on an inspection tour with Eyre Coote.

Major Coote tried to cheer his general. 'All the better if he defaults, sir, then we needn't spare any of our own troops to go to his aid.'

Clive gave him a withering look. 'Either you're a damned optimist or a damned fool, Major,' he snapped. 'In the name of all saints, consider the numbers alone. We shall field three thousand against the Nawab's what? Thirty? Forty thousand? Can one musket ball kill ten of the enemy? Can a sepoy with a bayonet prevail against fifteen swordsmen? Learn to be realistic, Coote.'

He strode on, hands clasped tightly behind his back. They were joined a moment later by Edmund.

'I've been discussing Mir Jafar with Coote here,' said Clive, 'trying to stress the weakness of our position should he fail us. What do you think of him, Edmund?'

Clive so manifestly sought reassurance that Edmund felt inhuman at not being able to give it. He pursed his lips and blew out noisily. 'A man committed to the betrayal of his own prince is hardly the kind of ally *I* would be inclined to trust . . . but this is no more than my personal opinion,' he added quickly. 'All we can hope is that his greed for the throne will force him to stand by his agreement.'

'More than likely he'll sit back calmly, let both sides commit massacre, then come forward to stake his claim from the winner,' Eyre Coote muttered sourly.

'For once, Major Coote, there is evidence of a brain under that flaming red hair of yours,' rejoined Clive with good-humoured sarcasm. 'Now put it to use by taking the fort at Katwa,' he added with less jocularity, leading the two officers into his tent.

'North of this point on the river . . . here,' his finger stabbed at the map set out on his plank table, 'is one of the Nawab's forts. It commands the river and will hold the frigate up. Without the frigate we'll be denied half our artillery . . . *and* control of the river.'

Major Coote grimaced at the figures Clive had scribbled by the side of the Katwa fort.

'That could never be taken by direct assault, sir, even were I to take the entire force,' he began, but Clive cut him short.

'Then substitute cunning for weapons and bluff for numbers, Major. Now's the chance you've waited for since you wept on my shoulder in England.'

Eyre Coote stiffened and coldly asked what forces would be assigned to him.

'Two hundred English foot soldiers, three hundred sepoys. I can spare you no more. Take Major Maskelyne with you as your adjutant and also . . . yes, Mathieson – it will be good for him,' Coote and Edmund exchanged meaning looks.

Two days later Major Coote's small force were within shouting distance of the fort overlooking the Bhagirathi. The protective wall of the fort was one mile in circumference, and was never less than thirty feet high.

'Bluff, the General says,' exclaimed Eyre Coote sardonically, instructing two cavalrymen and Mathieson to follow him under a flag of truce. He spurred his horse forward and halted before the main bastion overlooking the spike-encrusted gates. At closer range the fort was even more formidable.

The governor poked his head over the battlements and looked down at the strangers. Eyre Coote impudently called up, 'I propose to take this fort. Will you surrender?' and watched the turbaned head as it wobbled with indignation.

'I shall defend to the last!' came the answer.

Two startled pigeons nesting in one of the crenellations flew away in a scattering of dust. Major Coote bowed respectfully, and galloped back to his own small encampment.

'If he does indeed defend to the last, then we might as well walk back to Calcutta,' Edmund observed dryly, eyeing the thousands of dark heads which crowded the battlements.

'Take a hundred and fifty sepoys, Maskelyne,' Eyre Coote ordered, pointedly ignoring a remark which he considered in bad taste, and he outlined the scheme in detail.

At one hour before sunset, Edmund raised his hand. A drummer beat a stirring roll and at the sound a company of sepoys moved towards the main gate of the Katwa fort in three long lines. When they were within a hundred paces the drum beat changed. The front line dropped to its knees, aimed muskets and fired a tight volley. The heads on the wall ducked down in alarm. Then the second line fired, and then the third.

From the scattered nature of the fire returned it seemed obvious to Edmund that consternation had gripped the defenders though they grossly outnumbered the attackers. On the few occasions when muskets did point at the sepoys the men wielding them could hardly aim before ducking to cover again. By the time the sun faded only a few turbaned heads could be detected between the crenellations.

The gunfire continued in a desultory fashion right through the long hot night. It kept the defenders occupied while Eyre Coote crossed the river to launch the primary offensive against the weaker walls at the rear of the fort. The siege was pure comedy. Major Coote blew in the main gate, walked in and claimed the fort. Only a score or so of corpses were there to defy him. During the early hours of the morning the intrepid governor had fled with his entire garrison towards Murshidabad, and his mind was at this moment busy fabricating some yarn for the Nawab's benefit. Katwa was secured; the river open for the passage of the frigate.

'As I expected,' said Clive, when Eyre Coote reported to him two days later. 'Yet a fair job nonetheless,' he added deflatingly. 'I had heard of this governor and gambled he would have no stomach for a fight.'

Edmund came quickly to Eyre Coote's defence.

'Frankly, I consider it an outstanding and imaginative triumph,' he said. 'Even Stringer Lawrence – God rest his soul – never took a fort for the loss of only six men.'

The look of gratitude that Eyre Coote flashed him was sufficient reward. Edmund doffed his hat to Clive and was about to leave, when Clive said, 'Edmund, would you see me in my tent in a little while?' It was clearly a request and not an order.

'In an hour, Robert. Good-day, Major Coote – and again congratulations,' he added, sauntering away.

It was long past the hour when he approached Clive's tent. He was about to go in when he stopped and began sniffing the air. Cutting through the normal smells of dust, dung and decay, was a pungent odour he recognised immediately. He pulled aside the flap and hurried in.

Clive was sprawled on a canvas chair, his expression amiable and welcoming, his eyes bright and with narrowed pupils. On the low table beside him, thin blue smoke rising from its bowl, was an opium pipe. Clive lumbered to his feet and embraced Edmund, who remained stiff and unyielding. This was the third time he had caught Robert using opium.

'Come. I want you to see this,' Clive said, leading Edmund to a trestle table on which a map had been spread. It was badly drawn, possibly by Clive himself, for he fancied himself as a cartographer. He indicated a point where the river curled into a huge loop, not unlike a human intestine. Edmund peered at the small letters printed next to the east bank of the river.

'Plassey.' He said the name incuriously. Clive nodded.

'It's Palasi, really ... from the palas tree that grows there. Locally known as the Flame of the Forest because its shimmering orange blooms are supposed to look like a burning forest. Judging by latest reports on the Nawab's progress this is where I intend to meet him.' With his fingernail he etched a circle about the name. 'On the edge of the river here is the Nawab's hunting lodge, a substantial brick and stone building, and surrounding it a large orchard of mango trees ... there we shall make our stand.'

He was about to say more when he realised that Edmund was being unresponsive. He pushed the map aside and faced Edmund squarely.

'Edmund,' he pleaded. 'I do not know what the morrow will bring or what our fates will be after. I must talk with you. There is an ... an estrangement, a barrier, between us. It grieves me – for I know the fault is mine and I feel powerless to break it down. What has happened, Edmund? It isn't the disparity in rank. Wealth, rank, impress you less than ...' He made a helpless gesture. 'To me they are of value because I am what I am. What then is between us, dear friend?'

Edmund's face softened though he would not meet Clive's eyes. 'There is no quarrel between us, Robert,' he protested lamely.

'I said nothing of a quarrel,' Clive snapped, agitated by Edmund's deliberate obtuseness. 'Were it so simple as a quarrel I could remove the cause. It is rather a dulled impassivity where once there was understanding and sympathy. Of late I have felt when speaking to you that I must either command or else beg response. Is this the brotherhood we once knew?'

Edmund, shaken by Clive's direct appeal, impulsively flung an arm around the smaller man and said with a grin, 'Perhaps you destroyed too many innocent plants with your sword, Robert. I was never sure when next the blade might be turned on me.'

Clive jumped up in protest. 'Never! Never!' he declared passionately. 'I would as soon destroy ...'

'Perhaps there has been too much destruction,' Edmund cut in softly. 'Aye, and self-destruction, too, Robert.' His gaze went pointedly to the now cold pipe on the table. 'Do you think that opium enhances the image of Robert Clive?'

Clive gazed at Edmund, then stalked over to the table. He picked up the pipe, staring speculatively at it, then dropped it on the ground. He picked up a musket and smashed the butt on to the pipe.

'We shall try to go into battle tomorrow, Edmund, unsullied.'

38

THE ARMY of Siraj-ud-daula spread itself over the land and flowed south like multi-coloured treacle. The Nawab, with Sareen by his side, looked out from his large four-wheeled coach and sneezed explosively as a gritty cloud of dust enveloped them. To the horizon stretched the vast concourse, in the centre of which were sixty elephant, caparisoned and armoured with strips of leather and metal plates, great caps on their enormous foreheads from which jutted three-foot spikes. In the swaying howdahs on their backs nobility and captains were crowded in sea-sick anticipation.

To the left of Siraj were three divisions of 25,000 foot soldiers, richly-clad; behind them, carrying ancient muskets, were 10,000 less picturesque warriors. On the far, right flank were the mercenaries: 15,000 Pathan horsemen from the northern frontier districts, their dark-brown Mongolian faces scowling fiercely in their eagerness for battle. They were the finest cavalry in India.

In the rear, snorting under a thick coating of ochre dust, came the oxen towing cannon (fifty-two pieces of large calibre), accompanied by the blue-uniformed French artillerymen who had escaped from Chandanagar. And straggling behind lumbered the hundreds of carts and followers. The whole of India seemed to be on the move.

Siraj was in a foul mood. Since the news of the ignominious capitulation of Katwa he had hardly said a word. Not even Sareen could sweeten his disposition, though she tried hard to distract him.

'Is that my husband's division over there, my lord?' she asked, knowing that it was.

His heavy-lidded eyes stared balefully in the direction she was pointing. 'It is. And does he plan to fail me this day, Sareen?' he growled. 'I declare it is he that covets my throne,' he added, turning to her with a look of accusation. She stared fixedly out of the carriage.

'What would you have me say, my lord?' she cried helplessly. 'I wish only for your safety, yet would have no harm done to Mir Jafar.' She impulsively grasped his arm. 'You have so many warriors,

Siraj. What need have you of Mir Jafar? Return him to Murshidabad if you doubt him. There would then be no risk for him nor for Siraj-ud-daula.'

He impatiently shrugged her off. 'Were I to dismiss Mir Jafar then ten thousand of his men would follow him – and were ten thousand to go then the others would lose heart and flee after him. I would be left only with the Pathans, the Frenchmen ... and Mir Madan, my only general with courage and loyalty.'

'But Kassim would stay. *He* would be faithful,' she protested.

He sneered but made no comment. Then he asked her bluntly, 'Sareen ... will Mir Jafar betray me?'

She lowered her head and said softly, 'Were that knowledge confided to me, my lord, I should have warned you ... but first I should have urged my husband to flee from your wrath.'

He stared at her, perplexed. 'Do you then have real affection for me, Sareen?' he asked. She slowly nodded her head.

Accustomed to the submission of those near him, Siraj was astonished to discover one with genuine affection for him. It cheered him enormously. He embraced her, then stood up in the carriage, balancing himself with difficulty, and cried through the window to one of his captains, 'Move the army faster! On to Palasi! Let the Flames of the Forest be the funeral pyre of this Englishman.'

Two hundred yards away, an apprehensive Mir Jafar sat astride his horse at the head of his division. He sat with head bent and seemed lost in some gloomy reflection that made him oblivious to his surroundings. Only the horse seemed conscious of where it was going. He nervously rubbed his cheek with a sweating hand. Close behind him rode Kassim, resentful that he and his regiment had been placed under the command of his father. Often he glared jealously at the carriage where Sareen and Siraj-ud-daula reclined.

And all around them trudged the amorphous assemblage of the mightiest army in India, as the land tilted towards the mango and palas trees on the banks of the Bhagirathi where the sluggish river coiled itself into the shape of a human bowel.

39

THE THREE mounted senior officers with Clive in the lead made a thorough survey of Plassey, then rode through the unguarded gateway of the Nawab's hunting lodge. It was the only building of substance and style for miles around. Of Moghul-Moorish design, two storeys in height, wide, squat and with a flat roof, surrounded by slender columns and graceful arches, it had been used as a residence for the Nawabs of Bengal when they elected to go tiger hunting. In front of it was a courtyard, from which a broad flight of marble steps led straight down to the river. An acre of ground surrounded the whole, marked by a wall which offered but little protection.

'This will be my headquarters,' said Clive, dismounting and making his way to the roof via the outside stairway. Edmund and Eyre Coote followed him without comment: Clive had been in a withdrawn and brittle mood all day.

Major Coote, ever ready to find excuses for his commanding officer, winked solemnly at Edmund. His companion did not respond. Pre-battle nerves Edmund understood, but this grim melancholy of Clive's was becoming too permanent.

'The mango orchard, gentlemen.' Clive indicated the area with an outstretched arm. 'I would say it's half a mile long by quarter of a mile wide. It's open to the south, the river protects the west side, and on the north and east sides there is a dry ditch flanked by a mound of earth. Cover is good in the orchard itself but the primary line of defence will be the ditch.'

Eyre Coote cast a professional eye over the area indicated.

'Siraj has enough men to surround it entirely,' he murmured, thinking aloud.

'I'm aware of that, Major,' Clive said quietly. 'Hence my agreement with Mir Jafar. If he fails us we'll be trapped.'

'Even with the frigate to help?' Edmund imprudently queried.

Clive angrily grasped his arm and propelled him towards the side of the roof overlooking the river. 'Do you see a ship?' he cried, making a sweeping gesture towards the tranquil emptiness of the

Bhagirathi. 'Half my artillery is on that ship. We destroy forts to make the river safe, only to have some dolt of a captain run his craft aground.'

Later, having finished his briefing, Clive dismissed all the officers save Edmund.

'For mercy's sake, Edmund!' he cried, seizing his arm. 'Stop looking at me as if I were camel's dung. Have you no compassion? I apologise for my bad behaviour. If I do not have a friend to vent my spleen on – and to lean on – then I am lost. I need you, Edmund. Don't desert me.'

He released Edmund's arm and slumped on the low wall that fringed the roof. 'Still no news from Mir Jafar,' he said dully, after a pause. He glanced at Edmund and saw that he was squinting up at the darkening sky.

'The monsoon's ready to break,' was all Edmund said.

'Warn Mathieson about the powder barrels. "Trust in God and keep your powder dry," wasn't that what Cromwell preached?'

'Aye. And I'd better check that the rockets are protected as well,' smiled Edmund.

'Fizzy little squibs in metal tubes,' said Clive disparagingly. 'As much likely to kill our own men as the enemy.'

'I can't agree, Robert. A few rockets exploding in the middle of a cavalry charge can break up the whole effort. You yourself have seen their shock value among undisciplined soldiers.'

Clive stood up, thrust his hands into his pockets and walked back to that part of the roof overlooking the river.

'Do as you wish, Edmund,' he called over his shoulder. 'But for heaven's sake keep the damned things from landing in our own powder barrels.'

By nightfall Clive's force had been dispersed according to his orders. Eight cannon were laid side by side in the dry ditch facing north, while the remaining four were set to face east. Compared with the Nawab's fifty-three heavy calibre guns, Clive was brandishing a table-knife against a pikeman.

On the 23rd of June 1757 Robert Clive fitted his spyglass to his eye the moment the pink-striated dawn gave him light enough to see by. To the north he could just discern the grey mass of the Nawab's army. It was impressive. Drums began to beat and trumpets to sound as red-coated Britons knelt down in the dry ditch

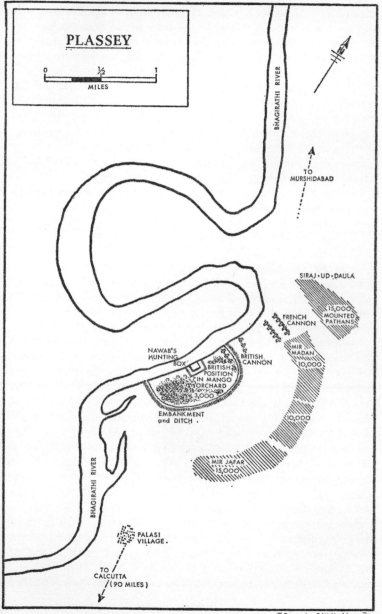

PLASSEY

0   ½   1
MILES

BHAGIRATHI RIVER

TO
MURSHIDABAD

SIRAJ·UD·DAULA

15,000
MOUNTED
PATHANS

FRENCH
CANNON

MIR
MADAN
10,000

NAWAB'S
HUNTING
BOX

BRITISH
CANNON

BRITISH
POSITION
IN MANGO
ORCHARD
3,000

EMBANKMENT
and DITCH

10,000

MIR JAFAR
15,000

BHAGIRATHI RIVER

PALASI
VILLAGE

TO
CALCUTTA
(90 MILES)

Drawn by G.W. Maddams

surrounding the orchard, loaded their muskets, or filled cannon with powder and basket-like containers of grapeshot. Behind them, camouflaged amidst the trees of the mango orchard, the sepoys in their brown 'John Company' uniforms took up positions, fitted bayonets to muskets and waited in trepidation.

Fifty thousand brown-skinned warriors marched towards that peaceful oasis of trees, fruit and flowers by the quiet Bhagirathi. Like their leader, most of them were of Turko-Islamic descent. Their ancestors, the barbaric Mongolians, had carved a bloody empire out of the greatest land mass on earth. Their descendants had swept through the frontier passes from Turkistan on to the plains of India, dismissing with ease the indolent and passive Hindu.

But the great invasion had taken place centuries before, and this warlike people had been corrupted by generations of contact with placid, indolent India. The Nawab's army was no more vital than the clumsy Hindu armies of the past. Its only strength lay in its artillery, the Pathans, and the sheer weight of numbers.

From the howdah of a war elephant Siraj directed a vast crescent of warriors around Plassey. At the southernmost tip he stationed Mir Jafar and his son with a division of fifteen thousand. The French artillery he sited at the northern end, and beyond the screen of foot soldiers he held the Pathan cavalry in reserve.

As the sun lifted clear of the horizon, heating the gun barrels to flesh-burning temperatures, the first shots were fired by the French artillery. Soon the noise became deafening as the cannon fired salvos in units of ten guns a time at ten-second intervals and continued on through the full set of fifty guns. Balls of hot metal whistled through the air to fall with resounding crumps into the mango orchard. Trees were struck and sliced in two; or they whipped backwards and forwards as they received a glancing blow. Columns of earth were flung upwards. Here and there a scream shrilled out as some unfortunate soldier was hit. After an hour the French switched to grapeshot, the forest was such an effective obstruction that the flying shards of metal found few targets.

Edmund, commanding all the British artillery, held his fire until the first regiments of the Nawab's foot soldiers started advancing towards the northern embankment. The enemy were so massed that at the first salvo they went down like scythed corn. They still came on but with less enthusiasm. The cannon fired again, and then again. The advance slowed even more, faltered and stopped. As if at a signal, the dark-skinned warriors dropped in terror to the earth as the hail of metal screeched through the sweltering air towards them.

Clive, from the rooftop of the hunting lodge, focused his telescope on the immobile columns of Mir Jafar's regiments. So far there had been neither word nor action from the senior general. With his free hand he rubbed nervously at his jaw.

Considerably shaken by the firepower of the British, and dismayed at the lack of fortitude in his troops, Siraj dithered as to whether he should use the fifteen thousand Pathan cavalry. Lacking the courage of decision, he tentatively ordered a single regiment of two thousand to make a charge.

The squat, flat-nosed, Mongoloid warriors willingly unsheathed their crescent-shaped sabres, and lustily yelling invocations to whichever gods they favoured, they spurred their horses forward. Bending low in the saddle, sabres waving in great circles about their heads, the two thousand Pathan mercenaries pounded towards the embankment on the northern side of Plassey. The sight was so stimulating that Siraj thumped fists against his thighs and made loud crowing noises in his throat.

Scores of noisily crackling rockets whizzed aloft – and dropped in the midst of the galloping Pathans. Little direct damage was done, but the effect was disastrous. The sharp explosions, the fearsome whizzing and fizzing, the long flaming tails of the squibs as they shot through the air, so terrified the horses that they reared up, unseating the warriors on their backs, and stampeded in all directions. That so major an attack should be so swiftly repulsed unnerved Siraj-ud-daula to such an extent that he screamed for his foot soldiers to retreat lest they, too, become part of the fiasco. This led to more confusion as one regiment pushed forward while other troops tried to push back.

'What is Mir Jafar doing? What is Mir Jafar doing?' he screamed when he saw that no aid was coming from that direction.

Mir Jafar sat astride his mount, sullen, withdrawn, out of danger, observing the scene from under glowering eyelids. He paid no heed to the messenger Siraj sent him. Kassim, fretting restlessly at his side, suddenly turned on his father with undisguised loathing.

'You vowed on the Koran you would aid the English,' he hissed, 'yet you hold back. You do nothing. Nothing!' He was tortured by his father's immobility – and he could do nothing.

'I also gave my oath of fealty to the Nawab on the Koran,' Mir Jafar at last replied miserably, averting his eyes.

'Then you are cursed in the sight of Allah no matter which course you take,' his son spat, jerking the reins and galloping away. Even his son's contempt failed to stir him to action. He sat immobile, brooding; and his fifteen thousand warriors remained watchful and inactive behind him.

'Mir Madan, Mir Madan! Send in Mir Madan,' cried out the now thoroughly agitated Nawab. And Mir Madan raised his sword, galloped to the head of his regiment, and led them forward.

With one accord a hundred conch shells were lifted to a hundred pairs of lips, and over the rattle of musketry and the boom of cannon, the plaintive, haunting sound made itself heard. In answer to the call a hundred drums began their throbbing beat.

As this drumming, wailing, discordant noise reached a crescendo, the Persian sword of Mir Madan levelled out and pointed at the enemy in the mango orchard. A great mass of ten thousand gaily-dressed warriors surged forward as if released from bondage. Some ineffective shooting began as those at the front excitedly discharged their weapons in their eagerness to start fighting, but most simply waved aloft their curved scimitars or spears and yelled and shouted as they ran forward.

Again the sheer congestion of numbers told against them. Muskets were as often as not discharged against their own men. Blades that swung too enthusiastically lopped off a companion's finger or hand. Many at the front found their courage seeping away and reduced their pace; the mass behind pushed harder, trampling on those ahead.

Edmund, with four cannon at his disposal, ordered grapeshot to be loaded, fully expecting the nearby Mathieson to repeat the instruction to his battery. Hearing nothing, he scrambled over the embankment and looked to where Mathieson should have been with his own artillery. There was no sign of him. Perplexed, he slid back.

'Find Captain Mathieson's battery,' he ordered a soldier. 'Tell whoever is there to load grape and alternate their fire with ours. We'll take the left flank, they the right.'

The first salvo from Edmund's guns cut four enormous gaps in the onward press of men, but before the other cannon had fired, Eyre Coote's voice rapped out commands to the light-infantry and grenadiers. Five hundred soldiers aimed their muskets and fired as one man, to be followed immediately by the shots of the sepoys who dodged from behind the mango trees to discharge their own weapons.

The effect of this triple blow on the attacking warriors was awesome. It was as if they had gone headlong into an invisible wall. A thousand men of the front ranks crumpled to the earth, staining it with their blood. Before the remainder could recover, the second battery of cannon had multiplied the carnage. The drums still beat in the distance but at a faltering tempo, and the wail of the conch shells acquired a dirge-like quality. The cries of the stricken rose above the martial sounds of drum and shell and were clearly heard even by the rearmost ranks of the Nawab's warriors.

The decisive moment came when an English soldier took careful aim with his musket and pressed the trigger – and Mir Madan, the Nawab's finest general, fell mortally wounded from his horse. At the sight of his fall a loud wail arose. The warriors paused in indecision, wavered, then started to push backwards. Volley after volley from the mango orchard and the embankment spurred them into flight.

Clive, observing all this from the hunting lodge, for the first time experienced the hope that he might yet still win – for Mir Jafar still watched silent and immobile from his position south of the crescent. If within the next hour or so he moved against the English, it would all be over. But, if he came to their aid, as arranged, the Nawab would be lost.

Clive sent urgent instructions to Eyre Coote to secure defences and make no attempt to follow the fleeing footsoldiers lest he be cut off by the Pathans.

But before the messenger arrived, Edmund blithely took it upon himself to initiate action. Elated by their success, he commanded that the cannon be dragged forward to a new position far behind the embankment where he felt he could better engage the French and bombard the reserve units of the Nawab's force. And as the guns were being moved to the new position a trembling Captain Mathieson was ordered by Edmund to follow.

Clive swore aloud when he saw the defence line ruptured by the advancing movement of the cannon.

'Tell Maskelyne to get back to his position!' he yelled at an aide. But it was to no avail. The officer was shot from his horse and the message never got through. To all effects, Eyre Coote was in sole command of the field. And Eyre Coote did not have Clive's military genius.

40

MAJOR COOTE was aghast at Edmund's reckless move. It was a basic principle of warfare not to be drawn from one's position by a suspect retreat. He looked appealingly towards the distant hunting lodge, but no advice came from that direction. He was faced with a terrible dilemma: if he were to order Maskelyne back to his original position, Siraj-ud-daula would certainly conclude that the British were retreating. This might stiffen his spine and encourage him to direct a full attack by the Pathans. Should that happen then neither rockets, grapeshot, muskets nor bayonets would prevail against fifteen thousand horsemen.

He leapt to his feet, calling to the men behind him. Scrambling through the ditch and over the embankment, he charged towards the new redoubt where Edmund was resiting his guns, followed by seventy large, hairy Highlanders swinging their broadswords and claymores in a bloodthirsty manner and howling ancient clannish battle-cries as they sped over the short stretch of ground.

From his howdah command post, Siraj-ud-daula was further disheartened by the sight of the cannons moving up. When this was followed by what seemed a major offensive by madmen in skirts, he screamed at the mahout to turn the beast around and head away as fast as he could, leaving behind the still formidable battery of artillery under the French command. The French, however, were made of sterner metal, and showed no signs of capitulating or of reducing the intensity of fire they had been keeping up since early morning.

Forty yards behind Edmund a sick-faced Captain Mathieson cowered at the bottom of a shallow depression in the redoubt. All about him ranged the Highlanders and his own men, now settling down in readiness for the counter-attack. He raised his head slightly and there was a sudden tug at his jacket, accompanied by a spitting, zipping sound. He looked down and saw to his horror that a hole had appeared in his tunic. The edges were frayed and charred by the passage of the musket ball. His hand trembled as he gingerly felt the hole. It was no more than a finger-thickness from his flesh.

His bottom lip quivered and his hand grasped a quaking jaw. Only a finger-thickness from his flesh! The narrowness of his escape all but paralysed him. He clasped both his hands to his face and sobbed. He must get away from here. He was going to be killed. No one cared. What was he doing here? They'd all be killed. His eyes glazed with terror.

His men were eyeing him strangely. Oafs! Scum! He castigated them in his mind, hating them for their dulled acceptance of their plight. Couldn't they see those hordes of barbarians? Were they blind to those curved blades? One of the men, a Sergeant Grimsby whom he knew well, a fellow with a plump face crimsoned by beer and the sun, ventured a cheerful remark.

'Soon be o'er now, Cap'n. We'll send all them 'eathen back-runnin' to Murshidabad.'

Mathieson almost jumped at the sound of the voice. 'What in Holy God's name do you know about it?' he exploded in a paroxysm of anger. 'Who gave you leave to speak?'

'Beggin' yer pardon, sir,' Grimsby returned stiffly. 'It just seemed that that bullet kinda upset yer. An' all I were ...'

'Damn you! Keep your infernal remarks to yourself.'

Grimsby held his tongue, but glared angrily.

Siraj somehow persuaded another regiment to go into the attack. Again the drums and the conch shells; again the thousands of warriors waving their swords and spears. And though some of this was bluff, it was still an awesome sight to those in the redoubt and the orchard. In the shallow depression behind the embankment, three hundred red-coats checked their muskets and tested their swords. The sepoys fixed bayonets. Soon the men could see brown-skinned attackers with twisted conches to their lips, blowing as though their lungs would burst.

Mathieson looked up – and all but reeled back at the sight. All around him, almost to the horizon, the earth seemed filled with warriors carrying weapons of every description. The dust kicked up by their feet rose high in flat-topped clouds. His nerve snapped. In a state of hysteria he scrambled to his feet.

'Run. Run ... They're coming!' he screeched, and he started to run back to the orchard. The image of the fleeing figure caught Edmund's eye. He turned and gaped. Sergeant Grimsby's eyes shot open.

'Come back! ... Come back!' he shouted after the fleeing officer, but Mathieson kept on running. Grimsby whirled round. His musket came up to his shoulder. 'Come back, you bastard, or I'll shoot!' he cried at the top of his voice. But Mathieson was insensible to anything save the urge to get far away from those warriors.

Grimsby fired. Flame shot out of the muzzle. Ninety yards away a ball of metal struck Captain Mathieson in the back and flung him forward. He sprawled to the ground, his superbly tailored jacket rapidly staining at the back. He raised his head slightly, an expression of disbelief on his face; then he flopped back and was still.

As Mathieson died, Clive caught sight of the frigate rounding the bend in the river. Its guns were run out and the first salvo struck into the massed thousands of the Nawab's army. Half of the French battery immediately ranged on the new threat from the river and a long-range duel commenced.

Edmund was so taken aback by Mathieson's execution that at first he could hardly comprehend it. And when he did, his impulse was to rush over and strike with his sword the infamous creature who had dared commit such an act. He clawed his way up the slight mound of earth, got to his feet – and was struck in the face.

There was no pain, yet he felt the globule of blood trickling down his cheek. His hand shook as he lifted it to touch the area where he had been hit. He felt the skin, then looked at his fingers.

It was water!

He raised his head and was struck again, and again. The drops of water were so large that they almost stung when they hit. 'The rains!' he cried, Sergeant Grimsby momentarily forgotten. 'Cover the powder and the guns!'

The cry was taken up. Artillerymen had tarpaulins at hand and it took only a moment to cover the barrels of powder and the gun breeches. The foot soldiers – in accordance with their training – took measures to keep dry their muskets and powder horn.

With the monsoon downpour came further disaster for the Nawab. There were only one skilled French artilleryman and seven Muslims to each of the fifty or so cannon. Confused by the language barrier, and hampered by the fact that the tarpaulins were on ox-wagons half a mile away, the Frenchmen stood little chance of protecting their guns. The splendid battery was put out of action within the first two minutes of the rainstorm. The barrels of gunpowder became containers of black ooze. The fire-holes in the gun breeches ejected little streams of rain-water, and the warriors with muskets simply wrapped their robes tighter around their bodies and forgot about their powder horns.

Still Mir Jafar watched and waited on the sidelines. Shrinking from an overt break with his master and a covert alliance with Clive, he adhered to his neutral position at a time when neutrality was the more loathsome form of betrayal.

Clive, soaked with rain, still stood on the roof of the Palasi hunting box, directing his forces with consummate skill by a relay of messengers. He decided the moment had come to take the offensive. Major Eyre Coote acknowledged the order. Edmund managed to send a signal rocket into the air.

Rising from the earth like several hundred spectres on Judgment Day, British and sepoy soldiers clambered over the embankment, levelled their muskets and bayonets, and charged. Across the churned-up muddy ground they plunged, leaping over the now saturated corpses of warriors, towards the dark wall of the Nawab's army. The combined effect of the barrage from the warship, the rain, the fire from Clive's cannon, the musketry of the British forces, Edmund's rockets, the treachery of Mir Jafar, the death of Mir Madan, had by this time completely demoralised the Nawab and his men.

Siraj climbed down from the elephant, rushed back to where his concubine was anxiously awaiting him, and leapt into the coach.

'We are lost, Sareen. We are lost!' He turned his haunted eyes upon her, and speechlessly stretched out his hands. She grasped them and held them to her breasts as if to give him comfort.

'We must go ... go my lord, now,' she urged with quiet decision.

The team of horses were turned; the war elephants were turned;

the army was turned; and the whole great mass lumbered back to Murshidabad.

There was much disaffection among the warriors. Already the blame had been affixed to the Nawab. They began to hiss and spit on the ground when his carriage passed, and only the presence of his personal bodyguard deterred them from outright attack.

'I am finished, Sareen,' he said quietly, on the second day of the retreat. 'I can call no more on the loyalty of my people. I am deposed. My throne is lost.' He touched her arm in strange affection and looked into her face. 'There will be a new Nawab, and you must go far from me, Sareen. For I will be killed when I am caught – and any who are with me. Go, my Sareen, go, and may Allah go with you.'

She returned his gaze with quiet compassion, making her decision even as she spoke. 'I will go only with you, my lord. If they who seek your throne intend you harm then I am ready to share your fate. If you are to die, then I must too. But speak not of dying while yet you have life. Bengal is large, and there are places other than Bengal in which we may find shelter.'

'Cease firing!' called out Eyre Coote, then he stood up and, under a flag of truce, trudged through the mud to the French redoubt. 'We have won this day,' he shouted to the listening Frenchmen. 'The Nawab is defeated. We offer you your lives, with honour, if you surrender.'

'What is to be done with us if we agree, Major?' an officer shouted back. Eyre Coote thought for a moment, and then took responsibility for his own promise.

'You may go where you wish or return with us to Calcutta – and from there you will be sent back to France if that is your desire.'

The silence that greeted this offer lasted no more than three minutes, after which a tall man in the uniform of the French Berchény Hussars climbed out and strode over to Major Coote. He saluted and offered up his sword.

41

THIS AMAZING victory opened a new page in history. As Clive's employer, the Honourable East India Company found itself feudal master of Bengal. The grocer had become Lord Mayor and Chief of Police and discovered that he wielded power equal to that of any Indian prince. The knowledge made him light-headed. He ruled as best he knew how, displaying compassion and a sense of justice, but some of the former grocer's assistants showed themselves unwilling to keep their hands out of the pockets of those they pretended to serve.

But as darkness fell on that day of achievement only Clive sensed something of what was to come.

'How many casualties did we suffer, Edmund?' he asked suddenly, during the celebration at the hunting box.

Edmund told him. 'But only four killed in the last attack ... plus Captain Mathieson,' he added heavily, looking squarely at his chief. Clive gave a slow deliberate nod.

Edmund put his glass on the table, hesitated a moment, then blurted out, 'Regarding that sergeant, Robert ...'

'Grimsby? The chap who got us over the wall at Madras, wasn't he?' Clive interrupted, with affected disinterest.

'That's the fellow. It's quite clear that he deliberately mur ...'

'Major Maskelyne,' Clive said abruptly, keeping his eyes fixed on the glass in his hand. 'In the heat of battle many things are done, the wisdom of which may only be questioned afterwards.' Every man in the room was silent, listening intently. 'As commander of the British forces in Bengal, I am content to declare that all those who fought this day with me, and who gave their blood, did so heroically.'

His gaze swept round the room, daring any man to challenge him. No one did. Then he looked straight at Edmund. 'If you harbour thoughts of retribution against any person whatsoever, dismiss them lest you do a graver injustice.'

Edmund, in a turmoil of conflicting emotions, prudently remained silent. General conversation flowed once more and he was left to his own thoughts. Retribution, Clive had said. But wasn't he using Grimsby as an excuse for his own guilt at finding his rival removed? Maybe. Yet the circumstances of Mathieson's death were criminal. For a soldier to slay his officer was the most heinous of acts – and yet, for an officer to display cowardice, to desert his post in the midst of battle ...

His head ached. Could he pretend remorse that his rival was dead? How contemptible to exult over the death of a brother officer. How should he tell Anna of Mathieson's death? Must he put on a despicable mask of grief?

Anna! Oh dear God, how could he tell her?

'Are you with me, Edmund?' Clive sounded pained. 'Edmund!' He came to with a jolt and discovered that he and Clive were the only people in the room.

'I disturbed your thoughts. I'm sorry,' apologised Clive. 'If you wish, I'll break the news to Anna myself,' he went on, to Edmund's surprise.

Edmund smiled his thanks but shook his head. The two men looked at each other for a moment, and then Clive, deciding his friend had no wish to talk on the subject, went on to a matter that concerned not only him but Bengal. He extracted a document from a leather case and handed it to Edmund.

'Read it. It's a sample of the missives the Council deign to send me – for my guidance,' he said blandly. Edmund's eyebrows inched up as he went through the letter paragraph by paragraph.

'Are they all as ... as ambiguous as this?' he asked.

'All of them,' Clive replied harshly. 'Each one so worded that however I may serve my commission and to what end, I may be reprimanded or commended according to the Council's whim. It is too much.'

He stalked over to a small table, took from his case a blank sheet of parchment, uncorked an ink-horn and dipped in a quill. 'Help yourself to the brandy,' he said over his shoulder.

A few minutes later he put his signature to the bottom of the document, burned a small quantity of sealing wax near his name, then pressed his ring into it. He hastily scanned what he had written, then tossed the paper to Edmund.

Edmund read it with greater dismay than he had read the letter from the Council.

'It's not lawful,' he protested. 'You can't do it, Robert. "I, Robert Clive, General, hereby declare Bengal to be in a state ... do take upon myself all rights and authority to make and administer laws according to the needs ... without sanction or permission of Council ..." '

Edmund took a large gulp of brandy and flopped into a chair. 'There is no legality ...' he began.

Clive laughed sardonically. 'Legality! Did the illustrious Members of Council prate the law in their sanctuary whilst fifty thousand heathen were planning to remove our heads? What long clauses did they spout whilst the Nawab took Calcutta and thrust you and a hundred others into the Black Hole? They powdered their wigs and shook admonitory fingers at Siraj, but they unsheathed no swords to defend Fort William.' His fist crashed on to the table, upsetting the ink-horn. 'No! They scuttled off to the boats to save their own skins – and with not a thought nor a prayer for the garrison they abandoned. Damnation to them! From this moment, Edmund, I, Robert Clive, will be the law and the power in Bengal. I shall answer only to the directors in England, or to my sovereign.'

Edmund wisely kept silent. It would be futile to argue with Clive in his present temper.

'Well?' Clive demanded. 'Have you no comment?'

Edmund squinted up at him. 'Frankly, Robert, if you seek my approval I cannot give it. If you want my loyalty and support, you shall have it – but only because I've a ridiculous faith in you, though I can't in all honesty see how it's justified by your proposal. According to my experience martial law is often used simply as a means to suppress opposition to dubious schemes. I agree about the Council ...'

'Oh, for the sake of Christ, Edmund! Stop preaching at me!' Clive cried, and at once apologised and topped up Edmund's glass.

Edmund adopted a cooler tone. 'I will argue no more with you, Robert. You must do as you see fit without constantly demanding my accord. Now, to change the subject, tell me your intentions regarding Mir Jafar.'

Clive was tempted to take issue with Edmund, but he thought better of it. There was a limit to how far Edmund could be pushed. Apart from that, Clive was loath to risk a breach in their friendship.

'He'll be here any moment,' he said, 'and I shall leave him in no doubt as to my opinion of his knavery.'

'Do you think he'll still expect your support for the throne – presuming that Siraj-ud-daula is ready to vacate it?'

'Siraj-ud-daula is finished,' Clive rejoined dismissively, and would have said more had not Mir Jafar and his son at that moment arrived.

Clive stood at the far end of the room, feet astride, hands clasped behind his back, head thrust forward aggressively. 'Show their highnesses in,' he commanded his aide.

Mir Kassim, a purple turban round his head, his robes still damp with rain, entered the room first. He looked round cautiously, casting about for any scent of danger, and only then offered Clive a casual salaam. Clive did not reciprocate the courtesy. When at last Mir Jafar appeared, the son immediately took his place behind 'him – almost as if he expected an assassination attempt on his father.

The obeisance Mir Jafar paid to Clive was excessive and commensurate with his sense of guilt. With an extravagant gesture he drew from his crimson sash a curved Arabic dagger in its sheath and laid it on the table. The hilt of the knife was thickly encrusted with gemstones.

'Accept this small gift, my lord Clive, as a symbol of the respect I bear for India's greatest soldier,' he declared unctuously. Clive took a pace towards the table and flicked the dagger so that it spun around several times.

'I would have placed more value on ten thousand swords, Mir Jafar, than this bauble you now offer.'

The nobleman gave a faintly deprecating smile and tilted his head as if at a humorous sally, then held out his arm towards his son.

'The treaty, Kassim.'

The scroll of white parchment was disdainfully slapped into his hand. He was about to present it to Clive, when the latter cried indignantly, 'Treaty! You dare speak of a treaty! I would rather a jackal sat on the throne of Bengal than a treacherous coward like you, Mir Jafar!'

The would-be Nawab blanched at the insult, and in a rage clutched at the hilt of his curved sword. Kassim clasped a hand over that of his father. It was clear that his father was only too happy to be restrained.

'Sahib Clive will not say these things – will not speak as he does,' Mir Jafar cried, shaking off Kassim's hand and adopting a threatening posture.

'The Sahib Clive will give tongue any way he chooses to that which he knows to be true,' Clive rapped back, taking a pace forward and standing challengingly within easy reach of Mir Jafar's sword. 'And, if once more you dare dispute my right, I shall straightway hang you from the nearest palas tree and bury your corpse in the skin of a pig, as a just reward for your craven perfidy.'

Mir Jafar swallowed the insult. Angry and deeply humiliated though he was – especially by the presence of his son – he was astute enough to judge that the crisis point had passed: the situation had been defused by Clive's outburst. In an astonishingly quick turnabout, his expression relaxed and he presented to the still simmering Englishman a dignified façade.

'If we are to work in harmony, my lord Clive, there must be respect between us,' he declared stiffly, conscious that his son was now staring out of the window, disassociating himself from whatever his father might say or do.

'Respect, Mir Jafar,' Clive sneered. 'Respect must be earned. I declare in all honesty that I would far rather have one such as Mir Madan on the throne of Bengal. Alas, he died in the ignoble cause of his Nawab.' He turned his back on the nobleman and said casually, 'I am left with no other choice.'

Returning to his seat by the table, he slumped into it, and, in a manner suggesting he was casting a coin to a beggar, said, 'I hereby appoint you, Mir Jafar, Nawab of Bengal.'

Mir Jafar gathered around him the tatters of his dignity and bowed, but as he made his way to the door he was stopped by the chilling voice of Clive.

'Note well the clauses of the treaty, and hear me now, Mir Jafar, that if there be default in any one, I shall raze Murshidabad so that one stone shall not sit atop of another.'

Kassim rounded on Clive, but his father laid hands on him and hustled him out of the door, muttering as he did so, 'If you must draw your sword, then do so against Siraj-ud-daula. Remember, Sareen is still captive and he may use her as hostage.'

42

LEAVING HIS army to follow at its own pace, Siraj and
Sareen took to horses. Even these were not fast enough for the
anxious Nawab. He had no illusions regarding his fate should
Clive or Mir Jafar reach Murshidabad first, and in his imagination
he saw the great Englishman disgorging troops into his palace.

Surrounded by a strong escort of Pathans sufficient in number
to discourage any overt acts of rebellion in the palace, he finally
entered the gates of the capital. Bad news flies swifter than good,
and his welcome in Murshidabad was less than warm. A carrier of
plague might have been better received. Peasants in the streets
turned their backs on him and remembered old grudges; few guards
paid him obeisance, and those only because of his Pathan escort;
and though the noblemen in the palace bent their knee, he found
later that they shirked the idea of taking up arms against either
Clive or Mir Jafar.

Siraj-ud-daula therefore abandoned the throne of Bengal.

Protected by his Pathans, he loaded four coaches with all the
treasure he could lay his hands on, and with a retinue of concu-
bines, servants and eunuchs, bid farewell to Murshidabad and
headed for some unknown destination in the north where he hoped
to find sanctuary.

Once Murshidabad had been left far behind, Siraj, with a
frightening lack of foresight, paid in full the wages of the Pathans.
It was the last he saw of them. Saddle-bags jingling with gold coin,
the squat, Mongolian-faced warriors saluted their honest employer
and galloped to their own land to dissipate their earnings. They
left Siraj-ud-daula with not one warrior to guard him.

'We must rest awhile, my lord,' Sareen begged him, when they
had travelled over thirty miles. She indicated a large building on
the crest of the hill some distance away. 'That should be adequate
enough to accommodate us, and I know the ladies are exhausted
by the journey.'

Her decision to flee with him had been irrational. She would
probably never see Kassim again, and though she grieved in silence,

it did not sway her from her sense of loyalty, and responsibility, for Siraj. She studied him out of the corner of her eye. He was such a child at times. While seething at his stupidity in paying off 'the Pathans so soon; worrying over the loss of his throne, his palace, his capital, his treasury, Bengal itself, he was clutching her 'hand for comfort and reassurance. It never occurred to him that he had earned such retribution.

'It would be wiser, my lord, for you to discard your rich clothes and wear those of a poorer man lest you be identified as the Nawab,' Sareen quietly suggested, and, when he made no answer, she proceeded to undress him herself. From one of the coachmen she procured garments that made Siraj squirm with shame. But he donned them at her insistence.

When the coaches pulled into the large inn yard and Siraj, his bones aching from the bouncing and the lurching, climbed down from his coach, the innkeeper was not taken in for a moment. When a traveller with four coaches and such a retinue arrives even the most doltish of innkeepers must conclude the visitor to be of rank and substance, whatever his dress.

Siraj imperiously waved aside one of the servants who had come forward to assist him, took hold of Sareen, and swept by the cringing innkeeper, saying over his shoulder to the chief eunuch, 'Pay him.'

The eunuch counted out several gold coins and dropped them into the trembling hand of the innkeeper. Sareen noted the innkeeper's nervousness and took a close look at his bent head, then 'hastened after Siraj. She was puzzled. She did not recognise the fellow, yet something about him disturbed her. He was too warrior-like for a simple keeper of lodgings.

While the party were eating, the innkeeper, unnerved by his suspicion as to the guest's identity, slipped out the back way and engaged in conversation with one of the eunuchs attending to the horses. The slave told the truth, and told it with pride. Why should he do otherwise?

The innkeeper's worst fears were confirmed. He would have given back all their gold and more besides to see the visitors ride from his inn. But the important visitor had no intention of leaving, despite Sareen's protest that they should be on their way as soon as they had rested.

, 'We are safe, my Sareen. It is a way rarely used. Perhaps to-morrow we shall go, or the day after,' he replied, contentedly spooning food into his mouth.

'Did you see the innkeeper, my lord?' she asked cautiously, not at all reassured. He shook his head vigorously, then luxuriously arched his back as if to say, 'Would you expect a Nawab of Bengal to notice a common innkeeper?'

'Something about his face disturbs me.'

'Well, should I chop off his head?' Siraj teased her, but she did not laugh with him. When the empty bowls were removed and others put on the table, Sareen scrutinised the warrior-like face, and was at once conscious that he was doing his best to avoid her stare.

'I am ill at ease, my lord,' Sareen murmured some hours later as she sat on the wide ledge of the window in the best bedroom.

Siraj yawned, screwed up his eyes, and said plaintively, 'It's the middle of the night, Sareen. The day has been long and I must sleep.'

She continued to peer through the window, but saw nothing save the slouching figures of two eunuchs appointed to stand guard, their chins drooped to their chests as they dozed in the pale light of a crescent moon.

'You must sleep too, Sareen. I swear on my oath that we shall resume our journey tomorrow. Is that enough for you?' he called across to her in mild irritation. She would not be comforted. The innkeeper's face jangled deep in some memory and all her instincts alerted her to danger. She persisted in talking, to Siraj's greater annoyance.

'This man, my lord, I feel he knows you. And I think that he would do you harm were he not so timid.'

Siraj propped himself up; pounded a cushion behind his head in vexation at being kept awake.

'Who in Bengal does not know their rightful Nawab?' he countered. 'And what is this dog to me? Such a man could do me no harm. When my eye lights on him he grovels to his knees. Must you see spirits in every shadow, Sareen?'

'You will be hunted and killed, my lord. Mir Jafar cannot allow Siraj-ud-daula to be a threat to his ambitions. He will take no rest until he has seen your body in the grave,' she pleaded.

Siraj, reluctantly bidding farewell to sleep, sighed extravagantly.

'So what would you have me do?'

In answer, she stole across to him, knelt by his side and put her hand on his forearm. 'Let us leave now, *now*, my lord. I have a premonition, a stirring inside me that warns of evil. Rouse the servants; take the coaches. By morning we could be far away. I fear this place, Siraj. Please, let us go ... wait not one minute longer ... please, my lord.' She bent her head forward and he felt her tears wet his chest.

With great tenderness he slipped an arm around her neck, forcing her head to rest against his face, and he fondled the lobe of her left ear with his ringed fingers. In a coaxing tone he said, 'Would you have me as timid as a Ganges fish, Sareen? Shooting away frantically at the first tiny stone that disturbs the surface of the water? Mir Jafar could not yet have reached Murshidabad, and when he does he will spend much time rushing through all the rooms of the palace to finger with avarice all the treasures we have left behind. But one treasure will be denied him.' He put his hand under her chin, lifted up her head and pressed his lips against her damp cheeks. 'Sareen, know you this always. I have taken many women – but only to you have I given my heart.'

Even as he was saying this, the innkeeper was quietly saddling a horse in the barn some distance from the house.

43

THE FRIGATE, its guns run out as a precaution, tied up at the quay in Murshidabad some three hours after Mir Jafar's triumphant entry into the capital. On the poop deck, Clive was discussing his own entrance. Edmund, Eyre Coote and the captain were set against such a provocative step until the new Nawab had established his suzerainty and could guarantee their safety.

'You can see for yourself,' the captain remonstrated, waving his arm shorewards where mobs of citizens were frenziedly rushing about.

'Give me two score of marines and I shall present you with Murshidabad itself,' said Eyre Coote facetiously.

'Give me two thousand and I'll take India,' Clive retorted with a grin.

An hour later, escorted by a squad of marines, Clive arrived at the palace. Mir Jafar greeted him effusively. The new Nawab was so impassioned with the success of his entry into the capital that he stuttered as he told Clive the news of Siraj-ud-daula.

'At first Sombrer, the Nawab's executioner, refused to believe it when the innkeeper arrived, but he called one of the guards who knew the fellow and he assured him that the innkeeper was indeed one of the prison guards whom my son, Kassim, had bribed to set free the Major Maskelyne when Siraj caused him to be brought to Murshidabad. And he knew that by coming here he would be rewarded – or at least pardoned – by telling where Siraj-ud-daula was hiding. The people have greeted me with great joy and the noblemen have given me their fealty as the new Nawab, and I doubt . . .'

'What have you done about Siraj-ud-daula?' Clive cut across his excited babblings.

'Done? I commanded Sombrer to take a party of guards and bring him back – but his head would suffice if Siraj resisted. And then I told my son a little later, and he immediately sprang on his horse and took off after the guards – no doubt to be present at the kill, for he owns to a vendetta with Siraj-ud-daula.'

Clive's face hardened. 'Your highness, I suggest you immediately send after this executioner and command him to stay his hand. The killing of Siraj-ud-daula is not to be tolerated.'

Mir Jafar smiled soothingly. He spread his hands apologetically, saying that the fate of the former Nawab was now in the merciful hands of Allah – and adding that he would indeed despatch a messenger though he was sure he would be too late.

Clive submitted the Muslim nobleman to a close scrutiny while he was speaking. Mir Jafar appeared too anxious to be friendly.

'There is something else you wish to tell me, your highness?'

The new Nawab pondered awhile, prevaricated, and finally got to the nub of the matter.

'The treasury is *empty*?' exclaimed the victor of Plassey.

'Of the forty millions, yes, your excellency. There never was such a sum as you claimed. And though I am told Siraj took with him four coaches filled with rich goods, there was little gold coin.'

'Then I shall see for myself,' snapped Clive, rudely pushing past and summoning his men to make a search.

Just as the sun tipped the horizon, Sombrer, with thirty men, surrounded the inn. The servants and eunuchs were brushed aside and as Sareen, awakened at the noise, sat up in bed, Sombrer burst into the room with six armed men.

'Sombrer!' she cried, recognising the state executioner immediately. 'Know you not your own Nawab, Siraj-ud-daula?' she exclaimed, in an attempt to bluff out the situation, confronting him in her nakedness before she snatched up a thin gown. Sombrer wavered, uncertain. He had encountered no difficulty in switching his loyalties from one Nawab to the other, but Sareen was a different problem altogether. She was the favourite of Mir Kassim, *and* the wife of Mir Jafar. The situation called for extreme caution.

He respectfully salaamed. 'It is for Siraj-ud-daula we have come, Sahiba. We intend you no harm. You will please go outside to my men.' He put out an arm to move her gently aside, but she stood firm. Sombrer looked over her shoulder to where Siraj was getting out of bed. Not three yards from him the ex-Nawab's sword lay over a chair.

Siraj drew himself up, strangely dignified despite the fact that he was naked. Former master and executioner looked at each other. Sombrer's expression, and the drawn blades of the men with him, left Siraj in no doubt as to why they had come. He glanced swiftly to where his own sword lay. It seemed a long way away.

'You may not touch him. Mir Jafar would have you executed if you laid a finger on the Nawab of Bengal,' Sareen screamed.

'Mir Jafar himself ordered it, Sahiba. *Jaayee!*' he suddenly yelled, sweeping Sareen to one side as Siraj sprang for his sword. 'Kill him! Kill him!' he shouted over his shoulder as he struggled with the screaming woman. 'Siraj! Siraj! ... Siraj!' she cried out, almost demented.

The six men pushed past, but halted warily at the sight of Siraj half-crouching naked, sword in hand. The room was too small for a concerted attack by all six. Two men leapt on to the bed and fell on the ex-Nawab. His blade sliced upwards and a sword clattered to the ground, a hand and forearm still attached to it; another assailant staggered back with a gaping wound in his neck, and a third collapsed screaming to the ground, disembowelled. But three others were upon Siraj in an instant. He fought them frenziedly. A sword tip laid open his chest, another hacked at his thigh and a third caught him across the face. As Siraj-ud-daula passed out of life he gave a long piercing cry in which the name of Sareen was heard. Still the curved blades rose and fell, hacking and slicing, until the bloody thing that remained was barely recognisable as a human being.

Kassim arrived in a lather of sweat, dismounted and rushed inside. He was too late. It was all over.

'Kassim! Stop them!' Sareen beseeched him in a frenzy of horrified grief. Sombrer dropped to his knees, pleading that he had obeyed his master's command and now awaited further instructions. Kassim brutally pushed him aside, flung his arms around Sareen and tried to calm her. He led her to her coach, commanded two maidservants to attend her, and returned to the inn.

He entered the bedroom, and recoiled at the sight that met his eyes. Even the ceiling had great splashes of blood smeared across it. One man crouched gasping in a corner; two others were moaning; yet another was unconscious and possessed only one arm; two were dead.

'Merciful Allah!' Kassim breathed, almost vomiting at the sight of the Nawab. All his hatred was swept away by the ignominious savagery of Siraj's assassination. He felt a strange emptiness inside him. Images of earlier years tugged at his memory, and as he looked down at the obscene heap of flesh an emotion verging on compassion welled up in him. Forcing himself to go closer, he picked up Siraj's garments, and from them something fell to the floor with a tinkling sound. It was the trinket, the golden Koran, that Siraj had taken from him so many years before. Holding it in the palm of his hand he gazed at it speculatively and sadly recalled the incident as if it had been the day before. He knelt by the brutalised body of his childhood companion and reverently fitted the trinket around its neck. That done he strode from the room, saying harshly to Sombrer as he passed, 'Take the body of His Exalted Highness to Murshidabad. Treat it with all honour. There he shall receive a funeral worthy of a prince of Bengal.'

Several days later the sailors cast off the ropes, and as the frigate slowly angled away from the crude pier in the three-knot current, a few square-rigged sails billowed in the freshening breeze.

Standing with Edmund in the stern of the ship, Clive silently watched as Murshidabad slowly vanished in the scorching haze. With a whiff of nostalgia he was reminded of when he had sailed with his new bride to England.

'I'll have to go again soon, Edmund,' he murmured, speaking his thoughts aloud.

'To Murshidabad?'

'By all saints, no!' he exclaimed with mock horror. 'This past week has stuffed my belly, if not my purse, with Muslim hospitality.'

'Aye, they're a barbaric people,' Edmund replied, thinking of Siraj-ud-daula's murder. Clive shrugged. Though at the time he, too, had been repelled by the news, his mind had been preoccupied with the phantom treasury. Two million had been unearthed – not the forty million rumoured.

'Three millions was the amount agreed on in the treaty – and three millions I insist we have. He has two years to make good his promise.'

Edmund loosened the button of his collar. Despite the river breeze the heat was still overpowering. 'I was engaged in conversation with Mir Kassim and Sareen when Omichand came to see you, and you haven't told me what happened.'

'That blackmailer! He's been skulking in Murshidabad ever since he tried his tricks with us. After the formal installation of Mir Jafar the impudent fellow brazenly made his appearance. Slipped into the audience chamber in that oily, obsequious way of his, made his protestations of obedience and loyalty to the Nawab – his fat belly wobbling with excitement at the thought of the millions guaranteed him under the treaty – and then made his claim.'

'And?'

'Mir Jafar's eyes nearly popped from his head. "What claim?" he screamed. I stood back, laughing to myself, and waited. Omichand wailed that he'd seen the treaty himself and that his claim had been formally entered on it. He'd seen the signature. Anyway, to be brief, Mir Jafar produced the real treaty and thrust it under Omichand's nose.'

Clive chuckled at the recollection. 'The fat swindler near collapsed. He shouted that the treaty he'd seen was on *red* parchment and that *that* was the genuine one, and that it clearly stated his claim – which indeed it did. By this time Mir Jafar was thoroughly exasperated, first by our own claim and then this ... it was too much. He struck him across the face and would have had him flogged had I not stayed his hand.'

'And so he's gone. The last of Omichand, eh?'

'Yes, he's gone. The Nawab gave him two days to leave Bengal.'

Edmund leaned his hands on the ship's taffrail and stared out over the hot landscape. The sails rustled and billowed above him and the timbers of the frigate groaned and creaked in the gentle swell of the wide river.

'Still, Robert, the red treaty was a fraud, even though I was the one to suggest it. Let's hope the news of it never leaks out. Think what your friend Dashwood could do with such a tasty morsel.' He struck a pose. 'The eminent Robert Clive coerces Calcutta Council into being party to a fraudulent treaty.'

44

'MAKE WAY for His Excellency the Sahib Major Maskelyne, a hero of Palasi; make way for His Excellency the Sahib Major 'Maskelyne, hero of Palasi; make way for His Excellency ...' The hurcurrahs conveying Edmund's palanquin shouted out his titles and achievements in a dull monotone as they carried him through the streets. There was nothing he could do about it without offending the status-conscious hurcurrahs. Though he wished they wouldn't mangle his name to 'Sahbmajmasslin'.

He chuckled at the recollection of their reception in Calcutta. The Council had turned out in force to welcome the victor of Plassey – prudently disguising for the time being their outrage at Clive's assumption of dictatorial powers. The adoration of the populace was sufficient to warn the Council against any confrontation, and so good-will and glacial smiles became the order of the day.

However, when Clive later made his appearance in the Council Chamber and with studied nonchalance told the councillors of the gifts he had brought, some of the good-will became genuine.

'From the Nawab of Bengal I have exacted certain compensations on your behalf,' he told them, waving a document in his hands as if he himself had no interest in its contents. 'For the army and the navy I have claimed four hundred thousand pounds. For damages to the city, one million pounds. For each member of this Council there will be a sum of money varying according to the individual's status from fifty to eighty thousand pounds.' The members gasped. 'And for each of the six members of the Select Committee there will be a further one hundred and fifty thousand pounds.'

At that point Clive was obliged to stop, so great was the uproar. Three members fainted. Only Warren Hastings – now a senior member of the Select Committee – preserved his calm.

'And what, if I may be permitted to ask, did the noble Clive reserve for himself?' he blandly asked in a voice loud enough for all to hear.

Clive tossed the document to one side and fixed the questioner with a scornful look. 'If the Member concerned desires to compare the fortune heaped on him whilst safe in Calcutta with that acquired by myself after facing thirty thousand of Siraj-ud-daula's warriors, then I shall grant him the information,' he said scathingly. 'Two hundred and thirty-four thousand pounds – no more, no less than any member of the Select Committee.'

Warren Hastings rose to his feet and bowed mockingly. 'Excluding the *jagir*, of course, your Excellency?'

Clive's face hardened. 'The estate was a personal gift to me from the Nawab – a gift worthy and fitting for the office I have assumed in the Carnatic and in Bengal,' he snapped, and he stalked out of the chamber.

Edmund rested his elbow on the window frame of the lurching palanquin. The shindig in the Council was nothing compared to his meeting with Anna. To bring bad news was a sufficient ordeal without having to lie about the manner of it. And lie he did.

When she learned of Mathieson's death, she collapsed to the floor in a faint. The flood of tears he had been prepared for. But during the weeks that followed, the tragedy of Mathieson's death consumed her very being. Only at the worst period in the Black Hole had she been so ready to give up life itself. Though he tried, in his pitifully bumbling way, to assuage the sharpness of her anguish, he met with little success.

He sent for a physician, but apart from attaching a few leeches to her arm and recommending a pipe of opium – which she refused – the doctor could offer no further advice than tenderness and understanding on Edmund's part until she should recover. This he certainly gave, to such an extent that he himself felt emotionally drained.

The palanquin halted inside the gates of Miss Wilkinson's residence. An hour later Edmund gave Jasmine's nude bottom an affectionate slap as she knelt to buckle on his shoes. Petal stood near him, pouring him a cup of tea. She looked scarcely a week older than the first day he had met her.

'Isn't it time you were married, Edmund?' she asked diffidently, noting a single grey hair near his temple. He squinted up at her and mouthed a kiss in her direction.

'One day, perhaps,' he rejoined, offhand, spluttering a little as the hot liquid burned his lip. Petal curled up at his feet and rested her arms on his knees.

'Listen, Edmund. I've known you for a long time now, and you know how fond I am of you,' she began, in a familiar preliminary. His eyes glazed. He could almost repeat the words of the lecture that was about to come. 'I accept that Anna was in love with that fellow, Mathieson, but really, Edmund, it's been two years since Plassey, and she goes on as if he were buried only yesterday. It's unnatural. And just look what it's doing to you!'

Two years. Indeed, it had been. Two years of visiting, sometimes four or five times a week. Each visit conforming to a fixed pattern: the greeting, the platonic kiss, the afternoon tea (or dinner), the sighs, the inevitable discussion of Mathieson's virtues, the detailing of how he had died so valiantly, and then the tears, during which she referred to Edmund as her 'dear, dearest friend'. On exceptional occasions she even compared his own sterling qualities to those of her 'near-betrothed'.

Edmund loyally matched her praises of Mathieson, for he would not have her disillusioned, but there were times when the unctuous words he felt obliged to utter stuck in his throat.

Of late, due mainly to Petal Wilkinson's high-flown sermons, he had begun to re-examine his relationship. Not, he told himself firmly, that he doubted Anna's sincerity. But there were times when he suspected that dearest Anna was indulging herself and obtaining a certain perverse gratification from the act of grief itself.

'It's quite ridiculous!' Petal's voice cut across his thoughts. 'She can't wrap her legs around a memory and neither can she make love to a wraith.'

'You've no idea of what Anna felt about Mathieson,' he protested stoutly, evading her arch look.

'And so you come here when you could be doing it with Anna – as a lawful wife if she were sensible enough,' she returned caustically, adding gently, 'Not that I mind your coming, you know that well enough, but it's wrong for somebody like you. Don't think we don't know that when you're lying with Lotus or Jasmine or me, in your mind you're really having it with Anna!' she teased him.

The next day, Edmund paid a visit to his sister. He found her in a bad mood though she tried hard to dismiss it for his benefit.

'It's the banquet we're giving,' she eventually confessed. 'The Plassey anniversary.'

'Jolly good idea, Margaret, so why the gloom?' Edmund returned, picking up his three-year-old nephew and bouncing him on his knee.

'You know what Calcutta banquets are like,' said Margaret, with a knowing look. 'But Robert insists. Probably he's right, Plassey deserves to be celebrated,' she went on dully. 'The news from London was quite gratifying. The newspapers have gone quite hysterical about it, and the Company shares went up a full ten per cent. Even King George sent Robert a letter of commendation and rather hinted about a peerage that awaits him when he returns to England.'

'Then, for heaven's sake, Meg, what are you so solemn about?' Edmund exclaimed, hoisting the squealing child into the air.

'Edmund dear, do put him down. He's just had his lunch and he'll be sick if you keep on.' Margaret frowned, touching a bell-pull to summon the infant's nannie.

'And where's Robert this morning, Meg?' Edmund asked, as he handed over the child reluctantly. Her face dropped a little and she gave a sigh.

'He's in the Council. Setting to rights the country, so he says – and more than likely earning for himself more enemies than he's got already. He's changed, you know, Edmund ... quite a lot, I think. Oh, he was always ambitious ... but now ... he's got everything he could possibly wish for – and still he isn't content. He broods a lot; worries about the country.' She averted her eyes as she added, 'And he's taken to – smoking.'

Edmund frowned. This was bad news. He had not seen Robert with a pipe of opium since that day before Plassey.

'Is he smoking a lot, Meg?' he asked gently, relieved to see her shake her head.

'A little ... usually when he's depressed about something, or, like this morning, before speaking to the Council. He's been up since dawn, stalking around, waiting for the time to confront them. He said he was going to nail them this time.'

While Edmund and Margaret were strolling around the ornamental garden, Robert Clive was striding over to the podium to face a full gathering of the Council. He came straight to the point.

'Anarchy, confusion, bribery, corruption and extortion, such was never seen or heard of in any country save this of Bengal!' he thundered, grasping the edge of the lectern with hands shaped into fists. 'Never have so many fortunes been acquired in such an unjust and in so rapacious a manner ... Once we were honest traders, content with honest profit; now we have become conquistadors in our conduct of business – greedily amassing fortunes to the impoverishment of this unhappy land.' If his accusations and remonstrances were delivered too vehemently, it was because his own conscience pricked him. The poacher had turned gamekeeper.

'I intend that these practices shall cease, and to this effect I have promulgated laws on which my signature and seal shall be affixed this very day.'

After the meeting he rode back to his home in the ragged state of mind of any businessman after a hard day. He sorely needed a brandy – or a smoke. His governorship of Bengal was successful, he tried to tell himself, but he well knew the number of holes to be sealed before the colander ceased to leak.

'Edmund, how are you, my friend,' he exclaimed happily when he entered Margaret's sitting-room. Edmund noticed that Clive's first move after kissing Margaret was towards the cabinet where he kept the brandy. It was disconcerting to see how much he downed.

'A touch of swamp fever ... always get it at this time of year,' Clive excused himself, when he saw his friend's look.

'How did the meeting go?' asked Edmund tactfully, going over to the sideboard and filling his own glass so that Robert should not drink alone. Clive told him briefly, passing a shaking hand across his face and pulling at his jaw as he outlined the main points.

'The Emperor's levy on his own people makes it too convenient for us,' said Edmund grimly. 'They pay forty per cent customs duty and we nothing. Permissible for John Company maybe, but not for private traders.'

'Would you have me forbid private trade?' Clive asked sharply.

'Eventually, yes – or else insist that the Europeans trade under the same tax rate as the native merchants. The Company can make up the difference to its employees by paying more than the pittance it does at present.' The discussion went on at length, moving by degrees to even larger issues.

'By no intent of ours, Edmund,' Clive said at one point, 'we have become a political force. And we can no more reverse that than we could hold back the Ganges. If we were to unburden ourselves of responsibility for the Carnatic and Bengal – become simple traders again – we should be swept from the country by any combination of princes, French, Dutch, Portuguese, the Pathans, the Marathas – anything. I tell you this, Edmund – and I believe it with all my heart and being – that should we abandon this land it would revert to its former condition. It would become a dying beast around which princely carrion and Gallic jackals hovered to tear the last shreds of flesh from it.'

He made an impatient gesture as if casting out the image he had conjured. 'No, Edmund. This I will not permit. I have visions, hopes, prayers, for India, that one day, with God's help, it shall become the brightest star in the galaxy of our Empire. I shall create here a new western civilisation based on the law and justice of England. And what was once desert we shall cause to bloom again ... However, enough of that. You won't forget the banquet next week, will you?'

'I shall be there, Robert, I promise ... but isn't it a little late for the Plassey anniversary?'

Clive smiled. 'Confidentially, it's more of a farewell party. Margaret, the child and myself will be leaving for England a month later.'

Edmund was taken aback. How could this accord with Clive's plans for India? How could the administration of Bengal be kept going without Clive to keep a restraining hand on the diverse factions that threatened to tear it apart? He voiced his fears.

Clive bowed ironically. 'An exaggeration, Edmund. Bengal is as stable as it's ever been. I think it should keep that way until I return.'

Edmund snorted. 'What guarantee is there, Robert, that you will return? Bengal is still a helpless baby, and if you withdraw, who knows what the devil it's going to succumb to in your absence?'

'I'm touched, Edmund, and I thank you,' Clive replied, adding somewhat portentously, 'Man is but mortal and countries have a genius for surviving in the absence of any particular one of them.'

45

THE ASSEMBLED noblemen, having given their fealty to the new Nawab of Bengal, whispered behind their hands to each other as his serenely beautiful wife was led into the audience chamber and knelt on the floor facing the ivory and gilt throne. The murmuring ceased as Mir Jafar rose to his feet, though several there sneaked a glance at the stony-faced Mir Kassim who was standing just behind his father. No one in the room was unaware of the story of Sareen and her three suitors.

'Sareen. For the injury you have done me, for the disgrace you have brought upon my name, and the shame with which you abused our sacred marriage, I will neither exact vengeance nor submit you to vilification, for many of your acts were performed at the command of the accursed Siraj-ud-daula against whom no one could prevail. Be it known therefore – and all here be witness to my deed – that you are free to live as you wish, to be concubine or to take husband according to your desires, and at all times to be shown respect as a princess of Bengal, but you will cease to be the wife of Mir Jafar.'

He paused, looking directly at her. There was neither tenderness nor understanding in her eyes, yet no hatred either. His left hand lightly touched the Koran held out to him by a Muslim imaum, and then he intoned the solemn words of divorce.

Sareen, kneeling on the mosaic floor, touched the cool marble stones with her forehead in humble acceptance of both indictment and divorce. It seemed to bother no one – nor even occur to them – that her 'guilt' was her husband's responsibility, for to the Muslim a woman was no more than a prized chattel to be petted or rejected according to the whim of the male.

'You will leave this house and take up residence where you will, but never again under my roof,' Mir Jafar went on, then turning deliberately and staring at his son he added, 'And I enjoin Mir Kassim to take due note of the Koran which forbids marriage with the former wife of his father.'

Kassim met his father's eyes and held them. 'Look not at me, your highness, to learn which of us holds the Koran in contempt,' he said in a low voice, so that only Mir Jafar could hear. The Nawab's lips tightened and he turned away. When he addressed Sareen again, his voice shook with suppressed anger. He waved a bejewelled hand, dismissing her.

Again she prostrated herself then rose to her feet and backed out of the chamber. What should have been a shameful ordeal for any Muslim woman, had left her unmoved. Since the brutal killing of Siraj, and her return to the capital, she had withdrawn completely into herself. She did as she was told without complaint, and without thought for the future.

This stupor had baffled and exasperated Kassim. He had taken her to his own palace, talked to her, pleaded with her, humbled himself before her, all to no avail. When he forced her to look at him her eyes were dead. Had he taken her to his bed she would have offered no resistance. Since Siraj's death she had spoken only when he addressed her.

He left the audience chamber as soon as he could and went to seek her. She was in her room at his palace, sitting quietly on the bed, staring unseeingly, an untouched bowl of food beside her.

'Sareen?' There was not a flicker of an eyelid to indicate she had heard him. He went over to her and, in a gesture rare for a Muslim male, crouched at her feet and took her hand in his. It was dry, cold, and limp in his grasp.

'Sareen. Believe me that I did not desire his death in that manner,' he began, averting his face from her. 'When we were children I swore an oath that I would kill him for what he stole from me. My hatred continued from that day – and had we fought I should have carried out that vow. But execution, no. He was my Nawab, and though I knew him to be evil, my oath of loyalty would have stayed my hand. I do not want to excuse my part in his death yet I do not hold myself responsible. All that I ask is that I be allowed to love you and that you, eventually, will learn to look on me with the same affection that you once did.'

He raised his eyes to her face and saw that she was weeping. It was a small sign and it gave him hope; not since that day at the inn had she wept.

In Calcutta the English residents were agog with anticipation as the day of Clive's banquet drew near. The clothing stores were doing a roaring trade; tailors and seamstresses were hard at work to have new finery ready in time. At the mansion itself some five hundred extra servants had been hired to augment the regular staff of five hundred. Although the immense dining-room could seat a hundred and fifty people other rooms had to be set aside for the remaining two hundred guests.

'Margaret's guest list reads like a roll-call of Bengal,' Clive told Edmund. 'Including her parents, bless them.'

'They're my parents too, don't forget,' Edmund grinned.

'Ah, yes. I think you visited them once this year and twice last year. A most devoted son,' Clive retorted dryly. 'By the way, Anna is coming, isn't she?'

'Yes, she's coming,' Edmund replied in a low voice, causing Clive to glance sharply at him. 'She insists on wearing black.'

'Why not! Margaret is, too. She calls it the Venetian style: something with a full skirt of black velvet and a kind of lace mantilla on the head – very lovely she looks, too. And I'm sure Anna is going to look equally beautiful.'

'Yes,' said Edmund, deflating him.

Margaret did indeed look superb, but after standing in the same place for an hour to greet three hundred and fifty guests, she was limp and bordering on collapse. Partway through the evening she pleaded the 'vapours' and slipped away to her bedroom.

Clive, presiding over the main table at the top of the vast dining-room, was at his best. On his right was Anna, who was next to Edmund; on his left was some widow, who seemed faintly bewildered by the illustrious company, escorted by Eyre Coote, now a colonel. Other principal guests included three senior officers who had fought at Plassey, their wives, plus six members of the Select Committee also with their wives – and finally Warren Hastings.

At nine o'clock the first hogshead of wine was trundled into the room, and by midnight, as the eighteenth course was served, the talk grew wilder. By then three hogsheads had been emptied plus four bottles of claret for each male guest. The din exceeded that of the battle itself.

Anna, sombre and very pale, listened demurely but spoke little. She ate sparingly and drank even less; Edmund's efforts to enliven her met with little success. Eventually she gave up entirely. Edmund drank morosely.

Clive was garrulous, banging the table and making declamatory remarks to which the inebriated Council members paid scant attention. Hastings sat silent, listening to the wild talk and storing in his retentive memory everything that might prove of value later. There were rumours of Clive's impending return to England; he intended that Bengal should be his the moment Clive's back was turned. It was time that a civilian took over as governor. Grudgingly he conceded Clive's talents as a soldier though he felt that as an administrator he concerned himself too much with legal technicalities. The time had arrived, he thought, when decisions were needed that would of necessity ignore the finer points of law.

Colonel Eyre Coote was in roaring form; the table was helpless with laughter at some of his more imaginative accounts of Plassey.

'And you only lost four,' someone exclaimed.

'Aye, four it was – and we had to kill one of them ourselves to puff up the Nawab's score.'

'Really? And who might that have been?' Warren Hastings swiftly put in, alert for scandal.

'Who!' Coote chuckled. 'Dear old Mathieson ... blighter ran terrified, like a chicken from the chopper.'

A thunderous gust of laughter greeted this, though it was unlikely that many knew what they were laughing at.

It took Edmund some time to register. Mathieson? Had he heard aright? Had Eyre Coote said something about Mathieson? 'A chicken running from ...' But they had sworn not to tell. Anna wasn't supposed to know.

He turned towards her. She was rigid. Her normally pale cheeks were now quite bloodless, and her lower lip trembled. At the same time her eyes had widened so that they seemed to fill her small face. They were riveted on the drunken Eyre Coote who, unaware of the calamity he had brought about, was leaning forward cradling a bottle of brandy inside his elbow. The liquid in his glass thrashed about as he raised it to his lips, and his head shook from side to side in sniggering hilarity at some shouted ribaldry.

Edmund, aghast at the thought of the effect upon Anna, was at first numbed, then sickened, and finally enraged. He staggered to his feet and, holding on to the edge of the table, swung his arm in a wide circle and smashed the glass from Eyre Coote's hand. Then, pendulum style, he swung back again, the palm this time cracking across the astounded colonel's cheek.

'You ... you ... you insult ... insult the ... memory.' It was as much as he could manage before he slumped down again into his seat and passed out, his head on his arms. As he went down, Eyre Coote stood up. Compared with Edmund, he was practically sober. His left cheek was crimson with the marks of his antagonist's fingers; his other cheek was deathly pale. One hand on the table steadied his body, the other reached out to grasp Edmund's unconscious form.

'You dare ... my seconds will call ... will call,' he stuttered; then he flung himself away from the chair, sending it crashing to the ground, and swayed an erratic course towards the door.

46

THREE HOURS later Edmund was seated in Clive's study, a wet towel round his head; a footman waved a fan over him. His irate host stood in front of him, his abusive tones having a dismal effect on the miserable 'hero'. Anna had long since been escorted home by some elderly member of the Council who happened to be less drunk than most.

'Of all the reckless, insane, madcap, foolhardy things to do!' Clive raved at him. 'To insult a man like Eyre Coote – and for no better cause than a damnable coward like Mathieson. I'll thank you not to slap *me* for what you well know is the truth,' he added vigorously. But the fire had gone out of Edmund.

'I had to, Robert, I had to,' he moaned plaintively. 'I couldn't just sit there ... Anna was so cruelly hurt ...'

Clive swore loudly.

'He was drunk, you oaf – didn't know what he was saying! He's been at Wandewash the past few months fighting the French, and he's possibly the only man in Calcutta ignorant of your fatuous worship of that woman.'

Edmund started to get to his feet. 'Do not ... refer to Anna in that way. Friend or not, I'll ...' He attempted a ridiculous posture of injured dignity.

Clive sighed, gave him a gentle push, and he subsided into the chair again. The footman replaced the cloth with a freshly dampened one.

'Edmund, can't you see the consequences of your action?' Clive's tone had become more reasonable. 'Eyre Coote would never have made that remark if he'd been sober.'

'Yet he made it,' Edmund persisted doggedly, 'and he must bear the responsibility.'

Exasperated, Clive dismissed the servant. Kneeling down beside his friend, he said with heavy patience, 'Dear boy, you with the brain of a mosquito; it is *you* who will take the consequences. You will be asked to choose weapons. If you select pistols, Eyre Coote can put a bullet through a man's heart at fifty paces – whereas you ...' He left that part unsaid.

'I shall choose sabres,' Edmund decided, with as much firmness as he could muster.

Clive gave him a pitying look. 'As for swordsmanship, Edmund, even the sergeant-instructor tries to be elsewhere when you appear in the gymnasium.'

Edmund set his jaw. 'I'm not that bad. I have been practising,' he insisted gamely. 'You have made no complaint of my soldiering in campaigns.'

He was sobering rapidly. His friend laid a hand gently on his shoulder and spoke with utter sincerity.

'Listen to me, Edmund. I have no officer whom I respect more than you and none whom I value more. Your bravery is legendary among the men; your leadership, your initiative in battle, your direction of artillery ... everything ... merits naught but praise.

233

But frankly, Edmund, with a sabre you couldn't chop the head off a chicken.'

He stopped, cursing his stupidity for using an analogy similar to Eyre Coote's offensive remark. This time Edmund did get to his feet. He faced his friend squarely.

'That we shall have to prove,' said he coldly; in formal tones he added, 'And now may I make request that you act as my second.'

The two men looked into each other's eyes for a few moments before Clive turned away.

'Regretfully, I cannot, Edmund,' he said quietly. 'As governor I am required to set my face against duelling, though I may not interfere where two officers are to settle an affair of honour. Besides' – he paused – 'as one who loves both protagonists I may second neither against the other.'

Despite his authority and his strength of purpose, Clive could do nothing to prevent the duel taking place. In defiance of the code that governed such matters, he called together the respective seconds and spoke urgently to them. It was clear to him that neither of them relished the prospect of a duel.

'If Colonel Coote would make an apology for his observation on the late Captain Mathieson?' one suggested tentatively; but the other fellow shook his head.

'He is unable to withdraw. He maintains it was the truth and as such could be no insult to either Major Maskelyne or the lady. But if your principal could offer an excuse for his ...?'

Clive listened with increasing weariness. 'Both men were so drunk that neither was capable of giving or receiving calculated insult,' he said with asperity. 'Were every brawl between carousers to end in a duel Calcutta's streets would be littered with corpses!'

Both seconds bristled in unison. 'Your excellency, may I remind you that my principal is unable to take such a light view of the matter,' they almost chimed together. And so the interview was terminated.

At five o'clock in a cool orange-tinged dawn on a field outside Calcutta, the seconds escorted their friends to the spot where honour was to be satisfied. A colonel of foot then arrived and took command as referee. He shook hands with the two adversaries, walked over to where a small table had been set and made a cursory examination of the weapons laid on it. After that he discussed with the seconds his interpretation of fouls and incapacitating wounds. With chalk he solemnly marked off a dividing line on the ground, checked that the surgeon was present, then directed the two men to take up their positions so that the points of their sabres in outstretched arms just touched over the chalked line.

Edmund and Eyre Coote then formally recognised each other with the curtest of bows. The seconds took their positions at each end of the line, and the weapons were inspected for rust or dirt that might poison a wound.

'Gentlemen, please be ready,' the referee said calmly.

The two adversaries, stripped to the waist, with silk handkerchiefs bound around the arteries of the wrists and with silk scarves around the neck to protect the external jugular vein, stiffened to attention, bowed, took their stance, stretched out their sabres at an angle to the ground, and waited.

'On guard!'

The sabres were raised until they were in line with each other, the points just touching. There was a moment of hesitation, then: 'Forward!'

Just beyond the perimeter of the arena an agitated Clive turned his face away. In a closed carriage, Anna sat rigid, all thoughts of Mathieson overshadowed by the vivid reality of this potential tragedy. Her hands were clasped together and she prayed, more fervently than at any time since she had been a child. She strained to catch the merest sound that told of disaster.

At the command to engage, Eyre Coote quickly stepped back, twisted sideways, raised his sabre and lunged in low down. Edmund parried clumsily what was obviously a testing stroke to gauge an opponent's skill. He sliced back a blow that Eyre Coote contemptuously dismissed. Several strokes later – after much haphazard swinging and lunging by Edmund – the truth dawned on Colonel Eyre Coote: that he was duelling with unquestionably the worst swordsman in Bengal. The revelation unnerved him. For perhaps a minute he adopted strictly defensive measures while he thought out the problem. Edmund's defeat, even his death, could be effected at any moment he chose. But did he want this? There could be no honour in such a victory; but he himself had no intention of getting cut to ribbons simply to please Edmund Maskelyne. How could he extricate himself from this damnable situation?

He changed tactics and went over to the attack: fencing with studied extravagance, using every trick of which he was master, performing fine gestures of lunging and cutting – yet to everyone's amazement his blade never once touched his opponent. Always it was made to seem as if the less skilful fighter had parried a stroke just in time.

Edmund, after his first enthusiastic showing, was now confused – albeit delighted at the fair performance he was giving. Then the suspicion took root that the colonel was deliberately playing with him to make him look a fool. He became even more erratic, indulging in ill-timed swings that would have cost him his life had Eyre Coote taken advantage of them. Yet, to all intents the colonel was hard put to it to parry his lunges, turn aside his slashes, dodge the head-splitters, and he made it seem arduous and a genuine struggle for survival. For to Eyre Coote, a man's honour and self-respect, as well as his life, were in the balance.

Clive, disturbed at the length of time the duel was taking, forced himself to watch, guessed immediately what was happening, and thankfully offered up a small prayer. Backwards and forwards the two men swayed until a quarter of an hour had passed and both were visibly tiring. Edmund, his suspicions now cast aside, exerted himself more and hoped that in his defeat he should die without shame – he had no illusions now as to his own swordsmanship. Eyre Coote, out of temper with the whole affair, sought only to end the charade. He found his opportunity when Edmund took a right-handed swipe at his head. Catching the blade on the hilt, he flicked his opponent's sword to one side, then bent low and lunged forward as if to thrust deep into Edmund's heart; but at the last moment he deflected his aim so that the point of the sabre cut into the fleshy part of his shoulder.

Edmund flinched. He grimaced with pain and staggered back.

'Halt!' both referee and seconds cried out in unison, and Eyre Coote dutifully lowered his sword, immeasurably relieved. The surgeon hurried forward to examine the wound.

'The contest is concluded,' the referee announced.

'No!' shouted Edmund, attempting to bring his weapon to the 'on guard' position. It flopped on to the ground from his weakened grasp – and a moment later he followed it in a dead faint. There he stayed whilst the surgeon attended to him.

Eyre Coote, playing out his role to the end, waited until Edmund opened his eyes and then came forward and raised his sword to his lips in the traditional salute to a worthy opponent. He caught Clive's eye. A look of gratitude passed between them, and then he addressed the injured man on the ground.

'Major Maskelyne, sir. If in my drunkenness I uttered certain scurrilous remarks that caused offence to either you or to Miss Vernier, I now tender my most abject apologies, and deeply regret what has since transpired. If you will allow me, sir, I should like to offer my wishes for a swift recovery from that most grievous wound. Never before did I fight against a man I more respected.'

Edmund, now sitting up, his face twisted with pain from the surgeon's administrations, acknowledged this most gracious apology. He could hardly believe that he was still alive and restrained himself from shouting aloud for joy. He controlled himself sufficiently to reply.

'I do accept your apologies, sir, though I myself am not without blame. Perhaps we should consider this affair to be over ... be forgotten ... and with respect, sir ... I ... am ... think I'm going going ... to ... faint.'

And so he did.

47

INSIDE THE vestibule of the House of Commons the Chancellor of the Exchequer stood nonchalantly, waiting apparently for his carriage. To the Members who greeted him he responded curtly, respectfully, glacially, or not at all, depending on the status of the Member or his potential value to Sir Francis.

'Ah, Sullivan, a word with you.' He held up a bony index finger in a peremptory manner. The man addressed was a red-cheeked tubby little man with a perpetual look of surprise on his face. He halted as if he had been apprehended by one of Fielding's Runners – and seemed little happier to discover it was Dashwood.

'Sir Francis. Always a pleasure, of course. You are well? The weather is not very seasonable, do you not find?' he babbled politely, warily eyeing the tall cadaverous figure that leaned over him like an undertaker viewing a lucrative corpse.

'I never find the weather of much consequence. It rarely disturbs me, but, to speak plainly, there are many other things that cause me acute distress, Sullivan,' Dashwood responded, holding his prey in his gaze.

'Really?' The tubby man gave a short, nervous laugh. 'And what would they be, Sir Francis?' Already his stomach was churning, for when the Chancellor announces that he is disturbed businessmen must needs watch out.

A long skeletal arm draped itself around the tubby man's shoulders and smoothly propelled him towards the massive gothic entrance of the Commons. 'Perhaps, if you are not otherwise engaged, you would accompany me to my club – the wine cellar is above reproach I do assure you.'

An invitation from Dashwood was in fact a summons. Sullivan accepted and a moment or two later entered Dashwood's splendid rig with him. The Chancellor was silent for the first few minutes.

'Bengal and the Carnatic,' he began, gazing out at the congested streets.

'Yes?' Sullivan asked innocently.

'You are content with progress there?' He still gazed out of the window. Sullivan shrugged. He had no idea what was expected of him.

'I think so. Certainly no complaints about Plassey or Madras or Wandewash. And when Pondicherry falls it'll be all over for the French. The Company will have a monopoly of trade in that area.'

'Yes. General Clive is indeed a remarkable soldier,' Sir Francis rejoined, the flatness of his tone giving the lie to his praise.

'And administrator,' Sullivan added, his mind struggling desperately to fathom where this was all leading to.

'Really.' The word was a gravestone on all further eulogies of Robert Clive; Sullivan mentally bowed his head and laid his own wreath. One step from the prime minister in power, Sir Francis was not a person to cross.

Sometime later in his club in St James's Place, the Chancellor stretched languidly in his reserved corner, casually examining against the light from the huge window the wine in his glass. Sullivan, warily sitting bolt upright opposite him, eyed him with growing apprehension. As chairman of the board of directors of the East India Company he was unduly sensitive to governmental pressure; his timid nature inclined him to sway with the wind.

'Naturally no blame could be attached to you, Sullivan,' Dashwood was saying, 'yet none must be more aware than you of the grave concern of the government. Bengal, as you must admit, is far and away the richest state in India and yet there is this lamentable fall in profits – a fall I must say that dates from the assumption of control by General Clive.'

The Chairman attempted a deprecatory smile that didn't quite come off. He took a quick sip of wine before replying.

'Oh, I agree that it isn't a state of affairs to be desired, Sir Francis, but one must expect a temporary fall in receipts. The condition of Bengal after Plassey and when Mir Jafar took over as Nawab, the restrictions that Clive felt compelled to place on private trade, the adjustments in the administration, the famine ...' He broke off when he saw Dashwood wagging an admonitory finger at him as though he were some naughty child, and the smile that he gave was like the touch of an icicle.

'Remember that I, too, am privy to many secrets. A protégé of mine – a certain Warren Hastings whom you doubtless know – lifts the veil on much that happens in that far-off country.' An expression of deep concern replaced the smile on the Chancellor's face, and he leaned forward in a confidential manner. 'The national debt is very considerably in excess of what it ought to be, Sullivan. It is my task to reduce it to a more acceptable level, and it is perfectly obvious to me – from what the worthy Hastings writes – that Bengal and the Carnatic are the logical means by which this may be accomplished. To put it in a more vulgar way, the door of a treasure house has been unlocked; I see no justifiable reason why we should not avail ourselves of it by means of increased trade.'

'We are in no conflict there, Sir Francis,' Sullivan replied, eager to please. 'The Council is alive to the possibilities yet they cannot ignore the problems. Political administration is often at variance with private trade, and I assure you that once the country has settled down after all this trouble the Company will once more start to reap its profits.' He stopped at the sight of Dashwood's glacial smile, then in a more conciliatory manner said, 'Naturally we shall impress these things on Clive whenever ...'

'Are you convinced, Sullivan, that Clive – as a soldier – possesses the qualifications to administer Bengal, to direct and expand trade to the degree we require?' Dashwood raised a hand to prevent Sullivan's possible objection. 'Would not such a person as Warren Hastings, a gifted administrator, be a more fitting choice?'

'Sir Francis. Were we to dismiss Clive the people in this country would raise an outcry of protest,' Sullivan objected lamely.

'Public opinion,' sneered Sir Francis. 'Must we conduct governmental affairs according to the whims of serfs and villeins? Is the Honourable East India Company responsible to its directors and shareholders, or to some Essex farmer or Devon pig dealer?' He leaned forward and tapped the tubby man on the knee-cap. 'Allow me to instruct you on the myth of this "public opinion", Sullivan. It is as fleeting as one day's newspaper following another. Already Plassey and its noble hero have been forgotten – superseded by the trouncing of the French at Minden, and Wolfe's epic battle at Quebec. Can these be compared with Clive's trivial skirmish? I promise you, Sullivan, should Clive return to London tomorrow he would be granted one day of glory, and then be relegated to the waters of Lethe.'

Dashwood beckoned to a steward to recharge their glasses. 'There is a move afoot in the Commons, I should tell you, Sullivan, for the government to take administrative control out of the hands of the Company ... not that it will come to anything, of course.' He let the thought simmer in the Chairman's mind, then added smoothly, 'I have a small retreat in the country, Sullivan, an old abbey in Medmenham. What say you to spending a little while there with me when we could thrash out this subject in more congenial surroundings?'

48

NEVER WAS bruised and bleeding flesh so content! He lay on the bed surrounded with pillows, his shoulder admittedly painful, watching with gratification while Anna bustled around ministering to him. She scolded the cook when the food was ill prepared; berated the punkah-wallah for constantly falling asleep at his task;

drove the servants to a frenzy of scrubbing; shouted to the dhobi for fresh linen each day. She herself tenderly changed his bandages and washed him.

The patient said little, but his eyes were constantly on her. She who had previously needed his care and protection was now a ministering angel and competent manager. Here indeed was the girl whose sturdy resilience had enabled her to survive the notorious Black Hole. Not once were the names of Eyre Coote, or Mathieson, mentioned. The past might not have existed.

On the third day after the duel Colonel Eyre Coote called to pay his respects; it was rare for the victor to behave so solicitously towards his erstwhile opponent, but the Colonel was that kind of man.

'I shall understand, Miss Vernier, if the Major is unwilling to see me,' he whispered tactfully to Anna in the vestibule; but he was promptly ushered into the patient's bedroom. Edmund attempted to prop himself on his pillows and regretted he had not shaved that morning. The visitor put up a restraining hand.

'Forgive me, sir, if I intrude without invitation, yet I desired to know your health and progress,' he said with genuine humility though without loss of dignity.

Edmund was a little embarrassed. 'I am comfortable, Colonel Coote, and there is no danger,' he managed to get out. 'Your concern is indeed welcome.'

Anna, hovering just outside the doorway, made her entrance on hearing this. The Colonel appeared to recollect what else he had come to say. He made her a bow. 'When in my cups, ma'am, I made an ungracious statement about a certain person, regretfully alive no longer. Believe me, Miss Vernier, when I say it was not true, and for it I stand shamed and do offer my most abject apologies.'

She instantly warmed to him, though her eyes filled with tears. She begged him to be seated and busied herself with pouring wine for the two men while she regained her composure. Then she filled a glass for herself. Eventually she spoke, almost in a whisper. 'You must not interrupt me, Edmund, until I give you leave to do so,' she warned, then turned her attention to the uneasy Colonel.

'Your apology is gratefully accepted, Colonel Coote; in this matter I believe you have behaved as a true English gentleman.'

'I am of Irish birth, ma'am,' he corrected her quietly.

'Very well; as an Irish gentleman. Now I have an important question to ask you and I must have your word of honour that you will answer it correctly.' She paused for a moment, and there was a tense silence in the room. 'Did Captain Mathieson meet his death while fleeing the battlefield?'

What it had cost Anna, Edmund could only guess. Eyre Coote unhappily fidgeted with his glass, unable to look at her. She stared straight at his bowed head.

'Your answer, Colonel,' she persisted softly.

Slowly the Colonel's head nodded. She took in a deep breath; but she had not finished with him.

'You were there; you saw it yourself?'

At this Edmund could restrain himself no longer.

'Anna, the Colonel has given you the truth. The only lie was in my reaction at the banquet.' He looked over at the bowed head of Eyre Coote, hoping the unstated apology would be understood. 'I placed him in an invidious position. It was ... as he said. Mathieson lost control and started to run.'

Anna lowered her gaze to the floor. She was silent for a few moments, but when she raised her eyes again it was as though a new woman were standing there.

'Thank you,' she said distantly, then appeared to force herself into a brighter mood and walked over to Edmund's bed. She sat on the edge of it – a gesture demonstrating her unity with him, it seemed to Eyre Coote. She flashed a smile at the colonel, saying as she did so, 'We shall be most offended if you do not stay to dine with us, Colonel.' She wrinkled her nose at the mildly astonished patient. 'I regret that it will have to be served in the bedroom.'

Eyre Coote, looking much relieved, responded with similar warmth.

'I should be honoured, ma'am. Indeed I am deeply honoured.' He clearly meant it.

Two weeks later both men were guests at a full meeting of the Calcutta Council. There was a low hum of conversation as Clive rose to his feet and walked over to the lectern. He looked resplendent in his full-bottomed wig, heavily embroidered Chinese-silk jacket of watered purple, lemon coloured blouse with lace neck and extravagant ruffles at the cuffs, his deep crimson breeches and his silver-buckled shoes. At thirty-five years of age he looked older, heavier, and less fit than he should have done.

'Better that he take to an excess of brandy than that opium. He does not look well,' whispered Eyre Coote with unmistakable concern. Edmund made no comment yet it disturbed him that others should know of Clive's smoking.

'Members of this Honourable Council,' Clive began. He spoke quietly for a few minutes before coming to the main point of his speech. Then he said in a low voice, '... and therefore I feel the necessity to return to England.'

There was immediate consternation, many exclamations of protest that Bengal could not be left without his guidance. Some members begged him to reconsider; others whispered furtively to their neighbour. Warren Hastings was silent, his face devoid of all expression.

Clive, undeniably touched, again explained his fears for the health of his wife and son that had forced this decision upon him. It was partly true.

'And when are you to return, your excellency?' someone called out.

When indeed, he thought, looking around at the comfortable over-indulged faces of the Council members. He despised them as avaricious, self-centred merchants with little thought for the land they plundered. This was only a little unfair; there were just a few who retained a sense of responsibility. His gaze met that of Warren Hastings. Heaven forbid that he should come to power, able administrator though he was.

'I cannot predict the future,' he rejoined flatly. 'When, or if, the need should arise for a return, then I shall make plans accordingly. Bengal and the Carnatic have peace, "John Company" flourishes, while despite the restrictions I was compelled to impose your own private enterprises continue to fatten your purses – and due to the brilliant victories of Colonel Eyre Coote, the French, the Dutch, the Portuguese, have ceased to be armed aggressors and are now simply minor competitors for trade. I leave you with no problems that wise judgment and administration cannot solve.'

'With the exception of the Nawab, your excellency,' put in Warren Hastings smoothly. 'Since your departure from Murshidabad Mir Jafar has offered not one gold coin towards payment of his debts – and I am inclined to suspect he may seek to repudiate those clauses of the treaty concerning the balance of monies.'

The mention of money had a marked effect on the Council. Hastings at once had its attention. All Clive's old contempt for them surged up again.

'Better you live with a complaisant Nawab on the throne of Bengal even though he beggars his debts, than with a tyrant who pays with the edge of a sword,' he rapped back.

'But Mir Kassim is no tyrant, your excellency, and it would surely be to our advantage to have him replace his father. He is a man of honour and would pay his debts.' Hastings noted with satisfaction how the mood of the gathering was inclining towards himself.

Clive was a little shaken to have this kind of confrontation with Hastings, and he had forebodings of how the drift would be when eventually he left Bengal.

'What honour do you find in a man capable of murdering his own Nawab with such savagery? What trust would you repose in the son who usurps his father's throne – steals his wife? Note you well, Hastings and Honourable Members, Mir Kassim is a man burning with fire. Were he to acquire the throne of Bengal, this land would be consumed with flames. Take heed of this warning: the son of Mir Jafar would be no puppet; he is a man of independence and a man of passionate feeling. With such a man on the throne you would sleep uneasily in your beds.'

There was only scattered applause. Warren Hastings folded his arms over his stomach as if respect for the honest, though misguided, beliefs of the failing governor would not allow him to make further challenge. He kept silent. Clive was on his way to England; this alone was important. Once his tremendous personality was removed, he, Warren Hastings, would bring his own not insignificant influence to bear on the Council. He looked round the chamber; Clive apart, he saw only mediocrity. He could afford to be magnanimous today. His face was a picture of good fellowship.

'I assume, my Lord Clive, that you will delay your departure at least until the nuptials of the excellent Major Maskelyne and the lovely Miss Anna Vernier?' he purred with much affability.

Clive shot him a suspicious glance, but allowed himself a smile. He saw that Edmund was gazing stolidly at the floor in a state of acute embarrassment.

'But of course; I am to be his groomsman. How could I leave

without first ensuring that this rapscallion bachelor is firmly shackled by the delightful chains of holy matrimony.' There was much laughter and considerable applause.

'Ah, so the date is actually set,' someone chuckled to even more hilarity. The story of Edmund and Anna was well known.

'In three weeks' time,' Clive grinned back, 'conditional, of course, on a warehouse being found for the bales of cotton stored in the church, and on our minister being agreeably sober.' But the joke had gone on too long; he added in a more serious tone: 'He is to be envied – for Bengal sadly needs men of such devotion and integrity.'

Three weeks later the church had at last been emptied. Edmund, very handsome in his new navy-blue uniform, waited nervously at the altar rail with Clive. Only a few seats remained unoccupied; three times the number were expected at the subsequent banquet.

A few minutes before the bride arrived there was a good deal of shuffling and whispering near the west door. Heads turned to peer at this unseemly disturbance; the ladies compressed their lips and glared at their husbands to follow suit. A few bachelors winked surreptitiously at each other. Clive himself turned, prepared to glare imperiously. Instead he simply stared with something akin to amusement at the sight of Miss Petal Wilkinson and her two 'assistants', Jasmine and Lotus, solemnly making their way down the aisle – heading for three empty seats in the front row. They were so fashionably dressed that they quite outshone most of the other ladies present – itself a reason to bring forth the frowns.

The groom also turned, and grinned his welcome as the trio with the gravest of expressions, offered him the most gracious of curtsies.

'Special invitation from me,' Edmund whispered, feeling a little less nervous.

'Does Anna know?' breathed back Clive.

'Oh yes,' Edmund replied nonchalantly.

The organ played a few chords and the congregation dutifully got to its feet as the bride made her appearance. Colonel Eyre Coote escorted her to the altar with massive dignity, formally bowed to the groom, and placed her hand upon his arm and stood back. Bride and groom smiled at each other before composing themselves to face the minister as he entered through the vestry door.

There was a slight gasp and then a quickly suppressed titter from those in the front pews when they became aware of his condition. He looked so haggard that it might have been a funeral he was to officiate at. He grasped a prayer book, looked at it sourly, scraped a raw tongue over dried lips and began the ceremony. Not once did he falter. His high-pitched voice was audible and his words distinct. His facial muscles twitched now and again as he glared at the bland face of the groomsman. Then it dawned on the congregation.

The minister was sober!

Determined to confound this reprobate who preached the Gospel, Clive had planted two of his officers to guard him from sunrise that day. With great courtesy they had kept the old soak from even a thimbleful of brandy. It was a notable moment in Calcutta's ecclesiastical history.

Six days after the wedding, Clive and his family bade a sad farewell to India.

49

IN THE vestibule of the abbey Sir Francis peeled off his monk's habit and tossed it to the slender young girl standing just inside the doorway. She was as naked as he, and both were perspiring and breathing heavily from their recent exertions. The girl watched him incuriously as he extracted his breeches from the dark wooden cupboard and started thrusting his stick-like limbs into them.

As he dressed she came up behind him, stretched out her arms and clumsily tied the tapes of his lace steenkirk under his greying pigtail, then stood back expectantly. Dashwood grunted his thanks, thrust two fingers into his waistcoat pocket, extracted a finely worked cloisonné sovereign-case, flicked it open, took out a half-sovereign and tossed it to her. She caught it expertly – as she had caught many similar. As she made to go back into the nave he called out to her, 'See if Mr Sullivan is finished.' She passed through the arched doorway, her bare feet padding softly on the ancient stones, and returned a few minutes later, giggling.

'Not yet, sir,' she simpered, 'and from the looks of him, abeggin' your pardon, sir, he's tryin' more'n he can manage.' She put her hands to her round peasant face to stifle her laughter. 'He's got

Molly – an' you know what *she*'s like.'

Dashwood growled some derisive comment and his eyes glinted with malicious amusement. 'Bring me two glasses and two bottles of wine while I'm waiting, Etti. There's a small cupboard by the side of the font in the left transept; here's the key.'

Etti took the key and hastened away to do his bidding. She passed down the left aisle of the nave, blithely unaware that, three centuries earlier, devout Cistercians had cloistered their lives amidst those aged stones for the preservation of their chastity, among other virtues.

She returned to her master with the bottles of wine, passing on the way a few vague shapes in Franciscan habit that writhed and heaved in odd corners; here and there seeing a flash of naked flesh as it emerged from the folds of the coarse brown cloth, an arm, a rump, a thigh; her eyes noting without inquiry the altar draped in black and the inverted cross where but recently Dashwood and his acolytes had performed an obscene travesty of the Mass. None of it disturbed her now. With the money she received on these occasions she was accumulating a tidy fortune. Think what she would have been paid as a common serving-wench, or bed mate, in some country squire's house.

Once she had overcome her initial shock, she had soon acquired a taste for the perverted sexual practices of Medmenham – actually she had discovered in herself a rare talent for licentious dancing and group fornication. Of course 'New Franciscans' was an awfully silly name – but they were all 'gentlemen': a little rough and demanding at times, but not like the village men. They liked to indulge in mock rape; it was so ridiculous, especially as she was supposed to struggle a little! What mattered was that they had no idea of money; they gave it out as if they'd been born with sacks of it.

Sullivan came wearily through the doorway just as Sir Francis was opening the second bottle of wine. He flopped down on the cold stone bench beside the Chancellor, his rotund body spreading out, his fat flesh hanging from him in loose folds of soggy exhaustion. He took in great gulps of air, and with the back of his hand wiped away the sweat from his forehead.

He drank the wine offered to him in one gulp, then allowed his body to reel forward, his arms sagging down between his fat naked thighs, shaking his head in bewilderment at what he had been doing. After eighteen months of visiting Medmenham, he was still a little frightened at the magnetic pull the abbey exerted on him.

'This is some devilry you've conjured, Dashwood,' Sullivan said – as he did after nearly every visit – in a tone of part wonder, part censure.

'Devilry? None, I do assure you, save that lurking in a man's own purpose,' Dashwood rejoined smoothly, refilling his companion's glass.

'You do talk rubbish at times,' Sullivan grumbled, finding these occasions gave him more licence with the Chancellor than he would dare take otherwise. Sir Francis seemed not to mind – not at that moment, anyway.

'We would not perform any act, Sullivan, if the need for that act had not been first implanted in our bodies by some being not of our ordering.'

He gave a dismissive wave of the hand. 'As for these girls, what would their lot be? Skivvies, scullery sluts, pan scrubbers, eventually married slavies to woodcutters, coke smelters, charcoal burners, navvies, producing broods of like creatures until they're worn into the ground. The money we pay them rescues them from such a condition,' he added virtuously.

Sullivan drained his second glass of wine, wiped his mouth and looked sideways at his companion. 'You're a magician with words, Dashwood. You could even tempt a saint from his rosary.'

Dashwood allowed himself a mirthless laugh; it sounded obscene in that place.

'It's tempted you, without doubt, Sullivan. As for saints, pure or impure, what of the saintly Clive?'

Sullivan got up and began struggling into his clothes. He wondered at times about Dashwood's hatred of the Governor of Bengal.

'He has been in England these past few months,' he replied, buckling his shoes. 'It's unlikely he'll give us further worry,' he added, hoping that would close the subject.

Dashwood sneered. 'And what of the day when he returns to India? Does it please the Board to employ such a man?'

'He will not return to India,' Sullivan said flatly, but not with any real conviction. 'Why should he? He has everything a miserable writer could wish for: money, rank; "Baron of Plassey", if you please. Why then should he go back to that pestilent Bengal!'

Sullivan was in fact in two minds. He had not openly supported Clive's autocratic assumption of power in Bengal; but who else had been better fitted? The facts of his achievements were there for all to see; and the whole of England had been ecstatic in his praise. To effect Clive's removal from Bengal (assuming that he decided to return there) would be as formidable a task as directing the king himself to abdicate. Of course, if corruption, abuse of power, or anything like that could be proved against him. . . .

It was as if Dashwood were privy to his thinking. He produced a letter from his inner pocket. 'This arrived a few days ago, Sullivan – from Warren Hastings. He declares, on the soundest evidence, that when the noble Clive sailed from Calcutta he had in his trunks gold coin to the value of £300,000. Now mark that sum, Chairman of the Honourable East India Company – three hundred thousand pounds – and ask yourself how it was possible to acquire this wealth in the few years that he was there. Is it not reasonable to assume that "John Company's" immense power and influence was usurped for private gain?'

Sullivan was astounded. He knew that Clive was a rich man, but this was several times the extent of his own purse. His indignation gave Dashwood no end of satisfaction. The Chancellor poured in a little more acid.

'Imagine if news of this were spread around: the effect on those already protesting against the nabobs. They would insist on government intervention in "John Company's" affairs. And there is more, too, Sullivan. Hastings refers to an estate that Clive, by some devious means, has acquired, which brings him the very handsome revenue of £30,000 per annum. Now when you compare this with the income of England's greatest magnate, the Duke of Newcastle, which is £40,000 per annum, you realise to what extent the noble Clive has been milking the brahman cow.'

'But this is monstrous! The revenue from *any* land within the Company's jurisdiction belongs by right to the Company. There may be some legal justification for his £300,000, Dashwood, but on the issue of the estate he could be impeached.'

'Impeached? Why not *indicted* if the Board find that what he has done is a criminal offence?' Dashwood returned. And when Sullivan seemed to hesitate, he continued with a hint of menace. 'It is against my nature to make threats; a warning perhaps, but never threats – and not to such a person as yourself, whose friendship I value so highly.' Sullivan glimpsed the axe above his head and prepared for the worst. 'There have been murmurs in the House, Mr Pitt himself being the most vociferous, that I, in my official capacity, should institute an enquiry into the Company's affairs; only a simpleton could fail to guess what such an enquiry might reveal,' he added, looking hard at his companion. 'Naturally I would try to lessen the impact of such an enquiry on certain directors whose worthiness impresses me.' His point was not lost on the now shrinking Sullivan. Dashwood went on: 'Therefore, it would seem to me sensible for you and your fellow directors to have one arch sinner nailed to his cross in advance of the Parliamentary report which otherwise might crucify the entire Board.'

Sullivan stood up, and somehow he seemed to have shrunk; the tall figure of Sir Francis loomed over him.

'I . . . I will give much thought to what you have said, Sir Francis,' he mumbled, attempting a dignity he had lost. 'It will be difficult but . . . but I suppose it'd better be done,' he added, averting his eyes from those of his companion, which gleamed in triumph.

50

NO HUMANE woman can indefinitely remain unmoved by the pleadings of a man whom she once loved, and still part-loved, without forgiving him his crime, and Sareen was not a woman given to vendettas. Kassim's constant protestations of love eventually broke down her resistance. For months after Siraj's death she had moved wraithlike through Murshidabad. It was not that her eventual affection for him had been particularly intense, yet having given it she had learned to love him as a mother might an adopted child. The gruesome manner of his death was deeply etched on her mind and she could still feel Sombrer's arms round her as he had carried her struggling from the scene of the murder.

Sombrer. The very name caused her to shudder; he was the manifestation of viciousness and mindless cruelty, the obedient instrument of any bad cause. She had not demeaned herself by pleading for his banishment, yet Kassim was left in no doubt about her feelings. Unable to overrule his father, he could only forbid Sombrer access to any part of the palace where Sareen was likely to be.

As for Kassim, he was delighted at having overcome the barrier between Sareen and himself, though he was conscious that the spectre of Siraj-ud-daula still hovered over them. By Koranic law they could not marry, and this offended his sense of rightness; but it did not prohibit him from taking her as a concubine.

Relations with his father were so strained that they rarely spoke. Since Mir Jafar had become Nawab, other causes had arisen to widen the gulf between them. Warren Hastings, whom Kassim detested, had now assumed power in Calcutta; ironically he seemed to prefer son to father. Already rumours had reached him about this Warren Hastings – that he would like to see a change on the throne of Bengal – but this Kassim had dismissed as so much gossip. Of more immediate concern to him was the nearby trading settlement of Patna in which a small colony of Englishmen lived. They had refused to pay their taxes and on two occasions had insulted and beaten the Nawab's revenue collectors – offering them the final humiliation of being returned to Murshidabad tied back to front on donkeys.

Would that he had the authority of the Nawab. He would teach those insolent people a lesson they would never forget. There were many ways other than slaughter or oppression by which a strong man could impose his will. To persuade Mir Jafar to take the necessary steps was all but impossible – the Nawab could never rid his mind of how a few red-coated soldiers had thrashed an entire army.

In England, Robert, Lord Clive, Baron of Plassey, carefully adjusted his new periwig in front of the Louis XIV silver and gilt mirror over his dressing table. The affairs of the East India Company were to be debated in the Commons that day and Clive, as a new Member of Parliament, was taking his seat for the first time.*

He tossed away the wig and tried on another. He caught his expression in the mirror; the corners of his mouth had begun to turn down making him look peevish. What was worse his face was swollen with over-indulgence; he had the beginnings of a double-

* As an Irish peer, Clive was in fact eligible for the Commons

chin – and a distinct paunch. He reminded himself that he was only 38. He flung down this wig, too, and turned away from the accusing reflection. At that moment a liveried footman bowed himself into the room.

'There is a gentleman to see you, my lord.'

Clive swore. Time was precious that morning, and he'd little enough to waste on casual visitors.

'Who is he and what does he want?' he snapped.

'He mentioned something about Bengal, my lord, and gave his name as Mr Maskelyne.' Clive started.

'Maskelyne! Here? *Edmund*?' he exclaimed, springing to his feet and rushed past the flunkey on to the broad landing. From the top of the curving double-flight of stairs he could see the familiar and much loved bulk of his friend, standing with his back to him at the front of the vast hallway below.

'Edmund!' he cried as he ran eagerly down the stairs, his pink satin dressing-gown flapping behind him.

The figure turned his head, and Clive could have wept with disappointment. The resemblance was indeed remarkable, though he could now see a number of differences. He momentarily closed his eyes as if to hide from this cruel prank, composed himself, and walked downstairs in a more dignified manner.

The stranger gave him a decent bow which Clive – still shaken – reciprocated.

'Forgive me, my lord, for intruding at this hour ...' (Even the voice was the same!) 'Allow me to introduce myself – Nevil Maskelyne at your service, sir; cousin of your friend Edmund, and of the Lady Margaret, of course.' His manner was respectful yet assured.

'Cousin!' Clive echoed weakly, holding out his hand. 'But I was not aware ...'

'Not surprisingly, my lord. It is difficult to keep track of all the branches of our family, and my contacts with the Indian branch have been less than frequent I do assure you. However, I hope you will forgive this somewhat abrupt introduction.'

'Forgive! I am delighted to see you. Margaret will be overjoyed to know that her cousin is here. Have you taken breakfast?' He was almost afraid that this extraordinary manifestation of his friend would vanish.

'Not as yet, my lord. I left my home too early both for my stomach and my servants,' he laughed, adding wryly, 'And as for the Lady Margaret, I have seen her but once – when she was seventeen months old.'

'No matter, no matter, you shall breakfast with us. I pray you allow me a few moments to dress and to tell Margaret.'

Later, the Clive family and the stranger stolidly ate their way through a large English breakfast. Nevil Maskelyne caught one of the surreptitious glances of wonder that Margaret kept giving him.

'Put it down to the robust strain in our paternal grandfather, Cousin Margaret,' he said jovially, guessing what she was thinking.

'And to what profession do you apply yourself, Mr Maskelyne?' Clive asked, enjoying the man's company almost as much as he would have done Edmund's.

'I am a scientist, my lord: a mathematician, an astronomer to be more specific, and a Fellow of the Royal Society,' he replied, without in the least appearing to boast.

'Gracious! I am indeed impressed,' Clive replied sincerely. 'But you hinted earlier that you had some specific reason for wishing to see me,' he said, adding rather hastily that he was welcome even if there was no motive for the visit.

In answer, the visitor took from his tail pocket a long folded envelope which he handed to his host.

'Edmund wrote me and requested that I give you this,' he said simply, adding when he saw Clive's puzzled frown: 'He felt more assured that it would be delivered safely in this manner. According to my cousin there are a number of men in high places, among them Sir Francis Dashwood, who have little regard for your dignity, and Edmund feared that eyes other than your own might see and take advantage of its contents. He mentioned also, in his letter to me, that this fellow Dashwood is in league with a certain Mr Sullivan – with what object he knows not, but he is certain it is not for your comfort.'

Margaret tactfully pushed back her chair and rose to her feet, saying as she did so, 'I'm sure Cousin Nevil would like to accompany me while I show him the house and gardens. We shall leave you in peace, Robert, with your letter.' She wavered a moment, phrasing in her mind words that would convey urgency to her husband without the visitor thinking it a hint to cut short his visit.

'The House of Commons, Robert,' she said. 'You're to take your seat there, today, remember?'

He glanced up at her. 'Yes ... yes indeed, my dear. Do not allow Mr Maskelyne to rush away – but you will forgive me for a moment.'

When they were gone he slit open the envelope impatiently. The writing was certainly Edmund's and the date was only seven and a half months ago – clearly the ship had had favourable winds. He read as follows:

Robert, my very dear friend, I do send you felicitations and warm regards from Calcutta, and trust that this letter shall find you and Margaret and your son in good health in the more gentle climes of England.

I write of matters here which may as yet be unknown to Parliament, the Board, or any in England; and there may indeed be some in that country who would prefer to keep it so. For a number of reasons I caution you to consider well what you elect to reveal of these things, and to whom. My dear Robert, all is not well either in the Carnatic or in Bengal for a new (and I fear, sinister) power is arising in this land which fills me with foreboding – and the name it bears is Warren Hastings. Though his official rank be modest he is the undisputed leader in the Council.

Within the year of your departure he had so bewitched the Council that – on the pretext of default in payments according to the treaty – they schemed to replace the Nawab, Mir Jafar, with his son, Mir Kassim. On the Council's orders (Warren Hastings really, for now they are little more than sounding brass for him) a Colonel Munro took three hundred troops to Murshidabad and demanded full payment of monies owing. On being contemptuously dismissed by the Nawab, this Colonel returned the next evening and by stealth took Mir Jafar prisoner and did install his son, Kassim, on the throne. Mir Jafar now rests in Fort William, and though treated well and with honour, he is prisoner indeed.

It grieves me to speak ill of this Mir Kassim, for once he saved me from Siraj-ud-daula's captivity, but he shows no more affection for the Englishman than did the Nawab just mentioned, though he is a much wiser man.

By devious means known only to himself, this Warren Hastings has cajoled great bribes from this Mir Kassim amounting to the sum of one million three hundred thousand pounds. These are for the blindness and silence of the new Vansittart, Drake the Governor of Calcutta, Watts in the Council, and Hastings himself. While Kassim, for an unknown reason, has taken his armies and self to a new capital two hundred miles further north of Calcutta, by the name of Monghyr.

We are plagued in this land by corruption and greed of the worst kind so that often I am shamed to think myself English – though there are still stout hearts who protest the evil, but too few, alas. It has been told me that soon you will be Member of Parliament for Shrewsbury, and though this must be of importance I do confess it a trifle to what you would be here in Bengal. Once, many years ago, I said in jest to you, 'India hath need of noble souls like you,' or some such words. Mark me well, Robert, Baron Clive of Plassey, this can no longer be thought of as jest or exaggeration. I, Edmund Maskelyne, and *India* itself, do entreat you ... RETURN.

To you, Margaret and your son – and to my cousin who brought you this letter – I send my love. Anna is well, as I am myself, and we are happy within ourselves, but heartsore for what we see around us.

Most affectionately,
Edmund.

51

MIR KASSIM, the latest usurper of Bengal's throne, was learning the responsibilities of sovereignty. He already looked much older. He stood at the window overlooking the inner courtyard of his palace at Monghyr. Down below, sitting quietly on a marble bench, was Sareen.

He watched her as she rose and began walking slowly towards the gardens. Her figure remained slender, and her softly defined features were unmarked by past ordeals; her carriage was gravely dignified. Yet he knew well enough that she was simmering with anger inside.

All because of Patna. Send a protest to Major Maskelyne in Calcutta, she had argued, in the belief that because he was known to be an honourable soldier he must perforce have influence with the Council.

'It is futile,' Kassim told her. 'Though kindly disposed towards me, he shared with the Sahib Clive the conviction that Mir Jafar should be Nawab. True, I might seek justice from Major Maskelyne – but Major Maskelyne wields no influence with the Sahib Warren Hastings who now is the real power in Calcutta.'

The argument had been long and acrimonious. Sareen's inclination towards the diplomatic approach was hotly contested by the more impetuous Kassim. Eventually he had lost his temper.

'I have sent letters to Calcutta before. Always they are replied to with soft words, yet the ills go uncured. The people of Patna pay no customs duty and are fattening themselves at the expense of my state. Everything we produce, or grow, or catch, they demand at the price they choose to pay – and when they sell, they sell at a price they determine. Betel-nut, rice, salt, gunnies, straw, bamboo, ginger, sugar, tobacco – they buy and sell everything, and always we lose in the exchange. Some day I shall command Sombrer and his men to teach a lesson to these feringhees at Patna!'

It was an empty threat and he knew it. But it had been made, and it was sufficient for Sareen. She rounded on him in anger.

'*Sombrer!* Neither Hindu, Muslim, Turk, English nor French, but some base mixture owning to the virtues of none yet with the depravity of each! And *you*, the Nawab of Bengal, grant him your ear!'

Shaken by her outburst, he put his arm around her in attempted conciliation. 'I listen to no advice of Sombrer's. I was angry and said only ...'

'It was enough that you spoke as you did,' she curtly interrupted him. 'If the Nawab of Bengal is given to hasty threats ...'

The argument had broken off as the chief executioner himself appeared at the door, kneeling and touching the floor with his forehead. At the sight of him Sareen pushed herself away from Kassim and flung out of the room.

Kassim started to upbraid him for his insolent entry, when the fellow raised protesting hands and stopped him.

'I have returned from Patna, your highness,' he said softly, a curious foreboding in his voice. The Nawab was at once apprehensive.

'Speak.'

'In obedience to your highness, I rode with two collectors and demanded payment. They sneered at this lawful request, and the divine name of your highness was insulted. So great was the throng about us that I feared for our lives. We were compelled to draw our swords to fight our way out of the village. Three of the hatmen tried to prevent us – and were slain.' The story was told with much sincerity and great humility.

Kassim felt the room spinning about him.

'You *killed*! Killed three *hatmen*! Has the sun burned into your head, Sombrer? Your life was not in danger. There are no weapons at Patna: not one musket, not one sword, not one spear. I insisted on this when the settlement came under my protection. They might have beaten you; they would not have killed you,' he stormed.

'Your highness, I was attacked; I was forced to use my sword,' he whined; his head snapped back as Kassim struck him about the face.

'Sareen!' Kassim cried, rushing out into the courtyard in search of her. 'Sareen!'

Several days later the Select Committee of the Council met to consider the long communication it had received from the Nawab of Bengal. Edmund (as honorary member and Clive's unofficial deputy) listened morosely as Warren Hastings read out the letter using various inflexions of tone that subtly adjusted its meaning to suit his purpose.

'A pittance is offered for goods worth infinitely more, and these goods are then sold by the agents of Patna for ten and twenty times their true value ...' the letter went on, and concluded with a detailed explanation and an apology for the deaths of the three hatmen.

Hastings folded the letter and placed his hands upon it in a cynical gesture of dismissal.

'The Nawab elects not to mention those foreign scallywags who, being no agents of ours, trade in our name and bring us discredit,' he observed sarcastically.

'Yet we are discredited and dishonoured, if there be but *one* agent of ours doing these things,' one of the members declared hotly, 'even though there be a hundred villainous fakes.'

Hastings gave a noncommittal shrug as if the point were hardly worth taking. Edmund, fearing Hastings' intentions – and amazed at the facile way in which he could turn so abruptly against his own nominee, Mir Kassim – quickly got to his feet.

'I am inclined to accept the truth of that letter – and the apology. And were Lord Clive heading this committee, I am content that he would order that we treat leniently and fairly with Mir Kassim and make efforts to right the wrongs of which he complains.' A faint murmur of approval followed this.

At the mention of Clive's name Edmund noticed a slight tic starting in Hastings' right eye.

'Undoubtedly we should give deep thought to what the sagacious Lord Clive would have advised,' said Hastings, giving each of the members there the benefit of his concern. 'Yet, as we may only surmise what this advice might have been – and while deploring that we ourselves lack his infinite wisdom and genius of foresight – we must decide upon a course of action with what inferior reasoning and judgment we lesser creatures possess.'

After this, Hastings had little difficulty in swaying the Council to his own way of thinking.

'Let it not be forgotten that three innocent people were murdered – *murdered*, whatever Mir Kassim's excuse. And lest this becomes habit with the Nawab when he wishes to show his displeasure, we have a duty to make our protest known with the utmost speed. I propose that we order a regiment to Monghyr, under the command of –' he looked directly at Edmund – 'Major Munro. Merely a show of force to express the Council's displeasure,' he added quickly, aware of the frowns of disapproval he was receiving. 'We must allow the Major to use his initiative in any confrontation with the Nawab.'

Later that day Edmund, with his one-year-old baby daughter in his arms, wandered moodily around the garden of his home with Anna.

'Hastings is a fanatic; obsessed with a dream of wielding Clive's baton, eager to prove his superiority at no matter what cost. Were I Mir Kassim I know what my reaction would be on learning that a regiment of soldiers were being sent against me. It's a downright challenge to his authority and his throne!'

The child was being bounced so much with his agitation that Anna stretched out a protective arm and took her from him. 'And the Council endorsed all this?' she asked.

'Only after a tussle. They did obtain one concession from him ...' He hesitated.

'Tell me,' she said dully, half knowing what to expect.

He took a deep breath. 'It was agreed that I – because of friendly associations with Mir Kassim – should take a small force of cavalry and ride on ahead to Monghyr and ... well ... act diplomatically ... well, soften the impact on the Nawab ...'

'And you *asked* them to send you,' she exclaimed in dismay.

'I was the only person fitted to go,' he offered lamely.

'What about Eyre Coote?'

Edmund shook his head. 'He's out of Calcutta for some time. Besides Hastings insisted on this fellow Munro, who's a jolly good soldier, I admit, but hard – he talks over the top of a bayonet. I suppose all we can hope for is that I'll be able to smooth the whole thing over before he gets close to Monghyr.'

Bad news travels fast, particularly in India. Long before the cavalry of Edmund Maskelyne and the regiment of Major Munro had covered the first hundred of the three hundred miles to Monghyr, Mir Kassim knew of it.

'They dare send an army against me,' he exclaimed.

'Indeed it is true, your highness,' purred Sombrer, sharpening his claws in revenge for his earlier humiliation. 'They have spurned your apology, treated with contempt your protests on the injustices done to your highness, and now threaten to destroy Monghyr. These are the white men you trusted, your highness; men without honour, determined they will have a puppet on the throne of Bengal. Think well, my lord, of what you should do to Patna – for these are the maggots now decaying the throne of Bengal.'

For days Sombrer distilled his poison and poured it into Kassim's receptive ear. Against him, Sareen was now helpless. Torn between them, and outraged by the thought that an English army was so unjustly marching against him, driven to distraction by Sombrer's urgings to prove to the British that *he* was master of Bengal and not they, Mir Kassim audibly expressed the wish to be rid of the people of Patna. It was no more an order that Henry II's exasperated plea to be rid of Becket.

52

SEVERAL MONTHS had passed since Clive received Edmund's letter but he still hadn't spoken to Margaret about it; it lay between them like a silent reproach. He was thinking of it when Pitt got to his feet and requested permission of the Speaker to address the House.

Pitt was always worth listening to if only for the pleasure of following his dialectical manoeuvres. He could use the English language as a rapier or a bludgeon. The issue on this day was the East India Company; the packed House included many nabobs and shareholders – it was therefore an occasion for a lesson in semantics.

In a few words Pitt sketched an outline of 'John Company's' history: its formation in 1600 AD when Elizabeth had granted it a charter for trade between England and the East, and how of late (during the past fifteen years) it had extended itself beyond the terms of its charter to become a major political power in India. At that stage he made no reference to Clive, though many heads turned to give the slouching figure curious glances. Then Pitt moved into the attack.

'How can we reconcile ourselves? How can we live with honour?' he went on, his voice becoming harsh. 'Consider so splendid a country as Bengal, yet with its fifteen millions of starving human beings – three times the number of inhabitants of England – it is controlled by a *trading company* – a company whose rules are dictated by a board of directors twelve thousand miles from the operative scene. Directors, I may tell you, concerned only with account-books and the enrichment of a few hundred shareholders. And it is for this ignoble purpose that Bengal and the Carnatic are given over to plunder and to misery. There are, sitting in this House at this moment, men of substance whose coin is smeared with the lifeblood of Indian peasants, whose wealth is founded on famine, whose riches came not from honest toil but from extortion.'

Clive kept his eyes firmly on the speaker, conscious of the drift in feeling of those around him. The long roll of evils was unfolded, and at the end of it the Prime Minister halted his flow of invective and dramatically levelled an arm and forefinger at the stone figure of Clive. The Members stared at the miserable offender who had been singled out. Yet when Pitt spoke again there was less aggression in his tone.

'There sits an Honourable Member of this House: the Lord Clive of Plassey. An undoubted hero on whom England has bestowed praise and given, too, its heart; a man of great courage, an administrator and an inspired leader – and one whose deeds in the field will forever be admired. Nonetheless, he is the one person on whose shoulders much blame for this evil state of affairs must rest. I seek not to accuse him of deliberate machinations, nor of initiating or directing this mischief in India ... yet neither will I grant him relief from allowing this pestilence to exist and spread under his governorship. There is indeed much evidence that the Lord Clive, by small example and wilful blindness, permitted this corruption to reach its present magnitude.'

Pitt took a sip from a glass that a servant handed to him, and thus refreshed, continued. But now his purpose had changed. Having flogged the outraged Clive, Pitt now applied the ointment.

'It is not my intention to impeach a man who, in many ways, has been a faithful servant of his company and of this country, and in the doing so, by a paradox, has been a saviour of Bengal and the Carnatic. His deeds are on record for all to see – and England shall not be lacking in gratitude. Towards the Lord Clive we shall neither be churlish nor serve him so ignominiously as did the French their own hero, Dupleix; nor shall we treat him with shame as did the French their own General Bussy; nor so cowardly as again, the French, their gallant Count De Lally – a victor over us on three occasions – whom, after an infamous trial, they did execute for high treason.'

Clive was moved. Even in the most bitter conflicts with the French soldiers he had felt their courage and loyalty to a cause they believed in. Now they were gone – cast aside by the nation whose honour they had striven so hard to uphold. He was so engrossed in these reflections that he barely heard what Pitt was saying next, until he heard his name mentioned again.

'... and though there is yet resistance in this House to bring this Company under direct control, I do hereby charge its directors to mend their ways and to make request of the Lord Clive that he return to this unhappy country and by his authority bring an end to these crimes that plague it.' He paused for yet another dramatic moment while the Member of Parliament for Shrewsbury glowered at him, and said slowly and with majestic emphasis: 'And in the name of our Lord King, George the Third, in the name of this House, in the name of England, and in the name of Christianity, I beseech the Lord Clive to ponder well on these things, to search his conscience, and to take first ship to India to do that which he ought.'

The Members rose to applaud him; even those hypocritical nabobs whom Pitt had so castigated stood up and cheered. But Clive was not appreciative. He was in a perfectly foul temper by the time he reached home.

'Then, after grasping me by the throat, screaming that I am the most satanic of monsters, he calmly pats me on the back and says "go back to India and be a good boy" ', he complained to Margaret. 'But I say, be damned to the Commons! Have I not spent my youth and my manhood in the service of that country? Must I forever bear its smell in my nostrils, its sweat on my body, its red dust on my feet, to spend my days treating with savages, and my nights fearing the knife or the spear. No, it is too much. I have a right to comfort after what I have done for India – aye, and for England!'

Margaret wisely said nothing. She had had experience of these outbursts many times before. Like all shrewd wives, she could extract meaning from protestation; the more Robert stormed about not going to India the more certain she became that the opposite was his intention. It saddened her.

In bed that night she put her arms around him and laid her head against his chest. 'I'm told that Warren Hastings is to arrive in England next year,' she said softly. 'Perhaps you would not need to go to India if you waited and spoke to him, telling him of your feelings about what is happening there?'

Clive pulled himself away from her and stared with disbelief. 'Hastings! God grant that Bengal carries not the burden of Hastings!' he said fervently. 'How such talent could be neighbour to such callous spirit, I will never know. And to see him Governor of Bengal....' He shook his head vigorously.

'Then you think you will go ... go yourself, Robert?' she asked with sinking heart. He put his right arm around her and pulled her face to his, kissing her lovingly.

'It calls to me, dearest. It calls – and I try to close my ears,' he replied tenderly, adding softly, 'I'm undecided, Margaret – quite undecided.'

53

THE CAVALRYMAN extended an arm and tried to estimate the distance, then galloped back down the hill to where the rest of the squadron of dragoons were drawn up in formation. He reported to his captain who duly conferred with Major Maskelyne.

'We take the fork to the right, sir. He thinks he could make out the Patna church three miles off.'

Edmund nodded. It had been a hard ride but at least they were three days ahead of Munro and his force – and he was sure he could smooth things over with Mir Kassim in that time.

He noticed the captain looking at him in an odd way.

'Something worrying you?'

'Over-stimulated imagination, I guess, sir,' the captain replied, his eyes searching the wooded area around them. 'I find it ... kind of unnaturally quiet, don't you, Major?'

Edmund also looked round him.

'Quiet? Yes, I suppose so. Why? Did the scout see anything?'

'That's just it. He didn't see anything – not even wood-smoke over the settlement. You'd expect to see at least a few peasants gathering around when a squadron such as ours comes by.'

Edmund thought for a moment or two before making his decision. 'Have a sergeant and six men ride to Patna as quickly as possible; see if there's trouble there, then rejoin us half a mile outside the village. Order him to fire two shots if he needs us in a hurry.'

The captain turned his horse and cantered back to the squadron. A moment or two later seven cavalrymen sped past him on the way to Patna. The rest of the Squadron trotted on in the wake of the scouts. Within twenty minutes they were on the outskirts of the village.

It was, as the captain had said, unnaturally quiet. Normally swarms of Hindu peasants and their children would flock round to gape at this spectacle of red-coats in their long black 'jockey boots' and black, red-trimmed leather helmets; but there was only one solitary naked child, and even he was swiftly snatched out of the way by a woman who suddenly appeared from among the trees, and as rapidly disappeared again.

There were two musket shots in quick succession, causing Edmund's horse to rear nervously.

'Draw swords!' the officer shouted almost before the echo of the shots had died away – and within seconds the squadron, with Edmund in the lead, was charging towards the open bamboo gates of the settlement.

'Halt!' Edmund yelled, waving his sword and reining in his horse. He was all but run down by the excited cavalry behind him as the horsemen struggled to obey. The sergeant of the scouting party was walking towards him, trailing his horse by its reins, his sword gripped in his hand. His eyes were blank, his mouth trembling.

'Sergeant!' Edmund shouted. 'What's the trouble?'

The sergeant came up to him, so distraught that he failed to salute. He just stared up at Edmund.

'They're ... gawn ... all of 'em. They're gawn ... butchered,' he stammered. Edmund felt a coldness in his stomach.

'Mount your horse, sergeant, and fall in behind,' he snapped, shocking the fellow from his stupor, then gave orders to the captain to divide the squadron into separate groups and search the whole village.

The massacre was complete. White-faced, nauseated, the cavalry combed the small settlement. The torn, mangled corpses of a hundred and seventy-five men, women and children were counted. They were scattered around the settlement in various attitudes of death. Many of the men still grasped the necks of broken bottles or sharpened staves or the broken legs of tables, the only weapons they could fashion against the swords and spears of Sombrer's troops. And though the numbers of Muslim warriors who companioned them in death testified to the terrible struggle that had taken place,

264

the outcome could never have been in doubt.

Here and there were the signs of ferocious individual combat – a sword still in a man's breast, the jagged edge of a bottle in his opponent's throat. A Muslim, his skull crushed, still lay over the bodies of two children he had stabbed; the father who had killed him lay a few paces away, a spear thrust in his back. One man with a sharpened stave was entangled with the corpses of three he had killed before he himself was slaughtered.

'Not one poor creature still alive,' reported the ashen-faced captain an hour later. 'In all my years I've never seen....'

'Yes,' Edmund cut him off. Hatred, real hatred for the Muslim, for the first time raged within him. After Patna there could be no compromise with Mir Kassim. A man who condoned such massacre was unfitted to live, let alone rule over millions. He motioned the captain to sit down beside him on the steps of one of the houses.

'Three hours' fast ride and we could be in Monghry,' the captain muttered. 'We could give those devils a taste of *our* blades. There isn't a soldier here who wouldn't give his left arm to pay them back with their own steel.'

Edmund slowly shook his head, and with his sword-sheath started drawing patterns in the dust underfoot.

'It would be a useless sacrifice, captain – useless. What can a hundred do against thirty thousand?' He rested his elbow on his sword hilt and pursed his lips thoughtfully. 'Major Munro has six hundred sepoys and two hundred British foot soldiers. I expect to meet him south of Monghyr in three days' time. We shall wait, and then there shall be a reckoning with this Nawab,' he replied quietly, scattering the dust patterns he had made with his boot.

But Major Munro had been held up for two days.

A hundred and twenty miles south of Monghyr, his elephant waited patiently, stolidly, indifferent to the drama as the six huge siege guns were unhitched and wheeled into line. Artillerymen moved swiftly in disciplined order as they swabbed out the barrels, then rammed in massive balls of metal with full charges of powder.

Out of two nearby tents came six sepoys. They were naked save for their dhotis and had chains on their wrists and ankles. Each prisoner was escorted by three armed sepoys and a tall, red-jacketed, mitre-capped English NCO. The prisoners dragged and shuffled their feet and stared around them in gradually heightening terror as they were led across the barren ground to where the cannons had been positioned.

Major Munro came out of another tent and strode across to take command. He was a bulky, red-faced, bewhiskered soldier of unshakable convictions. At his command each prisoner was grasped, lifted up and stuffed, feet first, into the gaping hole of the muzzle of a cannon so that eventually only his head protruded clear of the rim. Loud wails arose until they reached a pitch too ghastly to hear. They reverberated in the dry, searing air.

'Read the sentence,' Munro said to the sergeant-major near him, seemingly indifferent to the cries from the half-demented creatures in the cannons. Six heads, monstrous in the muzzles of the guns in the hazy dawn light, twisted round, the eyes panic-stricken. Six artillerymen, flaming port-fires in their hands, stood motionless and ready. The sergeant-major came to attention, his mouth dry, and read stumblingly from the scrap of parchment in his hand. When he had finished he moved to each gun and concluded the indictment by addressing individually each frantic head – though it is doubtful whether any of the condemned men understood what he said.

'... and in that you, in the company of others, did cause the deaths of three sepoy officers: an act accounted mutiny. And having been lawfully tried and found guilty shall now suffer death in the manner prescribed by army regulations.'

Shaken, the sergeant-major stepped back and solemnly drew his sword. His hand trembled as he raised the blade.

'Let the sentence be carried out,' Munro intoned. The sword lowered until it paralleled the ground – its point levelled at the condemned men. With one accord the six artillerymen touched port-fires to the breeches of the guns.

Six cannon recoiled from the blast as smoke, flame, metal balls belched from the muzzles – taking with them over the desolate and arid land the fragments of the six mutineers. Munro's gaze took in the entire scene: the ranks of men at attention, the smoking guns whose black shadows patterned the ground, the ashen-faced sergeant-major.

'Pull yourself together, man,' he muttered under his breath; then in his normal voice. 'Swab out and recharge.'

As the artillerymen rushed to comply, he said conversationally to the senior NCO, 'Get them moving faster, sergeant-major; we've twelve more to execute. This blasted mutiny's cost me too much time already. Major Maskelyne'll be getting frantic if I don't meet with him as arranged.'

A few days later the two British forces converged south of Monghyr. Here Edmund (at the Council's insistence, despite Hastings' objections) assumed overall command – to Munro's manifest displeasure.

'Every one of them dead!' He was as shaken at the news of Patna as Edmund had been, but made a quicker recovery and put his mind to the task ahead of them.

'I was in Monghyr a couple of years ago,' he told Edmund. 'I doubt it'll have changed much. The town itself has no fortifications worth bothering about but the palace is like a fortified mansion in England – on a bigger scale, of course. What I recommend – if you don't mind my making suggestions ...?' He glanced over at his senior questioningly.

'Not at all. Go ahead.'

'Well, I suggest I clear a passage through the streets with grapeshot, right up to the palace walls, then I'll lay down roundshot at the weakest point, and when I've made an opening you'll be able to get through with your cavalry.'

'Yes,' said Edmund dubiously, his resolve on the inevitable slaughter only stiffening when he recalled the terrible things he had seen at Patna. 'I assume you're aware of what forces the Nawab commands?'

Munro gave a derisive laugh. 'Ten to one by my reckoning; but I seem to recall that Clive took 'em on at twice the odds and the Nawab still ran.' Edmund was not sure how to take this. Munro certainly had a blunt way of speaking.

'This happens to be Mir Kassim, not Siraj-ud-daula,' he returned, heavily. 'However....' He rose to his feet to indicate the meeting was over. 'I'm reluctant to lay waste a town in order to bring two men to justice. For the past few days I've been giving Patna much thought. Something about it worries me: it just doesn't seem in character with the Mir Kassim that I knew.'

Munro flushed. 'I trust, sir, you've no intention of *parleying* with him,' he said angrily, his eyes manifesting his opinion of the spineless Maskelyne. Edmund stepped back a pace and coolly eyed him up and down.

'Major Munro. While I am in command of this expedition it shall be conducted according to my direction. Should you by any chance disobey my orders or show insubordination in any way, I shall have you put under arrest and returned to Calcutta to face a court-martial.'

The chill, dispassionate delivery of this threat had its effect on Munro. He started to bluster that such a thing had never been his intention.

'I am pleased to hear it, Munro,' Edmund rejoined calmly. 'Now. In the morning you yourself will take an escort of men under a flag of truce and demand audience with the Nawab. Before you deliver the message I am to give you, you shall insist that no person be present – other than the Sahiba Sareen. On no account are you to treat with the Nawab if the executioner Sombrer is there – mainly because I believe his hand to be behind this Patna affair. And, Major Munro, if this is proved to be so ... I ... want ... his ... head.'

54

MARGARET OPENED the door to Clive's study and shivered in the draught of cold air that met her. Exasperated, she closed the two windows that had been left wide open. Then she looked round the room, closed the two books he had been studying and put them tidily away; a thought struck her.

Robert hated the cold. He would never have stayed in the room with two windows wide open. She opened the bottom drawer of his writing-desk and felt around with her hand.

The pipe was still there. Her fingers shook as she touched the bowl. It was warm. From out of the drawer come the acrid sweet smell she recognised at once; no wonder he had been so relaxed that morning.

The discovery saddened her but she could not find it in her heart to condemn him. Such men as Robert Clive must be allowed their little frailties, she tried to tell herself, closing the drawer and hurrying off to see how young Edward was getting on with his new tutor.

In the board-room of India House, the headquarters of the East India Company, Clive took his seat with dignity. He was plumper than ever; his long wig brushed his shoulders, and his finery of silk and brocade outdid any other in the room. A jewelled sword hung at his belt and he carried a long silver-knobbed cane in his hand. Elegant, cool, foppish almost, yet the eyes still glittered with the passionate intensity of the hero of Arcot. He did not see the tall skeletal figure, with the face of a satanic undertaker and the eyes of a kite-hawk, who sat quietly at the back of the room.

The Deputy-chairman was clearly depressed as he called the meeting to order, while the Chairman, Sullivan, looked severe and stared at his fingernails.

'My lords, gentlemen, shareholders ...' the Deputy-chairman mumbled abstractedly, fingering nervously the paper in his hand. 'There is grave news from Mr Hastings ...' Only the rouge on his cheeks provided colour to his lined face. 'One of our trading posts, a place called Patna ... where once resided ...'

There was a moment of stunned silence when he had finished; in the uproar that followed could be heard threats and shouts for revenge. But a hush descended on them when Clive got to his feet.

'Mr Deputy-chairman, my lord, these are grave tidings indeed that you bring, and I speak for myself and for the meeting when I express the deep shock and revulsion I feel at such barbaric slaughter. To attach blame for the events which led to this massacre is not my purpose – not at this particular moment. Yet the Honourable Members of the Board are well aware of one in Calcutta in whose hands they have condoned the accumulation of power ... I will say no more on this matter,' he said in a respectful manner.

He lowered his head as if considering what next to say, and then raised it again, fixed his gaze on the glowering Sullivan, and began speaking again in an accusatory tone.

'It is no secret that the prime intent of today's assembly, under the instigation of its Honourable Chairman, Mr Sullivan, was to bring indictment against me. Thus, having thrashed and abused and maligned, and further reduced me to a cowering whelp, I would then be dismissed ignominiously to spend the remainder of my hangdog days in some obscure part of this country ... Therefore, let it be said, let it be known, let it be impressed on this meeting that I spurn this crimination of my governorship and will admit to none of it. I served always for the betterment of this Honourable Company. Consider the situation which the victory at Plassey surrendered to me. A great prince was dependent on my pleasure; an opulent city lay at my mercy; I walked through vaults piled high with gold and jewels which begged my taking; Rajahs and Nawabs offered me palaces; the richest bankers bid against each other for my smiles ... At this moment, gentlemen, I stand here astonished at my own moderation!'

A number there tentatively clapped their hands but were silenced by Clive himself as he turned on them his most imperious gaze. 'Now it is seen what has occurred during my absence from Bengal and the Board is preparing a volte-face to beg my return there – under pressure of Parliament and the frustration of its shareholders. Therefore I say to them that I reject the poisonous insinuations of the Honourable Chairman – and call into condemnation the machinations of that malevolent and odious crocodile, Dashwood – to whom Sullivan is mere lackey and obsequious toad.'

Here the outcries compelled him to be silent for a few moments – though it was difficult to tell if the voice of the meeting was for or against him.

'But guttersnipes and licentious knaves in public office are no concern of mine – what matters is Bengal. And to India I do incline myself ...' Heartfelt cheers greeted this, which again Clive silenced. 'Yet it would be futile for me to so exert myself – as indeed one must in that unhappy country – if my measures are to be thwarted and condemned here in England by this Board – due to the influence of a Chairman known to be my personal and inveterate enemy.' His gaze raked the line of solemn-faced directors before coming to rest on the fuming Sullivan, then addressing him and pronouncing each word as if it were a sword-thrust, he concluded with: 'It is a matter of complete indifference to me who fills the Chair – if Sullivan does not. But if he continues to occupy that seat, I must decline to go.'

Clive's ultimatum struck the meeting with an impact only a little less than that of the news of Patna. There was applause, insults were flung, challenges shouted, there was vociferous argument, cries of delight. The Deputy-chairman was almost helpless in the tumult as he banged on the table to restore order. And when eventually this was achieved he put Clive's declaration into a formal motion.

When all the votes had been registered and counted and the results announced, a smouldering Sullivan left the Chair – and his office – and stalked out of the room, to the sound of thunderous cheering for Robert, Lord Clive.

A few weeks later the Governor of Bengal and his family took ship back to India: the year was 1765.

55

KASSIM WAS unnerved by conscience. His self-esteem would not allow him to admit his mistake, and since Patna he had felt obliged to pretend that the massacre had been carried out on his orders; he suffered accordingly the scourgings from Sareen's tongue. But when Major Munro was brought into the audience chamber he saw before him Judgment itself come to pronounce against him.

Munro accorded him neither obeisance nor greeting. He simply handed him Edmund's note and stood back while he read it. Sareen, seated quietly at Kassim's side, observed the confrontation from under lowered lids.

'The insolence of these English!' exclaimed Kassim, preparing to tear up the paper, but Sareen gently salvaged it from his clenched hands and read it herself.

'It well merits your consideration, my lord,' she advised softly, setting herself to withstand his wrath.

He rounded on her immediately. 'You would have me renounce my throne – be taken to Calcutta in chains – executed in my own realm!' His voice rose in anger.

She faced him calmly. 'Rather would I die myself than have this happen, Kassim, but the Sahib Maskelyne makes no such demands. He asks only that you stand before a court of enquiry in Calcutta, and that the man who executed this deed, Sombrer, be at once put to death. When it is known that the killing was not your intention....'

She broke off when Kassim started to rave that nothing had happened which he himself had not ordered. She knew that he was not storming at her but at the possibility that others might not think him master in his own kingdom. Even at the risk of total disaster he was determined to inflate the image of himself as the omnipotent Nawab.

He stopped shouting, strode across the room and faced the major.

'Begone! Tell the hatman my answer is no.'

'My orders are that I must wait one full day for your answer,' Munro returned coldly, standing his ground. Kassim, infuriated by his insolence, drew back his hand to strike the Englishman across the face, but Sareen rushed across to him and seized his wrist.

'Go, Sahib Major, go,' she hissed, her head jerking back as Kassim smacked her hard to free himself. Munro hesitated, then swung on his heels and stalked out of the room, his face livid with rage.

Edmund listened with growing dismay to Munro's story. Even allowing for exaggeration, the challenge that Kassim had issued was unmistakable. At the end of the story he thanked Munro and was about to dismiss him when the second-in-command tossed down his gauntlet.

'Well, are we to attack?' he challenged.

For a moment Edmund thought what Clive would have done had he been in command. 'Yes,' he replied, 'since we have given him an ultimatum we must be seen to abide by our word. We shall adopt the plan you suggested, Munro.'

The glint of triumph in his companion's eyes annoyed Edmund but he refused to vent his spite on him. Instead he bowed his head and listened to the fellow boast. 'Give me thirty hours and I'll blast through the city and all the way from Monghyr to Oudh.'

Edmund did not check him. Munro was a good tactician, yet Edmund wondered at the nature of the man to whom the prospect of extravagant bloodletting made such an appeal. The next day his boast seemed likely to be fulfilled. The siege guns laid down a creeping barrage on Monghyr town. There was little resistance. The civilians fled while the soldiers retreated into the fortified palace. By noon the next stage of the attack on the palace walls was set to begin.

Pieces of masonry cracked and flaked off under the incessant pounding. The round balls of metal passed through the thinner sections of the curtain walls leaving behind gaping holes through which an ox might have strolled. On one corner of the palace a tower – a noble piece of architecture built two centuries before the Emperor Akbar – received a cannon-ball through its graceful triform window arches. With almost painful dignity the wall started to crumble and then bend outwards; finally with a resounding roar the whole tower split open and collapsed in a storm of rubble and a shroud of dust.

Ancient archways with their exotic foliations and grilles – the creations of long-dead craftsmen – shattered and fell to the dust; sturdy pillars cracked and toppled; great patterns of mosaics split into a million coloured fragments; historic tapestries and paintings were shredded or burnt. The palace of Monghyr, a testament to man's noblest creativity, slowly disintegrated under that terrible cannonade.

Inside the walls the defenders offered ineffectual resistance despite their superiority in numbers. Munro was right in his supposition. So deeply ingrained had the legend of white invincibility become that most of the defenders ran at the first barrage; and even those who remained were cowed. Kassim, who was made of sterner stuff, rushed about shouting threats and encouragement, trying in every way to stiffen the backbone of his men. The moment his back was turned they crept into shelter and peered longingly at the northern gate which promised escape. Ultimately, fear of the hatmen conquered fear of the Nawab: they set off at a shambling, crouching run towards the gate, casting aside their weapons as they went.

Edmund felt no joy as he watched the demolition of this lovely palace from his position at the head of the cavalry, but when the barrage ceased, he raised his arm and his men charged towards the broken walls.

Sareen, horrified by the suddenness of the attack, ran from room to room gathering the female servants in a frenzied effort to get them to safety. As she hurried down one of the outer corridors, a retinue of females screaming in her wake, she looked through a low window on the second floor and glimpsed Sombrer in the courtyard below.

Hatred for the man welled up in her, momentarily overcoming her fear. She stopped to watch him. With four other officers he was busily strapping leather satchels over the backs of five horses. It needed little imagination to deduce what was in the wind.

She saw a musket on the ground and without a moment's hesitation picked it up and rested its muzzle on the window ledge. She pointed the gun with a woman's aversion to firearms, closed her eyes and pressed the trigger. There was a click and nothing more. She flung the musket aside, weeping with frustration. A soldier pushed by, halted warily on seeing her.

'Kill him! *Kill him!*' she screamed, pointing through the window at the five men now climbing astride their horses. The bewildered man looked to where she was pointing then stared blankly at her. These were the Nawab's own men!

'Sombrer ... Sombrer,' she shouted at the slow-witted soldier. 'Kill him!'

With evident reluctance he knelt at the window, took careful aim and squeezed the trigger. The musket spouted flame. Either the musket or the aim was faulty. It was not Sombrer who fell from his horse but one of the other four.

Sombrer jerked his head round, spotted Sareen at the upper window and the soldier with the musket in his grip, and immediately dug spurs into his horse. The last she saw of him was the flapping of his robes as he and the remaining horsemen galloped through the north gate, scattering foot soldiers out of their way, their heavily loaded saddle-packs bouncing furiously.

As they passed under the stone archway, there came from the opposite direction the shrilling of trumpets. Clasping her gown tightly around her Sareen ran down the corridor to another window and looked out just as the cannons ceased firing. Less than a quarter of a mile away was a low cloud of dust and emerging from it like vengeful wraiths came a squadron of red-coated cavalry. Their sabres were held straight out and angled downwards as they headed for the broken walls.

The horsemen did not slow at the obstruction, but continued their charge, horses leaping over stones, fragments of wooden gates, bits of iron, the soldiers on their backs striking down any warrior rash enough to oppose them, heading resolutely for the main gateway of the palace itself.

Five of the Nawab's men, of nobler spirit than the others, rushed towards the invaders with their long spears. They were flung aside like so much discarded cloth, to be trampled over by the horses following.

Sareen's mind was in a turmoil. If the Sahib Maskelyne captured the Nawab he would be safe and would be taken to Calcutta to stand trial; but should he meet with one such as Major Munro he would not stand a chance. The English would be thinking only of what they had seen at Patna and would not stop to judge between Kassim and Sombrer.

For a moment longer she stood at the window, riveted by the sight. Hardly thirty feet from where she was standing, a Muslim thrust upwards with his spear at a cavalryman, impaling him with its point, but as he jerked to free his spear, a sabre came slicing across from behind him. The mouth gaped open, the head angled for a moment and then toppled from the body; it rolled in the dust, to come to a stop against a broken stone.

The shock released her from her temporary paralysis. She flung arms across her face – and screamed. And she ran. Yet even in her panic her thoughts were of Kassim and how she must get him away from this charnel house. She covered most of what was left of the palace in her agonised search until eventually she found him. He was alone in the great audience chamber, seated on his throne, head sunk deep on his chest, his gaze on the floor, in a posture of hopelessness.

She grasped him by the arm, tugged him to his feet and practically pulled him from the room and into the central corridor. He allowed himself to be led down flights of stairs and along narrow passageways until they reached the Nawab's private stables.

The volume of firing increased as sepoys and British infantry of Munro's force came over the walls and thrust their way into the courtyard. Soon the whole palace would be surrounded, and the last hope of escape would have gone.

Disregarding the lack of saddles, Sareen and Kassim mounted two of the stallions. The stable doors were wide open, the small outer gate unbarred, and in the searing heat of the late afternoon the two riders, lying flat across the backs of the horses, sped out of the palace.

By sun-set Major Edmund Maskelyne formally took possession of Monghyr and called a halt to the fighting.

56

THE BELLS of the churches in Calcutta rang when Clive's ship appeared in the Hooghly river. Clive stood at the rail of the quarter-deck, his arm around his young son, pointing out the features of the city – especially Fort William, and telling him, to the young-ster's joy, of how it had surrendered to three drunken marines. Margaret, in a deck chair behind them, watched him. She had had misgivings about their return to India, not least because of Clive's health – though he adamantly insisted there was nothing wrong with him. Fortunately the sea voyage, though tedious, had been good for him.

'There, *there* – now can you see him? The tall man over to your right,' Clive said to the little boy, his own excitement growing. 'That's your uncle – Edmund Maskelyne – your mother's brother.'

The child tried to look impressed, but of more interest to him were the ranks of soldiers drawn up on parade for the arrival of the new Governor. He pointed to a splendid fellow on horseback, and his father told him that was Colonel Eyre Coote.

'And who are those people there, father?' he piped up, indicating a score of richly dressed civilians, who clearly were not enjoying the torrid weather.

'The Council of Calcutta,' his father replied without enthusiasm.

The ropes were fastened, the ship secured, the gangway lowered, and, through a corridor of stiffly erect seamen and officers, Robert Clive passed from the deck of the Indiaman and once more on to the soil of Bengal.

There was much hugging and kissing, amazement in the change in each other (or at the absence of change in each other), laughing at one another's sallies, expressions of thankfulness at their safe arrival, and all the other banal, human things which are done and said on these occasions. Then followed in sequence the traditional inspection of the guard with Eyre Coote, the solemn address of welcome from the Council, the shaking of every important citizen's hand, the dramatic ceremony when Clive's personal standard was broken out over Fort William. Indeed royalty itself could not have received a more splendid welcome.

'Thank God that's over,' breathed Clive when finally they were allowed to climb into their carriage for the drive to his official residence. Next to him sat Edmund, opposite the little boy with Margaret and Anna – the women already engaged in animated conversation.

'Tell me of Patna,' he said quietly to Edmund, his eyes noting with ambivalent feelings the familiar drovers and bullock-carts, the beggars and bazaars, the proud Muslims and the abject Hindu, the ochre-red dust swirling about the baking streets, the off-duty soldiers in punch shops, the palanquins with their shouting hur-currahs, and the chariots and phaetons with their fashionably dressed passengers – all the same, all unchanging, the eternal canvas of India.

'Patna?' Edmund strove for an unemotional answer. 'It's quiet enough now. We're trying to encourage new arrivals in the country to go there and get the place functioning again. But it will be a long time before people forget.'

'And the Nawab?'

'There isn't one,' Edmund returned flatly. 'Mir Kassim escaped and fled to Oudh where they made him welcome. As for Monghyr, Hector Munro is still up there as officer administering the capital.'

'And where is the *real* Nawab, Mir Jafar?' Clive asked pointedly, causing Margaret to glance over at him in the way that wives do when their husbands threaten a breach of good manners.

'Still in Fort William,' Edmund told him, sighing as he saw Clive's obvious annoyance.

'All this time in Fort William!' Clive said, more to himself than Edmund.

'In all possible comfort,' Edmund replied defensively, refusing to wilt under the sharp look that Clive gave him.

'Twelve thousand miles away I sniffed the stench of Hastings. But *here,* it pervades the very atmosphere with its corruption,' Clive growled. Edmund kept silent. It was wiser to wait until this mood of Robert's had passed. He observed the faintest of tremors in the hand that Clive raised to his cheek.

'Does something ail you, Robert?' he asked solicitously, quietly so that the ladies should not hear him. He was aware for the first time of the yellowish tinge to his friend's skin.

Clive quickly put one hand on top of the other to still the tremor.

'It's of no consequence, Edmund. I was taken with a slight fever aboard ship. I think the medicaments that fool of a surgeon applied left their mark on the body. It will clear in a few days as soon as I get some fresh fruit and vegetables inside me.'

Edmund did not question him further. Every man was entitled to choose his own way to death; yet how tragic if Robert Clive had elected to choose *that* particular way. His volatile temperament, his moods so swiftly alternating between elation and acute depression, could be a frightening amalgam if compounded with opium.

Clive changed the subject.

'Petal Wilkinson? Quite well, Robert. She's still the best source of reliable information....' He stopped to ponder a moment. 'I had no intention of darkening your first day in Calcutta, Robert,' he gave an apologetic smile, 'but she says that Mir Kassim's friend, the Nawab of Oudh, intends to invade Bengal and attach it to his state. He's using Kassim's dethronement as an excuse.'

Clive was alert at once. 'Have you verified this, Edmund?'

'No. It's only a rumour that Munro picked up in Monghyr, but Petal confirms it.'

Clive thought for a moment. 'On the assumption that this rumour turns out to be true, have we enough troops to stop him?'

Edmund replied at once. 'No.'

Clive raised his eyebrows. Edmund went on to explain. 'Most of our sepoys are from Oudh families; it's as simple as that. They won't fight against this Nawab. We had an inkling of what might happen when Munro was on his way to Monghyr. The rumour got around that he was leading them against Oudh; there was a mutiny, and three sepoy officers were killed.'

Clive relapsed into a brooding silence until the cavalcade had passed through the wide gateway of the Governor's Residence. He assisted Margaret and Anna from the coach while Edmund lifted down the young boy, but as the ladies walked up the steps to the house, he caught hold of Edmund's arm. 'Time enough for chit-chat later. Come with me. To Fort William,' he called up to the startled coachman, then half pushed Edmund back into the carriage and climbed up after him. He leaned through the window and beckoned to a flunkey.

'Convey my apologies to Lady Margaret; inform her I shall be away for two hours,' he said, waving the coachman to proceed.

'At least let a little Bengal dust collect on your shoes before stirring up some more, Robert,' Edmund grumbled. Clive did not appear to hear him.

'When we get to the fort, contact Warren Hastings and tell him I wish to address a full Council meeting tomorrow, forenoon. Then ...'

'Hastings isn't in Calcutta,' Edmund interrupted, surprised that Clive had been unaware of this. 'He sailed for England several months ago. Either the Board or the government summoned him. He refused to say – simply told the Council he was taking leave for two years.'

'Hastings in London!' Clive exclaimed, then recalled that Margaret had said something of this before they left England. His mind began seething with conjecture at the witches' brew that Dashwood, Sullivan and Hastings might be concocting. No matter, he told himself, there are more immediate things to worry about. Then aloud to Edmund: 'Get hold of Eyre Coote and tell him I want a fully equipped force ready to move in ten days' time; he is to take no sepoys whose home state is Oudh. Scrape together every soldier you can. Leave in Calcutta only those men who are genuinely unfit. Have you got all that, Edmund?'

Edmund draped his arm over the leather squab of the seat and looked wonderingly at his friend.

'You sound just as you did before Plassey,' he rejoined with a huge sigh. Robert clapped a hand on Edmund's knee and with his other wagged an admonishing finger at him.

'If the Nawab of Oudh allies himself with Kassim and what's left of his army, Plassey might well be a skirmish by comparison. Just make damned sure, good friend, that every sepoy with us is going to fire his musket in the right direction.'

The commander of Fort William was put out but honoured by the Governor's arrival. He quickly recovered and prepared to lead him with much effusiveness towards his own suite of rooms. Clive stopped him.

'Go at once to where you are holding Mir Jafar prisoner, and request of His Highness that he grant me an audience in five minutes' time,' he said curtly. The bemused officer scurried away without further ado.

It was a much thinner Mir Jafar that made him a salaam – to which Clive respectfully doffed his hat – and then stood erect and stared with dignified coolness at his old adversary. Clive came straight to the point.

'It was not by my will – nor my knowledge – that you were dethroned and your son usurped your rightful place. And I grieved indeed that you were so sorely abused and held prisoner in this place. But all that is at an end now. By the authority invested in me you shall be forthwith released and installed once more as the true Nawab of Bengal.' The elderly man gave him a cynical glance but said nothing. 'You have been much abused, and for this I do now beg your forgiveness, and ask you to believe that I shall do all that I can to arrange compensation for this cruel and unjust incarceration.'

Clive paused for a moment, expecting some response, but when none came his manner hardened a little though his tone remained even. 'In ten days' time I shall be leaving for Murshidabad, Patna and Monghyr. I should be honoured indeed if you would decide to accompany me. Having attended to your re-installation as Nawab, it is my intention to continue further north to engage with Mir Kassim and the Nawab of Oudh.'

Mir Jafar studied his visitor with some curiosity before turning away from him and deliberately seating himself in the only chair in his room. It was a piece of princely arrogance in the presence of an underling – and Clive felt it.

'I am astounded at the honour you do me, your excellency,' he said with heavy irony. 'I am indeed grateful that you promise to restore to me that which should never have been stolen. As the victim am I now to cringe and beg favours from my erstwhile gaolers? And for how long shall I be permitted to occupy the throne of Bengal once the Nawab of Oudh takes up arms against the hatmen, and when my son returns to avenge his losses?'

'I have promised you compensation, Mir Jafar, and we shall say no more on that account. I have offered you apology for an offence not of my doing. As for the future, you are obliged to consider your fortune as inextricably bound with England's. Our cause shall be your cause, and yours shall be ours. Have no doubts; I shall hold the gates of Bengal secure against your enemies, and while my arms are at that gate you shall sit peacefully on Bengal's throne.'

The two men stared at each other, but it was the Nawab who first looked away. He tossed a speculative glance at Edmund as if only then being aware of his presence, and then he addressed him in a slightly amused tone.

'My lord Clive speaks well – and I do grant him honesty of purpose – but words alone will not push aside the mountain.'

Edmund bowed and replied evenly, 'Let your highness search his memory for Plassey; did not there the Lord Clive produce an earthquake?'

Mir Jafar looked at him, wondering if an insult was implied. Then he shook his head, rose to his feet, allowed the Baron of Plassey the merest glimmer of a smile, and said, 'So be it. I shall travel with you when you are ready.'

57

·EDMUND STRETCHED, rolled on to his side and playfully rubbed Anna's naked stomach. She firmly took his hand away and sat up, casting a glance at the clock on the wall.

'Enough, Edmund. Does time mean nothing to you?'

'Not a great deal,' he yawned; 'not for the next thirty hours at least. After that I shall no doubt fully earn my pay for the next few weeks,' he added ruefully, heaving himself off the bed and starting to dress.

Anna also slid off the bed and put on a robe. She watched Edmund pull on his clothes, smiling to herself at his efforts to button the waist of his breeches by sucking in his stomach muscles. He was getting to be a little heavy around the middle though his figure was still strikingly masculine.

'So you don't mind my going to see her?' he asked, dragging on his stockings.

'Not now,' Anna rejoined blandly. 'I'm sure her purpose is strictly honourable.'

'Well, would you rather that I asked her to come here?' he pressed, knowing well what Anna's answer to that would be. For what respectable household in Calcutta would dare entertain the owner of its most notorious bordello.

'I'm fully aware of the nature of your former association with ... with the lady in question. And I'm also sure that in her way she is a person of integrity.' Now she was being patronising. 'So if she makes an urgent request to see you then I must accept that it is for reasons that I could not possibly object to.'

Edmund hugged his wife. 'You're a stuffy old dear, but I love you,' he grinned, buckling on his sword belt. 'She said five o' the clock, so I'll be in good time.'

Some twenty minutes later his carriage drew up outside the familiar gates of the white stone mansion. His mouth twisted into a lopsided smile at the greetings he received from the chubdars, who hailed him as some long-absent patron.

'Edmund. How lovely to see you again.' Petal Wilkinson came forward, her hand outstretched, and as Edmund grasped it, hesitated for a moment and then came nearer and kissed him. He stood back and gave her an admiring look. The years seemed to have passed her by without leaving so much as a mark. Though the flamboyant Turkish pantaloons and Chinese jackets had been abandoned in favour of more conservative attire there was still an exotic air about her and a rare vitality that made her glow. 'How is Mrs Maskelyne?'

'Convinced you're up to some devious scheme to lure me back into bed,' teased Edmund, embracing her with great affection.

'Careful, Major, 'tis an honest woman you're speaking to,' she laughed.

'And Jasmine and Lotus?'

'Ceaselessly complaining that they never have anyone with the gallant, heroic gentility of their Edmund,' she tossed back, showing her white teeth in a flashing smile.

'Enough of that, Petal. I'm only a mere mortal – though I do admit, better than most,' he said, striking an attitude; then, in more serious vein, 'Now, a large glass of Madeira and then you can tell me what the summons is all about.'

Later, as they sat on the stone bench in the garden under the shade of an enormous fig tree, Edmund with a large glass of wine in his hand, Petal came to the point.

'There are rumours that Governor Clive is taking an army to

282

the north of Bengal – possibly to Oudh,' she said flatly, making it a statement and not a question.

'Why Oudh?' said Edmund cautiously.

'Please, don't treat me as a child, Edmund. I have eyes and very keen ears. Are you still determined on Mir Kassim – or is it the threat of Oudh?'

'Frankly, I don't know. Obviously I should like to bring Mir Kassim to justice, but the moment I mentioned to Robert Clive that he'd taken sanctuary in Oudh, he immediately made preparations for an expedition. For myself, I think it of greater importance to maintain peace in Bengal than to seek revenge on any individual.'

Petal studied him for a moment or two, then said gravely, 'Clive is a man of foresight, though I often suspect his humanity. For years he has been aware of the envy of the Nawab of Oudh for Bengal – and Kassim may now provide the touchstone to an invasion. Governor Clive knows that a swift show of force in northern Bengal may be sufficient to dissuade Oudh from stretching out greedy fingers.'

'Would that you were a man – and praise heaven that you're not, Petal,' Edmund breathed in wonderment. 'You would have conquered Bengal yourself.' She cast him a little smile.

They talked on at some length about the problems of Bengal, but Petal seemed abstracted, as if in her mind a plan was evolving to which the details refused to dovetail. Edmund had known her long enough to appreciate this and did not press her, but contented himself with providing inconsequential conversation.

'And you're very happy with Anna?' Petal asked, introducing a subject that she knew would keep Edmund busy while she attended to her own private thoughts.

'Very happy,' he assured her, 'though occasionally she makes reference to Mathieson and sighs a little. Otherwise we live together contentedly. Two days ago we went to the concert held in the Council House ...' He managed to stretch out the subject for a good ten minutes before he dried up.

Eventually Petal gave out a long shivering sigh. Ghosts walking over her grave, Edmund told her with a slight smile.

She pursed her lips in a silent kiss, then said quietly, 'I shall take a few retainers and travel north myself – to Murshidabad or Monghyr ... or even Oudh. If I leave tomorrow I shall arrive several days before you and your army.'

Edmund sat up in alarm. 'But for what purpose?' he asked sharply.

'First, Edmund, because of fear – fear that one day cannon will again destroy Calcutta and Bengal; fear for my own safety, for the lives of Jasmine and Lotus and my other girls, fear for all our lives. Do not think I have real nobility of purpose for I haven't – I simply want to live in peace.'

'But in the name of the saints, Petal! What can *you* hope to achieve?' Edmund expostulated.

'Somewhere in my ancestry I have blood ties with Alivardi Khan,' she said distantly, a revelation any white woman would not have dared make if she valued her status in society. Edmund made no comment, though he guessed at the effort it had cost her to tell him. 'Kassim and Sareen I have known – and loved – since birth, as I knew Siraj-ud-daula. You are looking at the only person in Bengal, Edmund, with the singular ability to speak with the Nawab of Oudh, with Kassim, with Sareen – with you, my dear friend – and even with Governor Clive, without any of them fearing my power or doubting my motives.'

Edmund gulped down the remainder of his wine and thought-fully wiped his lips with the back of his hand. 'If you are decided on going, Petal, then go and God be with you. But I don't think it would be wise for me to tell Clive of your intention – he might prevent you leaving as a precaution against advance notice of his move reaching Oudh.'

'Now I think you must return home to Anna,' Petal said, relieved that some definite course of action had been taken. 'You'd better give as an excuse that ...'

'That Jasmine and Lotus could tolerate my absence no longer,' he finished for her with a mischievous grin, and then he hugged her close to him and whispered sincerely, 'Take care of yourself, Petal. I'm not religious, but tonight I'll specially offer a prayer for you.'

58

THOUGH CLIVE had moved fast in putting together a force to meet the threat from the north, the Nawab of Oudh had moved faster. He advanced into Bengal with an army so immense that Siraj-ud-daula's at Plassey would have seemed but a segment of it by comparison, and had already laid siege to Monghyr and the small garrison it contained under Munro, by the time Clive left Calcutta.

From its previous battering, the huge and rambling palace at Monghyr bore the eroded, rubble-strewn appearance of ancient ruins. Inside, crouching wherever shelter promised, were a few score English soldiers and two hundred sepoys. Four days of constant attack by the advance units of the Oudh army had stiffened their resistance, and though nine thousand warriors prowled outside the walls, the attackers had brought no large cannon with them.

Striding through the crumbling masonry, Major Munro looked haggard but was still vigorously determined. His contempt for the fighting ability of the Muslim enabled him to view his plight with more sanguinity than another officer might have done. A pace behind him came a British sergeant-major with two English grenadiers, bayonets fixed on their long muskets.

Munro tried a door, found it locked and, without hesitation, kicked it open and barged inside. He was just in time to lay hands on a sepoy who was half-way through the window and to drag him back again. Five other sepoys sprang to their feet in guilty fear.

The recaptured sepoy squealed in panic when he recognised his assailant. Flinging the fellow against the wall, Munro pulled out his sword and nudged the point under the sepoy's chin, forcing the terrified soldier to keep his head pressed against the wall tapestry. In fluent Persian, Munro hissed, 'Any soldier, sepoy or British, who tries to desert under fire, will be suspended by his feet over the walls until the enemy blows him to pieces.'

He sheathed his blade, grasped the gibbering man by the scruff of the neck and sent him crashing to the floor. 'Now get to the window with your muskets, and start firing – ALL OF YOU!' he spat out, then stormed from the room followed by his escort.

'How many?' he asked the sergeant-major in a normal voice, taking an open space in the corridor at a loping run as a few musket balls spattered about them.

'Seventeen wounded or killed yesterday, sir – an' thirty-two deserted. I think most of 'em were from Oudh and they've no taste for doin' battle with their own folk.'

'I'll take no excuse for either mutiny or desertion, sergeant-major, and I meant every word I said in that room if I catch any of 'em. Do you think ...' The small cannon-ball splattered against a pillar, causing the party to duck involuntarily. One of the grenadiers gave a yelp of pain as a sliver of marble buried itself in his ear, drenching his face with more blood than the wound justified. Munro glanced irritably at him and told him to stuff a cloth against his ear, then again addressed the NCO. 'If those black-faced heathen had the guts to make just one resolute charge, it'd all be over. Just look at them.' He waved a derisive hand towards a gap in the wall over-looking the plain outside. 'Simply hanging back, hoping that some-one else will come along and do the job for them.'

'Yes, sir,' murmured the sergeant-major dutifully, flinching as another small round-shot struck the outer wall near him.

The group passed into the large, former audience chamber where seven English soldiers and fifteen sepoys were keeping up a steady and well disciplined firing. The sergeant in charge stood up the moment he saw the Major but was immediately waved down again.

'In good heart, sergeant?' barked Major Munro.

'It's ticking – that's the best I c'n say on it, sir,' replied the sergeant with a shrug.

'Well, be grateful. How's your powder and ball?'

'Well. That's a point, Major – not so ...' His answer was cut short by a yell from the window.

'THEY'RE CHARGIN' – whole lot of 'em!'

Kassim rested his elbow on the gunwale and moodily watched the yellow-green water of the Bhagirathi flow gently by. At least that lethargic Nawab of Oudh had discovered the ideal mode of travel in India. The vessel reminded him of an etching once shown him of an ancient Roman galley with its shallow draught, its two masts with their lateen-rigged sails, and its sixty oarsmen. This barge was similar except that the centre of the deck had been fitted with several top-heavy cabins, furnished hardly a whit less luxuriously than his own palace.

What folly this expedition was. Now was the time to attack, the Nawab had declaimed, now that Bengal was filled with dissension over the rival claims of Kassim and Mir Jafar. Well, if that was so, Kassim would withdraw. He no longer cared for the throne of Bengal. And even if he did, was it likely that the greedy Nawab of Oudh would kindly hand it to him after taking it by conquest? By no means! That sweating fat man in the bows of the ship – half a dozen men gently fanning him – sought only the extension of his own domain.

Kassim looked over the side. As far as his eye could reach there were solid masses of trudging warriors. He shook his head. He had seen it all before. Admittedly the Sahib Clive was no longer in India – but still the English soldiers were there, and he no longer felt inclined to engage them in battle. The Nawab's troops were now fighting at Monghyr, which should not prove difficult to take; yet the closer they got to Calcutta the closer they came to … he sniffed the air, and his misery deepened. Rain. The monsoon. Was it to be Plassey all over again? Any day, any hour, floods of water would come pouring down. And what Indian soldier ever fought well in the rain; what Indian ever fought at all in the rain?

He caught sight of Sareen – faithful Sareen who had insisted on being with him, even against the Nawab's objections. She also was staring with deepening despair into the distance. If only he had listened to her. She had been proved right on every occasion, and she had been so set against this new venture. In fact she had pleaded so fervently both with him and with the Nawab that eventually the Nawab of Oudh had forbidden her to speak any more on the subject. Well, maybe one day the fat Turk would discover just what kind of oracle Sareen was.

'Order the bargemaster to find a suitable place near the banks where we can anchor for the night,' the Nawab called out; 'otherwise we shall outstrip our own army.' Soon the odd-looking vessel had been manoeuvred to a high bank and tied fast. A gangplank was lowered, guards took up position, servants rushed about preparing the evening feast, and the rest of the immense force drew up in two great semi-circles on both sides of the river.

Sareen walked slowly over to Kassim and squatted down by his side. Kassim sneaked a glance at her. Her very silence was an accusation. Eventually, unable to bear it any longer, he turned sharply on her.

'It is not of my making, Sareen. You saw how I protested against this invasion, but Oudh is determined on war.'

He turned away, picked up a long boat-hook and peevishly began stabbing at their reflections in the glassy water between the boat and the bank. Their faces split into a myriad broken shapes as the pole plunged into the surface.

She was about to reply, when there came a sound of shouting and confused noises a little distance from the river. They shaded their eyes against the setting sun. Even the indolent Nawab raised himself from his brocaded couch to peer in the direction of the disturbance. Eight mounted soldiers forced their way through the jostling crowds of warriors on the bank. In the midst of them Sareen caught a glimpse of white cloth and then a woman's hat. She stood up to get a better view of this extraordinary sight. A woman ... a white woman, here!

'It looks like ...' she gasped incredulously. It was several minutes before the woman could persuade the guards on the bank to let her cross the gangplank.

'It's the Sahiba Wilkinson!' exclaimed Kassim, moving quickly towards the gangplank to greet her.

'Sahiba Wilkinson!' Sareen shouted. She rushed past Kassim to where the dishevelled woman was just stepping on to the deck and making some effort to brush the dust from her skirt.

'Sareen,' came the reply, and the two women embraced with obvious affection – though Petal managed to extricate an arm in order to touch the hand of the now smiling Kassim.

With imperious dignity, the Nawab of Oudh rose to his feet, his countenance severe at this breach of protocol. He was about to castigate the offenders when Miss Wilkinson tore herself from Sareen's embrace, and with consummate skill she gave her skirt a flourish and sank on one knee in a most perfectly executed curtsy.

'Petal Wilkinson, your highness.' She gave her name respectfully, hoping that his memory was good. Kassim pushed forward, intent on mediation if any should be needed, but the Nawab's upraised hand stayed him. He was staring at the white woman in perplexity, his mind searching for a connection.

'Sahiba Wilkinson,' he repeated her name to himself. A vain man who took pride in his omniscience, it was important to him that he should remember this woman. His face suddenly brightened.

'Alivardi Khan!' he exclaimed with obvious delight. 'Many years ago he was my guest in Oudh, and you, Sahiba Wilkinson, accompanied him ... Hah?'

'Your highness's gift of recall is the envy of all his subjects,' murmured Petal reverently, rising to her feet.

'Yes, yes ... I remember ... the Feringhee woman of Calcutta whom Alivardi Khan loved as though she were his own kin. But you are many days from Calcutta, Sahiba; what brings you here?' he asked with all the suspicion of an Indian prince for the white caste.

The moment had come. Petal had to make an acutely distrustful man believe in the altruism of her motives.

'I came for many reasons, my lord,' she began simply. 'First, because Alivardi Khan – a prince with undoubted affection for your highness – strove always to maintain peace between Bengal and her neighbour, Oudh; secondly, to avert a disaster in which both Oudh and Bengal would suffer; third, to save Mir Kassim and Sareen, whom I love dearly ...'

'Save!' expostulated the Nawab. 'Are they not safe here? Surrounded by a hundred and fifty thousand of my warriors?'

Petal hung her head as if too ashamed to contradict, then murmured, 'Because Alivardi Khan did love the Nawab of Oudh, I must also tell your highness this – that not too many days ago the great Sahib Clive returned to Bengal and is already marching north with an army of many, many thousands. Within one, two, or three days, he will appear and there will be a great slaughter.' A few drops of water fell on her face. She held out her hand and the rain splashed on it. 'Even as the monsoon begins, your highness, the English soldiers will be refreshed by it and will fight as tigers.'

'The Sahib Clive in Bengal! This I do not believe. It is false. News of this would have been brought me,' the Nawab maintained, but with no great conviction.

In answer, Petal Wilkinson drew from her blouse a sheet of newspaper, which she unfolded and handed to the Nawab. He took it, cast his eyes over it and disdainfully let it fall to the ground. 'I do not know the hatman's language,' he said dismissively. Kassim picked it up. 'It is a page from the Calcutta paper, your highness, the *Calcutta Gazette*. There is much in it of the Sahib Clive's return,' he said, adding softly, 'Perhaps, my lord, you should reconsider the wisdom of your intentions.'

It was clear to Petal, and to Sareen, that the news had been a blow to the Nawab, and though they took care not to gaze directly at him they could imagine the conflict taking place in his mind as greed for Bengal, confidence in the vastness of his army, competed against fear of the legendary Clive.

'No!' he shouted, 'No!' and stalked into his huge cabin.

59

OVER MONGHYR, too, the rain clouds had gathered but so far the monsoon had not broken. The ground was still dry dust as seven thousand foot soldiers and horsemen charged headlong for the palace. Conch shells set up their odd wailing and drum beats filled the air. The entire plain seemed to be dappled with scurrying figures as the sun, at intervals, broke through the clouds and rimmed them all with its dramatic back-lighting.

Though the Nawab's troops had brought with them only cannon of small calibre, it was nonetheless steadily pulverising the already battered shell of the once graceful palace. Smoke and dust hung over it; flames licked the stables and nearby buildings; a tall minaret toppled over and split into a million particles of rubble as a cannon-ball took out a supporting buttress. Ragged volleys of musketry still came from the palace windows as Major Munro urged on his men to greater efforts.

As the Muslim warriors began to clamber over the outer walls and to flow across the intervening spaces to the palace, the rain began to fall – but unlike Plassey it did not cause a general retreat though it did put out of action the cannon and the muskets of the attackers. The warriors still came on, surging up to the lower windows, their curved swords engaging with the swords and bayonets of the defenders. The English soldiers and the sepoys retreated to the inner parts of the palace, barricading the doors behind them. The rain began to fall solidly. Gulps and puffs of steam arose from the flaming stables before the fire was extinguished completely. Arrow points of lightning, fixing its image on the retinas of the eyes, drove into the earth with deafening claps of thunder.

This demonstration of supernatural power eventually cowed both attacker and defender. The sepoys shivered and hid their heads instead of loading their muskets, while the thousands of attackers in the belting rain found in this dreadful storm sufficient evidence of Allah's will. They began to falter, to hold back, to put their robes over their heads and to seek shelter. Rivulets of water cascaded down every wall and through every crevice in the ruined palace. Outside, what had been dust and parched earth became a quagmire several inches deep.

Yet fighting still continued in the shelter of the palace and the end was quite clear to Munro. He gathered about him the remnants of the garrison and retreated to the fortified keep of the palace. Here, without food and with very little ammunition, he held out for two days until – from a camp thirty miles south – a force of cavalry under Eyre Coote travelled through the storm (unaware that a battle was raging at Monghyr) and immediately charged right through the now thoroughly disheartened warriors.

It was all that the forces of Oudh needed to make them abandon their task. At the sight of these troopers on horseback making straight for them, swords and lances levelled, they began to run. They slithered, waded and splashed their way in any direction that promised safety. Within two hours all that remained of the attack on Monghyr were a few defenders inside the palace, and a soggy plain littered with dead.

Back at the British camp, some fifteen hundred soldiers emerged damply from their saturated tents and set about drying themselves during a break in the monsoon. From one of the largest tents a chilled and miserable Robert Clive came out into the hesitant sunshine. His shoulders were hunched together and persistent coughs racked his lungs. He hugged a steaming blanket around him.

Edmund saw his friend and hurried over, his face showing angry concern.

'Where's that servant of yours, Robert? You need a dry change of clothes.'

Clive paid him no attention, but concentrated on attempts to open a small jewelled container in his hand. Edmund coolly took it from him, opened it and handed it back, watching stonily as his friend took a pinch of the contents and snuffed it into his nostrils.

'Please, Robert, no more of that stuff. Let your servant give you a good rub down, some dry clothes and then we can have breakfast.'

Clive lifted his head in sudden anger. First Margaret with her frowns, warnings, insinuations, advice; looks of condemnation from Eyre Coote; raised eyebrows from the butler – and now Edmund.

'Since when do you presume ...' he began, but a harsh cough shook his body, and he tried to suck in air to allow him to speak again. 'Oh God, don't, Edmund!' he protested faintly. 'It helps to lighten the spirit when I am out of favour with myself; when the burden of responsibility weighs too heavily; when my head seeks relief from the multitude of problems that beset it. Are you not friend enough to grant me that?'

'Were I not a friend who loved you, I would make no issue of it; but as your welfare is dear to me I beg of you to cease this practice.'

Clive gave a shake of the head and returned to his tent to change. He removed his cravat and coat, and as his manservant came forward to help him off with the tight shirt, the pole of the tent quivered and then fell on its side – as did the manservant himself. His manservant opened and closed his mouth yet Clive could not hear a sound. Clive thought this very odd.

Then Edmund rushed into the tent. And he, too, was lying on his side; his mouth also was opening and closing. He wanted to tell Edmund to stop this foolishness and to order the soldiers to prepare to march. Yet, though all the words formed in his mouth, he didn't seem to have the strength to make them sound. He decided to close his eyes. When he opened them again this ridiculous situation would have righted itself.

When he did open his eyes he discovered to his puzzlement that he was lying on his camp bed, two heavy blankets over him; that Edmund was seated on a chair gazing fixedly at him; and that the surgeon was there.

'My lord, can you understand what I am saying?' the surgeon

said. Robert studied him, then, bored, he turned his attention to Edmund. His friend came over and sat on the edge of the camp bed, a strange look in his eyes.

'Robert? ... Don't try to speak but simply nod if you can understand me.'

Clive had no patience with such nonsense, yet he found himself doing as Edmund asked.

'Good,' said his friend. 'Very good. Now there is nothing to worry about. You have a slight fever, and you fainted. A few days' rest and you'll be back on your feet again and as healthy as you wish.'

'Major Maskelyne,' the surgeon broke in with some asperity. 'Pray, be good enough to allow me to deliver my professional opinion of the patient's health.'

The surgeon pointed his sharp little nose in Clive's direction; it gave him the appearance of a de-whiskered weasel.

'My lord Clive,' he said in a fluty voice. 'Major Maskelyne evidently does not wish to upset you and therefore pretends that your illness can be treated lightly. But to this deception I cannot be a party. Know now, my lord, that for the past three days you have lain upon that bed in a state of high fever and delirium ...'

'Three days!' cried Clive, making an effort to raise himself.

'Three days indeed,' said the surgeon. 'And were it not for the constant ministrations of Major Maskelyne here there is doubt that we would even be speaking with you at this moment.' He cast an appreciative nod in Edmund's direction before continuing in an even more severe tone. 'Now mark my words, Lord Clive. There are graveyards in India filled with men such as yourself who failed to take heed of the warning when it was granted them, who considered themselves bound by duty, and who refused to quit the tropics until it was too late.'

'I grant you your concern, doctor – but be damned to your warnings. Every man is entitled to suffer a little fever now and again without being urged to abandon everything,' Clive replied hoarsely.

'Be damned, you say, your excellency? Aye, but let none of us rush to damnation afore we need to. With all the authority of medical learning behind me, I advise you, Robert, Lord Clive, to clear out of this land before its poisonous air starts corrupting even more those weakened lungs of yours.' He raised a warning finger – a thing that few men would have had the temerity to do to Clive – and added, 'Opium is a drug of some complexity. I use it for my patients where the need calls. Yet when people smoke it with the habit and frequency of taking tobacco then they encourage their own destruction. And now you must rest, my lord, for at least two days, before we can arrange transport for you back to Calcutta.'

As the tent flap closed behind the doctor, Clive caught Edmund's eye.

'Is he a fool or simply a man who treats a thorn in the hand as a spear thrust?' Clive demanded.

'He is no fool,' Edmund rejoined levelly. 'And if your life be of concern to you – know that it is as much concern to Margaret, to your son, and to me.'

Clive lowered his gaze. 'Edmund, is it really three days that I have been here, three days out of my wits?'

'Three days it is, Robert, and in that time ... you have made history without being aware of it. Your name took the field and won a battle more convincingly than a hundred thousand troops could have done.'

Clive lay back, his mouth agape, as he listened to Edmund's story.

'We're not clear on all the details as yet, but after Colonel Coote relieved Monghyr and set out to return to camp, some of his scouts encountered Oudh warriors. There was a small skirmish. Coote persisted in trailing the warriors, and saw the Nawab's barge and the whole of his army going back the way they came. For the past three days he's had the cavalry out keeping a check that the Nawab really is fleeing back to Oudh.'

'Where is the Colonel now, Edmund?' Clive asked. He felt piqued that such momentous events should have taken place whilst he was unconscious.

'Out on patrol. I'm expecting him within the next hour or so.'

'Then kindly assist me off this damned bed. It's time I became commander-in-chief again and stopped acting like a child with the gripes,' Clive grumbled, thrusting his shaking legs from underneath the blankets and pulling himself to a sitting position. Edmund opened his mouth to protest, but he closed it again. It would have been so much wasted effort.

An hour later, seated on a large canvas chair that had been prepared for him outside the tent, huddled in a blanket despite heat that bathed others in perspiration, Clive looked like a cantankerous old man surrounded by anxious, overgrown grandchildren. He was still in this condition when Eyre Coote returned.

'They have gone, sir – without any doubt,' he assured Clive, after ascertaining the Governor's wellbeing. 'Monghyr is safe, and so is Major Munro – though the casualties were heavy. But the best news of all ...' – He made a pleasurably dramatic pause – 'We've caught Mir Kassim.'

60

PETAL WILKINSON'S bottom was sore; her back ached and her thighs felt numbed. For six hours she had been astride a horse and she complained to the troopers surrounding her that if Colonel Coote did not return soon she would lodge a charge with the Governor himself. In vain they assured her that without further orders they were compelled to keep the prisoners where they were. Miss Wilkinson's hackles rose.

'Prisoners!' she said starchily. 'Be good enough to summon Major Maskelyne and inform him that we're here and that we are most uncomfortable.'

A brown hand stretched out and touched her knee. 'Please do not worry on our account, Sahiba Wilkinson,' Sareen murmured, looking sadly towards the back of the bullock wagon where Mir Kassim lay, his feet and hands bound with leather thongs. Petal Wilkinson put her hand over Sareen's and tried to comfort her.

'It will be all right, I'm sure it will. After all, Kassim wasn't trying to escape. The Colonel must have known that by the direction in which we were travelling. Be of good cheer, Sareen. Major Maskelyne will be here soon, and then we shall be all right.'

Sareen smiled her thanks, but she had no illusions where Kassim was concerned. The British would exact their revenge.

'Petal! For God's sake!' shouted Edmund, thrusting his way

through the ranks of the mounted soldiers. He reached up and lifted her from the saddle. 'Come, both you and Sareen. Leave Mir Kassim here for a few minutes. Lord Clive wants to see you. Explanations later.'

Petal started slightly at the sight of Clive's gaunt condition and the pallor of his complexion, but a frown from Edmund restrained her from commenting. He offered no welcome nor any courtesies.

'Major Maskelyne has this moment informed me of your self-appointed mission to play mediator between the Nawab of Oudh and myself, Miss Wilkinson.' His voice was throaty and rasping, and his choice of words an implied rebuke to Edmund for lending himself to such a scheme. 'I accept his assurance that your intentions were motivated by the not ignoble desire to bring an end to this conflict in Bengal – and for this I thank you.'

If this was thanks, what would his displeasure be like, Petal wondered.

'Nevertheless, I cannot approve of such unwarranted interference in matters that are no concern ...'

At this Petal could contain herself no longer. 'No concern! No concern! Indeed it *is* my concern whether we live or whether we die. No concern, indeed. Your excellency, had I not taken it upon myself to intervene, you and your army would this minute be embroiled in bloody contest with a hundred and fifty thousand warriors. As it is – due to my *interference*, as you so rudely term it – the hand of the Nawab has been stayed; and with far more courtesy than you are at this moment showing.'

Clive was astounded at such effrontery – and from a woman. He lowered his head and studied his blanketed thighs, where his fingers had begun to drum an agitated rhythm.

'Madam, you will pray allow me to finish speaking, and have the good manners to remember that it is the Governor of Bengal who is seated in this chair.'

Edmund leaned over and whispered to him before he could say more. Clive raised his eyes to where Sareen was standing in great trepidation. Only at that moment did he seem to notice her. Very gravely he bowed in her direction. The movement caused the blanket to slip from his shoulders, and three people rushed forward to replace it. He shook them off in irritation.

'The lady Sareen is under no restraint whatsoever and I extend

296

to her our sincere welcome,' he said. 'Now, Miss Wilkinson, if we may continue – without further acrimony – perhaps you would favour me with an account of what has transpired with the Nawab of Oudh.'

Petal, her lips tight with anger, took a few moments before she deigned to reply, and when she did finally speak she addressed herself to Edmund.

'When I told the Nawab that the Lord Clive was in India and marching against him he was assailed by all kinds of fears. He seemed thrown into confusion, and though he declaimed he would take the field against the Lord Clive,' – she stressed the name slightly – 'he was, in fact, searching for a means by which he might honourably withdraw. Mir Kassim argued with him to such a degree that the Nawab, infuriated, simply told him to leave the barge.'

Clive looked enquiringly at Eyre Coote for confirmation of the last part of her statement. 'A patrol picked them up, my lord. They were heading in the direction of this camp,' the Colonel supplied briefly. Clive pondered on this. A thousand questions were flitting through his mind but in his present condition it was difficult to seize on the more pertinent ones. If only he could lie down and think – or better still, think of nothing, just simply go to sleep.

'Miss Wilkinson, do you seriously maintain that when the Nawab heard that I was marching against him – he simply fled?'

'Have no illusions, my lord, as to the effect the sound of your name has on the minds of princes,' Petal rejoined archly. Clive looked bleakly at her.

'Please be more specific, Miss Wilkinson,' he returned curtly.

'Very well, your excellency, I shall. It shall be for you to judge if the terms are fair – or if indeed the Nawab resorts to bluff. He is convinced that, having destroyed Monghyr, you will not rest until you have sought revenge on him by an invasion of Oudh. He therefore offers in compensation the formerly disputed districts of Allahabad, Corah, Orissa and Bihar, and he undertakes to withdraw from Bengal and to interfere no further in its affairs.'

'I cannot believe it!' Clive gasped. 'And what price does he demand in return for these concessions?'

'Nothing, my lord ... nothing, save that you guarantee to respect the independence of Oudh,' Petal returned, an amused look of triumph on her face.

'Heavens, Robert!' Edmund exclaimed. 'That's the richest volte-face I've ever heard of. Can you imagine ...'

Clive's upraised finger halted him in mid-sentence. 'Where is the Nawab at this moment, Miss Wilkinson?' he asked quietly.

'He intends to stay on the river some fifteen miles north of Monghyr and await your answer, your excellency.'

Clive gave an involuntary shiver as a shadow crossed the sun, and he huddled deeper into his blanket. For several minutes he remained deep in thought, and then he beckoned to Eyre Coote.

'Colonel. Take a squadron of cavalry and ride to the Nawab of Oudh. Ascertain whether these are the terms he offers; be not overly compliant with him, preserve a measure of authority, hint at but do not make threats, be reluctant towards anything he suggests – but eventually make agreement and document a treaty. But at all costs get him and his damnable army back into Oudh.' He wheezed. 'Sareen,' he addressed her gently. 'What was the intention of Mir Kassim when he returned to Bengal?'

Sareen hung her head, unwilling to let him see the tears brimming her eyes, and there was an uncomfortably long wait before she murmured, 'My lord, I am here to beg forgiveness for him and to plead for his life. He makes no more claim to the throne of Bengal, and what happened at Patna was not of his will. In his anger he cried out against the injustices done to him by the English at Patna, and his cry was taken to mean more than he intended or desired.'

'Forgiveness, Sareen? It is not a question of forgiveness but of justice: two hundred slain who cry for justice. Does not the Koran say: "Shall not the guilty be rewarded according to their deeds"? How can I turn my face from what has been done?'

Sareen sank to her knees in piteous appeal. 'He will not plead for himself, my lord, and I must do it for him. Seek not to punish him for the brief madness and evil spirit that made him utter words that were against his very nature. Kassim does not wage war on the innocent nor the helpless. He is a good and kind soul, your excellency, and bitterly regrets what happened at Patna. Should his death enable them to be brought to life again, willingly would he sacrifice himself ... and I, too, my lord,' she added softly.

'Your excellency,' Edmund intervened formally, 'it is no secret that my wife and myself are alive today on account of Mir Kassim, who risked his own life to rescue us from the prison at Murshidabad.'

'Two lives saved are little bargain for two hundred slain,' Clive rasped, then exploded into a fit of coughing. With some effort he clawed himself to his feet, blanket still around his shoulders, and in a voice that sounded like the turning of rusted cannon-wheels, he said to Sareen, 'Take him with you, Sareen. He is free. I care nothing for revenge nor for his fate. Blessed is he to have such an advocate as yourself.'

He walked unsteadily towards her, took hold of her arm and raised her to her feet. There was very little strength left in his body by this time. 'I shall require that he sign an admission that his father, Mir Jafar, is true Nawab of Bengal ... then you must take him from Bengal and never again return. Henceforth Mir Kassim is banished from this state.'

He took no heed of her protestations of gratitude. As he turned, Miss Wilkinson caught a glimpse of his face and saw his eyes slowly closing. She and Edmund sprang forward, caught him under the arms, and half-walked, half-carried him back to his tent. The doctor followed them, shaking his head with vexation.

A little later, Edmund poked his head inquiringly into the tent where Miss Wilkinson was acting as nurse to Clive.

'A high fever, but thankfully he's sleeping,' she whispered, at which the patient opened his eyes as if to give her the lie.

'Kassim and Sareen are leaving. They wish to say good-bye and to express their thanks to you,' he whispered back.

'Sahiba Wilkinson,' murmured Kassim emotionally, as he grasped her hand and pressed it to his cheek. Sareen clasped her other hand. Petal looked at the two of them for a moment and then flung her arms around them both. For some little time they stayed like this, allowing no words to destroy the tender moment. Eventually they broke apart, and Kassim and Sareen mounted their horses. As Kassim grasped the reins he saw Edmund looking reflectively at him a few paces away. The two men held each other's gaze, then Kassim said, 'In the sack on the cart, Sahib Maskelyne, I brought a gift for his excellency, the Lord Clive. When he recovers, please show it to him.' He hesitated before adding, 'I wished it to heal the breach between us.'

'The wound is too bloody, Mir Kassim, and the Lord Clive will accept no gifts from you,' Edmund rejoined, a little too stiffly.

'Be that as it may, Sahib – yet give it to him to dispose of as he will,' Kassim replied, and, waving farewell to those watching, he and Sareen cantered westwards out of Bengal. Edmund went to the cart, took hold of the sack, opened it and poured out the contents. The head of Sombrer rolled into the mud at his feet.

61

AT THE surgeon's insistence, Clive spent a few weeks at the palace in Murshidabad while a vessel was made ready to transport him back to Calcutta. Mir Jafar accorded him all the honour of a visiting prince: the best apartments were set aside for his use, the best of food and wine reserved for him. But the Governor of Bengal showed no signs of improving. His health remained as low as his spirits. Both Petal Wilkinson and Edmund had elected to remain with him: one as nurse and the other as secretary and friend.

Day after day Clive sat in his deep chair, blanket around him, disinterested in everything save the political future of Bengal and the Carnatic, dictating new laws which Edmund wrote down, ever aware that his time in India was fast running out. By the time the ship arrived, he was able to walk about with the aid of his cane and the supporting arm of Edmund or Petal.

'I don't think Margaret will be sorry to leave India,' Edmund observed to him as they neared Calcutta, trying to think of things to say that might lessen Clive's sense of failure. He sadly noted the thinness of Clive's wrists as they rested on the taffrail.

'No,' said Clive moodily, looking out at the desiccated landscape he knew he was seeing for the last time, at the temples and mosques, the toiling peasants, the broad sweep of the river.

'You know, in the short time you've been here, you've set to rights the Company, the throne, Bengal itself, halted an invasion ... really, Robert, what man could have done more?'

At this, Clive seemed to come alive a little. He was conscious more than ever before of the devotion of the man beside him. He slowly lifted a clawlike hand, dropped it on Edmund's huge fist and gripped it as hard as his slight strength would allow.

'India I shall miss, for a part of me will be buried here. But you, my dear friend, shall occupy a place in my heart greater than Bengal itself, for no other person has been so close to me,' he said quietly, his voice trembling with emotion.

A few weeks later, in the year 1767, Clive and his family took their leave of India. It was a burning hot day and even the Bay of Bengal seemed to have been ironed flat with a shimmering haze. The harbour was crowded. Colonel Eyre Coote was there with regiments of his men; the Council, scores of officers; Petal Wilkinson, Edmund and Anna.

Clive, with a shawl around his neck and shoulders, despite the heat, shook hands or embraced his friends, but when he came to Edmund those near him tactfully averted their eyes – for he was weeping. Though both men were comparatively young – only forty-two years of age – they both knew they were seeing each other for the last time, and tried to pretend otherwise.

Margaret and the child stepped down into the longboat that was to take them to the waiting Indiaman, and Robert followed after them. The sailors bent their backs to the oars and the boat moved away. When the craft was midway between shore and ship, Clive was seen to stand erect in the stern of the longboat and to face the land. He lifted his arms, stretching them out until they were level with his shoulders, as though he were both embracing and giving benediction to all those figures sadly waving to him on the quay, and also to Bengal itself.

It was a gesture neither blasphemous, presumptuous, nor affected: it was a princely blessing and a sign of grace, a small mark that Robert Clive – the greatest of Englishmen in India – was bestowing on the land he was leaving, a mark that has never been erased.

As the ship weighed anchor and left harbour, cannons boomed and church bells rang their salute to him, and those soldiers he had often led let fire volley after volley from their muskets in farewell.

Epilogue

A LITTLE of Clive's health returned to him during the years that followed in England though he was still subject to fits of melancholy. Instead of the public acclaim which he might have expected, he received venomous attacks from newspapers, slander from Parliament, scurrilous observations in Company reports – for Sullivan had again returned to power.

To meet this whipped-up public feeling against Clive, Parliament instituted an enquiry – and the devious Sullivan and Dashwood forged a spike for the crucifixion of the victim. The charges against Clive were many and had been well prepared. They regurgitated the old ones of bribery, stressing the item of the estate – *jagir* – given to him in Calcutta, and accused him of oppression. '... The very trees surrounding your estate at Claremont do whisper in the wind with the souls of murdered innocent Bengalis, victims of your maladministration,' the long indictment read, 'and is it not a fact that when you had in your power the slayer of one hundred and seventy-five people at Patna, Mir Kassim, you treated with him, offered forgiveness and allowed him his freedom?'

Even Clive's friends in the House looked askance at that.

'Now we come to a matter which in the annals of infamy can hardly be matched: the noble Lord Clive, in dealing with a certain merchant, Omichand, caused a false treaty to be prepared – with deliberate intent to defraud – and this was presented ...' The story of the blackmailing Omichand was related in full in damning phrases – against Clive.

'And who did sign this fake treaty?'

'Myself and Members of the Inner Council,' Clive answered, sick within himself.

'Including Admiral Watson?' Clive hesitated for so long that the interrogator then said, 'If that question causes you worry, Lord Clive, perhaps you will tell this Enquiry if the signature purporting to be that of Admiral Watson appeared on the red treaty?'

'It appeared on the document,' Clive responded dully, confessing minutes later that the forgery was by his own hand. 'I did what was necessary to outwit a rogue.'

A week later the enquiry was concluded and its members retired to consider what they had heard. Their judgment when given was cruel – though in mitigation of their condemnation, they added the rider: '... that Robert, Lord Clive, did at the same time render great and meritorious services to this country.'

If he had endured fits of depression before, in the months that followed the verdict of the enquiry he knew a bitterness that reached the depths of misery. To the proud and sensitive Clive it was a mortal blow. He recalled the ignominious treatment handed out to Dupleix, Bussy, De Lally, and cynically recalled his own Prime Minister's protestation that such could never occur in England. 'Better they had taken my fortune or life than my name,' he brooded.

One morning, even more dejected than usual, he wandered into his trophy room. On the vast walls hung the bizarre collection of bric-à-brac he had brought from India. One entire wall was given over to weapons that he had recovered in the many battles he had fought: swords, sabres, daggers, pikes, spears, muskets, bows and arrows, matchlock and flintlock pistols – and, hanging unobtrusively in one corner, the flintlock gun with which he had once attempted suicide in Madras so many years ago.

He took it from its hook and gazed at it with introspective bitterness.

'Who knows, Robert, Lord Clive, Knight Commander of the Bath, Baron of Plassey, what great and meritorious service you might better have rendered your country had this pistol been a more worthy weapon,' he said with mocking cynicism. And, on impulse, pulled open a cupboard and reached inside for powder and ball.

He loaded the gun and laid it on the fine Chippendale cabinet, and from a pocket he took out the cloisonné box in which he kept what appeared to be snuff. He shook his head sadly at the greyish powder, then snapped the lid closed and returned the box to his pocket.

'No snuff, no opium ... lest your enemies gleefully claim you were so drugged you were in ignorance of your act.'

His eyes fixed on a large wooden globe of the world. He walked over to it, spun it idly, then thrust out a finger to bring it to rest. He noticed where his finger touched, then he moved the globe and stared for a long, long time at India.

'Such a jewel,' he murmured, and picked up the pistol again. He straightened his shoulders, and there was no trembling in the hand that put the muzzle against his temple.

'As a just reward for your great and meritorious services, Robert, Lord Clive,' he cried aloud – and pressed the trigger. This time the ancient pistol functioned as it had refused to do two decades and an empire earlier – and Robert Clive, hero of Arcot, victor of Bengal and the Carnatic, founder of the British Empire in India, was dead.

REQUIESCAT IN PACE